A *New York Times* Notable Book

The
FOX'S WALK

ANNABEL DAVIS-GOFF

The
FOX'S WALK

A HARVEST BOOK • HARCOURT, INC.

Orlando   Austin   New York   San Diego   Toronto   London

www.HarcourtBooks.com

Library of Congress Cataloging-in-Publication Data
Davis-Goff, Annabel.
The fox's walk/Annabel Davis-Goff.—1st ed.
p.   cm.
ISBN 0-15-101020-X
ISBN 0-15-603010-1 (pbk.)
1. Girls—Fiction. 2. Grandmothers—Fiction. 3. Country homes—Fiction.
4. Social classes—Fiction. 5. Children of the rich—Fiction.
6. Waterford (Ireland : County)—Fiction.   I. Title.
PS3554.A9385F695 2003
813'.54—dc21   2003005400

Text set in Granjon
Designed by Cathy Riggs

Printed in the United States of America

First Harvest edition 2004
A C E G I K J H F D B

For My Mother,
Cynthia O'Connor
(1918–1999)

Acknowledgments

My mother spent part of her childhood at Ballydavid with her grandmother and great-aunt. When she died, she left an unfinished memoir that included an account of life at Ballydavid and a description of the lives of some of the local Waterford families. The background of this novel and a few of the characters and houses are taken from my mother's writing and from conversations in which she would recall childhood memories of life at Ballydavid. I have on two occasions, with great pleasure, borrowed a phrase from my mother's book.

I am grateful to Susanna Moore, Coco Brown, Julia Goff, Jenny Nichols, Frank Woodhouse, Sheelagh Goff, Robert Goff, and Max Nichols for help, advice, and details of Irish life of the period.

I am also indebted to David Hough at Harcourt for his tireless patience and attention to detail, and to my editor, Ann Patty, for her trust and support.

I wish to acknowledge the following books that I have consulted: *Ireland Since the Famine,* F. S. L. Lyons (Fontana); *Ireland 1912–1985,* J. J. Lee (Cambridge); *British War Administration,* John A. Fairlie (Oxford); *The Lives of Roger Casement,* B. L. Reid (Yale); *Roger Casement: A New Judgment,* René MacColl (Norton); *Roger*

Casement, Brian Inglis (Harcourt Brace); *The Black Diaries of Roger Casement,* Peter Singleton-Gates and Maurice Girodias (Grove); *Erskine Childers,* Jim Ring (John Murray); *The Riddle of Erskine Childers,* Andrew Boyle (Hutchinson); *The Life of a Painter,* Sir John Lavery, R.A. (Little Brown); *Kitchener: The Man Behind the Legend,* Philip Warner (Atheneum); and two articles about his father's career in the Chinese Maritime Customs by Perry Anderson, published in the *London Review of Books.*

The
FOX'S WALK

September 1965

ON A COLD DAY in March of this year, Sir Roger Casement was reburied at Glasnevin Cemetery.

His remains—he'd been buried in lime almost fifty years ago; what could they now consist of?—had been disinterred at Pentonville where he had been executed in 1916. He had lain in state at the Pro-Cathedral in Dublin before his ceremonial reburial in that part of the cemetery where patriots and heroes of the struggle for Irish independence lie. His grave is close to that of Michael Collins; the Countess Markievicz, too, is buried at Glasnevin. So is Erskine Childers.

The day on which Casement was reburied was (nature affirming the inconvenient character of the hero of the hour) not only bitterly cold but wet. Eamon de Valera, the Irish president, himself a former revolutionary, ailing, and now at the end of his long political career, ignoring his doctor's advice, stood bareheaded beside the grave.

Although I now live in Sandycove near the house where Casement was born and read about the ceremony in the *Irish Times,* I waited until the end of summer to visit his grave. The Republican graves are the frequent destination of nationalist pilgrims who consider that so long as the six counties in the north of Ireland remain part of the United Kingdom the struggle for Irish freedom is not over. For them, since I am a Protestant, I am English and therefore the enemy although my family has lived in Ireland for three hundred years. I am Protestant, Anglo-Irish, and I am not the enemy.

Today—1965, only forty-three years since Ireland became a Free State, and sixteen since she has been a Republic—the writing of Irish history is just emerging from the party line to become a more scholarly endeavor. Even so, the approved history books have always been studded with leaders and revolutionaries of the Anglo-Irish, Protestant, landowning classes who gave their lives in the nationalist cause. Roger Casement was one of these.

Casement's grave is marked by a slab of limestone, flat to the ground, inscribed in Irish. There is a tree beside it and the cemetery lies next to the Botanical Gardens. I think he would have been pleased. Despite a death cell letter in which he asked to be buried in the old churchyard in Murlough Bay, he might well have preferred Glasnevin; he could hardly have requested a hero's grave, and I doubt at that lonely time that he could have imagined one.

Casement's is a long and bitter story—some of which I am about to tell. Not because I ever saw him—I was nine years old when he was hanged—nor because anyone in my family had known him personally—which would have been unlikely but not impossible—but because he, as the personification of the Anglo-Irish nationalist patriot and martyr, outraged the values of the Protestant privileged class and also confused it. The Ascendancy—the aristocracy, landowners, and politically powerful stratum of society—already knew their days to be numbered. They saw Casement as a traitor, pure and simple, but they also saw the government in London, the government they thought

represented them, behave in a manner not only stupid but dis-
honorable. That behavior—the stupidity and lack of honor, not
the treachery—was one of the causes of an unpremeditated
choice that changed my future and would have affected the lives
of those around me had not the course of history swept away the
very foundations of the way we lived. In the end, the only life I
changed was my own; my choice largely invisible in that utterly
altered world.

May 1912–June 1915

Chapter 1

A S IN MOST HAPPY childhoods, my life consisted of long periods of boredom interspersed with moments of drama that did not have far-reaching consequences. The summer of my first memories I was five years old and still an only child. My mother was with me at Ballydavid—we were visiting my grandmother and great-aunt—and she must have been pregnant, carrying my brother Edward. Of her pregnancy, I remember nothing.

Instead, I remember moments of that summer—small scenes full of meaning that I couldn't then, with my limited vocabulary, convey to the grown-ups. I am not confident I can do so now. The largest of these fragments of memory begins on the avenue at Ballydavid. It says something about the benevolence of the Irish countryside in those days, and even more about the casual attitude toward children in my not overindulgent family, that no one noticed I had wandered away from the house—along the avenue almost to the wrought-iron and stone-pillared gates, on the other side of which lay the road leading south to the sea or north toward Waterford.

The entertaining of children was not, either in my family or in society at large, given the importance that it now is. There was nothing unusual about my being turned out of doors alone on a cold dark day with an airy instruction to play. The front door would then be closed, and the adult who had so instructed me would go back to sit by the drawing-room fire.

Usually I would loiter for a moment or two, hoping for a reprieve, before making the best of it. Ballydavid was not lacking in opportunities for the adventurous child I later became, but at five years old I was not tall enough to open the gates to the walled garden, nor was I encouraged by O'Neill to hang about the farmyard, under his feet or the hooves of the animals he cared for. I would be hard pressed, even now, to define in a couple of words O'Neill's exact position at Ballydavid, but all power over the farm lay in his hands, and his influence, although in a way not immediately apparent, possibly even to Grandmother, his employer, spread much farther afield. Very often Jock, the Highland collie, would be loitering around the front door, but that day he had found somewhere warmer and more cheerful to spend his afternoon. When it became clear I would have to amuse myself as best I could for the next hour or two, I wandered down the avenue with no destination in mind. And, with no particular enthusiasm, killing time until tea.

The avenue at Ballydavid curved and sloped gently downhill, disappearing around a bend where the mown-grass verges were interrupted by a clump of laurels. The house had been built on a hill overlooking the estuary of the river; the avenue, and then the road it led to, with stone bridges over streams and even a small hill on the way, gradually descended to the strand, a mere foot or two above the level of the sea at high tide; there it joined the narrow, sand-bordered road that followed the outline of the coast.

On either side, behind the neatly kept verge, were fields enclosed by iron railings. Only the tennis court in front of the house was not part of the small farm and garden that supplied most of the household needs. O'Neill and the two men who worked under his supervision maintained the avenue, raking the thin gravel and removing any weed that tried to take root in the stony earth. Although there was very little motorized traffic—the Sunbeam might travel up and down the avenue once or twice a week if Grandmother decided to call on her neighbors, or if the occasional visitor, reversing the process, called at Ballydavid—two worn, shallow parallel furrows lay on either side of the higher central ridge. The donkey dragged the water cart, full and heavy, up to the house every day; the wheels of the cart were metal and each day they wore a little deeper into the ground.

It was a gray dull afternoon at Ballydavid, but the sun lit the water of the estuary and as far out into the ocean as my eye could see. When I reached the bend in the avenue, I hesitated and glanced back at the house to see if anyone was watching me. But the house was closed and still, a column of gray smoke rising into the windless air from the fireplace in the library.

There was no explicit rule about being out of sight of the house, but my sense was that I was being slightly disobedient. And disobedient without any immediate benefit from my daring. I paused, considering a return to loiter outside the drawing-room window, hoping someone would take pity on me, when there was a rustling in some dry leaves under the laurels. Oonagh, my Grandmother's brindle cat, who had been prowling in the undergrowth, sauntered out. Normally, indoors, she ignored me, allowing herself to be stroked but, like most cats, not meeting my eye or quite acknowledging my presence. Now, however, she arched her back, stretched, and inclined her head toward me. I was suddenly aware of her feline grace and the shades of gray in the striped markings of her coat. It was, I suppose, the moment when I became aware of beauty; until then I had taken pleasure in the appearance of certain things—my mother when she came to kiss me goodnight, my first sight of the house as we turned the bend in the avenue, the garden in the blaze of midsummer glory—but implicit in these pleasures was their connection to me. Oonagh lying, as she now was, on the loose sandy soil at the edge of the avenue was beautiful in herself. Beauty—and, as I now understood, Oonagh—existed without me as a witness.

Naturally I lacked the ability to express this idea. Not only to communicate what I had discovered to someone else, but even the vocabulary to think it clearly. But I didn't consider that and, with one more glance at Oonagh, now scratching herself, I turned and trotted up the avenue toward the house. Instinctively avoiding the front door—knocking at it with my knuckles since I wasn't tall enough to reach the door knocker, waiting for a grown-up, and formulating an explanation for the necessity of coming indoors immediately—I made for the off-limits, but more accessible, kitchen door.

Tea was being prepared in the kitchen. Maggie, the cook, was standing in front of the large black iron stove, holding a skillet in her hands. I noticed a plate to one side, heaped with drop scones she had already made. Bridie, neatly uniformed, was waiting to carry the tea tray into the drawing room. Both women knew I was not allowed to visit the kitchen, but I had noticed that neither had much interest in enforcing rules when unwitnessed by adult members of the family. Neither really noticed me, but their lack of interest in the doings of children was different from the way I was ignored by Grandmother, or even by my mother. The maids included me, on a minor, powerless level, in whatever was going on; my presence, provided I was safe and well behaved, did not require any special acknowledgment. With my family, there was more often a feeling that I had not yet attained the right to be part of their self-contained and privileged society.

As I reached up to the china knob on the tall dark door to the

drawing room, some part of me remembered my own insignifi-
cance, but I was still too excited by my discovery to contain myself. It took me a moment or two to open the door, and as I
entered, my mother, having risen from her seat by the fire, was
crossing the gloomy drawing room toward me. Most of the light
in the room came from three long windows that looked out over
the damp tennis court and fields to the river estuary. The fire,
combating the cold of a rainy afternoon, was the only interior
source of light; it would be another hour or two before Bridie
brought in the lamps that marked the moment when I would be
taken upstairs to bed.

My mother, graceful though she must have been in the sixth
month of her pregnancy, looked rested and relaxed at Ballydavid
in a way that she rarely did in London. She was by nature
somewhat indolent and now, pregnant and in Ireland, took even
longer afternoon rests than she did at home while my father was
at the office. Her face still bore traces of amusement: Great-Aunt
Katie often made her laugh; Grandmother, though insightful and
witty, less frequently.

"Alice," my mother said, absentmindedly surprised to see me.

I realized that I needed to justify my presence, and I tried to
recount the moment of such importance that had just taken place.

"Mama, Mama, I saw a tiger on the avenue."

I knew, of course, that I hadn't seen a tiger, but the importance of what I had experienced could not be conveyed with the
words, *I saw Oonagh on the avenue.* It now seems to me—a memory recalled recently by an Etruscan mosaic of a pair of exotic,
predatory animals on either side of a tree whose fruit was large
and not concealed by leaves—that in one of the nursery books, a
tiger standing beside a tree heavy with brightly colored oranges
was smaller and less threatening than was another illustration of
a large black cat with long claws and teeth, hissing with a savagely

red tongue. It is possible that these illustrations may have misled me into thinking that substituting a tiger for a brindled cat was a less extreme exaggeration than it, in fact, is.

There was a sound of amusement, something a little lower and less than a laugh, from the end of the room near the fire, and I realized that Grandmother had visitors and that I had the attention of everyone in the room. *Children should be seen and not heard* was a familiar phrase in those days, the unoriginality of the remark equaled only by its sincerity. But my mother opened the door a little wider and I understood that I was meant to enter.

Grandmother and Aunt Katie were sitting in their accustomed high-backed chairs on either side of the fireplace. Sitting up straight in another chair—my mother had been sitting on the sofa beside a small and, at that stage unnoticed by me, elderly man—was a woman whose charms I could see, even at first glance, would be inexhaustible. The unrelieved, though by no means dowdy, darkness of my grandmother's and great-aunt's clothing—my mother was dressed in a loose pale blue frock and a cream silk zouave —only accentuated their guest's colorful and dramatic clothing. Blue, pink, gray, and red. Her gestures, too, were dramatic. As she turned to look at me—I had the impression that she had been the one doing all the talking—the osprey feathers in her large hat waved wildly, and a gesture of her hand agitated the strings of beads around her neck. I was utterly charmed and would have been happy to sit quietly and gaze at her.

But it seemed as though I would, for a moment or two longer, be the center of attention.

"A tiger, Alice?" my grandmother asked, her manner showing more interest than I was used to receiving when I spoke. I had the impression that my presence was welcome, though not because Grandmother had suddenly discovered my true worth.

"A tiger," she repeated. "On the avenue. Come here, Alice."

I crossed the room, now the recipient of rather more attention than I wished.

"And what did the tiger do?" she asked when I stood in front of her.

"It sat down and scratched itself," I said.

Adult laughter, affectionate and not too loud, made me regret having allowed myself to get so far out of my depth. After I had been introduced to Major and Mrs. Coughlan, my mother patted the sofa and I sat down beside her. She put her arm around me and drew me closer to her. I wondered why the tea tray I had seen in the kitchen had not yet arrived.

"Katie," Grandmother said in the polite tone she used to give domestic instructions to her sister, "please tell Bridie to dust Oonagh with some Keating's Powder."

Aunt Katie started to rise; the bell pull was on her side of the fireplace. But Grandmother waved her back to her seat.

"Later," she said.

As though it were a signal, Mrs. Coughlan rose from her seat, and after a moment her husband got up also. Good-byes were exchanged while I stood silently to one side. Aunt Katie accompanied the guests to the front door. As Mrs. Coughlan passed me, she paused.

"I hope *you* will come and see me one day," she said.

As the door in the hall closed, Grandmother turned to my mother.

"Mary," she said, "ring for tea."

BETWEEN THE AFTERNOON of my first memory—Oonagh and Mrs. Coughlan and the tea tray withheld until after the Coughlans' departure—and my next memory, this one not isolated but part of the jumbled montage I recall of early childhood, one chapter in the history of the world ended and another began.

The summer months of 1914 before the outbreak of war were the last moments before everything changed forever. There was no sense that the world was about to embark on the most terrible war ever fought. Instead, in London, there was an atmosphere of uncomfortable adjustment, and, in Ireland, a time of uneasy anticipation. My parents, both of course born during the long reign of Queen Victoria (by then it was unlikely there was anyone alive who could remember a time before she had ascended the throne) had adapted—happily, I think—to the freer and more worldly atmosphere of Edwardian society. Now, the popular, diplomatic, sensible, and reassuringly human king was dead; and society had once again changed, becoming a little dull with a less exuberant monarch on the throne.

In Ireland Home Rule seemed imminent; the question was when it would come and at what cost. My family waited and watched; we knew change was inevitable and hoped it would be peaceful and not immediate. Most of the Anglo-Irish tried not to think about it, and continued their lives as though their comfortable world would last forever. But there were exceptions.

Two men, both Protestant and from privileged backgrounds, felt a greater sympathy to the nationalist movement than they did loyalty to their own class and upbringing. At a glance, Roger Casement and Erskine Childers might have appeared similar. Both had served England with courage and distinction, both had received public recognition for their achievements; each loved Ireland with a patriotism intense enough to give his life in the cause of Irish independence. Both were executed: one hanged in an English prison, the other shot at a barracks in Dublin. The path each took to his patriot's grave could not have been more different.

Erskine Childers was the author of *The Riddle of the Sands,* a novel published in 1903 that has been read ever since as a literate thriller particularly attractive to anyone fond of sailing. At the time it was published it was also—and this was Childers' primary intention when he wrote it—a warning to England of her vulnerability to invasion from the North Sea should she engage in war with Germany.

Childers' wife, Molly, was an American from a good Boston family. She had been bedridden as a child and was never again to walk without a stick or to be free from pain. She adored her husband and loved sailing, and did not allow her disability to limit her more than was absolutely necessary. Childers' childhood had also, in a different way, been painful. When he was six years old, his father died of tuberculosis. His mother had chosen to conceal her husband's condition and to nurse him herself. After his death she contracted the highly infectious and, at that time, incurable disease and had to be separated from her children for the rest of her life. Erskine and his brother, Robert, were brought up by relatives in Ireland. As was usual at that time in Anglo-Irish families, the boys were educated in England. Childers served in the British Army during the Boer War and afterward became a hero in England for his gathering of the material—crucial to that country's intelligence—contained in *The Riddle of the Sands.*

A forty-foot ketch, the *Asgard,* had been given to Erskine and Molly Childers by her parents as a wedding present. On a July afternoon in 1914, just before the outbreak of war, the *Asgard* beat about Dublin Bay, waiting for a signal to dock at Howth; she was so laden with guns that she drew eighteen inches more water than she usually would.

With Childers aboard the *Asgard* were 900 rifles and 25,000 rounds of ammunition, and there were a further 600 rifles aboard the *Kelpie,* an accompanying yacht. Hardly enough to arm a revolution, but that was not Childers' intention. The guns for the Irish Volunteers were intended as a show of Southern Irish nationalist strength and as an answer to the—also illegal—April landing at Larne of 30,000 rifles for the Unionist Ulster Volunteers.

The crew of the *Asgard*—apart from two Donegal fishermen, ignorant until the last moment of the purpose of the journey—were Protestants sympathetic to the Southern Irish nationalist movement. Two of them were women. Despite a difficult and potentially dangerous voyage, there was an essentially English amateurism about the whole expedition. Gordon Shephard, a pilot on leave from the newly formed Royal Flying Corps, was at least an experienced yachtsman, although his attitude to their mission at times seemed less than serious. Mary Spring Rice, an inexperienced sailor but the innovator of the gunrunning scheme, kept a diary. In it she described Shephard's tendency to sleep late in the mornings and his wish to go ashore for a decent meal. The tone of Mary Spring Rice's account of the expedition is playful, but they all—Shephard the only one not to suffer from seasickness—made the twenty-three-day voyage and, during the night and while at sea, transferred the entire cargo of rifles and boxes of ammunition from the German tug to the *Asgard*.

As Childers and his tired crew strained their eyes for the signal to dock, Sir Roger Casement, in New York, waited anxiously for news of the success or failure of the *Asgard*'s mission.

Roger Casement, an Anglo-Irish Protestant, had been knighted for work in South America where he had exposed, as he previously had done in the Belgian Congo, virtual slavery and other atrocities in the rubber trade. Since his resignation from the British Consular Service several years before, he, like Erskine Childers, had espoused the Irish nationalist cause.

The arms were unloaded to the waiting Volunteers at Howth

on the afternoon of July 26th. On the 5th of August war was declared. On the 17th Childers received a telegram from the Admiralty telling him that his offer of service had been accepted; he left that night for London.

By then Casement, under a pseudonym and having shaved off his beard to alter his appearance, was on his way to Germany where he hoped to raise an Irish brigade to fight for Ireland against the British. With him traveled Adler Christensen, the man who was to become his nemesis.

THE FIRST SPRING of the war Uncle Hubert came home on leave from China. I was seven years old. My brother Edward had, eighteen months earlier and unannounced to me, arrived to share the nursery quarters. One day he wasn't there; the next he was. As far as I can remember, I accepted his presence without question and resigned myself to the inconvenience of living in close proximity to a baby with a loud voice and demanding habits.

Uncle Hubert was an official in the Chinese Maritime Customs. Although staffed at the senior level by foreigners (over half of them British) the customs service—which was administered with extraordinary efficiency and integrity—answered to Peking. Originally the Chinese Imperial Customs, the service had been created in 1860 and, after the Boxer Rebellion in 1900, was used to collect indemnities and to provide the Ch'ing Empire with about a third of its revenues. Over the years, the Customs had become a bureaucracy that, among other things, oversaw the postal services and waterways, and played a part in foreign affairs. Contemporary reservations about the connection between the Chinese Maritime Customs and Britain's morally dubious role in the Opium Wars were not shared by Uncle Hubert's family at Ballydavid.

My uncle's job was a reserved occupation that exempted him

from military service. The collection of revenues—mainly on salt—to repay a loan made in 1913 by England, France, Germany, Russia, and Japan was considered important enough to keep a young man who spoke fluent Chinese off the field of battle.

Uncle Hubert had written two letters to his mother, each telling of a death. The first he sent after the death of a baby that had lived only two weeks—the letter that announced its birth arrived after it was already dead—in the second he told her that his wife, weakened by childbirth and grief, had not been strong enough to fight off a sudden recurrence of fever. Grandmother and Aunt Katie went into mourning, although the difference in dress—both were in permanent half-mourning for their respective husbands—would have been noticeable only to those initiated into the rigid but scarcely visible rules by which we all lived. My father, who liked his wife to look pretty and welcoming, put his foot down when my mother took her black dresses out of mothballs: he saw no need for the new mother of a healthy little boy to wear mourning for a sister-in-law she had never met.

Uncle Hubert had six months' home leave every five years. Apart from a visit to Ballydavid and his mother and aunt, he spent this time in London. He used to come to tea; the timing of his visit, I now suspect, planned so he could spend time with his sister while my father was absent and to leave his evenings free for more amusing or livelier social arrangements.

My uncle was of greater interest to me in London than he would have been if I had met—or, more accurately, been shown or presented to—him at Ballydavid. The shape and constrictions of a London childhood made any departure from the dull and repetitive cycle of my days memorable. The rules at Ballydavid fell far short of anarchy, but there was a physical freedom that made me aware of the constraints of life at our house in Palace Gardens Terrace. The house was not small; by London standards it was open, light, and spacious, but the nursery quarters on the top floor were where Edward, Nanny, and I spent the greater part of our day. When we went for our afternoon walk, I was not allowed to stray from my place beside Edward's pram; and, if I had been permitted to do so, I could have wandered only along the paved paths, the grass and flower beds on either side a prohibited area, marked by a low edging of green-painted iron hoops. The clothing I was buttoned into before leaving the house restricted any spontaneous expression of energy or imagination— any possibility of play. Even in summer I wore black stockings and tightly buttoned boots; when the weather was cold, I also wore a stiff high-collared coat, gloves, and buttoned gaiters. I wore a hat throughout the year; it varied with the season, but it usually had an elastic band under the chin.

Uncle Hubert fascinated me. I had been shown in the schoolroom atlas where he lived when he was not home on leave, and my mother had traced with her finger the course of the voyage he had taken back to England. He was the eldest of three children and treated my mother with a teasing affection that both startled me and revealed a completely new aspect of her nature. I already knew that my mother loved Sainthill, her younger brother, to an extent that would not allow her feelings for Uncle Hubert to be described as more than a very strong affection. How did I know? I now think that because I was an eldest child, most of my instinct and a good deal of time and energy went into working out how the world—at that stage exemplified by my family and our household—worked. I already understood the realities of the nursery and had made a good start on the kitchen. Childhood is a time when one is presented with the pieces of a large and complicated jigsaw puzzle. I struggled to fit the interlocking parts together without knowing what the eventual completed picture was supposed to look like. And the picture changed with each new observation I made. Soon after Edward was born, I realized it was a puzzle he would never solve on his own, and I made it my business to inform him of some important aspects and to shield him from others.

Uncle Hubert's cigarette case was a good example of a piece of the puzzle that I recognized as significant without knowing, or having any way of knowing, its import. I still remember that case and the way his graceful fingers took a cigarette from it, closed its silver lid, and tapped the cigarette lightly before striking a match. It was not until my uncle Sainthill's personal effects were returned to his mother during an irony-filled Christmas visit by a fellow officer that I discovered the significance of these cigarette cases both as a gift and as a charm against the evil forces personified by a German bullet or shrapnel. The slim metal case, slightly curved to follow the outline of the body, was inscribed—usually by a woman—and kept in the breast pocket of the uniform of the man whose heart it was intended to protect. Did it ever save a life? Could it save a life? I don't know. And without knowing this, either, I imagine that the officers—and surely for so many reasons this was a phenomenon only among the younger ones— knew the cases would provide little protection but felt safer having them anyway.

Uncle Hubert: his moustache, his cigarette case (my father was clean shaven, regarding facial hair as an affectation and tobacco as a waste of money), his bantering tone with my mother, her difficulty in knowing what was a tease and what was not, and how he enjoyed testing her gullibility and humor. I remember, in particular, a Russian woman whom Uncle Hubert brought to visit.

Edward and I were with my mother in the drawing room. Edward, sweet and fat, sat on Mother's knee, and I perched on the edge of the sofa, brushed, curled, and uncomfortably dressed for tea. I don't know if my mother was expecting Uncle Hubert in the sense that an engagement had been made, but she was ready for him or any other visitor who might call.

The Irish maid announced Uncle Hubert.

"Mr. Bagnold to see you, ma'am, and Madame—" she hesitated as though she might attempt the name but changed her mind "—and Madam."

Uncle Hubert stood back at the door to allow a woman to enter. Although not as exotic as Mrs. Coughlan, of whom I still quite often thought, this was a creature who bore an encouraging similarity to her.

"Mary," my uncle said, "this is Madame Tchnikov."

My mother, putting Edward down on the hearthrug, rose slowly and approached the visitor. I could see that the time she was taking was designed to allow my uncle to add something—an explanation of who this strange woman was, of why she was accompanying my uncle, above all of why she was being introduced to my mother. But Uncle Hubert merely smiled; he looked as though he had arrived with a treat—something on the order of an ornately decorated tin of sweet biscuits. I, at least, was appreciative.

Tea was poured; small talk followed. The conversation remained general and superficial. Nevertheless, by the time my uncle and Madame Tchnikov left, we had gathered that she had lived in the Balkans, that she was of aristocratic birth, a refugee (someone close to her—not specified but referred to as *he*—had been political), and a widow. And that she had "suffered." I was curious to see how my mother would describe the visit to my father when he came home. Most events I witnessed gained a valuable dimension when I heard them described to someone else. I remained the epitome of a well-behaved little girl, silent and without fidgeting, in order to hear what my mother would say. I could see that she was confused and upset.

My mother was sweet natured and self-effacing. She was quiet, gentle, soft, and affectionate. Of the few times she had stood up for herself, the most dramatic was when she'd slipped out the side door of her parents' house in Philimore Gardens to meet my waiting father. They had gone to a Registry Office where she had married him. It now seems possible her action may be more an illustration of his will than of hers. My grandmother, who had had dreams and ambitions, was even more upset at the elopement of her beautiful daughter with a brash young New Zealander come to seek his fortune in England than was her husband, the General. My grandfather, though initially angry and disappointed, was at least aware of my father's strength of character and courage; he, himself, had had to make his own way. The elopement was now far enough in the past for the marriage to have become part of the pattern of our family, but my mother lived every day with a consequence for which she was entirely unsuited: a cultural—in this instance not only a euphemism for class—difference between her and my father, the difference more pronounced when witnessed by her friends and members of her family.

So Uncle Hubert was not alone in being more comfortable visiting my mother before my father came home; my mother was also happier spending time with her brother while her husband was absent. Now Uncle Hubert had introduced someone of unknown antecedents into her drawing room; someone who might be a most courageous and deserving refugee but who might also be what my mother called an "adventuress." And since my mother had given up the right to pronounce on unsuitable alliances when she had eloped with my father, she did not feel she could question Uncle Hubert's choice. What she could ask, or rather attempt to ascertain, was to what extent this unfortunate creature—by this time my mother had noticed dark roots below Madame Tchnikov's huge mound of red hair and color from her lip salve on her cup—had got her claws into Uncle Hubert.

My father, appealed to when he came home, remarked that Hubert had always given the impression of being well able to take care of himself. Even I could tell this offhand remark was intended to put an end to the subject. My father tended to be unsympathetic to problems peculiar to the privileged.

"It's just——" my mother said slowly, as she searched for the right euphemism, "in a few months he will be going back to China—for five years—and he doesn't have a wife. Maybe he's lonely——"

My father laughed.

"Do you think there aren't women in China?" he asked.

My mother drew in her breath, remembered my presence, and I was sent upstairs for my bath. But not before I had gathered, while not understanding the implications, that my father was suggesting for a man on his own, a beautiful, young, and undemanding Chinese woman might be more appealing than a shopworn and desperate Russian refugee. Or, I inferred, possibly even a suitable young Englishwoman of the right background.

Mother did not, to my disappointment, again require my company on the days when Uncle Hubert brought this exotic creature to call. After awhile, my uncle stopped bringing Madame Tchnikov to the house. When he came again on his own, he seemed to suggest, although nobody could ask—actually my father would have had no difficulty with the question but still showed no inclination to become involved—that he had brought Madame Tchnikov rather as a novelty that would interest and amuse my family as much as it did him. My mother breathed a sigh of relief. Rather prematurely as it turned out.

One damp April afternoon, as my mother was sitting in the drawing room, the maid announced Madame Tchnikov— Madame Tchnikov following close on her heels so there could be no question of my mother being not at home. Mother was at a disadvantage; she did not know if Madame Tchnikov was visiting at Uncle Hubert's suggestion or if he had perhaps arranged to meet her at Palace Gardens Terrace.

My mother, flustered, rose to greet her guest and glanced at me. I avoided her eye, fairly sure she would not insult Madame Tchnikov by immediately removing her daughter. And I knew, too, that Mother, guiltily, welcomed my presence as an inhibiting influence on the conversation.

"Mara," my mother said, "how nice. Is Hubert joining us later?"

"I don't know," Madame Tchnikov said. It was not possible to tell from the way she spoke whether she was unsure of the exact nature of Uncle Hubert's intentions for the rest of the afternoon or if she was declaring complete ignorance of his whereabouts and plans. It was not possible to rephrase the question, and my mother had no way of knowing if her guest was the vanguard of a fraternal visit or if she was acting as a free agent.

I, at least, was pleased to see Madame Tchnikov. She swept me up into a dramatic embrace. She smelled of powder and not quite fresh scent. And of a dark, mysterious femininity that I had never before encountered. My mother smelled of powder, too, but in a way that suggested lavender and fresh white linen. Madame Tchnikov evoked less innocent flowers: dark orchids or over-scented lilies.

The grown-ups sat down and my mother poured Madame Tchnikov a cup of tea. I had a feeling that cups of tea were not much in my new heroine's line. There was a moment of silence. My mother searched for some subject for small talk that did not involve Uncle Hubert.

"I visited Paris once. With my mother, before the war. Did you live there long?"

Even I could see that my mother's Parisian experience—her

mother, an English-speaking pension, Versailles, tea made with boiling water in a properly warmed teapot—was not that of a refugee from the unhappy Balkans. This knowledge, of course, was clarified and details added when later experience expanded childhood memory; I was a precocious child, but Swinburne and Montmartre were not yet among my terms of reference. Partly because I sensed the emotions and inferences that made this conversational gambit of my mother's almost inflammatory, I listened, remembered, and puzzled over each word and nuance. All the while sitting quietly with an expression that suggested incomprehension, mild stupidity, and dreaminess.

"It was a terrible time," Mara, as I was beginning to think of her—said, her voice and face tragic.

"I'm so sorry," my mother's social awkwardness now becoming sympathy. "I didn't mean to upset you."

"I was so young," Mara said, dabbing her eyes with a small handkerchief. I was fascinated but, like my mother, who seemed equally curious and embarrassed, I would have preferred to observe Mara from a distance.

My mother made a sympathetic sound. The tragedy of Mara's youthfulness was difficult to comment on, especially since, if she had, as she'd told us, just fled the oppression of the Austro-Hungarian Empire, this youthful tragedy would have had to have taken place in the very recent past.

"My——" Mara said, indistinctly, into her handkerchief.

"Your family?" Mother asked, her sympathy fully engaged.

Mara sniffed in a manner that suggested assent.

"Your mother?" my mother asked gently.

Mara said nothing, but shook her head behind the handkerchief.

"Your father?" My mother tried again.

Mara repeated her gesture. I watched, fascinated, prepared to have my mother run through every possible family permutation—I already had the feeling that, in some not yet imaginable way, Mother was on the wrong track—as far as second cousins once removed and the list of unlikely people one was, in the back of the prayer book, forbidden to marry. Fortunately for my mother, Mara preferred to avoid this ritual.

"My husband," Mara said, lowering her handkerchief a little.

"And he——is he——?" My mother was sympathetic but also curious. I was too fascinated to feel sorry for such a dramatic figure.

"He was a brute!" Mara said passionately.

Unfortunately, at this point my mother sent me up to the nursery. I could see her beginning to attempt, unsuccessfully, to stem the flow of information, every new revelation seeming, in Madame Tchnikov's mind, to form a bond—by which she meant an obligation on my mother's part—between the two women. I could see, as I dawdled toward the door, that Mara would have done better to reveal her story slowly, to have whetted my mother's curiosity with hints and barely alluded to mysteries. She had overplayed her hand, as I now suspect she had done all her life.

Although I was the one person who would have given my mother a sympathetic ear, she did not choose to confide in me. She, like all adults, assumed I understood less than I did. Even then this surprised me; would I, too, when I grew up, forget so completely what it was like to be a child? My parents underestimated my comprehension to the extent of sometimes saying in my presence, when one or the other glanced in my direction, the conversation having become interesting, "She's too young to understand." Useful though their belief sometimes was, it did nothing to allay my solitary moments of fear. I wanted information, but I also wanted reassurance. Not reassurance that my fears were groundless—I knew they were not, even when they were not specific but inferred from the unspoken or from conversations I did not understand—but I wanted some indication of the worst that could happen.

Money and the death of my parents were the principal sources of my fears. I knew that my parents sometimes worried about money; my father, whose family had been badly off, worried more than my mother did. Sometimes they argued when my father thought my mother extravagant or careless. What would happen if we ran out of money? We would be poor, but how poor? Poor like my nursery maid who had, at least, a roof—ours—over her head and plenty to eat? Or poor like the old soldier who, an arm missing and a row of medals on his chest, sold matches from a tray beside the gate to the park? His professional cheerfulness, suggesting that there was nothing about his condition unusual enough to justify bitterness, did nothing to allay my fears. Then I would think about the beggar women trudging up the avenue at Ballydavid, always with a silent ill-nourished baby under their shawl. These women would go to the back door where they would be given food and a small sum of money. They came at what seemed to be self-regulated intervals. Some enjoyed a status superior to others, and I would from time to time see one sitting at the kitchen table with a plate and a cup of tea in front of her. But I never chanced upon anyone admiring the baby.

This image of mother-and-child poverty, distressing though it was, was related to a consoling thought: if my father proved unable to provide for us, surely my grandmother would intervene and take at least me back to Ballydavid. My grandmother was also the image I invoked, late at night, when I imagined either or both my parents dead. She and Aunt Katie were still alive; surely that guaranteed the lives of my parents, who belonged to a younger generation. But in my heart, with the evidence of war around me, I knew this was not true.

My mother came to fear and then resent Madame Tchnikov's visits. She was unwise enough to complain to my father. He saw her problem as amusing and lacked sympathy for either my mother or her increasingly frequent caller.

"Tell her to go away and not come back," he advised unhelpfully.

"Oh, Bobby, I couldn't possibly do that. You don't know what the poor thing's been through."

"So it looks as though you're stuck with her." My father, whose life had not been privileged enough to induce guilt, lacked imagination or sympathy for this kind of problem. "Just don't ask her to dinner or give her money."

My father, having lost interest in what he considered a self-induced problem of my mother's, retired behind the *Times*. He missed Mother's guilty expression; I knew that small sums of money had already passed from her to Madame Tchnikov.

After a time Mother complained to her brother. Uncle Hubert had brought me a book. The book provided cover for eavesdropping, and I kept my head down as though I were puzzling out the difficult words while listening to the grown-up conversation.

"But Hugh, she's such a bore," my mother said.

My uncle laughed lazily and picked me up and put me on his knee. I continued looking at the pictures, and from time to time he would point out some detail. The book was about a Chinese family.

"Hugh," my mother said, her casual tone abandoned. She was beginning to sound desperate.

"I wonder if you would think her such a bore if I told you she had murdered her husband."

My mother's gasp was the only sound for a moment or two. Then my uncle laughed. His laugh suggested Mother was being teased, but it didn't necessarily mean that he had made up this shocking, to my mother, and thrilling, to me, piece of information.

"Really, Hugh!" my mother said, predictably adding, "Alice, I think it's time you———"

"Nonsense, Mary," Uncle Hubert said good-naturedly, "How do you ever expect the child to learn to read if you keep interrupting her lessons?"

So I was allowed to stay a little longer, though my feelings were hurt. I did know how to read and had thought my uncle had been taken in by my occasional guess—inspired by the illustrations—at the harder words.

"Are you sure, Hugh?" Mother asked, adding, to prevent his pretending she was asking a question about my education, "That she—that that's what she did?"

I remembered that Madame Tchnikov's husband had been a brute, and admired her all the more for having dealt with her problem so decisively.

"That's what she told me—I've no reason to doubt her word. On that particular count, at least."

"Well," my mother said, fussing with the hot water jug, "I don't know what to say."

"I gained the impression that he was no great loss to society," Uncle Hubert added.

"But still," Mother said.

And Uncle Hubert laughed again.

"Now, Alice, take your book upstairs. You can read with Nanny before your bath."

I looked up at my uncle for a further reprieve, but he seemed to have forgotten about me. I went as slowly as I could toward the door. Neither of the adults spoke; my uncle, relieved of my presence on his knee, took out his cigarette case and opened it. After I closed the door, I leaned against it, listening.

"Really, Hugh, if you knew this, I think you should not have brought her here."

"I thought you'd be amused."

"Amused?" My mother's voice was a little higher, but I knew she was mostly outraged because she didn't know how to get rid of this woman whom Uncle Hubert seemed effortlessly to have discarded.

I heard footsteps coming from the kitchen. At the same time the front door opened and Kathleen went to help my father out of his wet overcoat. Here my memory fails me. Was my father in uniform? Was he home on leave? In my mind's eye he is dressed as though he had come back from his job in the City, although this is not possible since the Stock Exchange had been closed for the duration of the war. I loitered silently. Kathleen took the damp coat and hat back to the kitchen quarters, and my father looked at me benevolently and slightly quizzically.

"Hello, Blossom," he said. "What're you doing here?"

"I was on my way upstairs," I said. I hoped he might stop and talk to me, but he just asked, "Where's your mother?"

"In the drawing room."

"Is anyone with her?"

"Uncle Hubert."

"Anyone else?"

I shook my head. I wondered if I should tell Father that Madame Tchnikov was a murderess; I am afraid I was ready to sacrifice my heroine for my father's attention, but he had already turned away.

"All right, Blossom," he said as he put his hand out to open the drawing-room door. "Run along upstairs."

For the next two weeks, my mother went to bed with a headache every afternoon. After a while Madame Tchnikov stopped coming to call.

———

SIR ROGER CASEMENT was a homosexual, and he kept a diary. At the time I am describing, I had not heard of Casement and, equally unsurprisingly, *homosexual* was a word I would not come across for some years. I did, however, own a diary.

As the first born, I was sometimes given presents which, though flattering, were more suitable for an older child. My first diary has my name in pencil, a couple of poorly written lines in January, and not much more. In subsequent years I developed the knack of recording events with a line or two. There was space for little more and no need for it: My day-to-day life was uneventful; I was not given to introspection; and, had I been, I would, I hope, not have been so foolish as to commit secret thoughts to paper. These diaries sometimes serve as an *aide-mémoire* as I attempt to reconstruct the events of the years I am trying to describe, but more often I turn to one of the books written about the early years of the war or about Casement himself. There are more of these than you might imagine. My nursery diaries and these books show me something that is always true but almost impossible to keep in mind, that our everyday lives—in the main part dull and lacking in important event—are lived in an historical context.

My early childhood, which seemed, and was, a recurrent round of boredom, starchy meals, uncomfortable clothes, and rules of no apparent benefit to me, was lived in a terrible moment of history. The First World War. Men from almost every family in England were in France, fighting and dying in horrifying conditions. In London, the experience of war was not limited to fear and mourning; I have dim but thrilling memories of Zeppelins and the glow of night fires.

And in Ireland a revolt against British rule was brewing. Since the fates of both islands were even more closely connected than they now are, the lives of the inhabitants of both countries were affected by the war and the incipient rising. Although my daily life in the nursery, at school, or on walks seemed as solidly settled in dullness as the only slightly more interesting lives of my family, history, intermittently and with no warning, would from time to time change or destroy some integral aspect of our lives.

I now teach English literature and grammar at a Protestant girls' school in Dunlaorighe—from which you may infer I am a widow of modest means; were I unmarried I should probably be a governess. I am grateful that teaching my pupils the history of their country is not among my duties, since my own life, suddenly and forever, was changed in a moment in history which I do not choose to expose to a partisan or politically expedient interpretation. Since I was not quite ten years old when Casement was executed, my description of the last years of his life and my thoughts about his behavior are those formed during the fifty years I have had to think about his actions. Fifty years to read about, as history, some of the events immediate to my childhood; to study the causes of those events and the random, fortuitous influences— largely human weakness and human error—that changed their course and altered their resolution; to consider my own choices; to form opinions and regrets.

Casement was, as I have said, a homosexual. And he was unwise enough to keep a diary. Homosexuality was probably no less common that it is today, but it was considered by the greater part of the heterosexual population to be an odious sin. A surprising level of conspicuously effete appearance and behavior was tolerated among the English upper classes and—perhaps because of the seriousness of the offence—not openly considered homosexual. Nevertheless, once the charge was leveled, the legal implications were, then as now, grave and the social consequences impossible to survive.

Adler Christensen complemented Casement's emotional weakness and shared his taste for drama. A Norwegian sailor, out of work and desperate, he had accosted Casement on the street in

New York City. Christensen was young, tall, blond, and destitute; Casement was susceptible and sympathetic. He was habitually generous to those in need and, although short of money himself (the Foreign Office could have been more generous in the matter of his pension), told Christensen to visit him at his hotel the following day. He became the patron and employer of the manipulative young man; at what stage the relationship became a sexual one is not known.

Casement didn't speak German when he left for Berlin in the summer of 1914, and it seems he didn't learn much during the increasingly unhappy sixteen months he spent in Germany. Adler Christensen traveled with him as his servant and translator. That Casement should have given the additional power that comes with the role of translator to his dubious companion seems not only self-destructive and unwise but in keeping with the extraordinary lack of judgment he displayed throughout this futile, depressing, and ultimately tragic mission.

Casement's journey and stay in Berlin were arranged and financed by the Clan na Gael, an Irish-American organization, formally connected to the Irish Revolutionary Brotherhood, whose aim was an independent Irish Republic. The most powerful member of the Clan na Gael was John Devoy, an Irish-born, well-organized, clearheaded revolutionary. He was a tough, bitter man who had spent two years in the Foreign Legion and five years in prison for his revolutionary activities in Ireland.

One has the impression that the Clan na Gael was comprised of similarly well-organized, clear-headed Irish-Americans devoted to the cause of Irish freedom but devoid of that romantic, idealistic, unrealistic quality so often found—and almost as often with disastrous results—in the homegrown Irish patriot. It goes without saying that every member of the Clan na Gael was Roman Catholic. It is possible, though not likely, that one or more of these supporters of the revolution would have been tolerant of Casement's choice of companion, but it is not possible that any of them would not have worried about his lack of judgment. Casement must have been aware of what they thought, and it is hard to imagine that efforts were not made to dissuade him when he insisted Christensen should accompany him on his mission to Berlin.

The tone of schoolboy adventure was set even before Casement and Christensen arrived in Germany. Traveling on a Norwegian ship, the *Oscar II,* they had several adventures before they arrived in Germany. Casement elected to disguise himself by shaving his beard and, even though there were United States citizens on board, posing as an American. His behavior drew attention, especially from the Americans, and it was assumed he was an English spy. The neutral ship was stopped by a British naval vessel, and several passengers who were German subjects were taken off for internment. Casement raised a small subscription for those taken away, diffusing the feeling against him but, of course, drawing even more attention to himself.

In Norway, a neutral country, the dramatic stakes were raised. This story has two sides: one told by Findlay, an English diplomat, the other by Christensen and, secondhand, by Casement. Findlay reported to his superiors that Christensen had presented himself at the British Legation and had offered to sell information about "an Irish-American-German conspiracy." Visits of this kind were, it seems, a frequent enough occurrence for a procedure, including a scale of remuneration, to be followed. Findlay interviewed Christensen who, without offering any concrete information, received encouragement and a small fee. Findlay afterward claimed that he had had no previous knowledge of Casement's activities and had assumed that he was still a member of the British Consular Service.

Christensen couldn't wait to return to the gullible Casement with his improbable story. He said he had been approached by a stranger and, entirely in Casement's interests, had gone with that stranger to the British Legation where he was offered money to watch and report on his traveling companion. The effect on the vulnerable, self-dramatizing Casement can be imagined.

Encouraged by Casement, Christensen returned to the Legation the following afternoon. At this stage the story starts to build on itself; not only does Casement seem to have accepted without question Christensen's penny-dreadful account of his dealings with a British career diplomat, but eventually that career diplomat, Findlay, was persuaded by Christensen to put in writing an offer to pay him £5,000 for the delivery of Casement into British hands.

Assuming, as I think one must, that Adler Christensen acted as an *agent provocateur,* it does not seem that he did so from any more noble motive than self-aggrandizement or the wish for attention and small sums of money. Nevertheless, by persuading Findlay to put in writing their agreement, he placed the British in the position of having abused the hospitality of a neutral country and having provided evidence of their intention to assassinate or kidnap a former colleague of their own. It was a wrongdoing that Casement was to return to obsessively each time he failed to achieve one of the goals for which he had come to Germany or when he was disappointed in one of the increasingly unrealistic schemes he had developed once he got there.

Findlay was embarrassed, his superiors angry. But in the end, who really cared? The war continued; Casement's Irish-American comrades had more heinous crimes to lay at the feet of the British; and his new German allies soon became bored by his morbid insistence on the importance of this "outrage."

In the end, perhaps the saddest aspect of this farcical behavior is that it makes one question Casement's previous achievements.

Were his triumphs on the part of suffering humanity a result of his high-minded sense of justice? Or had he, casting about for something on which to focus his always smoldering sense of outrage, just happened to fix his sights on two noble causes? The kindest and most probable answer, I think, is that not only had the hardships of the Congo and Putumayo broken his physical health, but the horrors he encountered there had affected his sanity.

Chapter 2

I REMEMBER MY—OUR—next visit to Ballydavid more clearly than I do the summer when I met Oonagh on the avenue and Mrs. Coughlan came to visit. But I have come to understand that, as when we recount a dream we adjust the images, events, and emotions of which it is comprised into a neater narrative form, so do we, when our memory fails, without knowing that we do so, use the probable to bridge the gaps between those events we remember clearly (although not necessarily accurately) and what is lost forever. Shortly after Uncle Hubert went back to China, without an unsuitable wife—or a suitable one either—we went to visit Grandmother and Aunt Katie.

We traveled second class on the train. My father, who was not with us and therefore had no idea of what was involved in taking two small children on a long journey, thought traveling first class an affectation. We lived comfortably enough at Palace Gardens Terrace, but luxury and even the purchase of the nonessential was actively discouraged by my father. My mother bought good writing paper, scented soap, kid gloves, and made charitable contributions, well aware that Father would have forbidden the expenditure had he known about it. We had, fortunately for my mother's self-respect, a large, solid, and well-situated house. Father had bought it cheaply before the war as an investment and because he thought possession of the house made him appear, as it did, solid and well situated.

We boarded the train at Paddington in the early afternoon. At the outbreak of war, railway services had been taken over by the government and a reduced timetable had come into effect; travel by rail had become progressively less comfortable and more expensive. But it was a warm sunny day and for some time I, at least, was full of a sense of adventure. Edward was asleep but Mother, though putting a good face on it, was undoubtedly apprehensive. She suffered terribly from seasickness; and, apart from her anticipation of a miserable crossing, she must have worried about her ability to care for us while she was in that state.

I watched, full of anticipation and excitement, as the train seemed to come to life, sigh, and roll slowly out of the busy station. It was not the first time I had been on a train, but it was the first rail journey that I can remember. Soon we were passing through poor neighborhoods with rows of small houses backing onto the railway line. Behind each house was a small sooty backyard that contained nothing but the occasional sooty washing line. I remember a large black-and-white cat lying on a fence between two houses, self-contained and seemingly oblivious to the discomfort of its narrow perch and the proximity of the noisy train passing only yards in front of its face.

Then came the beginning of the suburbs, the houses a little more prosperous, although well short of substantial or handsome; no one who could afford to do otherwise was likely to live beside a railway track. The train stopped at suburban stations. Commuters got off and other passengers boarded, some with serious luggage and probably also traveling to Ireland. A few were in uniform—soldiers on leave.

A station at a small rural town. Then the beginning of the open countryside: fields, crops green and still close to the soil, and small farmhouses. When I had finished admiring the scenery— inferior in my opinion to what we would see in Ireland, but a step in the right direction—I turned to my illustrated story- book. Edward slept on, and my mother sat quietly, her hands in her lap, a small smile on her lips; I had no idea what she might be thinking.

After a while, the train stopped, but not at a station. I leaned out the window to see what was happening. Some passengers, men in tweeds, women in beautiful clothes, got off the train and stood on a small platform. From further down the train came men and women in plain dark clothes—valets and lady's maids—who fussed around the luggage as it was loaded onto a smartly painted horse-drawn cart. As well as suitcases, there were gun cases; hat- boxes; and dressing cases that I imagined contained jewelry and sets of glass, silver, and enamel jars of powder, hairbrushes, and chamois nail buffers that the maids would arrange on dressing tables when they arrived. The younger women were beautiful or at least pretty, the older women handsome or distinguished, the men well fed, confident—all completely indifferent to the gaze of the passengers still on the train, many of whom clustered at the windows in open curiosity.

"It's Badminton," my mother said. "The Duke of Beaufort is having a house party. When he has guests, the train stops here to let them off."

She didn't rise from her seat to look out the window, but she was watching the activity outside as much as she could without betraying curiosity. It is a moment that I can remember with complete clarity and in minute detail; although all the activity and all the most interesting characters were outside and the well-dressed guests were now getting into a series of smartly

turned-out horse-drawn vehicles, it is my mother's attentive, expressionless face that is for me the center of the scene. I realized
later that, had my mother not nipped out the side door of her parents' house and gone to Caxton Hall, throwing in her lot with my
overbearing New Zealand–born father, she might have been one
of the women on the platform. At that moment, too, I learned
that to show curiosity about the lives of those more privileged
than oneself was to suggest that they were in some way superior.
Mother had learned this—by example or osmosis, it is not possible that words would have been employed—from her mother.
Grandmother would never show, or I imagine feel, interest in the
life of anyone who would not be equally curious about her own
circumstances. She showed no more interest in the aristocratic
Irish families who had retained their money and estates than she
did in the day-to-day life of the solicitor's wife who spoke with a
thick Cork accent. Grandmother acted as if the world in which
she lived, that of the landed gentry, was the most admirable and
desirable; to think otherwise would be to admit inferiority to
someone. Although my mother may have been secretly wistful
when she looked out the window of the second class carriage, I
believed—believe—Grandmother to have been right.

After a minute or two—no one was boarding the train at this
stop—we continued. I slept for a while; I was still young enough
for the motion of the train to have a soporific effect. When I woke
up we had the carriage to ourselves; and my mother unpacked
our picnic basket, a handsome wicker affair, the kind people then
used to give as wedding presents, although wedding presents
were probably something else my mother had missed out on
when she eloped with my father. There were ham sandwiches,
hard-boiled eggs, barley water, and a thermos of tea for Mother.
And apples—their skin wrinkled by winter storage—to clean
our teeth and freshen our mouths afterward.

The spring evening became night. It started to rain. Wind, foretelling a rough crossing, spattered large drops against the grimy windows. Outside there was nothing but rushing darkness broken by occasional lights, glittering in the wet night. The lights inside the carriage were dim and I alternately dozed and listlessly looked at my book.

"Don't strain your eyes," my mother said. She sat with her head resting on a neat, white antimacassar attached to the dark plush upholstery, as beautiful as the women we had watched alighting at Badminton—pale, tired, but not relaxed enough to sleep.

"Are we nearly there?" I asked.

My mother glanced at her watch and then outside at the darkness.

"No," she said, "We've only just crossed into Wales. Why don't you try to sleep a little?"

"I can't," I said.

But I must have fallen asleep again, although I had no sense of having been woken when I became aware that we had stopped at a large station. The noise outside also woke Edward: doors slamming, the stationmaster shouting, porters loading and un-loading baggage, good-byes. My mother was stiff with tension; I knew she dreaded crossing the Irish Sea, but her present disquiet seemed more immediate. As the train started to pull out of the station, she seemed to relax a little. We heard the hiss of steam, a clank of metal as the wheels engaged, a slow chunk-chunk-chunk that became faster, and then the familiar rhythm of wheels on tracks. We had left the noise and light of the station and were rushing through the unbroken dark of the Welsh countryside when the door of the carriage was pushed open. Again my mother's sigh of relief had been premature. It occurs to me now that this may have been more than just bad luck; she had, I think, a tendency to focus only on the problems of the next moment. It would have accounted for her marriage to my father. As she had slipped out of the house in Philimore Gardens, her heart had pounded with fear that she would be caught and prevented from making an unsuitable marriage, not that she would one day find herself looking out the window of a train at what her life could have been and wasn't.

A man stood in the doorway of the compartment. In one hand, he held a brown beer bottle; with the other he supported himself against the swaying of the train. He stood there for a moment, surprised and pleased, as if he had come across friends in an unexpected place. He smiled a weak, slightly guilty smile and came into the carriage. My mother glanced past him at the corridor, hoping for the conductor or fearing the man might have a companion. But we were alone, just the four of us. Edward had gone back to sleep.

Our new traveling companion sat down beside my mother. He lifted his bottle to his lips, drained it, and put it with exaggerated care on the floor. Although I was a little nervous, I was also curious. This was not a situation where Mother could send me upstairs when it began to be interesting. My mother sat up a little straighter, an aloof half-smile on her lips and an expression that, while not encouraging our new traveling companion, would not provoke his belligerence. I flicked my glance from my mother to the man; he caught my eye and winked. It was a friendly wink; I thought he might have children of his own. I looked down, simulating shyness; although I had been taught to stand up straight and be polite to those adults who acknowledged my presence, my mother's silence told me that this was an exception to the rule.

As I pretended to study my book, hoping that this interesting stranger would be impressed by my ability to read, he spoke. I could not understand him and I looked up, startled.

"He's speaking Welsh," my mother said. "I don't think he speaks English."

This was even more interesting than I had imagined. It was my first exposure to a foreign language. And my mother seemed more open to conversation than she sometimes was.

"Of course," she added hastily in a low voice, "he may understand it."

I studied the man's face. I did not have the impression that he comprehended my mother's words, but I could tell that his lack of reaction might be a result of his condition—I understood the principle of intoxication, although not to the extent of being able to recognize it; but in this case the brown bottle was a clue—rather than an ignorance of the English language. As I watched, his eyes began to close; they half-opened once or twice, and then he sank into an uncomfortable sleep.

I was free now to study our traveling companion. Before I did so, I glanced toward my mother. She smiled a half-hearted, reassuring smile and put her finger to her lips. I understood that she hoped the man would continue to sleep, at least until the conductor came. He was dressed in dirty clothes, but I could see that his clothing and the grime on his hands and face were the consequence of work, not of vagrancy.

We continued silently on for a long time. Edward slept; I stared at the unconscious man; my mother sat up straight with a benevolent expression, her demeanor confirming that she was a pillar of respectable society. From time to time, the whistle blew; the train left the blackness of the open, raining night and passed under hills though dry, dark tunnels. I began to feel the need to visit the WC at the end of the corridor, but I said nothing.

We passed though a dimly lit small station without stopping, and as the train slowed down to follow a curve of the tracks, the empty brown beer bottle toppled over and rolled across the carriage and under my seat. The man sat bolt upright, said something in his mysterious language, smiled apologetically at my mother, and patted her reassuringly on her knee.

I was already adept at pretending not to notice awkward moments or inconvenient facts. Partly because I gathered that was how one was supposed to behave, and partly because the less I seemed to notice or understand the more likely I was to be in a position where I could watch interesting things happen and gather necessary information. Nevertheless, my mouth opened in astonished disbelief at this extraordinary liberty, and I felt, for the first time, a twinge of fear. It was not often that the conventions of society did not work, and if they didn't, it meant that other rules—the kind that guaranteed safety—also might not hold true.

My mother, without relinquishing her protective ladylike posture, shrank as far as she could into the ungiving upholstery of the Great Western seat. Our traveling companion patted her knee again. I looked at his hand, its ingrained dirt, the black under and around his fingernails, the grimy, frayed cuffs of his shirt; despite his unnerving behavior, I still had the impression that he was a laborer and that his appearance was not a result of an intrinsic lack of cleanliness. The man also regarded his hand, resting on the lavender gray of my mother's spring coat. My mother, dignified and frightened, looked above my head, seeing nothing.

After a moment, the man lifted his hand and looked at it with a puzzled expression. Then he turned to look at my mother. At first it seemed as though he were about to apologize; then his expression changed and he began to smile. I thought, and I am sure my mother thought, that he was about to kiss her. We both froze, holding our breath, my mother, I am sure, as frightened as I was. The man sighed, his eyes began to close, and he once again fell asleep. This time with his head on my mother's shoulder.

"It's all right, Alice. He's harmless." Mother didn't speak again until we reached the next station. As the train drew into the noisy, brightly lit platform, the man woke up and, without a glance at any of us, stood up and left the carriage. I looked out the window and saw him make his way slowly across the platform, through a gate, and out into the darkness.

I slept for most of what remained of our journey. When I awoke briefly, Mother was sitting as upright as she had been before. On her face was an expression I had never seen. Angry, resentful, and determined.

O'NEILL WAS WAITING for us on the Quay at Waterford. The warm, sunny day with a mild fresh breeze seemed to begin when we reached the dock. Tired, dirty, pale, we walked down the gangplank into paradise.

The crossing had not been particularly rough. But it had been unpleasant—particularly for my mother who, seasick herself, had had to look after an overtired infant. Even though I had tried not to be any trouble, I had, to my shame, vomited on the cabin floor. During the night, I had woken and heard my mother weeping quietly and, I thought, angrily. After the boat had turned into the early morning calm of the river, strong tea had been served. Our fellow passengers availed themselves of its dark reviving powers. My mother added some more milk to hers and told me to sip it. My stomach, still tender, revolted against the strong pale liquid, and I retched; to this day the idea of stewed milky tea in a thick white cup revolts me.

O'Neill welcomed my mother as though she were a returning princess. He seemed impressed by how I had grown and pronounced the pale and grizzling Edward "a fine looking lad." O'Neill worshipped my mother. She had a good seat on a horse; and, on the rare occasions that she now enjoyed a day's foxhunting, the overconditioned hunter still kept at Ballydavid was shown to O'Neill's credit.

Patience, the pony that pulled the trap, was for me one of the great attractions of Ballydavid. I hoped to be allowed to ride this summer and I sometimes pretended that Patience was my pony. O'Neill found our luggage, loaded it into the trap, and we were on our way. There was a smell of salt in the air; noisy seagulls circled overhead, and pigeons, sidestepping horses' hooves, pecked at spilled grain between the cobblestones.

Ballydavid was six miles from Waterford; in cold or wet weather it seemed a long journey, but on a sunny morning like this it was only pleasure. Color came back into my mother's face as she questioned O'Neill about people and places and asked after his family—his son Tom was fighting in France—and about my grandmother and great-aunt.

It seemed to me—a minority view, I was aware—there was more of interest to look at in Waterford than in London. Soon we left the wide streets around the river and the Mall and drove past small gardens with monkey puzzles and the large stone gates of a school where I could see a games field; chestnut trees held large pink and white candles, and a cherry tree in pale bloom stood inside the gates of another large house set back from the road and partially obscured by trees. We passed children and dogs, and a middle-aged woman in a mackintosh, to whom Mother waved, walking two sleek greyhounds. Leaving the town behind us, we descended the steep hill, from which we could again see the river and the island in the wider part of it, home to a Hassard whom my great-aunt had once referred to as "Bluebeard." I watched for the carved milestones on the side of the road, half-concealed by weeds, an unspecified superstitious advantage to be gained by seeing all six.

Then we drove up the avenue and saw Ballydavid in all its spring glory. The house was no more than a good Regency villa, but I thought it the most beautiful place in the world. That morning the sun on its ivy-covered walls, the spring grass, and the trees in new leaf made it seem magical.

Grandmother and Aunt Katie were waiting to welcome us. They stood in the shade of the veranda, tall and straight, the skirts of their dresses—Grandmother's black, Aunt Katie's a dark brown—touching the gray flagstones. They were both widows, and had been for some time, Aunt Katie for longer than Grandmother. Both seemed immeasurably old, but, looking back, I now realize that Grandmother, the elder by a year or two, was probably only in her late fifties.

I looked at the two old ladies and felt admiration, respect, a little fear, and certainty that there was no limit to their power, their authority, or their ability to make safe those within their keeping. Without glancing at my mother, I knew she felt the same way.

Oonagh, Grandmother's tigerish cat, and Jock, the Highland collie, were waiting with them; Jock, enthusiastic and playful, rushed out to jump up at us while Oonagh, tail in the air, paraded back and forth, stroking herself on the skirt of Grandmother's dress. Bridie, the housemaid, stood behind them, alerted to our arrival by one of the men, or perhaps she had been watching from an upstairs window. When we got out of the trap and were embraced by Grandmother and Aunt Katie, Bridie, smiling, stepped forward to help O'Neill with our luggage. Protocol dictated that her welcome should take place a little later. For me, it might be that afternoon when I crept into the kitchen or when she gave me my bath before I went to bed. My mother and she would exchange a few affectionate words when next they found themselves alone, perhaps when Bridie carried up a jug of hot water to my mother's room. Mother would ask after Bridie's family and accept her congratulations on how big and strong Edward and I were becoming.

After I had washed and changed my clothes, I found that I was ravenously hungry. Mother and I sat down to a late breakfast and Bridie swept Edward away to the kitchen. My mother and the two old ladies remained at the table; I was sent up to bed. I protested that I wasn't tired, but minutes later, lying between the cool sheets in the saggy comfort of the old bed, with a feeling of utter, complete, and all-surrounding well-being, I fell deeply and blissfully asleep.

From time to time I woke up, once to find Bridie sitting on my bed, stroking my hair back from my forehead. She had brought my lunch up on a tray. I ate it gratefully and went straight back to sleep. When I next woke, the color of the light told me it was late afternoon. I lay still, lazy and happy. I wondered if Bridie would bring my tea. The feel of the old linen sheets, a down-filled pillow, and a horsehair mattress kept me in bed, although I was thinking of the pleasures that awaited me downstairs and, even more, out-of-doors. A cool breeze from the open window touched my face; it smelled of spring rain and the freshly opened buds green on the trees outside.

My dreamy laziness was interrupted by a crunch of feet on gravel. The crunch became footsteps followed by the scrape of a chair leg on stone. Whoever was below—two people—had stepped onto the veranda and sat down on the old wicker chairs below my window. I was surprised that I could hear them so clearly. It seemed likely that the footsteps were my mother's and those of one of the old ladies.

After a moment I could hear the murmur of voices, although not clearly enough to hear what they were saying. Then something in my mother's voice—I still could not tell which of the old ladies was sitting with her—caused me to listen more intently. It seemed to me I could hear a tightness in her tone that suggested she was worried, and it sounded as though she were asking a question.

If my mother had questions, I wanted to hear the answers. I

climbed quietly out of bed and crossed the room to the open window.

"What will happen?" My mother asked.

"We don't know." The other voice belonged to Aunt Katie. A wicker chair below creaked.

"But Redmond is sound?" My mother seemed to want to be reassured.

There was a pause before my great-aunt replied.

"Yes. He's behaving well and bravely. But both sides have guns. How long can it be before they use them?

There was another silence, broken only by one of them sighing, and after a little while the chairs creaked again as they rose and went indoors.

From the window one could see the river estuary, a calm tidal body of water, and beyond it, in the distance, the Atlantic. As I leaned on the windowsill, in the fading early evening light, I could hear the cry of a curlew. A flight of mallards came in low over the trees, on their way to one of the many small ponds that lay below us in the marshy ground close to the estuary. I could hear the companionable evening sounds they seemed to make to one another as they passed overhead.

AS THE LONG DROWSY summer began, I was aware of drama and tension in the air and, to some extent, I knew where it came from. There were four sources: the war, the unresolved future of Ireland, a quarrel between my mother and father, and the day-to-day pitfalls of living in my grandmother's house.

The war affected me less than did the other three. Every day the *Morning Post* arrived, a day late, from England. It was eagerly and anxiously read and then discussed by my mother and the old ladies. Occasionally, perhaps once a week, a letter would come from my uncle Sainthill serving in France. It seemed as though time stopped while Grandmother opened the letter and read it. Mother and Aunt Katie watched her closely, trying to deduce its contents from her expression. When she had finished reading her son's letter, Grandmother would hand it to Aunt Katie and she, in turn, would read it and then pass it to my mother. Every fact, nuance, and inference of the letter would be discussed then and for the rest of the day.

I understood that the unstable political situation in Ireland was the subject of the conversation that had floated up from the veranda to my bedroom the afternoon of the day we'd arrived in Ireland. Redmond, I knew, was the leader of the Irish parliamentary party. He had succeeded Parnell, whose glorious political career and, with it, the prospect of Irish Home Rule, had disappeared when he was cited in a divorce case. Redmond was popular with the Anglo-Irish because although he supported Home Rule—the question of Home Rule for Ireland having been shelved for the duration of the war—he also supported Irish involvement in the war. At the beginning of hostilities he had suggested that the defense of Ireland should be left to the Volunteers (those of the North and South, both now illegally armed the first by the rifles landed at Larne, the second by the shipment brought into Howth by Erskine Childers in the *Asgard*) in order to leave the English soldiers stationed in Ireland free to fight. The offer had been declined—an insult similar to Kitchener's resistance to forming specifically southern Irish regiments—and whole regiments of English soldiers, who, had the offer been accepted, would have been sent to the front, instead spent tours of duty safely and comfortably in Ireland. Young officers, instead of going to France, spent a season in Irish society, shooting and hunting in winter, attending race meetings in summer—a welcome resource for hostesses with unmarried daughters of a dancing age.

My parents' quarrel was also conducted through the Royal Mail. It was a more private affair than the war. One morning I watched my mother take a letter, unopened, from the breakfast table. She went upstairs to her bedroom and she didn't come down for some time. Three days later there was another letter; I recognized my father's handwriting. When we rose from the table I followed the adults into the hall and watched my mother hesitate for a moment at the foot of the staircase. It was a warm day and the front door stood open. I did not follow her when she went outside but ran upstairs to my room to watch from the window where she would go, what she would do. I saw her standing on the gravel in front of the house, the letter in her hand still unopened; the black cat from the stable yard was setting off on a predatory errand to the woods and Mother was superstitiously waiting to avoid its crossing her path. When the cat disappeared into the dark of the woods, my mother sat down on the bench under the beech tree beside the tennis court. She paused a moment before opening the letter—one side of a single sheet of paper. Father came straight to the point and it was always his point; he didn't have much interest in the opinions or reasoning of those who disagreed with him. My mother read the letter twice, then refolded it and put it back in the envelope. She sat still for some time, gazing out over the woods and fields toward the estuary, her expression sad, angry, and confused. And stubborn. A characteristic I think she had developed as a reaction to my father's overbearing ways. She was gentle and not short of courage; a better or more sensitive man would not have reduced her to this state.

The fourth source of drama and tension, that of everyday domestic life at Ballydavid, affected me most directly, and, apart from the time spent lying awake in the pale darkness, frightened about what would happen to me if my parents' quarrel continued forever, it gave me the greatest food for thought. And worry. My nervousness was most often caused by the lack of warning before an eruption or a cold reprimand for the infringement of some never-before-invoked rule. Ignorance of the law is at the best of times an inadequate defense, and at Ballydavid I could not plead it without raising the question of how my mother was bringing me up. I came to realize that she was often indulgent when she was distracted, preoccupied, or unhappy. It did nothing for my confidence, while negotiating the everyday, to discover—in addition to the Ballydavid rules that must be obeyed and those that could be discreetly disobeyed—another rule which forbade complaining or showing fear. And I was often afraid.

It was some time before I realized I could carry these fears to the out-of-bounds kitchen, where they would be listened to and taken seriously. Perhaps too seriously. I would go to the kitchen for company and to postpone the moment when I would have to make my way to bed, the flickering light of my candle summoning looming shadows from the doorways and heavy dark furniture that lined the corridor. My fear was not specific and would disappear once I was safely in bed, reassured by light from the window and the sound of the rooks in the trees as they settled down for the night. In the kitchen, I was given a sympathetic ear; my fears were listened to, understood, and confirmed. Those that were vague were given form, shape, and provenance. The dark shadows were replaced by the ghost of a weeping woman apparently seen by both Maggie and Bridie, and I was told of the banshee who could be heard wailing when someone in the house was about to die. Both the maids volunteered that nothing would induce them to sleep in the room I occupied. I would leave terrified and with a glimmer of understanding why I was not encouraged to hang around the kitchen.

One cool early summer day I was standing by the window in the drawing room. It was shortly after breakfast, and I was watching my mother sitting alone on the bench by the tennis court. She was smoking a cigarette, something I had never before seen her do. It was, I knew, an act of defiance against my absent father. I noticed with some surprise when I next saw my mother light a cigarette, sitting on the veranda with my grandmother and great-aunt, that neither showed disapproval.

The window by which I stood was open a few inches and my bare legs were cold. Watery sunshine shone on my mother; she had a light shawl around her shoulders. I was hoping she would come indoors and wondering if it would be all right to join her, when there was a ping of metal touching wood, the bounce of something soft on the carpet, and Oonagh darting, in simulated self-induced fear, across the room.

I turned quickly to see the no longer young cat lightly touch the arm of the sofa as she leapt onto the cushions, continue over the farther arm, turn sharply, and return to the small Turkish rug in front of the fire. On the hearthrug lay Grandmother's knitting: three inches of the ankle of a gray sock, one needle no longer attached, and a ball of gray wool. I was still laughing at Oonagh's progress around the room when she made a dive at the ball of wool, leaping on it and sinking in her claws as though she were slaughtering a small, soft, gray animal. I laughed again, and was still laughing when the door from the hall opened and Grandmother entered the room. She was carrying a small branch of blossom. She often returned from her walks with booty that was usually turned over to someone else to take care of—Aunt Katie, in this instance, since it was she who arranged the flowers for the house. I stopped laughing, aware—as I should have been a moment later even had I not been reminded by an adult presence—that Oonagh had damaged or destroyed Grandmother's work.

There was a short silence. I looked aghast at the gray mess on the hearthrug. Oonagh gave the ball of wool another tap with her paw and then again leaped on it. Grandmother's face was cold and set. Aware suddenly that my presence had apparently made me responsible for what had happened, that I had been found a spectator entertained at the scene of the disaster, I darted forward. Oonagh, startled, but incorporating my action into her game, leaped onto Aunt Katie's chair, a strand of wool caught between her claws. All three needles were now separated from Grandmother's knitting, and every move Oonagh made unraveled what remained of the sock a little further.

"Really, Alice," Grandmother said, and left the room, closing the door behind her. I was in disgrace.

The rest of the morning passed slowly. I felt ashamed but not guilty. I knew that I had done nothing wrong, and I thought that the grown-ups, even Grandmother, understood that I had not caused or encouraged Oonagh's moment of wanton destruction. Nevertheless, as scapegoat, I had to keep a low profile until some time had passed.

I remained silent and scarcely visible for two or three hours without even my mother coming to look for me to say a reassuring word. I considered visiting the kitchen but was afraid that the instinct there to dramatize would leave me feeling even more of a pariah than I already did. It also occurred to me that, if I were caught creeping into that forbidden territory, I might seem defiantly to be breaking another rule before I had been forgiven my last infringement.

I went outdoors. There was no one in sight; a bored Jock lying half-asleep by the front door opened one eye as I passed. I thought that if I went for a little walk he would accompany me and I should not be so alone. I started to stroll away from the house, down the avenue that led to the front gate. After a moment, Jock heaved himself up and ambled after me. I reached the corner where I had once watched Oonagh emerge from the laurels and remembered that day and the fuss that had been made of me by the grown-ups in the drawing room. I remembered the completely admirable Mrs. Coughlan and her words as we had parted. "I hope you will come and see me one day." Surely there could be no better time.

Large trees and bushes grew on either side of the avenue, with areas of carefully mown grass between them. Soon we came to where the wood began; it lay at the base of the hill and ran along the southern and eastern boundaries of Ballydavid. Jock and I turned off the avenue onto a footpath. The trees, with fresh green foliage, gave the narrow path the daytime darkness of a fairy tale; to either side there were brambles and stretches where dead leaves lay under sunless, bare, brown lower branches. I began to feel afraid and was glad to have Jock's company. My fears were based on nothing specific, but they were not nameless. Jock and I were on the Fox's Walk.

The Fox's Walk—I don't know how it came by its name and there is now no one left alive who might know—was a path that ran through the woods from the front gate to Rowe's Lane at the other end of Grandmother's property. Rowe's Lane wandered between high thick hedges to a large farm and an unpretentious farmhouse belonging to Nicholas Rowe, the most prosperous of Grandmother's Roman Catholic neighbors; to either side of the lane stood the cottages of the men who worked on the Rowe farm and of some who worked at Ballydavid. The Fox's Walk was a little more than a quarter of a mile in length, and its terrain was uneven. Part of it had once been landscaped, and although brambles and indigenous scrub now largely obscured the exotic flowering shrubs that been planted during a more affluent period in the family's past, this stretch of the walk was wider than the footpaths that lay at either end. It was the first time I had been on the Fox's Walk by myself.

Jock and I passed overgrown azaleas and crowded tufts of pampas grass and entered an alley of overgrown yews. At the end of it we took a path, no wider than the one we had taken from the avenue, which ran downhill toward the Woodstown road. I knew the path beneath my feet and Jock's paws might once have been a trail used by animals, but now it was human feet—workmen and maids using it as a short cut to the farm or house—that had packed down the mud beneath our feet. I knew what a fox looked like, and I also knew that, in the unlikely event Jock and I met one, the fox would flee and Jock would chase him. Even so, I was aware that I had left the world of houses and humans and had invaded the territory of unseen woodland life and nocturnal animals. And of mythic beings. I glanced nervously at Jock, but he was still slouching along behind me, his head down, too lazy to sniff at the scent of small animals.

After a while it became lighter and I could see a space between the trees beyond. In it was a stile, built into the overgrown bank that was the boundary of Grandmother's land—low on the Ballydavid side but with a drop of four or five feet down onto the road below. I climbed over the stile and scrambled down into the ditch and onto the main road. Jock squeezed himself under the low branch of a sapling that had taken root in the bank and jumped down beside me. We set off along the road toward the house where Major and Mrs. Coughlan lived, leaving behind the unfairness of being held accountable for the misdeeds of Grandmother's cat.

As we turned the corner, Jock, for the first time, began to react to his surroundings. He growled. A low, provisional, warning growl—the kind he might make if a familiar but infrequent beggar were coming up the avenue. But now we were in full sunlight and I had no fears. I was in a hurry to present myself to Mrs. Coughlan, to be fussed over and offered refreshment.

We continued along the deserted road—we had seen no one since we had left the house—and Jock growled again, this time deeper in his throat. And he slunk a little closer to my side, as though afraid, or at least apprehensive, in the presence of the unknown.

At first I could see nothing, but I began to become aware of an unpleasant but not identifiable smell. Soon the smell became stronger, and I put my hand over my nose and mouth and breathed through my fingers. The wide grassy area on the side of the road was where the tinkers had camped.

I had heard the maids talking about the tinkers: They were afraid of them. A fierce tinker woman had come to the front door, begging, a day or two before. Aunt Katie had given her money, but had avoided the further ritual conversation—sympathetic inquiries on her part and promises that she would be remembered even more fervently than she already was in the prayers of the recipient. The woman had whined, pulling back her heavy black shawl to reveal a pale and comatose baby, her thanks quickly becoming an aggressive demand for more money. Aunt Katie had tightened her lips, looked coldly at the woman, wished her a good morning, and closed the door firmly. She had watched from the drawing-room window until the woman turned the corner of the avenue and went out of sight. O'Neill had reported two pullets missing from the hen house and, listening to his talk with Pat and Ned, I had gathered that the local farmers were getting close to the moment when they would unite to move the tinkers on. The tinkers, whose senses, it is likely, were tuned toward such a moment, had made a round of last-minute thievery and disappeared during the night.

They left behind—like pieces of cloth on a bush beside a holy well—scraps of rags on the hedgerow, the ashes of their fires, some animal droppings, and the lingering and unidentifiable smell. And, mysteriously, among the cold ashes of their fires, I saw the burned shells of fifteen or twenty snails. Did they eat snails, I wondered, or had they burned them as a gratuitous act of cruelty? Or did the snails have some practical use of which I was not aware? Or perhaps the charred shells were the remains of a ritual or had a superstitious significance. Each possibility was disquieting, and, although I wondered, I knew I would never ask about it for fear the answer would be one of those previously unimagined distressing facts that, once heard, I could not dismiss from my mind.

We hurried past the site of the encampment. The road ran uphill and the day was growing warmer; I began to feel tired and thirsty. At last we reached the gates to the Coughlans' house. They were closed.

I was taken aback by this unforeseen obstacle. The gates were large and heavy. With no anticipation of success, I tried to lift the black, paint-encrusted latch; I could not move it. The obvious thing would have been to return home and to say nothing about my clandestine and premature attempt at adult social life. But I was tired and full of the anticipated pleasure of a visit to the gaudy world of Mrs. Coughlan. I was also reluctant to repass the place where the tinkers had camped. I sat down on the sparse gravel and leaned against the closed gates; after a moment Jock slumped, bored, beside me and closed his eyes. Without a plan, I waited to see what would happen next.

For what seemed like a long time, nothing did. Then a small cart drawn by a shabby donkey came along the road. It travelled slowly. There was a large milk churn on the cart, and the donkey was old, with worn misshapen hooves. A man sat on a front corner, paying no attention to the donkey. A daily routine: The donkey knew where it had to go, and the man knew that no action of his would get them there any faster. He had plenty of time to observe me and Jock as they came closer. Without any instruction to the donkey, he stepped down from the cart; the animal took a couple more paces and then stopped. Jock woke up.

"Locked out, are ye?" the man asked. He sounded amused. He spoke, of course, with a local accent. It is not possible to put in writing what he sounded like, and an attempt at an approximation tends to read like the dialogue of a stage Irishman. Without waiting for an answer, he opened the gates and allowed Jock and me to proceed up the avenue.

Although I had often passed the gates on the way to Waterford and knew who lived behind them, I had never seen the Coughlan house before, and I was, for a moment, disappointed that it looked like the other houses in the neighborhood that belonged to the gentry. The avenue was shorter than that at Ballydavid and, unlike Ballydavid, where the gardens were enclosed in faded red brick at the rear of the house, there was to one side of the avenue a lawn with a narrow gravel path and flower beds, to the other a tall hedge that presumably concealed the kitchen entrance and outbuildings such as the laundry and dairy that serviced the house.

We approached the front door. This should have been another moment when I hesitated to ponder the wisdom of my unannounced visit, but instead I wondered how I was to make myself known. I was not tall enough to reach the door knocker, and it seemed unlikely that the noise of my small soft knuckles on the door would attract the attention of the inhabitants, whom I imagined as pale attentive beings in thrall to Mrs. Coughlan, circling in her colorful orbit.

The door was slightly ajar. First I knocked, but, as I had anticipated, this produced a less than adequate sound. Then I called out. This presented two problems: I was not sure what words would be appropriate and, were I to keep my voice at a polite level, it was unlikely that I would be heard.

"Hello, Mrs. Coughlan. Is anybody there?" I called out, self-conscious and ineffectual.

There was no reply. I could hear the ticking of a grandfather clock in the hallway and the pleasant early summer sound of birds behind me. Leaving Jock outside, I pushed open the heavy green door and stepped into the hall and looked around. The furnishings of the hall were exotic, but in a way that, since I came from a military family that had served in India, were familiar to me: a brass gong, a carved wooden chest, even a python skin, similar to the one at Ballydavid, mounted over one of the two doorways that, on either side, led off the hall. A tiger-skin rug lay on the large stone flags. I went over to it and looked down; it stared back at me with yellow glass eyes.

Outside, Jock began to bark. I recrossed the hall and reached the door just in time to call off my dog and welcome the rightful owners of the house.

"Hello," Mrs. Coughlan said with a smile. She didn't recognize me.

"I'm Alice," I said. "I've come to visit you. This is Jock."

Mrs. Coughlan's smile became even more welcoming.

"It's the little girl from Ballydavid, dear," Major Coughlan said. The only words I heard him speak that day. When Major Coughlan had married the woman I heard Grandmother once refer to as "a Jewess he picked up in Cairo," he had committed himself to living forever in his wife's colorful shadow.

"You're just in time for lunch," Mrs. Coughlan said. She was wearing a dress in two shades of deep pink, with a fringed Chinese shawl over her shoulders. She carried, unopened, a parasol she clearly hadn't bought in Waterford which she now put into a brass umbrella stand beside the front door. Crossing to the looking glass over the hall table, she pulled out her hatpins and took off a large shady hat with dark pink feathers that had brushed one of her shoulders.

"Why don't you tell Norah there will be one more for lunch," she said in a kindly tone to her husband, who disappeared through a green baize door that led off the hall. He was shorter than she was.

"Well," she said, "you must tell me all about yourself." And she took my hand and led me into the drawing room.

My life seemed pathetically banal beside hers; besides, who knew when I would again have an opportunity to talk to her? I was wondering how best to frame a question about her experiences as a Jewess in Cairo when a door, not the one we had entered through, opened and an Indian servant, in a white jacket and a turban, announced: "Luncheon is served."

I was, fortunately as I now realize, speechless in the face of this new and exotic sight. I had never seen a male house servant before. I hadn't known that they existed. I knew that there were such things as Indians and I had seen pictures of them in books, but I had never expected to have the great good fortune of seeing one in the flesh.

I followed Mrs. Coughlan back through the hall. The dining room, the one with the python skin over the door, was a room of the same size and shape as that we had just left. Major Coughlan was there already, standing by the sideboard, sharpening the carving knife.

"Sit here," Mrs. Coughlan said, putting a cushion on one of the three chairs at the end of the dining-room table. "Now, what would you like to eat?"

It was the first time I had ever been consulted about what food I would prefer; unfortunately, since all the choices were unknown to me, I could not take full advantage of the opportunity. I looked at what I now know to be curry, a bowl of rice—at Ballydavid more often met in a milk pudding—and many little dishes filled with interestingly colored chutneys, relishes, and the other traditional accompaniments. I didn't know how to answer and remained silent.

"How about a little of everything? You don't need to eat anything you don't like. Unless, of course, like my Ancient Husband, you'd prefer cold mutton and pickles."

I shook my head and glanced at Major Coughlan. The knife and sharpener still in hand, he was sizing up the cold meat as though considering how best to go about carving it. His lack of reaction to his wife's description of him suggested that the nomenclature might be a nickname.

Mrs. Coughlan helped me to the colorful food, carefully keeping each portion separate on the plate. The spicey smell made me look forward to trying the curry. But it was not to be.

The door of the dining room was flung open. Grandmother came in, in her wake Mother and the Indian manservant. I glanced at Mrs. Coughlan; her expression was one of mild surprise and welcome. But before she could speak, Grandmother had crossed the room.

"Alice," she said, her voice cold and angry as she took my arm and slid me off the chair. No one spoke as she led me to my mother who clasped me in her arms, then followed Grandmother to the hall door. Behind us I could hear only the rhythmic sound of the bone-handled knife being drawn once again over the steel sharpener.

WE MARCHED SILENTLY back to Ballydavid. My grandmother, head in air, drew ahead of us, although my mother, holding my hand, was already walking too fast for me. "We thought the tinkers had taken you," she said, quietly enough for Grandmother not to hear her.

I didn't reply. It thought it likely that if I spoke I would draw Grandmother's wrath, and it seemed wise to allow a little time to elapse before the full extent of my transgressions were discussed.

They never were. I was sent up to bed as soon as we reached Ballydavid. That I hadn't had my lunch was an oversight rather than a punishment. I was tired and overexcited—as were Grandmother and my mother—and I shouldn't be surprised if they both had retired for a prolonged rest that afternoon.

Their fears were real, although I didn't then understand their source. When I woke up from my nap, I wondered—there was no clock in my room—if enough time had elapsed for me to go downstairs. I lay in bed for a little time, not reluctant to put off the moment when I would face the reproaches of the adults I had inconvenienced and, apparently, frightened. I considered my mother's words and thought her fear that I had been stolen by the tinkers illogical. When we had driven past the tinker encampment several days before, I had observed them as carefully as was possible while obeying the injunction against staring. It seemed to me they already had more children than they needed. So why had my mother been afraid? Had they some other use—unknown to me—for children? Did they sell them? Or was it possible that I might have served the same unidentified purpose as the snails whose charred shells had suggested some sinister meal or ritual? Might they have eaten me? I had now frightened myself enough to get out of bed, dress quickly, and go downstairs.

I opened the door of the drawing room a little and slipped in. Mother was sitting on the sofa, Edward crawling around at her feet. She smiled at me and beckoned. I crossed the room quietly and sat beside her, close enough to feel her warmth. Neither Grandmother nor Aunt Katie seemed to notice my arrival, but I did not have the feeling that I was being pointedly ignored. Avoiding my mother's habit of premature relief, I waited to see what would happen next. Tea had been brought in some time before, and empty teacups and small plates with crumbs had been put back on the tray. My mother put two cucumber sandwiches on a plate. The upper side of the sandwiches had become dry and started to curl at the corners, but I was hungry and ate them happily. When I finished, Mother silently cut a slice of Madeira cake which she handed to me with a gesture that cautioned me not to drop crumbs on the sofa.

I ate and watched. The room was very quiet, the silence broken by the scratching of Grandmother's pen and the cards that Aunt Katie was laying out for one of her ritual games of patience. Grandmother, at the table beside the window, engrossed in her task, had covered several sheets of writing paper. I glanced at my mother. Her face was calm and relaxed, the expression one of the near happiness she attained when not faced with the demands of others. I, too, was happy that I seemed to have been forgiven or forgotten, grateful for the peace of the late afternoon, the day winding down, the changing color of the light, the quiet of the approaching evening.

"The nine of spades," Aunt Katie said dramatically. She stood up and left the room quickly.

"Oh dear," mother said sympathetically, but not as though she shared her aunt's sense that something tragic had occurred. Grandmother did not even look up from her task. I had the impression that she was now writing more quickly and with greater urgency.

Mother, Grandmother, and Aunt Katie were intensely superstitious, but each had her own taste in superstition. What seemed to one a portent of great weight was merely indulged by the other two, each having some more reliable method of her own to ward off disaster or to predict the future. Grandmother would not allow hawthorn or marigolds inside the house, the stricture against the former at least having a good pagan origin. Aunt Katie depended on cards and symbolic messages from a wide variety of inanimate objects that came unexpectedly into her line of vision. My mother's foible was a series of small anxious rituals, superstitious and neurotic, the rewards of their observance as unspecified as the disasters that would surely befall if they were ignored.

Grandmother laid down her pen and read through her list. When she finished she nodded with the satisfaction of one completing an arduous, subtle, and physically exhausting piece of work.

"Katie—" she said, and then, noticing for the first time that her sister was no longer in the room, turned to Mother.

"I thought," she said, "we might have a tennis party. I've made a list."

Mother smiled, a little weakly I thought. Later I would understand the principles and procedure for entertaining at Ballydavid. Grandmother drew up the invitation list. If one took into account geography, religion, and Grandmother's social beliefs and prejudices, there were a finite number of people who could be invited. For most families living close to Waterford, the cast and characters of their modest and occasional parties would be fairly consistent; there would be a wider range of those asked to, say, a garden party than to dinner. The guest list varied only when the young English officers stationed at the garrison behind the city were posted elsewhere and a new wave of young men took their place. Grandmother's variation on this otherwise unquestioned social procedure was to take the conventional list, add a name or two—nothing dramatic, something on the lines of allowing a person who could expect nothing more than a garden party to come indoors—and, this her main contribution to the entertainment, to strike off the names of one or two neighbors who might have expected to be invited. The withholding of an invitation might be temporary, but, since entertaining among the far from affluent Anglo-Irish was not constant, it might be months or even a year before the offending—and not unreasonably offended— party was restored to his rightful place. Having drawn up the list,

Grandmother turned all other arrangements over to the capable hands of Aunt Katie.

Aunt Katie had had time only to instruct O'Neill to prepare the tennis court and to read through the invitation list—the Coughlans the only omission, a cousin to whom Grandmother had not spoken in several years restored in order to make the omission more pointed—before rumors began to arrive of an unimaginable disaster.

NEWS AND INFORMATION from the outside world came a day late—or sometimes two if the mail boat was delayed by weather—from the *Morning Post*. In addition to the war news so carefully read by my family, the conservative English newspaper often contained a leading article about the trumped-up grievances of the ungrateful Irish.

More personal communications came by mail. There were two mails a day, though the second post was not delivered, and someone would have to ride or walk for it to the post office at Rossduff, a cottage three miles away on the side of the Waterford–Dunmore road. There was a telephone in the hall at Ballydavid, but the connections took time and were generally unsatisfactory. I never heard it used socially. The maids were afraid of it and ignored the ringing; even Grandmother, on the rare occasions she used the instrument, held it a little away from her ear and raised her voice to the loudest level consistent with ladylike behaviour.

But there was another way that information arrived, a Gaelic form of bush telegraph. Sometimes this news was local; sometimes it came from as far away as Dublin; sometimes it was secret (secret in the sense that it was communicated gradually and by hints); sometimes it was what we would read in the newspaper the following day.

The first rumor of a disaster—brought by a stableboy return-ing with a horse from the blacksmith's and not given much cre-dence—came during the early evening. It was followed by others after I had been taken up to bed.

The evening was still light and, aware of the excitement below, I could not sleep. Bridie, who had been turning down the old ladies' beds, catching sight of me peeping around the door of my room, told me there had been a terrible shipwreck. The hor-rors of war had come closer to Ballydavid than any of us could have imagined. The *Lusitania* had sunk only seventy miles away, just out of sight of the Irish coast, torpedoed by a German sub-marine in the full sunshine we had seen over the sea on our way back from my unofficial visit to the Coughlans.

The liner, flying the American flag (America was then still a neutral nation), sank in circumstances that should have made pos-sible the survival of the greater part of her passengers and crew. She went down quickly, only eleven miles off the Old Head of Kinsale in three hundred feet of water. The sea was not so cold that those who survived the explosion need have died of exposure for several hours. There were enough lifeboats for everyone, but the angle at which the ship tilted prevented the launching of those on the starboard side, and several of the lifeboats that could be lowered were, in the panic, launched so ineptly that the passen-gers already in them were spilled into the water. Half those on board perished, the number proportionately equal between pas-sengers and crew.

Immediately after the explosion, fishing boats set out from Kinsale and, shortly afterward, larger boats were launched from Queenstown, some miles farther east. These boats at first rescued those clinging to wreckage and later carried back the bodies. The dead were laid out in lines on the quays; the resources for caring for the survivors were stretched far beyond the capacities of the small fishing villages such as Kinsale, or even Queenstown, the port adjacent to Cork, where transatlantic liners—although not the *Lusitania,* which was making for Liverpool—sometimes called. For weeks later, the tide would wash up bodies on the beaches and rocks along the coast.

At the time of the shipwreck, horror and outrage at the tragedy prevented questions being asked, but not for long. When they were, too many were unsatisfactorily answered. The Admiralty had set out a procedure designed to minimize the danger from submarines: full speed ahead and a zigzag course. The captain of the *Lusitania* had taken a bearing on the Old Head of Kinsale and steered a direct course at a speed that did not employ all the boilers, in what was afterwards described as an economy measure. Unanswered, also, was the question of the second explosion. Most eyewitnesses described only one torpedo, and the inference was that something stored below deck had exploded when detonated by the torpedo. Since the *Lusitania* had been flying the neutral American flag, arms or weapons of war would have been contraband, and she would have forfeited the protection of her neutral status. If this had been the case, the German U-boat that had sunk her would, under the articles of war, have been, however horribly, technically within her rights. Since one hundred and twenty-four citizens of the neutral United States had died that afternoon, these unanswered questions were of some importance.

By the time I said my prayers and climbed into bed, the first fishing boats would have reached the lifeboats rowing toward land, and as I lay in bed, listening to the rooks noisily settling down for the night, fishermen were dragging cold, shocked, sodden survivors from the water.

Twelve hundred men, women, and children perished in the disaster. Some are buried at Saint Multose, the twelfth-century church in Kinsale; some in small, close-by parish cemeteries; others at Queenstown where a long grave was dug and coffins marked with chalk—some with names, others only with numbers—were arranged like a macabre puzzle. Many of the dead, their bodies disregarded while the living were rescued, were never found and drifted or sank, eventually eaten by fishes; others, killed by the explosion or trapped inside the liner, went down with it; a few, already in the water, were sucked down when the ship, fourteen minutes after the second explosion, released her last breath and, with a sigh, sank to the ocean floor.

THE TENNIS PARTY was to have taken place in the second week in June, rather earlier than was usual for an outdoor entertainment; it was now postponed until the middle of July. Also postponed was Grandmother's intended snub to the Coughlans; deprived of immediate revenge and wound up for social intercourse, she became restless. One morning, she announced that Nicholas Rowe was coming to tea—the announcement not an invitation to the rest of her family.

Nicholas Rowe was a neighboring strong farmer with openly nationalist sympathies; he was said to be the local head of the Irish Revolutionary Brotherhood. When he came to tea, once Bridie had carried in the heavy tray, the door to the drawing room was closed. It is difficult to imagine what he and Grandmother talked about. Their opinions, I should have thought, were not only diametrically opposed but lacking any common premise upon which to base an argument or discussion. Tea itself would have underlined the difference in their assumptions. For Grandmother, tea took place at half past four in the drawing room. A maid wearing a neat apron and a small cap carried in a tray, on it a silver teapot, cucumber sandwiches, and whatever cake Maggie had baked that day—a light sponge with a raspberry jam filling, perhaps. Nicholas Rowe, whom I now realize owned more land than Grandmother and was materially better off than she was, would have been served tea at six o'clock on his own kitchen table. The only refreshment in common would have been the tea they drank, his being a good deal stronger and without a slice of lemon offered as an alternative to milk. Tea as a meal took the place of dinner, so, although the main meal of the day for the Rowes, confusingly also called dinner, took place at midday, tea would have been substantial enough to see them through to breakfast. Cake also would have been served at his meal, but it was cake in the rural Irish sense of the word: a round flat unleavened cake of soda bread.

Grandmother was the daughter of one man, and the widow of another, who had both distinguished themselves in the service of the British Empire. It would be unreasonable—especially at that moment in history—to expect her to question the merits of the Empire or of its colonial history. Although at that moment a number of the Anglo-Irish Ascendancy were embracing the image of a glorified Hibernia, my grandmother was not among them.

Nicholas Rowe would have seen that the end of direct English government of Ireland was in sight, the statute for Home Rule already on the books in Westminster and theoretically waiting only for the war to end for it to be enacted. He was a man who had managed to prosper under what he would have considered a foreign government, but that did not prevent him holding extreme nationalist views.

What were the subjects Grandmother and Nicholas Rowe would have found to agree upon? I think they might have argued about history and morality but would have agreed pragmatically, unemotionally, and with a not overexamined respect for habit and tradition that any alteration to the delicate equilibrium of the farming and agricultural economy and culture would have unforeseen dangers. Both of them knew how the world worked and how dangerous theory, sudden change, and sentimentality could be; the sentimentality in particular would have been distasteful to both. (Sir Roger Casement, still unhappily and ineffectually in Germany, had maddened Devoy, the hardheaded Clan na Gael leader in New York, by his habit of referring to Ireland as "the Poor Old Woman"; Grandmother and Nicholas Rowe would have been equally appalled and for not dissimilar reasons.) Both knew that the beliefs they held exacted a high price and the occasional extreme sacrifice.

My grandmother's insistence on observing conventions had prevented me from considering whether she had had any experience of the tragic or dramatic. I imagined her life had always been as it then was, rigid and uneventful. I was too young and lacked the imagination and information to understand that experience, as well as observation, had taught her that the tragic and unthinkable might occur at any moment. As a young army wife in India, her husband away on a tour of duty, her first child, a little girl, had suddenly developed a fever. Grandmother, with only servants to provide help or comfort, had waited through the night for a doctor summoned from a distant station. He arrived too late; the child, who had been happily playing on the grass in front of the house that morning, was already dead. Grandmother, young and heartbroken, had understood that, although the loss of her child was the single most horrible thing she could imagine, it was in no way unusual.

And Nicholas Rowe. His name tells me he was of Norman origin; like many of the Catholic Irish, his family was descended—the ancestral blood over the years somewhat diluted—from the tough, hard-minded, and energetic Normans who had in the twelfth century invaded Ireland and, almost simultaneously, adapted to and been assimilated into the life and customs of that

country. It would be naïve to imagine that the Rowes, while holding their Catholic beliefs, had managed to retain or replace their
land without compromise, hardship, sacrifice.

Once or twice a year, Grandmother and Nicholas Rowe
reached over the chasm of class, religion, and political thought.
On one side, the waning Protestant Ascendancy and on the other,
the understated strength of the Catholic farmer. I think Grandmother and Nicholas Rowe each may have been, for the other, the
only adversary with whom it was worth arguing—or, it is possible, negotiating. But what did they talk about? They could not
have spent the whole of each visit debating the current and future
political situation. Crops, the families, and the welfare of their
employees—a form of enlightened feudalism might have been
one of the few beliefs they shared. After all this time, I am still unable to imagine their conversations. Or at least the conversations
they had in the summer of 1915. Later, there would be plenty for
them to talk about—a time when their friendship, if friendship
it indeed was, would have allowed them to help, or possibly en-
danger, each other, a time when it was not always easy to tell the
difference. Or perhaps theirs was only an inarticulate form of intelligent friendship, like two old men who, without much in
common, meet regularly and wordlessly to play chess.

My predilection for eavesdropping was hampered by a strong
streak of timidity. The afternoon of Nicholas Rowe's visit, I was
loitering in the no man's land of the passage that ran behind the
drawing room. Parallel to the front of the house, it led from a
dining-room service door on the east side of the house all the way
to the back stairs on the west. The doors on one side led to the
kitchen, butler's pantry, and a small room next to the side door
where we left our muddy boots and wet coats; on the other side
lay the dining room, the drawing room, and access to the hall and
front stairs. I was listening and watching, scurrying along the cor-

ridor whenever I heard a sound, since I was reluctant to be asked to account for myself and sent off to do something that was supposed to be improving. I knew instinctively that this was not a day to sidle into the kitchen, the maids far less likely to be colorfully and imaginatively indiscreet about a Roman Catholic neighbor than they were about the affairs of one of Grandmother's heretic visitors.

After a long and uneventful wait, there came, simultaneously, the sound of the kitchen door opening and of someone descending the front stairs. Cut off from the bolt hole of the back stairs, I quietly opened the door to the empty dining room and slipped in. The advantage of my position now was that I could spy on the hall from a room no one was likely to visit; the disadvantage was that, if someone did happen to come in, I had not even the flimsiest reason for being there. I could no longer keep an eye on the kitchen to drawing room connection—it seemed likely that Grandmother had rung for more hot water—but now I could hear someone hurrying downstairs and then footsteps crossing the stone flags of the hall. There was a pause, and I considered opening the door to the hall a crack to see what was happening, but a crunch of feet on gravel drew me to the window. A boy, adolescent but not fully grown, was walking down the avenue away from the house; I did not recognize him, but his flat cap and shabby clothing suggested that he had come on an errand. I was still puzzling about why he would have come to the front door rather than the kitchen entrance when a combination of muted sounds drew me back to the door to the hall. I heard a moan, as though an old animal were in pain, and the rustling of clothing that meant the presence of either Aunt Katie or Grandmother, a muffled thud, and another moan.

It was the silence that followed the second moan that made me carefully open the door enough to see what was happening.

Aunt Katie lay crumpled over the lower steps of the stairs; Grandmother, followed by Nicholas Rowe, was coming out of the drawing room. They seemed to move very slowly, as though they were floating in one of my dreams. Grandmother eventually reached the foot of the stairs and crouched beside her sister, Nicholas Rowe standing to one side. It seemed to me that they were frozen in a dark and strangely beautiful tableau. It was one of those moments when time hesitates before everything is changed forever. Aunt Katie, even I could see, was unconscious. Grandmother's immobile back was to me; Nicholas Rowe's was the only face that I could see; it lacked all expression. I, too, remained motionless, as detail after detail of the tableau became clearer. The crumpled piece of paper in my great-aunt's fist, the light of the spring day from the open hall door, the ticking of the grandfather clock.

Then, still slowly, my mother drifted into the picture. Coming down the stairs, she saw what lay below her, raised her hand to her throat, and became, also, still. The tableau, the composition changed, again became static, broken only by the small movement and faint sound of her lapis beads trickling, bouncing, and rolling down the stairs, some of them becoming caught in the folds of Aunt Katie's dark clothing and some of them rolling across the stone flags of the hall until they were lost under the furniture or in the gray shadows of the corners of the hall.

July 1915–November 1915

Chapter 3

I SAT IN THE FINE SAND, sheltered by the sea grass. Although the sun shone, it was beginning to be chilly as the late afternoon wind came in over the wet sand, and I hugged my arms around my legs in an attempt to keep warm. I was wearing a washed-out cotton dress and a cardigan that Aunt Katie had knitted; my legs were bare and I had taken off my sandals to walk on the beach. My mother was walking away from me, just above the line of shells the receded tide had washed up. She, too, wore a jersey over her dress. Her arms were folded across her chest, her head bowed. She had been walking all afternoon, back and forth the length of the beach—about a mile and a quarter. I had at first amused myself collecting shells, building canals, and damming streams in the mud, but now I was tired and hungry and becoming cold. Once or twice during the afternoon, I had tried to get her attention, but she had seemed not to recognize me; now I sat, as the sun sank, in the dunes and waited for her to remember me.

The texture of the sand at Woodstown varied, depending on how far one was from the sea. The sand on the crest of the dunes, blown about by the wind so that the resilient dark green sea grasses were sometimes buried halfway up their stems, was yellow and fine. On the strand the sand was an uneven coarse gray, gritty with pieces of broken shell; at the water's edge, swept up by the tide, the shells were often whole and sometimes pretty, though most of them were hard, sharp cockles.

That afternoon the tide was out. It had left behind almost a mile of wet muddy sand, little streams, puddles, and ripples drawn by the retreating water. On the mud were small coiled heaps excreted by worms; beneath the sand lay the cockles. A few women, cockle-pickers, had been at work; they had walked bent, digging into the wet sand, reaching down to pick up the cockles and throw them into the wet sacks they dragged with them. Now they were leaving the beach.

I felt helpless and guilty. Helpless because Grandmother, Aunt Katie, and my mother were stricken with grief. If I weren't watching my mother pacing the strand at Woodstown, I would have been watching my Grandmother at Ballydavid, sitting on the bench beside the tennis court, gazing, without seeing, over the fields. Aunt Katie was not often visible, although I was always aware of her closed bedroom door. There had been tears in the kitchen when Maggie and Bridie had heard of my uncle Sainthill's death. Maggie had known him since he was a little boy, and Bridie referred to him, through her sobs, as "a lovely gentleman." The next day, although subdued, their tears were over, and they continued with their lives—their lives of serving and looking after us. My family, after Aunt Katie's first moans as she lay at the foot of the stairs, grieved silently and separately. Alone, each lived with her grief, and, when one met another, after a blink of bare recognition, each veered off to return to her solitary mourning. I could do nothing to help or comfort; when I tried to show affection toward my mother, she barely saw me. And I felt ashamed because I could not remember my uncle. And since I couldn't admit that I had forgotten him, I was left pretending to mourn the loss of someone who was only a name and a face in a silver-framed photograph.

The sun went behind one of the puffy white clouds drifting slowly across the fading sky, and I was now cold enough to feel that some action on my part was necessary. My mother had reached the end of the strand where an outcrop of rocks extended into the bay, and turned. As she came in my direction, I stood, holding my sandals in one hand, showing myself clearly as a child waiting to be taken home. When she was almost abreast of me, I took a couple of steps toward her, ready to meet her if she came to join me. But she walked past without noticing me. I looked at the beach in the direction she was walking; there was more than half a mile before she would turn again. Now I began to be frightened. Since my mother seemed unable to behave as a mother should or even to register my presence, it was time for me to seek the help of another adult, someone who could look after me. And my mother.

We were, by road, more than a mile away from Ballydavid, and even if I got myself there—I felt less confident about my ability to make the journey than I had about the far less justified excursion to Mrs. Coughlan—I would find two old women who were no more accessible or competent than my poor mother. The maids, it is true, would look after me, as they increasingly had while my mother mourned. But I had never seen either exercise authority outside the kitchen, and even there only over boys coming to the back door with messages or selling game. (Game that had probably been poached from the Ballydavid woods, according to Aunt Katie.) I tried, and failed, to imagine Bridie, with her starched muslin cap, white apron, and blue print dress, on the strand taking a firm line with my mother.

Appealing to neighbors, I didn't even consider. I knew my family's grief was too private to expose to anyone not part of it.

Then I thought of O'Neill. I had never seen a limit to his authority, and he even had a means of transporting my grief-frozen mother back to Ballydavid, where she would be given tea and a warm fire and the silent sympathy of the maids. Not that it would comfort her, since escape from the proximity of the two old ladies and the weight of their similar devastating emotions was the very reason for her sojourn on the strand. Be that as it might, neither she nor I could spend the night on the beach; the sun was now close to the cloudy horizon, and the wind colder on my legs.

I knew that I was supposed to announce my intention to my mother. Walking on the main road alone was forbidden (a rule it had never been considered necessary to formulate before my elopement to the Coughlans), and I was proposing to travel more than a mile by myself. But my mother was a pale, small figure at the end of the strand still walking away from me; I knew a gesture in her direction would be pointless. Carrying my sandals, I walked along the dunes to where the beach road joined the main road that turned inland. I wanted to keep my mother in sight for as long as possible, just in case she came to her senses. But a light mist rolling off the sea made her seem even less substantial.

Sitting on the coarse grass beside the road, I did up my sandals. The wind had blown sand, yellow and fine against the asphalt, onto the road itself. A motorcar—still rare enough to be remarked upon—came down the Waterford road toward me. It looked very like the Ballydavid car, but, although I was always prepared to be interested in a car, I couldn't tell the difference between one make and another. And Grandmother's car was a vehicle I had rarely seen outside its garage. It was O'Neill's proudest possession: He assumed that he was in a sense owner of anything used outdoors at Ballydavid as, on some level, did my family and the rest of the household. Polished to a high gloss, the Sunbeam was kept under a cover of old bed sheets in the garage. I realize now that O'Neill was not an accomplished driver and, for day to day outings or those (such as meeting us at the boat) where it was necessary to have completely reliable transport, the pony and trap was always dispatched. He preferred, I think, to drive my grandmother on her afternoon calls or her visits to the graveyard when he would have plenty of time to turn and have the car pointed in the right direction when she was ready to go home.

I watched the motorcar pass me and turn along the beach road which, behind the dunes, followed the outline of the coast. O'Neill was at the wheel and there was someone beside him. Even in the moment of overwhelming relief—it was as though I had accidentally summoned the necessary genii from a bottle—I wondered who his passenger could be. It seemed equally as impossible that one of the family should be sitting in front beside him as it was that he might be giving a lift to either of the men who worked at Ballydavid. My relief turned to despair as I understood that he had failed to see me, or that he had seen me and thought me one of the local urchins sitting at the side of the road. There was no longer any reason for me to trudge back to Ballydavid. I sat despondently for a little while as I tried to think what to do; the road was sheltered from the wind coming in from the sea and was a little warmer than the strand. I had begun to think about going to the nearest farmhouse and knocking at the door, but what could I say? I didn't know how to explain my predicament or to describe what was wrong with my mother.

After a little while, not bothering to unbuckle my sandals, I climbed back up the dune behind me, the sand slipping away beneath me as I scrambled to the top. It seemed better to be able to see my mother than not, and, since I now could not think of anything to do, I thought I would sit in as much shelter as I could find and weep.

At the very end of the strand I could now faintly see two new figures. One was moving along the beach toward my mother who was walking away from him—both the new arrivals were men—while the other stood near an opening that led onto an area of thin grass and sand under a windswept sycamore. That opening was where we usually drove to if we came in a pony and trap; if we arrived on foot, as we had that afternoon, we gained the strand through the closer opening near where I now waited.

It was the way he stood—straight backed, still, his weight on one foot—that made me to realize that the closer man was O'Neill. And I suddenly knew, although he was only a shadowy figure in the heavier mist rolling in, that the other man was my father. Magically, it seemed, transported from Tidworth, the officer training camp where he was now stationed.

My father had been wounded and decorated for bravery during the early months of the war. He referred to his wound as a small one, and to his medal, too, as small. Even so, the wound and decoration must have been important and dramatic events in our family. I have no memory of them. My encounter with Grandmother's cat on the avenue at Ballydavid and my meeting with Mrs. Coughlan took place before my father was invalided home from France, yet I remember that afternoon—although nothing before or after—and not my father's wound, my mother's fears, or her relief at having him safely back in England. The wound had not been life threatening, but it kept him from seeing any further action. His decoration established his courage and no one could imagine him reluctant to "do his bit." Since he had also seen action in the closing months of the Boer War, he did not have a romantic or unrealistic view of war and felt no particular regret that, through no fault of his own, he was unable to return to the battlefield. He had fought as a noncommissioned officer, and since he was tough, strong, intelligent—although not imaginative and completely lacking in an aesthetic sense—it should not have been difficult to find something useful for him to do. And for some time he had had a job connected with military supplies. He had a practical, tidy mind with a great capacity for concentrating on detail and the kind of determined common sense that can cut through, or circumnavigate, bureaucracy. I think that, in his way, he liked the work and I am sure he was good at it. But his father-in-law had been a general, and someone, though not Father, thought my father should become an officer. Strings had been pulled and that spring while we were staying with Grandmother, he had begun his training at Tidworth.

I stood on the beach, still, with my arms wrapped around me in an unconscious imitation of my mother, watching Father, in the distance, stride after her. She was still walking away from him and I thought she had not seen him; it seemed unlikely that even in her grief and shock she would ignore him. My mother was a little afraid of Father, her attitude not quite that of a normal wifely deference, since on some, perhaps many, levels she would have considered herself superior to him. She knew herself to be better educated, better bred, better mannered, better connected, and she knew that he thought these qualities mere female attributes and secondary to her beauty and sweet nature. When Mother was with her family, she was in the position of silently defending him from their silent criticisms, these unspoken thoughts batting around the room like shuttlecocks, inhibiting and coloring even the occasional remarks of day to day family life. It was only when Father was safely in England and Mother had settled in at Ballydavid that everyone relaxed.

In London, at Palace Gardens Terrace, my father's values ruled. He had come from New Zealand, his family originally farmers from the north of Ireland who had emigrated during the nineteenth century. He had returned to the British Isles with values learned from two generations of brutally hard work and poverty: frugality; common sense; infrequent, inexpensive, simple, and unsophisticated pleasures (he had a weakness for music halls and would on occasion quote catchphrases from comics he had seen there); and a lack of frills or airs. The moment he was out of the house, my mother's suppressed gentility sprang back into place. Because I spent most of my day in the nursery and because of my father's time as a soldier, he had so far played a comparatively minor part in my life.

Although I was never quite at ease with him, his attitude to me at best momentary benevolence, I now welcomed another approach to life—one with clearer rules and fewer surprises—than that which ruled Ballydavid; I was relieved to see an adult who had not abnegated authority to grief. It seemed, as I warmed to consideration of my role, that the advent of a sentient adult would be followed by a full appreciation of my courage and stoicism and by the realization that I had been neglected by the matriarchal side of my family. I turned over some phrases in my mind—modest disclaimers that in no way suggested that I had not suffered—and prepared myself to be congratulated, apologized to, and, in some manner, rewarded. I started to walk toward my parents.

My father had now caught up with Mother. Their movements seemed part of an informal dance; although I was slowly getting closer, a new wave of mist drifted over the beach. My father in silhouette turned toward my mother, both of them still walking. Then they stopped, Father gesticulating, as though he were trying to get her attention—I knew what that felt like— Mother motionless as if she had not quite noticed his presence. He laid a hand on her arm; she seemed for a moment as though she were going to continue her pacing. I was now close enough to see her shoulders suddenly slump, and my father put his arm around her and lead her slowly, as though she were immensely frail, toward the opening where the car was waiting. It seemed to me the spell had been broken and that I could now claim my father's attention and be looked after myself. No longer frightened, I felt the full extent of my cold, hunger, and exhaustion. I looked forward to being petted, cosseted, admired, congratulated, lifted up into the motorcar onto my mother's knee, and driven back to Ballydavid, where I would be made a fuss of by the maids. Tea and a bath in front of the nursery fire and then an adult member of my family, perhaps even my newly restored mother, would read to me before I climbed into bed.

I followed as fast as my tired legs could carry me over the loose sand; ahead of me my parents disappeared into the dark opening that led to the Sunbeam. The early summer foliage had formed walls and a roof of leaves that reduced the now faint light of early evening. O'Neill had disappeared and I could now hear him cranking up the engine of the Sunbeam.

Clambering, although the slope at the top of the beach was not in fact steep, I was now really tired, and, despite my intention of presenting myself as brave and uncomplaining, qualities given great value in my family, a wail escaped my lips. It was not quite loud enough; I reached the scrub that separated the strand from the road just in time to watch the car turn the corner and drive away toward Ballydavid.

FOR A LONG TIME I harbored an unjust yet understandable belief that it was during those hours that I had been abandoned on the beach that my family hatched the plot for a greater abandonment. Since, as usual, I was neither consulted nor informed of the plan as it developed, I don't feel any remorse for my suspicions. It was a time when the convenience of children was not taken into account and their wishes rarely solicited. In my family and, I imagine, most others of that time and place, this cavalier attitude—one that I sometimes consider when I wonder how one small island nation managed, without any apparent moment of self-questioning or loss of confidence, to rule half the world—was accompanied by the assumption that those without power had little need for information. I look back now and see, without much surprise, that my parents, whose boat was in low emotional and financial waters, decided to lighten their load by throwing me overboard. Especially since there was a comfortable lifeboat alongside—or, at least, in a nearby country, one not at war.

It was Bridie who noticed that I was missing and I was lucky it was not longer before she did so. The Sunbeam came up the avenue more quickly than did a pony drawing a laden trap, and, by the time she came out on the porch, the motorcar door was open, and she had assumed that I'd already been let out and had gone about my business elsewhere. It was not until she carried the tin bath into the nursery that she realized it was some time since she had last seen me. Instinct rather than logic—there were many places I could easily have been—told her that I was missing.

My father came to look for me. He came by himself, driving the Sunbeam. Later, when I understood how much he enjoyed being at the wheel (he was a beginner and it is just possible this was his maiden voyage), I thought it likely that he experienced neither anxiety about my loss nor imagination about what I must be feeling. It was an unexamined belief that, since children hadn't the information that caused fear in adults, they neither understood nor feared those dangers. At the same time, they were supposed to be able to apply adult logic and not indulge in childhood terror of the dark, of ghosts, of abandonment. I wonder if my father would have been worried if, when he arrived at the beach, he had found it deserted and dark. As he would have, had he not seen me sitting on the back of a cart about to turn in at a farm-house gate.

He stopped the car, briefly and casually thanked the farmer who had found me wailing on the sea road, and cheerfully told me to hop in. I had never ridden in the front of the Sunbeam before, and I hesitated, unsure whether to get in beside him or to climb into my accustomed place in the back. My hesitation was long enough for me to catch a flicker of impatience cross his face and to see the queer look the farmer gave this unnatural English parent.

Nothing was said during the first few moments of our reunion. I was silent because I felt I was due either praise or an apology; my father was silent because he had overestimated his driving skills and underestimated the width of the country road on which he was now attempting to turn the Sunbeam. The farmer, who had stopped to open the gate, now stood watching while his horse pulled the cart far enough along the stony track to allow his master to close the gate behind it.

An already disapproving audience did nothing for my father's performance. He had misjudged the width of the road, not understanding that the lushest, darkest green part of the grassy verge grew out of a drain from the marshy field behind the hedge. Father turned the wheel sharply and drove the Sunbeam onto the verge; he had intended, I suppose, to back up to the farm gate, turn sharply again to the right, and return to Ballydavid. Instead there was the strange sensation of the car in motion without a corresponding forward progress as the wheels failed to engage in the wet earth of the ditch.

My father became red in the face and I sat very still; whatever moral advantage I had earned by my ordeal at this moment counted for nothing. Father ground the gears into reverse and put his foot on the accelerator. The wheels spun, digging themselves deeper into the boggy soil. Out of the corner of my eye I could see the farmer who had rescued me leisurely close the gate, bolt it, and take a clay pipe from the pocket of his jacket. He, at least, was enjoying himself. Father had, in a dramatically short period of time, shown himself as unmannerly, neglectful, and arrogant; the farmer would have seen him, not in any way accurately, as rich, upper-class, and Protestant.

After a moment, my father turned off the engine and got out of the car. Standing in the stagnant mud of the ditch, he cursed as he heaved his weight against the bonnet of the Sunbeam. It did not move. After a moment, he returned to the car and disengaged the gear. Now the motorcar responded to his pressure, but only for as long as he strained against it. Each time he let go to return to the driver's seat, it sank back into the soft mud. He knew, I knew, and the farmer knew that sooner or later he would have to ask for help. I flicked a glance at the farmer. His face was utterly expressionless as he struck a match and lit his pipe. Drawing on the tobacco, he leaned on the gate and seemed to give the evening sky the same amount of attention as he did my straining parent.

In the end, of course, help was requested and given. But the comedy was not quite over. The combined strength of the two men easily pushed the Sunbeam back onto the road. The farmer reopened the gate to give my father more room to turn; Father backed up, ground the gears, and stalled. Now he had to get out again, reach under the driver's seat for the handle, return to the front of the car, and crank the engine until it again started. I sank down in the seat and tried to disappear; the farmer, still holding the gate, still expressionless, permitted himself a couple of slow, thoughtful nods.

Nothing was said as we drove back to Ballydavid. As soon as we were out of sight of the farmer, my father pulled a handkerchief out of his pocket and mopped his face. When he had replaced it he glanced at me and looked mildly surprised. I felt as though I had changed since he had last seen me and not for the better, but he said nothing.

When we had turned into the avenue at Ballydavid, Father stopped the motorcar and opened the door. Fortunately, he had not got out completely before we began to roll slowly backward, and he angrily wrenched the brake into place. For a moment, I considered asking if I could walk the rest of the way, but, seeing his scowl, I thought better of it. He walked around the Sunbeam, inspecting it. The rear did not engage his attention for long, but when he got to the front he crouched by the engine grill. I stretched myself to my full height and saw that he was wiping the muddy evidence of his adventure off the chrome and mudguards with his pocket handkerchief. When he got back in the motorcar his face was again crimson; this time he wiped his brow with the sleeve of his jacket. I remained completely still and silent, although I was uncomfortable. Since my legs were not long enough to reach the floor, I had to brace myself with my hands in order not to slip about on the seat. And for some time I had needed to urinate.

Father sat for a moment before he set off again, and we drove up the remainder of the avenue at a dignified speed that did not require the changing of gears. An anxious group of women stood on the veranda—Aunt Katie, Grandmother, and Bridie—and, to one side, a stern-faced O'Neill. Mother was, I think, lying down and unaware that her elder child had been misplaced. A dark cloud heavy with rain had formed over most of the sky, although the horizon was pale and light; the dark sky and a low strong wind announced a gale coming in from the Atlantic. I imagined, and I think the distraught women on the veranda did also, myself alone on the darkened strand, battered by the storm wind, and drenched by the rain. Father and O'Neill, I am fairly sure, were preoccupied with the welfare of the Sunbeam.

The women and O'Neill were presumably reassured: the women by the top of my head visible over the dashboard through the windscreen, O'Neill by the lack of immediately visible dents on the Sunbeam. As a collective sigh of relief was emitted, Father drew up in front of the house and braked too abruptly, spraying a shower of gravel at the feet of his audience and throwing me from my insecure perch on the front seat against the polished wood of the dashboard.

UNCLE SAINT WAS DEAD but the war went on. In trenches stretching from the English Channel to the Swiss border, Allied and German soldiers faced each other; behind four hundred miles of barbed wire troops dug into mud.

During the Boer War, Major John McBride had raised an Irish Brigade to fight on the Boer side against the British; Sir Roger Casement now attempted to raise another Irish Brigade from the prisoner-of-war camps in Germany. At the beginning of December 1914, the German authorities began to separate Irish prisoners of war from their English comrades. The Irish prisoners were taken from their various camps and assembled in one large group at Limburg. Many of them had come from the Sennelager camp, where for some time they had been softened up by the Germans with speeches and promises of improved conditions: fewer rules, better food, Mass every morning. Suspicious and possibly mystified by the historical and political references made by their now curiously placatory captors, the Irish prisoners responded in a memorandum that they did not wish to avail themselves of these concessions unless their fellow prisoners also benefited, "as, in addition to being Irish Catholics, we have the honour to be British soldiers." Nothing subsequent appears to have altered this position, and their suspicion of German motives extended to Casement and to his attempts to recruit them to fight for Irish independence.

From the beginning, Casement faced a disillusioning task. The Irish prisoners of war were at first bewildered by and then antagonistic to his proposals. He himself was discouraged by a report in the *Times* in which Germany, while making peaceful overtures to the United States, omitted Ireland from its list of small nations who should be free to decide their destinies when the war was over.

The reluctance of the prisoners to change sides was not a reflection on Casement's powers of persuasion or a result of his Protestant origins and former career in the British diplomatic service. Two Irish priests brought from the Irish College in Rome had no better luck; and when an Irish-speaking priest sent from America took a more aggressive approach, there were complaints from the prisoners and talk of a boycott of his services. Casement's initial speech to a group of NCOs produced only two volunteers, and it was obvious even to the idealistic and self-deluding Casement that neither was of sterling character. His second visit in January 1915 was even more discouraging: he was jeered and booed by the Irish prisoners. Never short of courage, Casement returned to the camp every day of his stay at Limburg, but contented himself in following around Father Crotty, the more sympathetic of the two priests who had come from Rome.

In the spring, Casement sent Adler Christensen back to the United States. Some time before, Christensen had been involved in a scandal, referred to but never specified—almost certainly of a homosexual nature. It had been forgiven by the generous and pliable Casement, although the scandal must have made even more awkward his life in Berlin. One imagines that whatever sadness Casement felt at parting with Christensen, it was diluted by exhausted relief.

The formation of the Irish Brigade brought no consolation. Eventually fifty-two men were recruited and given privileges and smart uniforms designed by Casement. Their fellow prisoners resented the rewards of their treachery, well aware that most of the recruits had signed on for the comforts and benefits that went with belonging to the Brigade. The soldiers of his new brigade did not rise to Casement's imagined ideal; they drank, and they got into fights with their fellow prisoners, particularly the French and Russians, and eventually—since they were free to go to beer gardens—with German soldiers who also despised them. By August, the discouraged and increasingly ill Casement was considering returning to the United States. Instead he was joined in Germany by Robert Monteith.

Monteith had served in the British Army as an ordnance store conductor and had fought in the Boer War. He was realistic, competent, and experienced, qualities that Casement lacked to an unusual degree. Devoy, in New York, saw him as the ideal man to deal with Casement and the Irish Brigade. Christensen, still—but not for long—in the employ of the Clan na Gael, accompanied Monteith on his crossing to Norway. Their ship, too, was stopped by a British cruiser and boarded, then detained in the Orkneys for five days. These days allowed Christensen further scope for his dramatic talent: While Monteith moved from empty cabin to empty cabin, Christensen alternated between spreading false alarm and distracting the searchers with, one suspects, a heavy-handed performance.

Monteith revered Casement, and together they tried to raise enthusiasm and morale in the brigade. To what extent they succeeded may be judged by the reception of a later deranged scheme of Casement's. In December of 1915 Casement suggested to the German authorities that his brigade should be dispatched to help fight with the Turks in the Dardanelles—where Erskine Childers was now an officer aboard a primitive aircraft carrier, the *Ben My Chree*—but the Germans thought it unwise to give arms to such men.

Chapter 4

UNCLE SAINTHILL HAD been killed in May. My parents, with Edward, returned to London in the middle of June, leaving me behind as part of a household incapacitated by grief. Why did they do it? At the time I looked no further for an explanation than that they didn't love me enough to take me home with them. After a while I amended this belief, deciding bitterly that they had given me to Grandmother as a pet to distract her from her mourning.

In hindsight I don't think I was completely wrong on either count. I understand now that my father thought my mother incapable of looking after me, he worried about how he himself would take care of his family, and they both probably thought it not only beneficial to me but faintly patriotic to leave me in a country where food was not rationed and where there was no danger of nighttime bombs. If so, one could applaud their prescience, for the air raids became more frequent as the war went on, and by the beginning of 1917 England was experiencing severe food shortages as the German blockade cut off shipping in an attempt to starve the island into submission. One might have admired my father's foresight were it not that he took my stunned and grieving mother back to London and almost immediately impregnated her. It might be argued that he should not bear the full blame for this pregnancy, that my mother—or possibly even Nature, desperate for male children to replace the men dead in France—might share the responsibility for this new mouth to feed. But I am a product of my times and hold the man accountable.

It was a summer of fear, sorrow, silence, and almost unbearable loneliness.

It was not unusual—indeed it was an aspect of privilege—for children, especially boys, to be separated from their parents and sent away to school. Their new circumstances would invariably be less congenial than those in which I found myself. But such children, despite bad food and cold showers, were in the company of other children. They knew why they were there; boarding school was an unpleasant but apparently necessary part of growing up. To be left behind in someone else's house at the end of a visit was not. I was afraid that the atmosphere in which we lived would not change and that I would live out my foreseeable life as an insignificant character awake alone in Sleeping Beauty's palace. I was dimly aware that the war would in time come to an end and with that end would come change, but that might be—and, in fact, was—some years in the future. And if England did not win the war, that change would be for an unimaginable worse.

I have had a better life than most. I live in congenial surroundings. My marriage, although too short, was happy. Mine would appear to be an average life affected by the time and place in history in which it has been lived. As I have told you, I am a teacher and I live in a little house on the seaside fringe of Dublin. From that you may infer that my life did not follow the conventional lines one might have expected from my upbringing. As in every life, what might have been can be no more than an educated guess. Would mine have been different if my parents had not so casually abandoned me at Ballydavid? Had I returned to

England, it is not unreasonable, since my family survived the war, to assume I, too, should have done so. But it is hard for me to imagine that my untaken path would not have eventually led me back to Ireland.

Ironically, even if I had remained loyal to the privileged Anglo-Irish society to which I belonged, the circumstances of my life would be, on the surface at least, much as they now are. By the time I was grown, the world of the landowning Protestants—the world I, when I had to make a choice, instinctively, and in an instant, rejected—no longer existed.

My parents left me at Ballydavid in the summer of 1915. Seven years later the world of the Ascendancy ended. In 1922, after two ghastly and brutal years of revolutionary killing, burning, and menace on the Irish Republican side, and reprisals, often random and even more brutal, on the part of the imported-from-England Black and Tans and Auxiliaries, Ireland became a Free State. A civil war ensued. Many of the Anglo-Irish left the country; it would be hard to say whether Independence or the Civil War was the greater cause for the exodus. Certainly those whose houses were burned during the Troubles before Independence, or during the Civil War afterward, were among those who could no longer imagine a future for themselves in Ireland. Ballydavid survived, and it may have survived because one of the Republican soldiers owed me his life. At any rate the house still stands, although it no longer belongs to my family.

The Anglo-Irish who remained gradually adapted to a new way of living. Had I not thrown my lot in with that of an eleven-year-old Catholic boy after a tennis party on a hot August afternoon and, as a result, later eloped with him, there would be no perceptible difference between me and those of my contemporaries with a similar upbringing. My husband was killed in the early stages of the Second World War—it seemed inevitable:

he never lost his streak of boyish recklessness and his love of adventure. But I am, even so, grateful that my marriage seems to explain the divide between me and my upbringing. Although the elopement and marriage outraged and scandalized both families and both religions, it was only one consequence of an earlier, more serious, secret, and still invisible decision. One I would not have had to make had I been taken back to London with my family.

For almost a month I wandered about the sad silent house, not knowing what to do with myself and largely unnoticed by its inhabitants. Then Grandmother and Aunt Katie began to come out of their trance. Gray-faced, they sat once more on either side of the fireplace in the drawing room.

Each afternoon, Uncle William, Aunt Katie's stepson, drove over for a largely silent visit with her. Uncle William lived alone at Ballinamona Park, maintaining the standards of domestic comfort established by Aunt Katie. He was a middle-aged man of enormous personal authority. Ballinamona Park was a perfectly run gentleman's residence, the model to which O'Neill aspired in the day to day management of Ballydavid. The stables (Patience and my mother's hunter were fed the same diet as Uncle William's horses, both of which were hunted twice a week all winter); the lawns and avenue; the fencing and drains; the cattle; and the garage were maintained along the lines of Ballinamona. Improvements and modernization were of great interest to Uncle William, and it was he who had introduced the Sunbeam into the lives of the old ladies and O'Neill.

Long silent meals were served. Both Grandmother and Aunt Katie had become thinner and older. Neither ate much, while I, afraid not to finish everything on my plate, self-consciously cut up and chewed my food as quietly as possible. Gradually the familiar rhythm of life was resumed, punctuated by Aunt Katie from time

to time rising from her armchair or the dining table and leaving
the room with a handkerchief to her face.

When I had been told I would be staying for a while at Ballydavid, one of the seeming (not actual, since I was powerless in the
matter) inducements offered was that O'Neill would teach me to
ride. Patience was already in fantasy my pony; now it seemed that
she would be so in practice—at least when she wasn't between
the shafts of the trap.

Riding was not as I had imagined it would be. I had dreamed
of riding—like a little princess—on a calm, obedient, and docile
pony. Instead there were lessons. It was O'Neill's charter to prepare me for the hunting field and to instill in me courage, a good
seat, and other qualities of horsemanship that would reflect well
on his stable. Unflattering comparisons to my mother's gentle
hands, erect posture, and her fearlessness gave me to understand
that I would never attain the standards she had set.

And my fear was not groundless; at least once during every
lesson I would either slither forward on Patience's neck, over her
shoulder, and headfirst onto the packed dirt surface of the paddock or, once O'Neill had started schooling me over low jumps,
land rather harder on my bottom. The first time this happened I
was as much surprised as I was hurt. Tears were instantaneous.
Weeping was discouraged by my family and usually met with an
admonition to be "a brave little soldier." (With the maids tears
were a little more effective, probably because they had no investment in building my character.) For O'Neill, tears, let alone the
loud wails with which I accompanied them, were merely another
way I had found to shame him and Ballydavid, on a par with my
hair coming down on the hunting field, or allowing my pony to
tread on a hound.

"Git up," he would say, "and stop making a holy show of
yerself."

The first time, the shock of his lack of sympathy or concern—how would he have liked to have had to tell Grandmother he had managed to break my neck?—stopped my tears instantaneously, but thereafter most lessons ended with my sniveling into a soggy handkerchief.

I was full of regret and aware that I had made a bad deal that did me no credit. The level of desperation in every member of my family—Grandmother; Aunt Katie; my mother stunned with grief; and my father reluctantly, and without qualifications, responsible for his distraught wife, his hitherto largely unnoticed children, a military career he was socially unsuited to, and the financial pressure of a large establishment that the war and rising prices had left him unable to maintain—had encouraged them all to maneuver me into what must have seemed the only tenable position. A step that would help them all to keep going until time and changing circumstances would allow life gradually to regain its own rhythm and become normal again.

My mother had taken little active part in my abandonment. That her condition did not allow questions, appeals, or explanations was maybe the strongest reason for me to do what I was told and hope that my acquiescence would gain me favorable treatment from the less indulgent Irish side of my family.

I had also been, I soon realized, too easily seduced by the promises of material benefits and the pleasure of my new status. I had not understood that after I had enjoyed the novelty of being the pet of Ballydavid and the daughter of the house, everything would not snap back into its previous—if not comfortable, then at least familiar—mode.

What I had been offered was not insubstantial. The nursery was to be made into my own bedroom, with rearranged furniture and a pretty bedspread; I would learn to ride and have a pony; Jock would be my companion on walks; there would be lessons rather than school and a little girl nearby I could play with; and, once I could ride well enough, I could go by myself on Patience to visit her. I seem not to have been aware of my parents' and my brother's departure although I had the evidence of trunks, suitcases, and tissue paper before me, or perhaps I understood that they were leaving but not that I could not simultaneously enjoy my new privileges and go home with them. While I was contemplating Patience and my new bedroom, my father packed up Mother and Edward and took them back to England.

AT THE END OF JULY, approaching the Devil's Birthday, as the anniversary of the outbreak of war was known, life at Ballydavid began again. It seemed as though the clocks again ticked, Oonagh again purred, Bridie's broom again swept the flagstones in the hall, hooves and wheels could be heard on the gravel outside the front door, the sparks flew up from the turf fire that was lit every afternoon, and the swallows once more swooped over the summer lawn in search of evening insects.

The resumption of something approaching everyday life was marked by two activities, each a futile refusal to admit the finality of an untimely death. The arrival of the artist who was to paint my uncle Sainthill's portrait occurred in the same week as I became aware that Grandmother and Aunt Katie were attempting through spiritualism to bridge the gap between this world and the next.

The painter came down from Dublin on the train. He was not a painter of the first water, and I suppose Grandmother must have been aware that his availability at short notice to paint a portrait from a photograph suggested both a lack of worldly success and a journeyman attitude toward his art. For a day or two before he arrived, he was the subject of several long discussions between

Grandmother and Aunt Katie. Should he eat meals in the dining room or should he be fed separately? It was a tricky question that could not be resolved until Mr. McLeod arrived and they could see and hear him, but I think the feeling was that a painter bore the temporary status of a governess and would eat breakfast and lunch in the dining room and have his dinner on a tray in his room.

The painter, when he eventually arrived, was Scottish, with a red nose and sandy beard. Before Grandmother and Aunt Katie could withdraw to reassess the placement, he managed—I no longer remember how, but doubtless he had had years of practice—to establish that he would eat his lunch ("with a bottle of stout, if you would be so good") in the room where he would be working and the other two meals at a location chosen by his employer, but alone.

Relieved, but vaguely insulted, this snub was quickly translated into a lecture to me by Grandmother about an artist's need for quiet and privacy, and I was told not to bother Mr. McLeod while he was working.

I was bored and lonely; the stretch between breakfast and lunch seemed interminable. The next morning, soon after Mr. McLeod set up his easel in the drawing room, I crept into the room with a book and, seating myself on the sofa at some distance from where he stood, settled down to watch.

The photograph of Uncle Sainthill, from which Mr. McLeod was to paint, was a conventional studio portrait—my uncle in uniform, dignified, a little stiff, a row of medals on his chest. McLeod's commission was not only to place my uncle at Bally-david, but to alter the trimmings on his uniform to reflect his promotion to major during the last month of his life, and to include among the medals his Military Cross.

I watched, holding my book on my knee and making no pretence of reading it—it was a dull book; the bookshelves at

Ballydavid had little to offer me—as the painter angled his easel, attached the photograph a little above the canvas, placed his paints on a small table covered with a thick cloth to his right, and propped the other photographs he was to consult on grandmother's desk to his left. He then stood back a little and looked out the window. The downstairs windows at Ballydavid were large, the upper and lower halves each divided into nine panes. Shutters, plainly carved, were drawn back into the wall on either side. As Mr. McLeod began to sketch the outline of the portrait, I crept a little closer. I remained silent and, as he appeared not to be aware of my presence, I considered myself technically obedient to Grandmother's instruction not to disturb him.

From the vertical lines on the right of the canvas and the lighter horizontal lines to the left, I could see that the portrait was to show Uncle Sainthill leaning against the shutters. The angle of the easel was such that he would not be shown in profile; he would be looking out the window, though not at the view shown in the background of the painting. Behind my uncle, the carved white shutter, its line broken by the border of the dark velvet curtain on the right; to the left, the Ballydavid fields with the woods beyond and, in the far distance, the sea.

Although the photograph was of conventional proportions (about five inches in height and three in width) the canvas on the easel was long and narrow. I watched and waited to see what Mr. McLeod would do next. After a little while he took a pipe and a pouch of tobacco from his pocket and, without looking away from his work, stuffed the tobacco into the pipe and pressed it down with his fingers.

No one ever smoked in Grandmother's drawing room. I was unsure what I should do. Clearly it was no concern of mine, but I remembered how I had been held responsible for Oonagh's destruction of Grandmother's knitting. When Mr. McLeod lit his pipe, I cleared my throat gently. He appeared not to hear me. I stood up and crossed the room to where he stood.

"Would you like me to open a window?" I asked.

"Certainly not," he said. "It's bloody cold already."

I regarded him with some curiosity. I had heard Bridie telling Maggie that she had found an empty bottle in the wastepaper basket in his room that morning.

"What are you doing?" I asked.

"Waiting," he said abruptly, drawing on his pipe.

"What are you waiting for?" I supposed that I was disturbing Mr. McLeod in just the manner I had been told not to, but I sensed that this particular artist was a less sensitive flower than Grandmother had imagined.

"Waiting for the light to change."

I looked out the window. A morning mist was rolling in from the sea. By eleven o'clock, it would burn off. Coming out of the mist at the bottom of the field, I could see a man, walking slowly up toward the house. After a moment or two, I saw that it was not a man but rather the red-haired youth who sometimes came to the kitchen door with messages.

Leaving my book on the sofa—I would return later—I quietly left the room. Before closing the door I glanced back. Mr. McLeod had not moved; he stood gazing despondently out the window, a cloud of evil smelling black smoke drifting closer to the velvet curtains.

In the kitchen, Maggie was reading tea leaves. I stood quietly beside Bridie, whose cup was being read, and watched happily, while listening for a knock at the kitchen door.

I preferred the more social and usually more optimistic superstitions of the kitchen to those of my own family. Although Maggie's tea leaves would sometimes warn against treachery or disaster, they more often foretold dark strangers, journeys across the water, or a letter. Whenever possible, I would creep into the kitchen to witness this magic; historical evidence to the contrary, the shadowy promises of good fortune suggested faith in distant outside influences.

The kitchen was pleasantly warm, and, even more than the heat thrown off by the range, I was aware of the soft comforting warmth of Bridie, against whom I was leaning. But there had not been a knock at the door. After a moment I let myself out the kitchen door into the yard. Even at the time I was surprised that I would leave the cozy atmosphere of the kitchen—where, although the reading of the tea leaves was over, I could perhaps have climbed into Bridie's lap—for the chilly damp of the yard and a chance to see the red-haired boy at closer quarters.

But I was, apart from a red hen scratching about between the cobble stones, alone. It was too late in the morning for there to be activity in the dairy, and it was the wrong day of the week for laundry. The bleak gray of the morning—no colder than it had been in the drawing room—and the stillness and silence that surrounded me contributed to the illusion of a household, if not frozen, then lagging in time.

I buttoned up my cardigan and waited. After a moment I began to stroll about the kitchen yard, since I didn't want the boy—who should have been there by now, had this been his destination—to find me standing pointlessly by the kitchen door. But even in motion I began to feel silly. If he had come into the yard and asked me what I was doing, I could not have answered him in a way that wouldn't have made me appear half-witted. My situation had a certain familiarity: on cold afternoons Grandmother would send me outside for fresh air and exercise, and invariably I would be asked by one of the men who worked at Ballydavid what I was doing—as though I didn't have enough sense to stay indoors and keep warm.

But this time I had gone outside through my own volition. And I had not, even in my imagination, taken my acquaintance-ship with this boy so far as a conversation. I had, I suppose, wanted to see him at close quarters, maybe to smile at him and to have him acknowledge my existence. I was lonely enough for this to seem important.

There was a shortage of children in the neighborhood of Bally-david—by which I mean there seemed to be only one Protestant child of my age among the local families with whom Grand-mother was on visiting terms. The child's name was Clodagh, and, in September, soon after my birthday, I would be sharing a gov-erness with her and taking lessons each day at her parents' house. In the meantime, Ballydavid in indefinite mourning, social life was suspended, and no one considered whether I, just separated from my family and without a friend or playmate, might be un-happy and lonely.

It now seemed that, if the boy had come up to Ballydavid, he had not come to deliver a message to the kitchen door. I wan-dered, as nonchalantly as I could, into the stable yard. The stables were separated from the smaller courtyard behind the kitchen by a covered passageway, to either side of which lay the O'Neill's house. As I hesitated in the dry sheltered area, I heard a voice behind the door of the room where the O'Neills lived and ate. The sleeping quarters were on the other side of the passageway and above their house were haylofts and, what had been during more affluent times, the attic quarters of grooms and stable boys. When I visited Mrs. O'Neill, I could sometimes hear the surpris-ingly loud movements of what I liked to imagine were squirrels but which were more likely rats, overhead. The voice I heard was Mrs. O'Neill's, but I assumed it was O'Neill to whom she was speaking, so I hurried on toward the stable yard. It, too, was de-serted. Rather than retrace my footsteps—with the possibility of finding myself face to face with O'Neill as he came out his front door—I left the yard by the main gate and strolled past the bleaching garden and onto the back avenue.

I understood, although I didn't wrap the thought in specific words, that now Grandmother was bereaved, O'Neill stood at the moral center of Ballydavid. He said very little about anything that took place beyond the boundaries of his small kingdom; after the frank and respectful traditional words of condolence, "I'm sorry for your trouble, your Ladyship," he showed by word or expression no reaction to the permanent grief following my uncle's death. Nor did he ever volunteer any information about his own son, Tom, who had now been in France for almost a year. In the same respectful way that he had acknowledged Uncle Sainthill's death, he would reply briefly to enquiries about the well-being of his elder child. The lack of emphasis with which he did so did not encourage further conversation on the subject. He knew, as well as we did, that Tom's life expectancy was even shorter than had been Uncle Sainthill's. I imagine he maintained this distance among his social equals, some of whom would have been strongly opposed to Irish men enlisting in the English Army. Conscription for Ireland was in the air and threatened to fan the smoldering violence of nationalism, always beneath the surface, to flames.

I glanced toward the passageway as I reentered the kitchen yard from the avenue. But the yard was still empty. I scurried across it, now aware I was more likely to have an awkward encounter with O'Neill, whom it was my intention to avoid until my riding lesson, than to meet the red-haired boy.

I was about halfway across the yard, the cobbles slippery from the early mist and uncomfortable beneath my indoor shoes, when the door to the O'Neill kitchen opened. I considered retreat, and, as I hesitated, the boy with red hair came out of the O'Neill's house. He paused for a moment at the entrance to the passageway, as though drawing a deep breath, then he slipped an envelope into the inside pocket of his jacket and put his cap on.

Although this was the moment for which I had been waiting, I felt deeply embarrassed and foolish. I could not look at the boy as I muttered, "Hello."

When I raised my eyes I saw that he was still standing, hands in pocket, balancing on the edge of the step.

"Good morning, miss," he said, taking his cap off with a flour- ish and a slightly mocking but, I thought, good-natured smile. Then, putting his hands back in his pockets, he set off across the kitchen yard, whistling as he went. I watched him go. He seemed to me in that moment infinitely valuable, heroic. Desirable.

It was my first experience of romantic love. It would be easy to disown that description of my feelings with a laugh and an af- fectionate backward glance at a child too young to know what love is except by what she had overheard in adult conversation. But then I could ask myself at what age such a love would not seem laughable; unsuitable affection before the age of eighteen in those days was dismissed as "puppy love." And soon after that, in our world, girls married suitably, and romantic love was either repressed, discreetly handled within the conventions of Edwar- dian society, or became a scandal. One might also say that I didn't know the boy—his name was Michael, but I didn't know that yet, and looking back I find that I still think of him as the red- haired boy—well enough to love him. I loved him on the basis of inadequate available knowledge, a similar basis to that of most people of our class in those still chaperoned days. Physical appear- ance and a moment of charm: Many hearts have broken for no more than that.

My love was, of course, a product of my fear and loneliness. And because—although no one, except perhaps O'Neill, treated me badly—I was starved of affection. I was, I suppose, casting around for someone to love. And the red-haired boy had stood still for a moment.

BY THE END of the week, Uncle Sainthill's portrait was finished. I have it now, hanging in the front room of my little villa overlooking Dublin Bay, where each day the tide uncovers a flat, wet, muddy expanse and I am reminded of Woodstown strand. The painting has stood the test of time; Mr. McLeod had been better than any of us thought. In my house it looks larger than it did on the wall of the drawing room at Ballydavid—the sole object from childhood that in life is not smaller than in memory.

The choices the uncouth Scottish painter made at the time had seemed daring. It was as though he had abandoned the attempt to re-create the photograph before him in oil and had, instead, tried to give an impression of his subject—a man whom he had never seen. It was, I now know, less of a gamble than it had seemed at the time. He had known what he was doing.

Although the background of the portrait shows an interior— the window and shutters I had watched Mr. McLeod sketch— Uncle Sainthill is wearing his military greatcoat over his uniform. The coat hangs open, the collar turned up. My uncle stands leaning against the shutter, looking out the window; in one hand he holds a silver cigarette case, in the other a cigarette he has just taken from it. McLeod had elected to paint the portrait in the darker light of early morning—he had at one moment had me stand on a footstool against the shutter while he looked at me with an expression of critical attention. The expanse of khaki and my uncle's air of prescient restlessness make the portrait unsettling.

To everyone's surprise, Grandmother liked the painting. When it was finished, she looked at it for a long time, then nodded, said "Yes," and left the room abruptly.

By now spiritualism—the other symptom of Grandmother's and Aunt Katie's inability to accept that Uncle Sainthill was not only dead but gone—had become part of life at Ballydavid. The drawing room, dominated by the portrait, would be darkened on sunny afternoons, the heavy velvet curtains drawn to provide an atmosphere that would coax the spirits to visit or, at least, to assist a suspension of disbelief. Grandmother and Aunt Katie experimented with table turning and automatic writing. " Ectoplasm," "aura," "the other side" became part of the vocabulary at Ballydavid. The old ladies once even traveled to Dublin to consult a medium. Mother, I gathered later, was kept abreast of the results of these activities by post; she in turn wrote about the séances she attended in London and about the celebrated mediums she had seen or consulted there.

This activity was, in theory, kept from the maids whom, they supposed, would regard it as devil's work. It scared the wits out of me when I first discovered its existence; and even more so when I improved my reading with literature from the Society for Psychical Research, which arrived regularly by post at Ballydavid. I even dipped into one or two books by the society's founder, Sir Oliver Lodge, and found the descriptions of communications from the other side alternatively frightening and boring. The women of my family—along with women and some men all over the British Isles—were searching for evidence or, at least, hope that there might be a life beyond this one. And that that life would offer a reunion with a lost son or husband—more often a son, the unnatural reversal of the generational order inspiring these desperate measures. And, in the meantime, they looked for a message or some other form of reassurance.

The maids did, in fact, consider whatever happened in the forbidden, darkened drawing room an attempt, more than probably successful, to conjure up the devil. I could have told Grandmother that they were not as shocked as she might have imagined. Since my family were Protestants, we were automatically going to burn in hell for all eternity, so whatever took place in the drawing room after tea merely anticipated—and only slightly, given the age of the two old ladies—their inevitable meeting with the Prince of Darkness. Illogically but, I think, understandably, I was more frightened of meeting the devil at Ballydavid than I was of a future, and apparently guaranteed, longer acquaintanceship on his home ground.

Between them, the maids and Grandmother and Aunt Katie drove me out of doors most afternoons. To where O'Neill waited to give me my daily riding lesson.

THE LONG SAD SUMMER drew to a close. It would be going too far to say that I had learned to amuse myself, but my days developed a rhythm, and each no longer stretched before me like an endless desolate waste, broken only by meals and moments of predictable anxiety. I still missed my mother terribly, especially at night, and I thought more affectionately and less critically of Edward than when he and I had shared the night nursery at Palace Gardens Terrace.

September began mild, warm, and still. It was the month of my birthday. Despite their grief and the unrelieved atmosphere of mourning at Ballydavid, both the old ladies rose to the occasion. I was to have a birthday party.

The procedure for entertaining at Ballydavid left Aunt Katie in charge of the arrangements for my party. Grandmother, of course, composed the guest list. It was a division of labor that, I think, suited both. My great-aunt had a talent for the practical aspects of entertaining, and a prodigious memory. She remembered the culinary likes and dislikes of everyone who had ever eaten lunch or dinner at Ballydavid. "Major Gibbon is coming to lunch," she might say. "His favorite is roly-poly pudding." And roly-poly pudding would be served. Aunt Katie was famous for her light hand in the making of pastry, and for special occasions she would make a steak and kidney pie.

When Grandmother visited the kitchen, which was not often, she would stand just inside the door, staying only for as long as it took to make a pronouncement or to inspect some aspect of domestic life that could not be brought to her in the drawing room. One had the impression of skirts drawn in to avoid the contamination of the lower things in life. But Aunt Katie, when the occasion warranted it, would push back her sleeves and, surrounded by an admiring audience, roll out pastry on the floured kitchen table. It was the performance of an artist. Maggie, the cook, herself talented enough to satisfy the standards of Grandmother, watched with respect.

Aunt Katie had married late in life. She was childless, a second wife, and an affectionate stepmother. When I was grown up and married myself, my mother hinted that Aunt Katie and Uncle Jack had entered into a *mariage blanc*. A mutually convenient arrangement that gave her the status and power of marriage and him an unusually accomplished housekeeper to whom he turned over the upbringing of a son—my uncle William—for whom he felt limited affection.

To be Mrs. Martyn of Ballinamona Park was certainly preferable to life as an aging spinster on a small fixed income but, given my great-aunt's nature, it is sad that in all likelihood she died a virgin. A certain wistfulness and a liking for romantic novels—she would refer to one she was enjoying as "a pretty story"—suggested that she might have valued love and sexuality to a greater extent than did, say, my grandmother. And her gentle nature made her more motherly than was her sister. Aunt Katie to a large extent brought up Grandmother's children. My mother, Uncle Hubert, and Uncle Sainthill, the three that had survived early childhood, had come back to live with her at Ballinamona Park until Grandfather finished his Indian tour of duty.

I watched Grandmother approach the guest list in her usual hard-minded manner. Ready to consult her last and socially precise record in order to elevate some child who would glow with happiness and gratitude (or at least its parents were meant to) with the unexpected pleasure and privilege of an invitation to Ballydavid. She was ready also to strike from the list some child who might reasonably expect to be invited but whose parents had incurred Grandmother's displeasure, often in some quite arbitrary way, since the last party. The problem was that there was no last party of this kind and no list. There had not been a children's party at Ballydavid since my uncle Sainthill was a child. Many of the boys who had been at that party now lay, as he did, in soldiers' graves in France.

Grandmother was driven to consult Aunt Katie, who, more in touch with the lives of their neighbors, explained to her that most of her candidates were already in uniform while others were still in their cradles. Eventually even I was consulted. My only suggestion, once the maids had been vetoed, was Mrs. Coughlan. Grandmother gave me a sharp look, but, since her guest list now consisted only of names scratched out, she wrote Mrs. Coughlan's name at the top of a clean sheet of paper.

In the end, three children were invited. One was the little girl with whom I would be sharing lessons, and the other two were sons of neighbors. I knew none of them.

On the morning of my ninth birthday, I came down to breakfast as usual. I was curious about what my presents would be and when I would be given them. Several packages had arrived during the past few days, one from London and two from Dublin.

They had been whisked away before I could test their weight or consistency. Grandmother and Aunt Katie were already at table when I entered the dining room a little breathlessly.

"Good morning, Alice." Grandmother said. "Happy Birthday."

"And many happy returns," Aunt Katie added. Her tone was the warmer of the two. Grandmother seemed subdued rather than chilly. I sat down and tapped the top of my boiled egg with an egg spoon. Aunt Katie engaged me in conversation; evidently the convention that I should be silent and invisible at meals had been suspended as part of the celebrations of the day.

"You have a new frock for your party," Aunt Katie said. "Sent down from Switzer's. I think it will fit you, but you should try it on after breakfast so I can put a stitch in it if needs be."

A party dress was a very satisfactory solution to the mystery of one of the parcels, and there still remained one unaccounted for. I lost the little appetite I had but knew better than to leave food on my plate. Grandmother was paying me more attention than I was used to, so I sat up straight and was careful with my table manners. When I looked up she was still watching me, her face expressionless. She made me nervous and I dropped a finger of buttered toast down my front. Although her eyes were on me, she didn't seem to notice. I glanced at my great-aunt; very often her expression would provide encouragement or reassurance, or she would, with a tactful word, let me know what I should, or should not, do.

"I thought, Alice, we would have egg-and-cress sandwiches, chocolate biscuits, and a sponge cake. Maggie has made her special birthday cake. Do you think——" and she went on to discuss details of the party. It was a subject of some interest to me and, I think, to her. At the same time I could feel that she was deliberately diverting my attention from Grandmother and that she was doing so to avert some awkwardness or embarrassment that I could not imagine. Not one, I had the impression, for which I was responsible.

Breakfast ended and we got up from the table. Grandmother used to sit in the drawing room after breakfast and read the *Morning Post* which came in the first mail. Sometimes Aunt Katie would join her with her needlework so that Grandmother could read aloud the parts that most outraged her—usually pertaining to the grateless and feckless Irish in whose midst she had the misfortune to live. I hesitated by the door, hoping Aunt Katie would take me to her room to try on my dress. She had just turned toward me when Grandmother spoke my name.

"Alice, come here."

She spoke gently, and I did not feel the usual twinge of alarm that came with the full weight of her attention. I went over to her. She was sitting in her straight-backed chair beside the fireplace.

I stood in front of her and waited to see what she would say next. I could feel my great-aunt's immobile presence behind me. Grandmother looked at me long and searchingly. After a moment she took my hand gently and I dropped my eyes. Her hand was cool and dry; I tried not to look at the veins that stood out on the back of it. I heard Aunt Katie's skirt rustle behind me. Then Grandmother raised her hand and took my chin between her finger and thumb to turn my face toward the light of the window. Outside a lovely late summer day boded well for my party. I was aware of a harmony between the color of my grandmother's dress, the upholstery of her chair, and the heavy, faded velvet curtains that framed the window. After a long moment she kissed me on the forehead, sighed, and let go of my face.

"Now run along. Don't keep Aunt Katie waiting."

My great-aunt led me silently up to her room and waited until I was standing on a footstool in my new dress before she spoke.

"Just a dart on either side and it will be perfect. What a skinny little thing you are."

I held my breath while she stuck two pins into either side of the bodice of the white linen dress. I would have chosen something frillier and more colorful, but I could see that the lace insets made the dress pretty and there was a gratifyingly wide sash that tied behind me in a big bow. Because of my father's financial reverses, it had been some time since I had had a new dress.

"Grandmother...I don't think you know," she said, from somewhere around my knees as she tugged at the hem to make sure it sat straight, "but today would also have been your uncle Saint's birthday. He would have been twenty-three."

I now faintly remembered having been told (before it had its present associations and while it was still merely a pleasant coincidence) that I shared a birthday with my uncle. My uncle and I had the same coloring and there was, I knew, a family resemblance. I noticed then that my great-aunt's eyes were pink and swollen, but she was smiling up at me. Grandmother ate lunch in her room on a tray and did not reappear for the rest of the day.

The morning passed slowly. Aunt Katie and the maids smiled encouragingly each time they saw me, but there was no planned activity until my guests arrived for tea. Aunt Katie allowed me just to pick at my lunch, and I was sent to my room to rest. I can't imagine anyone thought I would sleep, and I spent an hour leaning on the window sill, watching Patience, head down and tail flicking away flies, grazing in the field below the lawn. Then I brushed my hair in front of the looking glass and regarded my reflection with largely unwarranted satisfaction. Soon it was time to get dressed. Bridie came to my room, arranged my hair, and did up the buttons down the back of my new dress and tied my sash in large crisp bow. I was ready.

Downstairs, the atmosphere was suspiciously calm; I wondered for a moment if my party had been forgotten. But tea for four children had apparently been taken in stride by Aunt Katie and the maids. I sat quietly on a footstool with my dress and sash spread out behind me so that I should not crush them before my guests arrived. The needlepoint felt rough and scratchy on my bare legs, but I had lived long enough at Ballydavid not to fidget. Now, for the first time, I began to worry about the tea party. I had never met any of my guests and was unable to imagine what would happen after the introductions. Would we stand about awkwardly, looking at our feet? Or would my guests be sophisticated enough to come prepared with the small talk that adults employed on these occasions? Or, worse still, and the most likely, might not the other children already be friends, delighted to see one another, and ignore me, their hostess and a stranger?

Nervously, I excused myself and went upstairs to the bathroom. Aunt Katie, matching a strand of wool for her needlework, nodded approvingly at my foresight. When I came back, the first guest had arrived, but none of the mortifying scenarios I'd imagined had taken place.

Mrs. Coughlan, resplendent in pink and gray—her dress more beautiful and less eccentric than the first time I had met her, although a good deal more interesting than one had any right to expect in County Waterford—was sitting in the drawing room, talking to Aunt Katie. Her face lit up when I came in; I was delighted to see her and flattered that she seemed as pleased to see me. It is possible that I was the only person in the neighborhood who fully and unreservedly appreciated her vulgar, generous nature, her sense of the dramatic, and her demand that life should provide a little more color than that offered by provincial Protestant society. She handed me a package conventionally wrapped but tied with the largest ribbon bow I had ever seen. I glanced at

Aunt Katie, well aware of the convention that presents should be unwrapped all at the same appropriate time.

"Open it, Alice," she said, a slight nervousness in her voice suggesting that I should do so quickly, before anyone else arrived.

I pulled off the ribbon, and, while I tore open the paper, Aunt Katie undid the knot, smoothed out the ribbon, and wound it round her fingers into a neat coil. There was tissue paper inside the wrapping; I opened it carefully to find a small ornately embroidered reticule. I held it up, both delighted and baffled; I was very pleased to own it but knew that my chances of being allowed to carry it in public were very slight.

"Thank you very much, Mrs. Coughlan," I said in the conventional way I had been taught, but my face showing my enthusiasm for this evidence of an exotic world into which she seemed to think I would fit. "It's beautiful. Is it from Cairo?"

Mrs. Coughlan looked surprised; Aunt Katie pursed her lips.

"No. Singapore. Look inside."

From outside came the sounds of a pony's hooves on gravel, the creaking of wheels, and an impatient "Whoa."

Aunt Katie rose and moved toward the door. I had just time to open the little bag, to see two half crowns nestling in an inside pocket, and to register Mrs. Coughlan's finger conspiratorially at her lips before I followed my great-aunt to the front door.

Fortunately all three of my guests arrived at much the same time. Two were neatly and uncomfortably dressed, the boy's hair slicked down, the girl's in finger ringlets at the back of her head; each carried a present. The third, Jarvis de Courcy, his hair already untidy, his sailor suit far from neat, was not carrying a present; his mother, an untidy harassed woman, delivered it from her own hand to Aunt Katie with the air of one who has learned not to take an unnecessary risk. Jarvis was a boy with an engaging expression and the confident smile of one who expects to have a good time in almost any circumstances, although well aware that he may have to provide his own fun. A moment's silence of the kind I had feared followed introductions. It was broken almost immediately by an angry meow, followed by a hostile hiss, from Oonagh. Jarvis had given her tail a tweak, hard enough to be unkind but still short of cruelty.

Oonagh was probably more shocked than hurt, but her reaction was unhesitating. Before Jarvis had time to let go of her tail, she had bitten his hand just below the thumb and, for good measure, scratched his wrist. Blood, although very little, had been spilt during the first minute of my party. The silence was broken as Mrs. de Courcy gave Jarvis a good smack on his bare leg; he reacted to neither attack and, still grinning, was led away by Aunt Katie to have iodine applied to his wounds.

The ice was broken. Mrs. de Courcy cut short her apologies and left; Aunt Katie was no longer there to receive them. I had the impression that his mother was more angry than surprised at Jarvis's behavior.

"The de Courcys are Catholics," the little girl to whom I had not yet been introduced said.

"How do you know I'm not?" Mrs. Coughlan asked. She had come to the door of the drawing room in response to the disturbance in the hall. It was a good question. It didn't seem likely she had been brought up as a member of the Church of Ireland if she'd been born in Cairo.

Her question silenced the little girl—whose name I now remembered was Clodagh. The only sound was that of Mrs. de Courcy's pony and trap driving away from the house. I had the feeling that she was on her way before Jarvis did something that would require more of her than a passing slap. Or, maybe, she had to hurry home to care for her other children; since she was a Roman Catholic there were probably lots of them.

The silence—not awkward, we were all too pleasantly shocked by the dramatic start to the party—continued until Aunt Katie led the still grinning Jarvis back to us. Dark patches of iodine covered the bite and scratch; there were other small scars and nicks on his hands that seemed evidence that his sense of adventure was greater than his instinct for self-preservation.

"All right," he said, rubbing his hands, "when's tea?"

Aunt Katie was rather taken aback by this forthright approach to the afternoon's entertainment.

"Don't you want to play a game before we have tea?"

"No," Jarvis said firmly.

Clodagh's mouth was even more disapproving than Aunt Katie's, but the first part of the party was at least postponed. Jonathan, the other little boy, seemed nervous. I stole a glance at Mrs. Coughlan; she seemed very amused. Although I shared all their emotions, what I mostly felt was deep admiration. Especially since Jarvis appeared to have no sense of having behaved in an in-any-way-unusual manner.

"Chocolate biscuits. Good," he said approvingly, and sat down on the chair closest to them. I sat beside him; Clodagh sat on the other side of the table, as far away from him as possible; Jonathan, without quite pulling his chair out from the table, slid into the other place beside Jarvis.

Having only a cultural connection with the Church of Ireland, no one in our family said grace before a meal, but even so the speed with which the first chocolate biscuit traveled—before he was quite settled on his chair and without pausing for it to touch his plate—to Jarvis's mouth was unusual. Clodagh took one of the small sandwiches with exaggerated delicacy and put it on her plate. Bridie circled the table, carrying a jug of milk and, as a special birthday exception, one of lemonade. When she had poured my lemonade, she moved on to Jarvis.

"Will you have milk or lemonade?"

"I'll have a cup of tea." Jarvis pronounced the word differently from the way my family did. He said "tay" and it made me think that he was expecting something darker and stronger than the China tea that had been set out for Aunt Katie and Mrs. Coughlan in the drawing room.

Bridie glanced at Aunt Katie.

"I'll bring a cup of tea from the tray," Aunt Katie said, and indicated with a wave of her hand that Bridie should continue serving those of us with more conventional tastes.

Mrs. Coughlan followed Aunt Katie back to the drawing room and the tea tray. Aunt Katie would have poured tea for her guest before she returned with a cup for Jarvis. Bridie may have also have taken another cup and saucer to the drawing room; if she did so, it would account for her longer absence from the dining room after she left to fetch more lemonade.

When Aunt Katie returned she found one child missing. The chair to the left of Jarvis was empty, the place in front of it leaving a convenient space for him to set the remaining half plate of chocolate biscuits. Clodagh was still nibbling her sandwich. She had asked for milk instead of lemonade and I despised her for her premature allegiance to adult values. Without quite understanding her point—and she may have merely been parroting what she had heard from her mother—I didn't like the suggestion that Jarvis's lack of discipline could be laid at the feet of his family's religion. Clodagh's hair was scraped back from her face; she looked like a middle-aged Protestant mouse.

Aunt Katie looked to me for an explanation of what had happened. Without emulating Clodagh, I was not brave enough to throw in my lot with the breathtaking Jarvis and I hid behind an expression of astonished lack of comprehension.

"Where is—ah—Jonathan?"

Clodagh permitted herself a downward glance, Aunt Katie not necessarily exempt from her extreme disapproval.

"Whatever is he doing there?"

Jarvis grinned; Clodagh and I remained silent. Even if I had wished to do so, I would have found it hard to describe what had happened. Jonathan, instead of playing it safe like Clodagh and eating the requisite number of sandwiches or pieces of bread and butter—in our family, two—before helping himself to something more interesting, had elected to follow Jarvis's lead and reached out for a chocolate biscuit. Although Jarvis had done nothing more than bare his teeth, Jonathan—not, I thought, without reason—had felt himself lucky to escape with his hand intact. Jonathan had frozen until Jarvis had growled some words I couldn't hear, although the sound was that of an aggressive warning, and Jonathan had slid slowly down in his chair until his head was just above the level of the table. Having seen Clodagh and me staring at him, his face had turned red and, still slowly, he had continued his descent until he had disappeared.

"Jonathan," Aunt Katie said firmly but not unkindly; this was, after all, a festive occasion. "Please come back to the table."

Clodagh and I looked at Aunt Katie; Jarvis helped himself to another biscuit from the now almost empty plate.

It was unusual for a day to go by at Ballydavid without my learning something about rules, manners, conventions, and behavior. I didn't think them as important as the war, death, or my father's financial woes, but they were more immediate to my life. I also had begun to understand that small gestures, such as allowing a sandwich to rest for a moment on one's plate before picking it up again to eat it were more than meaningless conventions; they were the minute bricks that built a solid wall around our way of life. That protected us from the barbarians and the Protestant merchant classes.

These invisible rules would be hard to explain, and harder still to justify, to anyone who did not from early unquestioning childhood subscribe to them. That was, to some extent, the point. It would be easy and inaccurate to equate the resting-the-sandwich-on-the-plate convention or the emphasis on good posture with the idea of female delicacy or an empty life; late-Victorian women were tough. Grandmother had traveled to India, a journey that in those days took several weeks, and I don't for a moment imagine she loosened her stays when she reached the tropics. She would have taken in her stride seasickness, the squalor, and the heat of the subcontinent with her hair in place and a starched blouse. She had lost her eldest child, and though she mourned her little girl I am sure she wore her mourning without any display of emotion; as she now, an old lady, mourned the death of her youngest son. The small conventions weren't a substitute for life; they held those lives in place in the same way that the whalebone in the women's corsets defined their figures.

I had not, needless to say, thought this out by my ninth birthday, and it is only now that I see how illogical it was for any of us—me, Aunt Katie, or Clodagh (Jonathan having other things on his mind)—to expect Jarvis to subscribe to, or even to have been taught, these conventions. They weren't protecting his way of life—to the contrary. It was thrilling nonetheless to see the total disregard with which he trampled underfoot social maxims unquestioned by us.

I saw Aunt Katie's eyes flicker to the plate on which there now remained two biscuits before she addressed her more immediate problem. Jonathan had not answered when she called him, and she had only Clodagh's gesture on which to base her belief that he was hiding beneath the long linen table cloth. She tried again.

"Jonathan," she said, this time with a note of exasperation. "Jonathan, please come back to the table immediately."

I was delighted; my party was turning out far better than I could ever have hoped. I cared nothing for Clodagh's disapproval and was very interested by my aunt's lack of a secondary plan to which she could fall back if she were not immediately obeyed. That Jarvis did not see me as, if not an ally, an admirer and supporter of his anarchy only impressed me further. Not only did he not care that he had driven a fellow guest under the table; he seemed not to find it interesting.

After a moment, my aunt descended to her hands and knees and out of my sight. Inspired by my hero's nonchalance, I pulled up a large handful of table cloth and, without getting off my chair, leaned down to peer under the table. Aunt Katie's head and shoulders were draped in starched folds of white linen. Jonathan was crawling toward her. She withdrew and stood up; I watched for a moment longer. As Jonathan came into range, Jarvis kicked him. Not particularly brutally, but hard enough for him to squeal and scurry closer to Clodagh's feet. It was not impossible for him to emerge at a point outside the range of Jarvis's foot, but this attack by his oppressor, Aunt Katie's wrath, and his loss of face all combined to keep him in what I now suspected was a familiar retreat.

"You'd get him out fast enough with a yard brush," Clodagh said in a matter-of-fact tone.

My great-aunt ignored this callous but practical suggestion. I had, for a moment, an image of O'Neill summoned with the stiff-bristled brush he used around the stables and thought that he could probably deal with not only Jonathan but with Jarvis as well.

Aunt Katie did not intend to spend the rest of the tea party on her no longer supple knees, and there was Mrs. Coughlan, another unpredictable guest, abandoned in the drawing room. So

Jonathan stayed put until we left the table; I could hear Jarvis's heels from time to time kicking the crossbar of the chair, but I thought this was merely a bad habit unchecked by his mother, who undoubtedly had more immediate problems on her mind.

"Where do you go to school?" Jarvis asked me.

I was flattered that it was my, rather than Clodagh's, education about which he was curious.

"I'm going to be sharing lessons with Clodagh," I said, realizing that my romantic anticipation of a best friend in my schoolmate was less than realistic. "I used to go to school in London."

"Kindergarten," Clodagh said, helpfully and inaccurately; but since my school catered only to younger children, it was close enough to the truth to sting.

Jarvis ignored her. He seemed somewhat interested in both my pieces of information, and I risked a question of my own.

"Where do you go?"

"Christian Brothers."

The Christian Brothers provided a good, if often brutal, education; I didn't know it then, but their schools were considered the breeding grounds of nationalism. Jarvis seemed philosophic about the undoubted hardships of his schooling. I wondered if the Brothers were confounded by his cheerful resilience.

I don't remember a birthday cake, although there must have been one, and I must have blown out nine candles, with Jarvis and Clodagh as witnesses and Jonathan silently cowering at my feet. But I do remember Jarvis, his tea drunk and the biscuits finished, getting to his feet. After a moment I, too, slid down from my chair, not something I usually did without a murmured *"Puis-je m'en aller?"* to Grandmother or Aunt Katie.

"Right," Jarvis said, in a businesslike voice. "Where are those presents?"

THE EVENING OF the day after my birthday Grandmother and I went for a walk. To be taken for a long walk by a forbidding old lady might not seem to a modern child much of a treat, but to me it was an indication of my place in the household. Grandmother would not herself have taken a child for a walk in order to make sure that child was getting enough exercise.

As I went upstairs to change my shoes, I considered my apparent new status. The cause seemed simple: my age and my appearance. I was uncomfortably aware that this benefit—if benefit indeed it were—had not accrued through any action or virtue of my own. I had been living at Ballydavid for some months and enough time had passed for my birthday to occur. How I looked was again an aspect of myself over which I had little control. Grandmother had, the day before, held my face to the light in search of a resemblance to her dead son. Over the years I used to study my face—age would now make it a fruitless exercise—comparing my features with those of Uncle Sainthill in old photographs. Beyond a mild family resemblance I cannot find what it was that she saw there, the quality that persuaded her that I could, if brought up under her auspices, in some ways take his place.

Since I had come to live at Ballydavid, I had gathered evidence with far greater urgency than I had ever found necessary in London, and now two overheard words seemed to me to provide significant clues—both to my present domicile and to my invitation to accompany Grandmother on her evening constitutional. The words were "pretty" and "heiress"; the former overheard at Ballydavid, the latter—with an ironic overtone—at Glenbeg.

That my future—if I were to have one at Ballydavid—depended so little on my own effort or moral worth was a circumstance not individual to me. There was no virtue to which Grandmother ascribed greater value than she did to family or, in a woman, to classical features. On the latter qualities she had definite opinions: A short upper lip and straight features were her criteria. She had no time for the *jolie laide* or for standards of beauty valued by other cultures. Nor was she among those who valued simple faith over Norman blood. Family backgrounds were also judged by her rigid standards; a title was an asset, more so if it were an old one. She considered a good family to be one who had lived in the same house for four or more generations. The house did not need to be architecturally distinguished, but a certain amount of land was a requirement. What she admired, I suppose, was the landed gentry. Money was not a factor she took into consideration. Unless it had been too recently acquired.

Unimaginable—and, in reality, unlikely—benefits seemed implicit if Grandmother were to develop the habit of evening strolls during which she might solicit my advice on small decisions to be made at Ballydavid. I came downstairs with a few words already prepared on O'Neill's disregard for my safety during my riding lessons, and on Patience's shortcomings as a suitably obedient mount.

We did not, to my surprise, set off down the avenue but instead turned to the left when we came out the front door. Jock raised himself indifferently from where he lay on the porch and followed us. The graveled area in front of the house extended about twenty yards to a narrow strip of lawn and the edge of the Ballydavid woods. To our left, a flat, beaten-earth track led to the stables and the farmyard beyond, and, for a little time after we entered the woods, I could hear cows lowing and the clucking and crowing of barnyard fowl.

The path was wide enough for me to walk beside Grandmother. Although the sun was setting, the sky would be light for some time, and the woods were gloomy but not dark. I did not speak, partly because I knew Grandmother felt children should not speak until spoken to and partly because I thought there might be something special she wanted to talk about.

For a long time she did not say anything, but paused occasionally to drag at ropes of ivy that were strangling trees close to the path. We came out of the woods and found ourselves at the edge of a steeply sloping field. There was a view over the top of the trees below us of the estuary of the Suir. A narrow path on the outside of the fence had been beaten down by the feet of workmen and anyone else approaching Ballydavid over the fields. I had not known of its existence and had thought that the path Jock and I had taken when I visited the Coughlans was the only shortcut used by the household staff and men who worked on the farm.

The path was narrow and Grandmother walked quickly; my bare legs were scratched—leaving white marks on my dry skin—by the stubble of the weeds and grasses that I trotted through to keep up with her.

"A fine old beech," Grandmother said, indicating a tree a little larger than the one beside the tennis court and not to my eye remarkable. "See how light the leaves are. Soon you will find beechnuts under it."

I regarded the tree without expression and glanced up at her to see if a response was required. I decided that it probably wasn't and instead nodded and tried to look as though I understood why she was telling me this.

"This oak is the oldest tree at Ballydavid," she said, pointing to another tree, when we had walked down the length of the field. "It is more than two hundred years old. They can live for longer than that. After the first frost there will be acorns."

This time my interest was not entirely simulated. Acorns suggested squirrels—small, reddish brown, and seen rarely enough to be remarked upon. An English king had hidden from his pursuing enemies in an oak tree. I remembered the story which had been read at the little school that I attended—had attended—in London, although not well enough to remember which king. I had been relieved that he had not been caught. I assumed—with an almost complete ignorance of geography, botany, or probability—that the tree from which Absalom had been fatally suspended by his hair was also an oak.

At the bottom of the hill, a loosely constructed arrangement of stones allowed a small stream, at this time of the year no more than a wide strip of darker colored grasses growing out of wet black soil, to run under the path, which was about to end in the wider one that we were now approaching. As we crossed this crude bridge, I became aware of an unpleasant smell. The stream was most likely fed in part by the stable yard drains.

Grandmother spat. I was astonished. And deeply shocked. Spitting, until that moment, was an activity confined to poor, disgusting old men—not only a revolting habit but one associated with disease. Tuberculosis was not unusual in those days; it was incurable and usually fatal.

"Always spit when you pass a bad smell," Grandmother said. "Germs."

For some moments I imagined the dramatic effect to which I could put this newly authorized activity when I returned to London.

The path we were now taking was wider than the one we had left and seemed older, although that may merely have been because it was better defined, the shade of the trees—we had reentered the woods—inhibiting the growth of encroaching vegetation. We passed an overgrown clump of pampas grass, and then another; we were on the Fox's Walk.

"I used to come to Ballydavid for parties when I was a child," Grandmother said, breaking a silence of several minutes.

I looked up at her with unfeigned interest and equally genuine apprehension, certain that there had been no teasing of cats or fugitives under the table at the parties she had attended. I had thought that Aunt Katie, for everyone's sake, would have kept some details of the party from Grandmother. The official position at breakfast that morning had seemed to be that the party had been a great success and all three guests appropriately cognizant of the honor bestowed by an invitation to Ballydavid. I thought of Jarvis and tried not to smile. But when I looked up, Grandmother was smiling, too.

"It was where I first met your grandfather," she said. "My mother—your great-grandmother—brought me. Grandfather was, of course, too grown up for a children's party; but it was there that we first met."

For one wild moment I thought she might be inviting a confidence, or telling me that my birthday party had been the first step toward finding me a suitable husband. I wondered whether Grandmother could really be the one in whom I would confide my affectionate admiration for Jarvis de Courcy.

"These woods must never be cut," she continued in what seemed to me a non sequitur but probably wasn't. "If necessary, grazing can be let, but we don't sell land."

I nodded solemnly.

"When my ship comes home," Grandmother said, "I would like——"

We were walking very quietly—the path tramped-down earth and dark moss—and we saw the youths some time before they saw us. The two boys were standing, talking, where the yew alley was intersected by the path that led steeply down to the stile over the boundary wall to the Woodstown road. When we were close enough to see their faces, one glanced in our direction and muttered something to his companion. Without acknowledging us, they moved quickly down the path and disappeared into the overgrown shrubs and brambles.

I was surprised. Most of the families that lived in the neighborhood not only would have recognized Grandmother but also would have known that they would be welcome to take a short cut over her fields or through her woods. There would usually have been a raised cap and greeting; country people in those days had exquisite manners. I looked up at Grandmother, but she did not say anything.

"Were they poachers?" I asked hopefully, the possibility of local criminal activity an interesting one. My question was not only based on wishful thinking; Bridie had told me that it was the red-haired boy—I had not, despite judicious loitering in the kitchen yard, seen him again—who sometimes during the winter months brought pheasant and other game, perhaps dubiously acquired, to the back door. My question was, in part, intended to lead the conversation in his direction.

"I don't think so, Alice," Grandmother said, her voice low and steady—thoughtful, rather than surprised by my question.

I barely had time to register that my line of enquiry had been stifled before the boy himself came running lightly down the track from the direction of the farm. He paused on the wider, more defined, path, looking around for his companions. When he saw Grandmother, he raised his cap.

"Good evening, your ladyship," he said, and glanced at me. I thought his expression amused and slightly admiring. I was, I suppose, a fairly pretty child, my appearance enhanced by the veneer of privilege.

"Good evening," Grandmother said, her nod familiar and gracious.

The boy crossed our path—he was still a little distance ahead—at a pace not much faster than ours, but, when he reached the stony track on the other side leading down toward the stile, he seemed to bound, his gait varying with the rough ground beneath him as he disappeared after his friends.

I glanced at Grandmother.

"He's one of the Clancys," she said. "His family works for Mr. Rowe."

I now knew half of my hero's name and that he lived on the Rowe farm. I couldn't tell if he was young enough still to be at school or over fourteen, in which case he, like his father, would have been a farm laborer. But I was sure that, whatever the source of the game he purveyed, it wasn't poached from Nicholas Rowe.

"His brother is in the army—the same regiment as Tom O'Neill. He comes up to see Mrs. O'Neill whenever he has a letter," Grandmother said. After a moment, she added, "Or, I suppose, if he hasn't had a letter, to see if she has any news."

We continued in silence along the path. Grandmother's expression was thoughtful, and she did not speak until we reached the avenue and turned toward the house.

THE FIRST OF November—All Souls' Day—was warm, golden, autumnal. A touch of crispness in the air during the past two weeks had filled me with energy, and I got out of bed each morning with the same enthusiasm I noticed in the animals at Ballydavid. Patience and Benedict, my mother's old hunter, in the evenings no longer loitered at the far end of their field but waited at the gate for O'Neill to take them in, looking forward to a sheltered stable and a scoop of oats disproportionate to the probable calls on their energy. Even Jock was alert, as though waiting for a man with a gun over his arm and a game bag on his shoulder to follow to the marshy fields and desolate bogs beside the river.

I had started lessons with Clodagh the week after my birthday. Our schoolroom hours were shorter than those I had been used to and included such pleasant diversions as nature walks and bathing during the first warm afternoons. But the conventions of term time and holiday were the same as those observed by real schools. Clodagh and I were much of an age; her initial claim to seniority disappeared when it became apparent that my education was somewhat further advanced than hers. She wasn't stupid but she lacked imagination, and already her mind was locked into the narrow conventions and beliefs held by her mother. And I had the advantage of having spent two years at a proper London school—the one she had unwisely dismissed as "kindergarten."

I came down to breakfast that morning silently spelling some of the words we had been set for homework—"choir," "perceived," "catastrophic"—and making a list of words whose roots came from the Greek. Grandmother already sat at the head of the table; Aunt Katie was still upstairs.

"Today you and I will go to the Abbey and Slieverue."

I opened my mouth to say that I was supposed to go to Glenbeg for my lessons and then shut it again without speaking. I had learned during the past months not to question Grandmother's decisions; I was now trying to teach myself not to ask her any questions at all.

"I sent a note to Miss Kingsley."

The previous day I had been given a letter to deliver to my governess; it still lay at the bottom of my school satchel. To admit this to Grandmother would be proper, honorable, and unimaginable. My mind raced as I nodded obediently. Tomorrow I would throw myself on Miss Kingsley's easier to imagine mercy, and, I decided with deceit born of fear, if by some chance Grandmother found out that my absence had been unanticipated, I would pretend that I had not associated the envelope in my satchel with this announcement of my absence. I kept my face expressionless and waited for my stomach to unclench.

When we eventually left a couple of hours later, the Sunbeam, polished and shining, was outside the front door, and O'Neill was wearing his chauffeur's uniform. He had a long gray overcoat and a peaked cap; his demeanor, too, had changed with the role he was playing. He assisted Grandmother, who carried two sprays of flowers from the garden, into the back seat, his manner formal, deferential, and courtly. I scrambled in beside her.

"The Abbey Church first, O'Neill. And then Slieverue."

"Very good, my lady."

I looked at the back of O'Neill's head. This uniformed man, punctilious about observing the formalities, was the same person who had, only yesterday, cursed at Patience and hit her with a switch after I, through cowardice, had allowed her twice to refuse a small jump. Shocked by O'Neill's sharp cut, Patience had gathered herself and cleared the jump; I had not, and two dark bruises bore witness to my sudden and involuntary descent. But this was not the time to tell Grandmother of this hypocritical double standard.

There was plenty to think about. First I reassured myself that there was nothing sinister about this expedition. Grandmother's initial announcement might have meant anything, but the addition of the word "church" in her instruction to O'Neill seemed a guarantee that this outing would not end in a surprise tonsillectomy. And surely, if something unpleasant were involved, Aunt Katie would have been the one sent with me. Unless, of course, we were embarked upon something so terrible that Grandmother could not trust my great-aunt's sentimental nature; I thought, not seriously, of Snow White and the huntsman instructed to take her into the darkest forest and to cut out her heart. If that were the purpose of the outing, presumably I would have been alone with O'Neill, the very man for such a job. But where was Aunt Katie and why hadn't she been at breakfast? Both the old ladies made a hobby of their health, and it was not unusual for one of them to stay in bed, "resting" until lunch. Might not there be another explanation? The flowers that Grandmother held suggested that my great-aunt had been well and functional that morning, or at least the evening before. The flower room was her domain, and not even Grandmother would have dared to gather so many flowers from her cutting garden.

I glanced at Grandmother. She seemed lost in thought, but I was fairly sure I was not the subject of her contemplation and I turned my mind to less threatening subjects. During the two months since my birthday party, there had never been a full discussion of the behavior of my two male guests. I didn't even know if Aunt Katie had told her sister the full story. I searched for a way to introduce my hero's name into the conversation.

"Clodagh says that Jarvis de Courcy is a Catholic."

That hadn't come out the way I intended. I sounded much the way Clodagh had when she had offered the information as an explanation for poor behavior. She made Jarvis's Catholicism sound like a malady of suspect origin—unpleasant, infectious, and one for which the victim had only himself to blame. I was immediately aware of O'Neill, for whose brutal behavior I did in part blame the Catholic Church, directly in front of me. It was as impossible that he should react as it was that he had not heard my *bêtise*.

But Grandmother seemed to find nothing amiss with what I had said; it was possible that her lack of reaction was on O'Neill's account, but I don't think so.

"We are all Catholics," she said. "The de Courcys are Roman Catholics. The oldest families in Ireland—the Norman families—were all Roman Catholics. It is only the families who came after the Reformation that are Protestant. Many of the Roman Catholic families had to convert, of course. In order to keep their lands. Miss Kingsley will teach you about that soon, I expect."

Miss Kingsley. My fears of surgery or abandonment were replaced by the greater likelihood of being found out in cowardly deceit.

"We are doing English history—we've got to the Romans and Boadicea."

Grandmother nodded approvingly in a way that told me she considered our conversation at an end.

I knew she was not telling me that she considered the harassed Mrs. de Courcy or her undisciplined son her social superiors, but I thought she might be telling me that Clodagh and her family were not necessarily her—our—social equals and that their opinions and taste were open to question or at least confirmation. I remembered now that I had heard Aunt Katie refer to Captain Bryce as a "temporary gent"—a term I had questioned my mother about later. She had reluctantly—so that I should understand the expression should not be repeated—explained the phrase was sometimes unkindly used to describe someone from a modest background who had been given a wartime military commission.

By now we were on the outskirts of Waterford. I had accompanied Aunt Katie there several times during the summer and although the city no longer seemed the magical place it had when I had arrived, sick and bedraggled in the spring, I had begun to think of it as a place that contained a large quantity of children my age, one or two of whom, with a little luck and a proper introduction, might become my friends.

We passed the Quaker school at the top of the hill overlooking the city; the De La Salle college, concealed by tall stone walls; Waterpark, a boys' school; to the left, on the other side of the park, the Christian Brothers, Jarvis de Courcy's education their responsibility; and went over a small bridge and onto the Mall. I was pleased to be sitting beside Grandmother in such a fine motorcar; I felt like royalty and my grandmother, at least, looked the part. We drove along the Quay. On our left were shops, banks, and offices; on our right a cargo ship unloading coal, and behind us a ship loading horses on their way to the war in France. We crossed Waterford Bridge, passed the railway station, and—now on the Kilkenny side of the river—drove a little farther until O'Neill drew up in front of the Abbey Church.

He opened the gates to the neglected churchyard and then stood back. Grandmother and I went inside. She led the way along a path of damp hard earth and moss, strewn with small twigs and leaves from the tall elms that grew to one side of the church, sheltering it from the north wind. I glanced back and saw O'Neill standing outside beside the Sunbeam, under the trees. To either side of us were Irish yews, evergreen and the dark color of mourning. We passed carved stone monuments, worn by wind and rain, and gravestones encrusted with lichen. After a little while, Grandmother turned in from the path, and we walked through long grass and shrubs until she stopped by a grave.

I saw now that she carried only one bunch of flowers; the other, without my noticing, had been left in the Sunbeam. The autumn flowers, Michaelmas daisies and Japanese anemones, were loosely bound with raffia. She untied the flowers and, with two or three graceful movements of her arm, scattered them on the grave.

"Your grandfather is buried here," she said.

I looked at the headstone: plain gray, and rounded at the top, the lettering carved in small capital letters without ornamentation of any kind. GENERAL SIR PERCIVAL BAGNOLD, ROYAL ENGINEERS 1852–1910. He had died when I was three years old. I was surprised: It was difficult to imagine a time when Grandmother and Aunt Katie had not lived together at Ballydavid. Even now I have to remind myself that Grandmother at this time was probably much the same age as I am now.

Grandmother stood quietly for a moment—not, as I now think, in prayer. I stood a little behind her, my head bowed respectfully but my eyes on her. After a little time had passed, she sighed deeply and turned aside to point out the nearby graves of a previous generation of Bagnolds. Then we walked silently back to where O'Neill was waiting with the Sunbeam.

The cemetery at Slieverue, perhaps six or seven miles away, was beside the road, separated from it by only a low wall and iron railings. Again O'Neill waited by the car. Grandmother pushed open the rickety gate which stuck a little in the gravel, and we walked up a narrow path. To either side, the roughly cut grass was turning yellow. There were rows of headstones, polished granite, shiny black or white marble; in front of some were wax flowers under glass domes.

I was too young to have developed much sense of the aesthetic, but this orderly graveyard, its bleakness broken only by touches of vulgarity, seemed an unlikely place for Grandmother to visit. I observed her closely. Halfway up the path was a stunted Irish yew, beyond it a tall stone Celtic cross. Grandmother stepped into the grass and I followed her. She stood for a moment in front of the cross and then she laid her flowers on the ground in front of it. I read the inscription, SACRED TO THE MEMORY OF MAJOR LAURENCE BURKE, LATE OF THE 90TH LIGHT INFANTRY.

"This is my father's grave. He was MP for Waterford."

"But why is he buried here?"

By here I meant this dreary cemetery, too close to and unprotected from the road. I thought of the dead lying in rows under the coarsely cut grass. At the Abbey Church I could imagine them as part of the life of the overgrown churchyard. Where eternity might be spent with the wood pigeons nesting in the heavily ivied elms, the elderberry bushes and hawthorn growing in the boundary hedges, and the visiting rabbits and friendly, mysterious, nocturnal animals.

"Because he was a Roman Catholic," Grandmother said. After a pause but with no particular inflection, she added, "He fought for Home Rule with Parnell."

I had then only a vague idea of who Parnell had been and an even hazier notion of the significance of Home Rule, but I knew that my great-grandfather's politics were not those of the *Morning Post*. Or of my grandmother. Even so, there was pride in her voice when she spoke of him.

We drove silently back into Waterford. I now had to consider myself one-eighth Catholic. I was offended by Clodagh's bigotry and ashamed I hadn't seen it as such at the time. There was no excuse; my mother regarded religious intolerance as insufferably bad manners, particularly between Protestants and Catholics in Ireland. On the Catholic side, she said—not intolerantly, though perhaps condescendingly—it could be put down to ignorance, perhaps fostered by the priests, but on the Protestant side it was simply smug and very middle-class.

"Where is Uncle Sainthill's grave?" I asked.

"He's buried in France. All the soldiers killed in the war are."

She seemed unsurprised by my question. He was never far from her thoughts, and on that day it was not possible that she shouldn't have been thinking of him. Even I could feel the dead crowding in.

December 1915–March 1916

Chapter 5

THE SECOND WINTER of the war came—bleak, wet, and cold. The slaughter in France continued; Gallipoli was evacuated. The normally subdued colors that Anglo-Irish women wore became darker. And not only the Anglo-Irish mourned. There was no conscription in Ireland, but by the end of the war—still a long way off—two hundred thousand Irishmen would have volunteered. For some, the King's shilling was a means of earning a living and of feeding a family at home, but there were others who volunteered through loyalty to the Crown—and for all the confused reasons that young men have enlisted throughout history.

I was less aware of the war than I had been when I first came to Ballydavid. The newspaper arrived every day, the war was discussed each time adults met, but it seemed farther away and of less immediate concern to us than it had been when Uncle Sainthill was still alive.

Christmas, a subdued affair, was celebrated modestly in the cold, sad house. Grandmother observed the traditional rituals despite mourning; not to have done so would have been as out of character as to have ceased wearing stays after her favorite son was killed. We came from a military family and courage was expected on the home front as well as in battle.

The Christmas tree in the murky hall glimmered when Bridie passed it, carrying lamps for the drawing room. Beneath its branches lay a few carefully wrapped presents. The holly on the chimneypieces came from the bushes behind the bleaching lawn; I had gone with Aunt Katie to cut it and helped her carry it back to the house. A sprig decorated the plum pudding at Christmas lunch, and, for my benefit, brightly colored Christmas crackers containing favors and paper hats were set in front of each of our places. Christmas away from my real family had increased my feeling that I was abandoned and adrift. I missed my mother that day, as I still often did at night, but I had already begun to think of Ballydavid as my home.

Uncle William came to lunch on Christmas Day—and to tea, two days later. It was a grim little tea party and at it I made only a token appearance. A letter had arrived just before Christmas; short and straightforward, it had been pored over and discussed as though it were encoded or open to interpretation. An officer from Uncle Sainthill's regiment was on leave with his family at Dunmore; he asked if he might call and return a few of my uncle's personal effects.

I do not know what Grandmother and Aunt Katie expected, although I am afraid there was an underlying hope—probably not articulated—that Major Somerville would suggest that Uncle Sainthill might not actually be dead: that he was missing in action, the chances that he might still be alive so slight that his commanding officer had decided not to foster false hope. Or maybe Somerville would bring a last message, even though Grandmother had been told that her son had died instantly, killed by a piece of flying shrapnel.

Although I was as bored and curious as ever, and, as always, seeking information to help understand the rules and reasons of my new life, I would have preferred to have been—to use one of

Aunt Katie's expressions—a fly on the wall rather than to be briefly and silently present when Major Somerville arrived.

Poor man! How he must have dreaded the visit. It is possible that this was not the only one of its kind he made during his leave: two stricken women in mourning, a pale and apparently orphaned child in a silent gloomy house, a Christmas tree in a corner of the dark hall adding an unnecessary touch of irony to his task. And the pathos of the possessions he returned: a fountain pen, a wallet, an address book, some letters, a photograph or two, and the cigarette case. He must have been grateful for Uncle William's presence and for the courage of both the women, courage that did not allow them to break down or show emotion until after he had left; each spent the remainder of the day and evening in her room.

The next morning, when I came downstairs, the cigarette case was in the glass-topped cabinet in the drawing room. Neither Grandmother nor Aunt Katie had come downstairs for breakfast so, after a moment or two, I turned the small dark brass key and carefully lifted the lid of the cabinet. Beside the silver cigarette case lay Uncle Sainthill's Military Cross, its brightly striped ribbon flat above it. The cabinet also contained other, to me meaningless, mementos of family history: three other medals, older than the Military Cross; a miniature of a cardinal; a mother of pearl case for visiting cards; a small, leather-bound prayer book with gold-edged pages and a silk ribbon book mark; and a large, old-fashioned gold watch. There was also a small rough flint arrowhead and the heavy crude head of a Stone Age axe; both had been found late in the previous century when the path through the Ballydavid woods had been cleared and landscaped.

I listened for footsteps in the hall before picking up the cigarette case, but there was only silence. Uncle Sainthill's regimental crest was in raised silver on the front lid; I ran my fingers over its rough outlines before I pressed the catch to open the case. On the right-hand side an elasticated tape stretched from top to bottom, and there was still a flake or two of tobacco from the cigarettes the tape had once held in place. On the left was inscribed, in Aunt Katie's handwriting: *S.F.B.*, below it, *9.9.1914.*, and her initials, *K.A.M.* Aunt Katie had given the cigarette case to Uncle Sainthill on his twenty-first birthday, just before he left for France.

Grandmother and Aunt Katie came downstairs in the late morning. During the course of the day—it was wet and windy and I spent much of it in the library with them—they talked about Major Somerville's visit. They seemed to take some comfort from the conventional words he had used to describe the respect and affection Uncle Sainthill had inspired in the regiment. They used also, I remember, to refer to the stock phrases in the letter Grandmother had received from his commanding officer. Imagining the words that he must have written, time and again, to bereaved parents, to have been inspired by my uncle's unique qualities.

I think sometimes of Major Somerville: He epitomized those inarticulate men whose courage lay not only in their deeds but in their silence. Probably not even Uncle William, who had himself been a soldier, could accurately imagine the conditions that Major Somerville had chosen not to describe—how Uncle Sainthill had lived and died, what he himself would return to, and where he, too, would in all probability die.

The winter passed slowly. The days became shorter, and the time I spent indoors trying, not always successfully, to amuse myself became longer. It froze during most of January that year, but February was warmer, and on the second Wednesday of the month, the hounds met a little less than three miles from Ballydavid. It was decided that O'Neill should take me and Patience to the meet.

I hardly slept the night before, my excitement equal parts fear and eager anticipation. I was afraid of getting hurt, making a fool of myself, or of incurring O'Neill's wrath. I was well aware that these disasters were not mutually exclusive. Hunting was a privilege, one of the pleasures of growing up, and I was eager to claim it. There was no prestige attached to attending a meet on a leading rein, rather the reverse, but if all went well—if I didn't fall off, if Patience didn't kick a hound, if I sat up straight and looked neat—there was a possibility that the next time the hounds met close to Ballydavid I would be allowed half a day's closely supervised hunting.

I was dressed as smartly as though I were to accompany the hounds to the first covert. My new jacket and the small bowler hat had been Christmas presents from Grandmother and Aunt Katie. O'Neill, riding Mother's hunter, held Patience on a leading rein. We set off down the avenue and onto the main road. Both horses danced nervously, overfed and anticipating the excitements of the field. I was unhappily aware that the road below me was considerably harder than the ground of the paddock where Patience usually deposited me. I was frightened, and both the animals simulated fear at whitewashed gates, farmyard geese, and passing bicyclists. O'Neill cursed and threatened them as they tossed their heads and tried to shy. I remained quiet and hung on tightly.

The hounds were already in front of the pub at Herald's Cross when we arrived. I could feel Patience's excitement; her hooves touched the ground as though there were springs in them, and her nostrils flared. When we arrived at the meet, she and Benedict became even more excited, but they behaved in a disciplined manner as though they understood the importance of the occasion and were proud to be part of it.

The pub at Herald's Cross—a side road came over the brow of the hill opposite the pub to cross the main road, its continuation the thinly gravelled area where the horses and hounds were now gathered—was a low whitewashed building with small deeply set windows and a thatched roof. Above the door, in white on the dark brown lintel, was painted in neat National School handwriting the words: *Patrick Horan, Licensed to Sell Wines, Spirits and Tobacco.* There was a small tin sign outside the front door that also identified the pub as a sub-post office.

The Gaultier Harriers was not a smart hunt. I had hoped for pink coats and ladies in elegant habits on perfectly turned-out horses. In the album at Ballydavid I had seen a photograph of Grandmother as a young woman thus attired. She was wearing a silk hat with a veil, and I could see that she had once been beautiful. The members of the Gaultier hunt were disappointingly ordinary. An older sister of Jarvis's, on a skittish bay mare, conversed with one of two young English officers from the garrison at Waterford. These young soldiers had drawn one of the more enviable tours of duty, a season's hunting and shooting in Ireland before they were inevitably posted to France. But I did not reflect on the nature of their reprieve; I was too young to have much sense of the future. Perhaps they were too. Instead I noticed how Jarvis's sister sat on her mare and admired the neat and attractive way her hair was pinned into a glossy coil below the rim of her bowler hat.

I was pleased and proud to be well turned-out and present at a meet, but there seemed to be no further pleasures or benefits. I wasn't admired or made a fuss of; I evoked no curiosity and was offered no hospitality. The meet seemed to have much in common with tea with Grandmother and Aunt Katie; I should be seen and not heard, sit up straight and not fidget. Even though the sun was shining, it was a February morning and I could see the breath of the horses in the bright chilly air. My hands and feet were becoming increasingly cold.

Only a few of the men and women dressed to hunt were on horseback; grooms held horses while the owners mingled outside the pub drinking and talking. Some of the men—farmers, I thought—held their own mounts casually by the reins as they stood around; there was the sound of masculine banter and laughter, the yipping of hounds, the pawing hooves of horses.

O'Neill had dismounted and, no longer looking in my direction, was holding in one hand Benedict's reins and Patience's lead; in the other, he held a glass. The glass was, I now think, more a statement of status than refreshment. Farmers held glasses in their hands, grooms did not; whether the grooms would take a drink after the hunt moved off and before they followed with replacement horses was another matter.

I had, I suppose, hoped there would be other children there. By now, even more than missing my family, I missed having someone to play with, someone to talk to, someone to discuss the mysterious ways of adults, or even someone more conversant with the rules to explain some of the nuances. There were two other children at the meet, but both were older than I was, and they handled their ponies with casual efficiency. Not a leading rein in sight.

After twenty minutes, during which O'Neill walked about talking to neighbours and I alternated between boredom, fear, and self-consciousness, there was, without any visible signal, a general movement toward horses, mounting, and a greater sense of anticipation and excitement. It seemed as though my first exposure to the pleasures of foxhunting was almost over. I had experienced cold and fear; it didn't seem quite enough.

But there was still time for something to happen, and two things did; neither would have been of much interest to a modern child nor, indeed, to any of my contemporaries less isolated in an adult world than I was. I had expected to see at least one person whom I recognized—not with an expectation of conversation or even necessarily of acknowledgment, but in order to put hunting in context and to connect it to my life at Ballydavid.

As the hounds, now beside themselves with excitement, began to move onto the road, Nicholas Rowe came out of the pub, wiping his mouth on the back of his hand. As he passed O'Neill, he acknowledged him; a word or two may have been exchanged, but the lack of expression on his face gave the impression of powerful adversaries meeting on neutral territory. I watched to see, when O'Neill turned again toward me, if there was any further clue. But when he turned, so did I, our attention—and that of the horses—drawn to a motorcar braking and stopping noisily on the other side of the road.

Motorcars were no longer a novelty; this was, after all, 1916, and Uncle William, for instance, had owned a series of them during the past ten years. But this car was large and stately and in every way superior to the Sunbeam. It was the kind of vehicle from which royalty might have emerged. Instead, a woman carrying a riding whip stepped out into the road. She was wearing riding clothes, but, unlike Jarvis's sister whose riding habit skirt covered her boots, this woman wore what appeared to be men's riding britches, although they were largely concealed by a long-skirted coat which came to the top of her boots. This was the sort of person I had hoped to see at the meet. Unfortunately, Patience, her controlled excitement getting the better of her, danced sideways into a sturdy brown cob.

"Careful, he kicks," the middle-aged man on the horse's back said, not unkindly. I recognized him as the Resident Magistrate. A less temporary representative of the Crown than the young officers, Major Spenser was responsible for overseeing the rural courts in his district. The perennially popular stories of Somerville and Ross made it inevitable that an element of the ridiculous was associated with his position. There was a small red ribbon attached to the top of his horse's tail. I yanked Patience's mouth in the direction we had come from and saw with relief that O'Neill had returned.

The woman, who was wearing dark red lipstick, crossed the road to where a groom was standing with her horse. No words were exchanged as he gave her a leg up and she struggled onto the back of a solid gray hunter. Everyone knew that a Master of Foxhounds in County Cork had, not so long before, taken his hounds home rather than allow a woman who rode astride to hunt with his pack. The groom then retreated to stand beside the car parked carelessly on the road. He lit a cigarette and watched, expressionless. O'Neill, too, was expressionless, not acknowledging this last minute arrival.

The horse danced around as the woman turned to follow the hounds.

"Stop that, damn you," she said. It was the first time I had heard a woman curse; I was very shocked. I didn't recognize her accent; it was neither English nor Irish. The old ladies within earshot had pursed lips and disapproving eyes; I couldn't tell whether they were more shocked by her words or her painted face. Every man at the meet, whether looking at this strange woman or not, was expressionless, and I knew she had their full attention.

"Who is that—lady?" I asked O'Neill.

"That's Mrs. Hitchcock, miss," he said, and added after a telling pause, "She's an American."

It was the first time O'Neill had called me "miss," and it was the first coded exchange between us. The horses and hounds were moving off, and we watched as they streamed along the stony dirt road leading up the hill to the first covert. Soon they were out of sight and we turned for home. From time to time, we could hear the huntsman's horn and the baying and crying of hounds; Benedict and Patience were reluctant to leave them as was, I think, O'Neill. He was short-tempered with them and impatient with me all the way back to Ballydavid.

Mrs. O'Neill was waiting in the stable yard. It had started to drizzle, and she was sheltering in the whitewashed archway outside her house. Her hands were worrying the apron she wore over her black dress, clasping and unclasping the crumpled, worn material. She did not step into the yard, but both O'Neill and I were aware that she had something important to tell him.

"You run along now, Miss Alice," he said. "I'll see to Patience."

I was curious, but I was very cold. My string gloves were damp and my fingers were stiff and sore from holding the reins; Patience had become suddenly enthusiastic about going home when we reached the front gates of Ballydavid. I dismounted and stretched my aching legs. O'Neill took the ring of Patience's bit, and I walked stiffly through the passageway into the kitchen courtyard. The dairy and the laundry were both sources of familiar and not entirely pleasant odors. It was now just after midday, and the predominating smell was that of carbolic soap and the heavy cooling damp of the morning's wash.

Using the scraper and mat outside the kitchen door, I cleaned as much of the stableyard mud as I could off my boots and went into the warm and welcoming kitchen. At first it was hard to see, the overcast day outside far brighter than the large room lit only by small windows and the glow of the kitchen fire. I glanced up at the drying rack held overhead by two stout cords. On it were sheets and pillowcases, and among the jumble of household wash I could see one of my night dresses.

"Run along, Alice, your Uncle William's come for lunch and it's ready to set on the table."

Bridie was ladling steaming potatoes out of the pot into a serving bowl. I hurried up the back stairs, wondering why I should be Miss Alice outdoors, presumably on the grounds of one very slight exposure to hunting, but indoors still addressed as a small child.

I changed my clothes quickly, brushed my hair, washed my hands and face, and was in the drawing room five minutes later. My fingers and toes were still cold and, since I had forgotten my handkerchief, I sniffed surreptitiously to keep my cold nose from dripping. But I did not place myself in front of the smouldering turf fire. Instead I kissed Uncle William, avoiding as best I could his prickly gray moustache.

Grandmother, having noticed that I had changed properly and was in time for lunch, gave me a small nod. She did not ask how I had enjoyed the meet or even if I had managed not to disgrace the family. I perched on the edge of a chair and waited for the grown-ups to continue with their conversation.

There was the short silence that told me my arrival had necessitated a change of subject. I looked sideways and saw the suggestion of an enquiry on my uncle's face, and then in the other direction to witness an even slighter shake of my grandmother's head.

Uncle William turned to me and smiled; I knew then that whatever they had been talking about pertained to me, rather than it having been one of the myriad largely innocuous subjects that were either none of my business or from which I had to be sheltered.

"Not blooded yet?" he asked; it was a rhetorical question.

I shook my head shyly, thinking that the previous subject was less likely to upset me than was the reminder of the ritualistic smearing of fox's blood on my face that would take place the first time I had ridden well enough to keep up with the hounds and be in at the kill. I preferred not to think about the blood-spilling aspects of blood sports and reminded myself that it would take some time and many riding lessons to gain the proficiency that would bring me to the point of that disgusting ritual. To change the just-changed subject I offered a small piece of news of my own.

"Mrs. O'Neill was waiting for O'Neill when we got back." I knew what I had seen held a significance that I would not be able to work out for myself.

The short silence was broken by Aunt Katie when she realized that neither her sister nor her stepson, to both of whom she was in the habit of deferring, was going to comment or explain.

"Tom O'Neill has been wounded," Aunt Katie said. "Mrs. O'Neill got a letter while O'Neill was at the meet."

"Oh," I said, surprised and confused.

Again no one spoke for a little while. Straining to remember, I thought that the last time I had seen Tom O'Neill had been when I'd seen Oonagh on the avenue and described her as a tiger. My memories of him were clear but limited. I knew that, while Grandmother and Aunt Katie wished the O'Neill family no misfortune, they were imagining a life in which my uncle Sainthill had been wounded, rather than killed.

During this silence, Bridie came in and announced lunch. Enough time had passed since the steaming potatoes were spooned from the huge saucepan for me to know that she had delayed lunch a few minutes so that I would be in time. I looked at her with silent gratitude.

"Not the worst thing that could happen," Uncle William said when we were seated in the dining room. I knew him to be literal-minded and not particularly sensitive, but I was surprised to hear such a callous remark.

"It means that he's safe—at least he won't be killed in battle now. And he'll come home. On some level his mother must be, even now, relieved. And perhaps it won't be too severe a wound— and, of course, there'll be a pension."

I thought he was right. Mrs. O'Neill's expressionless face could well have concealed mixed emotions, emotions she might not want to articulate, even to her husband: horror that her son had been wounded and was in pain, and full of hope that she would soon have him safe at home.

I was hungry and lunch—the food at least—held no pitfalls. Steak and kidney pie (Aunt Katie must have spent the morning in the kitchen), Brussels sprouts, and floury boiled potatoes, and then canary pudding with a sauce made from red currants bottled during the summer. When I finished eating, I was pleasantly sleepy and no longer cold; I stifled a yawn.

"You may be excused, Alice, dear," Grandmother said. "Why don't you go and sit by the drawing-room fire?"

There was a certain irony that this was the one afternoon I would have welcomed the usual instruction, following my dismissal from the luncheon table, to go straight upstairs for my afternoon rest. I thought it might mean another small change in my status, but no sooner had I curled up on the sofa beside the fire than Aunt Katie followed me into the room. I considered for a moment the possibility that she too had been "excused" by the two stronger personalities still lingering over the Stilton, and then, as she spoke, I realized that in a sense she had not been excluded from dining table conversation, but instead delegated to speak to me.

"Alice," she said, sitting herself down beside me, "before you go upstairs for your rest I wanted to tell you that you have a new little sister."

I looked at her blankly, unable to imagine what she could be talking about; the information proffered directly to me seemed more obscure than much of what adults, imagining their conversation incomprehensible to my immature ears, talked about in front of me.

"Your mother," she added gently in explanation, "has a new baby—a little girl."

I was still too young and too shielded to know the facts of life or even the barest principles of procreation and assumed—an assumption Aunt Katie probably would have confirmed had I asked—that my mother had had the baby delivered from one of the better department stores. This misunderstanding increased my sense that my mother had permanently replaced me. Now I would never go home. I had no home other the one provided by my grandmother and great-aunt, the former at least as mysterious and frightening as she had been at the moment I was abandoned to her terrifying care. I started to weep quietly.

"It's a baby, a sweet little baby. She's your younger sister."

Since this was unanswerable I blew my nose, tried to stop crying, and went upstairs to rest.

Uncle William was still there when I came downstairs swollen eyed after two hours of deep sleep. Again I interrupted an adult conversation. This time the adults chose not to allow my presence to censor their conversation. Aunt Katie patted the sofa beside her and I sat down close to her. She stroked my hand and smiled.

"The priests speak against it, but it doesn't make any difference." Uncle William seemed as confused as he was outraged.

"O'Neill would——" Aunt Katie said tentatively.

Uncle William shook his head silently—a small gesture—and suddenly I remembered the exchange of glances outside the public house between O'Neill and Nicholas Rowe.

At that moment Bridie came in with tea and the subject was dropped. Uncle William turned to me.

"Next month we're having a lawn meet at Ballinamona. Maybe you'd like to come. There's a stall for Patience, so you could ride her over the night before."

My usurping sister, fox's blood, rumors of rebellion, falling off Patience and disgracing myself and O'Neill—all fears and unpleasant thoughts disappeared as I began to imagine my future as a brilliant horsewoman with an athletic and obedient Patience beneath me and about the admiration evoked by my courage and smart appearance. If there were any further references to the political unrest all over Ireland, I did not hear them. I had started to think of life at Ballydavid in the long term.

Chapter 6

I DON'T BELIEVE IN psychic phenomena. I don't believe in supernatural explanations for the inexplicable. I don't have faith in séances and mediums, in clairvoyance or automatic writing. I don't now, but I did then; and I have come to believe that what is untrue now may at times have been true then. That there may have been—during and for some time after the war—inexplicable answers and supernatural responses to the questions and searching of those who did believe.

In the spring of 1916 many events, not at first apparently connected, occurred more or less at the same time. The invisible ripples following each were enough to give me greater access to the adult world than I would otherwise have had. Winter lasted into the early weeks of spring that year, the cold keeping everyone indoors and as close to a fire as possible. This enforced proximity lent itself to indiscretion, to forgetting the presence of a child playing quietly out of sight.

To take the sequence of events loosely in order, one has to start with the medium. Her presence was first a rumor; then it was confirmed. To make her acquaintance without appearing importunate or crossing class barriers became a matter of strategy.

All Waterford society wanted to meet the Countess, a tragic refugee from Manchuria with a Polish title—not only a countess but a medium with extraordinary powers. An introduction should not have been difficult; hospitality and a helping hand for a deserving refugee would have obviated the need for formality, had it not been that her hostess was Mrs. Hitchcock, a woman pointedly ignored by the female Anglo-Irish.

This story I gathered over time from two sources: my usual way of solving a puzzle. I availed myself of inaccurate and often improbable information in the kitchen and modified it with the drawing-room version, censored but more reliable.

As it happened, chance intervened, and Grandmother and Aunt Katie were not obliged, as were so many of their neighbors, first to compromise themselves and then to be humiliated when their belated overtures to Mrs. Hitchcock were ignored. A rumor intended to console and save face began to circulate: that the medium was a fake. It was said that Mrs. Hitchcock looked upon séances and the Ouija board as entertainment and that both were accompanied by the usual level of hard drinking believed to be maintained in her house.

On the day of the Ballinamona meet, when I returned from the stables where I had gone with a lump of contraband sugar to ingratiate myself with Patience, I saw, standing on the gravel in front of the house, Uncle Hubert's unsuitable woman friend, Mara.

I had a moment or two to wonder what Mara could be doing at the lawn meet as I made my way to the front door, my new boots crunching the frozen gravel. I took a good but discreet look at the pale, dramatic woman who, although still Mara, appeared to be younger than the Mara I remembered from London—I was not old enough to be precise about ages—and more beautiful in a colorless, undefined way that the earlier Mara, despite the dyed hair and lip rouge that had so fascinated me, had not been. I also had enough time to realize that the subtly different Mara must be the Countess. I hadn't known that Mara was a countess and I was certain my mother had not known she was a medium. And my uncle? He had, doubtless, known more that we did about his colorful friend's past and talents—but if he had not felt the necessity to be discreet about a murder in her past (had her victim been the count?), why would he not have mentioned these other two fascinating attributes?

Confused by the changes in Mara's appearance and not sure how properly to address her, I lowered my eyes until I came close enough to greet her. When I looked up, I saw her attention was completely focused on me.

"Mara," I said, my voice tentative and low.

She didn't seem to hear me.

"I am the Countess Debussy, I've come all the way from Manchuria—what is your name?"

I felt myself start to blush, but, even while I was trying to decide whether Mara—the Countess—was snubbing me for addressing her by her Christian name or was telling me that I was mistaken in her identity, it crossed my mind that Grandmother, at least, would have considered it vulgar for the Countess to refer to herself by her title. Doubtless things were done differently in Manchuria.

"I'm Alice. Don't you remember——?"

"Alice. Alice in Wonderland." My name appeared not to mean anything to her, but her expression was preoccupied and, it seemed to me, suggested recognition, not necessarily welcome. I thought it might account for the banality of her reply. That I still had her entire attention suggested it would be all right for me to take the conversation a step further.

"Are you——?" I am still not sure what my question would have been had I not been interrupted. I think I might have been going to ask her if she were Mara's sister.

"Yes," she said, as Aunt Katie arrived at my side. "Yes, I am. And, I think, so are you. Even though you are a little girl, I can see you have the gift."

"Alice," Aunt Katie said, and then, turning toward the Countess, extended her hand. "I'm Katie Martyn."

The Countess neither took her hand nor offered her own name to complete the introduction. Instead, she looked at my great-aunt for a moment and nodded her head.

"Yes," she said, "the cigarette case."

As we stared at her, she smiled with an otherworldly sweetness, turned, and drifted away from us toward the hall door. We watched her go.

The way the Countess had chosen to dress was original, almost eccentric. I was conscious that she had in some way managed to look exotic, elegant, and ladylike. No mean feat when one considers that the conventions of how one dressed not only to hunt but even to attend a lawn meet were strict, class defining, and not flexible.

Women, to hunt, wore black riding costumes, top hats or bowlers, fat white stocks, and riding boots largely obscured by their long black skirts. The exception to this rule was Mrs. Hitchcock, who immodestly rode astride, and dressed accordingly. The women on foot seemed dowdy in comparison: tweed coats and skirts, attractive only on a young woman with an eighteen-inch waist, sensible boots, and an equally sensible hat.

The Countess, a second but contrasting exception to the rule of dress, was wearing a skirt of soft beige; it was of a thinner, more fluid material than were those of the other women, and her boots were not sensible. She did not wear a jacket but instead was draped in a variety of shawls. There was nothing flashy about her appearance; it was just that she wasn't dressed for outdoors. It seemed that, stepping through the French windows from the drawing room for a moment, she had thrown something warm over her shoulders. The effect seemed foreign although not contrived; the soft drapery of subdued colors was flattering to her tall, straight figure and small waist. Her face was pale and her hair a light brown. She seemed oblivious to the fact that she was the center of attention.

I glanced up at Aunt Katie, not knowing whether I had broken some rule by being found in conversation with a stranger. But Aunt Katie was still gazing after the Countess.

Shortly afterward, O'Neill brought Patience up from the stables, and I stopped thinking about Aunt Katie or the Countess as I concentrated on coordinating my scramble onto Patience's back with O'Neill's leg up and my pony's determination to practice a complicated dance step. Although there was an instant when it seemed as though I had turned into a sack of potatoes, O'Neill saved the day with a second shove, and I landed, if not lightly, at least in the saddle. Soon we were moving off.

It is difficult to make interesting an account of one's sporting experiences, and rather than describe my first day's hunting field by field, bank by bank, ditch by ditch—all of which I remember with the clarity that the old reserve for certain magical or terrifying events in their childhoods—I will try to describe what it felt like. And my first day's hunting was both magical and, at first, terrifying. During the next few hours—I was only out for half a day—I shed two fears. Both were lost during the first run. The fox broke covert soon after the hounds had gone into the bracken to flush him out. I had ridden up an overgrown boreen, frightened and excited. But, hearing the baying of the hounds and the huntsman's horn, I felt a new kind of exhilaration. I had tucked myself and Patience a little away from the other horses and riders, determined neither to be in anyone's way nor to be hurt by a sudden move from one of the huge, overexcited horses. The hounds, following the scent and encouraged by the hunting horn and the whips of the hunt servants, set off—tails up and noses down—across the frosty field into a stony lane with heavy, bare hawthorn growing on its banks. Soon we turned into another field and the pace picked up. It was then I understood that Patience was a pony whose more usual work was to pull a trap and that I was in no danger of being in at the kill or being blooded. By the time I had arrived at the first five-barred gate, I found it open; Patience and I were not the only ones incapable of jumping such a barrier, or the only ones happy to avoid ridiculous risks. I began to realize I would not be called upon to make death-defying and foolhardy attempts to emulate the experienced riders on large athletic horses. As I urged Patience to gallop as fast as she could, I felt my fear slip away. By now I was trailing behind, but I was not alone. Clodagh, who I knew hunted—one of the many sources of unexpressed envy on my part—but whom I had not seen at the meet, was also among the five or six of us who were not keeping up with the better-mounted, hard-riding group. We could see them, Mrs. Hitchcock among them, disappearing over the hill. I followed some older women and a courteous middle-aged man on a sturdy cob who dismounted to open gates or to lower the top pole barring the entrance to a field. I was so excited by this time that when I miscalculated a narrow grass-topped bank on which Patience touched down before clearing the ditch on the other side and I tumbled off, I felt neither fear nor pain. Before I knew it, I had got myself back on board and was galloping after my reassuring companions. I had fallen and not been hurt, and I had remounted; I had felt excitement, not fear. I knew that I would make mistakes and would take more serious falls, but I would not again fear the hunting field, and, if I were to disgrace Ballydavid, it would not be there.

O'Neill was following the hunt in Mrs. Hitchcock's motorcar

with her groom. The groom carried refreshments—sandwiches and a flask of Irish whiskey—and probably her lipstick and face powder; O'Neill was keeping an eye on me and ready to take me home at the end of the run closest to one o'clock. To follow a hunt by car successfully requires not only a good driver (less in terms of attaining great speeds or taking sharp corners than judgment as to where one can or cannot take a car) but a knowledge of the geography of the narrow roads, small lanes, and mud tracks of the countryside, the coverts, the fox's habits, and the place to where he was most likely to make his run once he had broken covert. It was no surprise to me that O'Neill, who knew the countryside like the back of his hand, should be comfortably ensconced in the front seat of Mrs. Hitchcock's motorcar, but I was interested to see, when we assembled at the next covert to be drawn, that one of the grooms following with remounts was also leading Benedict.

It was time to go home. I was tired, muddy, and very happy. Clodagh wasn't going home after half a day, so I muttered something about Patience not yet being fit. We were now some miles from Ballinamona and O'Neill and I set off across the fields and down the lanes until we came to the road. I knew enough not to burble or boast, and O'Neill was a man of few words, none of them employed in compliments. But his slow, judicious nod confirmed that I had done well enough in his eyes. And, when we rode into the stable yard at Ballinamona Park, he said he would brush down Patience and feed her himself and that it would be better to leave her at Ballinamona overnight—thus excusing me the otherwise mandatory long hack home.

I brushed as much mud as I could off my boots on the doormat before I went into the house. Aunt Katie had stayed at Ballinamona—indeed she had no way of going home since O'Neill was out following the hunt—and had presided over lunch from her former place at the head of the dining-room table. Now she sat beside the fire in the library with the Countess. They looked up as I came into the room, though I did not feel that I was interrupting an intimate conversation. The Countess had her feet tucked up under her and was reclining in the corner of the sofa nearest the fire. Her back was to the window and I couldn't see her face clearly. It occurred to me I still didn't know how to address her.

"There you are," Aunt Katie said. "You must be exhausted. Come closer to the fire and we'll get you something to eat before O'Neill takes us home. Now tell me all about it."

Although no less self-centered than the next child, I was far more curious about what had taken place between Aunt Katie and the Countess at Ballinamona while I had been gone. I gave them a short account of the hunt, ending with a grateful reference to my new boots; I knew them to be a generous extravagance on the part of Grandmother since I would outgrow them by the following year.

A little later, after I wolfed a boiled egg, fingers of toast, and a pot of tea, I climbed into the Sunbeam with Aunt Katie. Apart from her smile and an expression of interest while I'd briefly described the hunt, I had had no further conversation with the Countess. I would have liked to ask Aunt Katie about her but thought I would wait. I was fairly sure my great-aunt would have something to say on the subject.

"What," she said, relaxing as O'Neill successfully steered us between the Ballinamona gate posts and turned onto the Waterford road, "did—ah—Countess Debussy say to you?"

"She just asked me my name and said I had a present and then something about a cigarette case, but that was to you."

"Nothing else?"

"No. Well, she said Alice in Wonderland after I said my name."

"I see," said Aunt Katie.

We did not speak again until we arrived at Ballydavid. We both had plenty to think about. When we got home I was sent into the kitchen to have my boots pulled off; Bridie had already put two cauldrons of water on the range to heat for my bath. I went upstairs to a bedroom where a fire had been lighted and towels were warming on the fireguard. The bath tub had been set on the mat in front of the fire—the temperature perfected by Bridie, who, sleeves rolled above her elbows, was ready to give me a bath.

A more independent child might have felt that, since she was now a fully fledged member of the hunting community, she was old enough to wash herself, but I did not. A bath in front of the fire with Bridie squeezing hot water from a sponge over my back was the most sensuous pleasure I had ever experienced or could imagine. I lay back and allowed my tired muscles to relax. Afterward Bridie wrapped me in the warm towel from the spark guard. I remembered nothing more until I woke up in the dark; I was in bed, lazy and content, the curtains open to the now black sky.

When I went downstairs I found Grandmother and Aunt Katie in the drawing room. The tea tray had already been taken away. Despite my midafternoon meal, I was hungry and hoped some alternative arrangement for me had been made. Since I went to bed early, I usually had only a glass of milk and an oatmeal biscuit between tea and the time I went upstairs.

It appeared my needs had been anticipated; in response to my glance toward the table where the tea tray no longer sat, Grandmother said:

"We thought, Alice, that, since you had an inadequate lunch and we let you sleep through tea, tonight you would stay down for dinner. Run along and tell Maggie you'll be eating with us."

On the way to the kitchen I considered why Grandmother had not rung to summon Bridie, her normal way of conveying minor instructions. Evidently, I had interrupted a conversation not intended for my ears.

Bridie was sitting at the table peeling potatoes, and Maggie was in front of the range, lifting boiled eggs out of a saucepan with a slotted spoon, when I came into the kitchen.

"I'm to stay down for dinner—tonight," I said, both proud and apologetic.

"Potato and hard-boiled eggs gratin," Maggie said. "There's two extra boiled for the kedgeree for lunch tomorrow."

Bridie took another potato from the sack.

"Look at your boots," she said. When I was in the kitchen, I was in the habit of pronouncing the word *your* as "yer"—as Bridie just had—but I could not have attempted Maggie's *boiled*; the *i* emphasized, the *o* more hinted at than pronounced.

"Did you——?" I asked, wide-eyed with gratitude. My boots stood just inside the kitchen door, the polish even deeper than it had been when I had first taken them out of their box. Wooden trees held them proudly upright.

"O'Neill did your boots. No one but himself is let do the hunting boots. He did a grand job of it altogether."

He had done a grand job of it. And of making me understand that the torch had been handed to me—temporarily, at least. If my mother decided to take up hunting again, I knew how quickly I would take second place. But she wasn't going to come to Ireland and hunt. She was going to stay in London and look after her new baby.

I changed my dress for dinner. I put on the pink and beige wool dress I wore at Christmas and when Uncle William came to lunch on Sundays, but I was careful to make sure that the rest of my appearance was plain and neat; I wanted to seem cognizant of the honor accorded me without seeming to dress up or show off. Grandmother looked at me searchingly when I returned to the drawing room; after a moment she gave me a small nod of approval.

The heavy velvet curtains were drawn in the dark dining room when we sat down, the table lit by a pair of candelabra, each of which held three candles. Nothing else was changed, even the meal was one we might have been served for lunch, but the candlelight reflected on the wood of the table, as richly and deeply polished as my boots, made dinner seem dramatic, exciting, sophisticated.

"Aunt Katie tells me you and she met the Russian woman who is staying with Mrs. Hitchcock."

"She said she comes from Manchuria." As soon as I closed my mouth I realized that I had contradicted Grandmother. I had no reason to assume that Manchuria was not in Russia. My geography lessons so far had been limited to an intensive study of Ireland and a general impression of the pink on the map of the world that denoted the length and breadth of the British Empire. Russia and Manchuria seemed more the names of places in myth or story books.

"What did you make of her?"

I felt as though I had grown up five years during the course of the day. The change in O'Neill's demeanor, staying down for dinner, now being asked for my opinion on an adult—I put it all down to my new status as a fox-hunting woman. At the same time, however flattering it was to have my opinion solicited, it raised an awkward question: Should I or should I not mention the startling resemblance the Countess bore to Mara? I could not help feeling they must be connected.

"It felt," I said slowly and a little reluctantly, "like I had seen her before."

"*As though* I had seen her before," Grandmother said. She was in the habit of correcting not only my grammar but my way of expressing myself. But she said it automatically. She and Aunt Katie caught each other's eye in a way not perceptible to anyone who had not studied their expressions and habits as carefully as I had.

I had considered mentioning Mara but, after another hesitation, I thought I had said enough. Until I understood better the nervous excitement that lay just beneath the surface of every word and silence since we had met the Countess, a demeanor of innocence and a simulated lack of interest seemed prudent.

I forget now what else we talked about or when I went to bed; not surprisingly, it is all a long time ago. The moments I describe are those that stand out either for their significance or for one of the invisible, seemingly arbitrary reasons that some moments of childhood remain with us forever.

I do, however, clearly remember waking later with a start. I had the sense that I had not been asleep for long. I imagine I woke because I had gone to sleep with an unaccustomed and undigested meal in my stomach, but at the time it seemed that I had woken up because I remembered that my boots were still standing by the kitchen door. It suddenly seemed important that I should not leave them there for O'Neill to see in the morning. I thought it would appear ungrateful after the masterly job he had done of polishing them. It also seemed a casual way to treat a present of Grandmother's. I did not like leaving my room after dark, but I had the sense that I was not the only one still awake.

I lit my candle and climbed out of bed. There was an ever present fear of fire at Ballydavid and at all other houses of a certain age that depended on turf or wood fires for heat and on candles and oil lamps for light. The condition of the interiors of the chimneys, perhaps never repointed since the house had been built in a previous century—not necessarily the one before—was, like an overdraft or the political situation, one of the small-hours-of-the-morning terrors of an anxious or imaginative householder. Nevertheless, a candle and matches were left in my room—many rules, warnings, and injunctions surrounding them—in case I woke in the night and needed to go along the corridor to the WC.

I put on my dressing gown and, steeling myself to look under my bed, the most likely and terrifying place for a monster to lurk, I found my bedroom slippers. If I met anyone on my way to the kitchen, I did not want to add the misdemeanor of not being warmly enough wrapped up to that of being found out of bed in the middle of the night. As I put on my slippers, I remembered one of the rare moments when my father had concerned himself with a detail of my upbringing. "Why isn't that child wearing bedroom slippers?" he had asked, interrupting my mother who was scolding me for some more serious offence.

Shielding the flame of my candle as best I could from the draft, I put the box of matches in the pocket of my dressing gown and went downstairs. The back stairs would have provided a quicker and more discreet route to the kitchen, but they creaked and the stairwell was darker and there were corners and doorways from where some faceless horror could lean out and whisk me in, never to be seen again. Fortunately for my family, I thought, bitterly and not completely logically—I was halfway down the *front* stairs at the time of the self-pitying thought—my mother had a new baby to distract her, so my loss would not be a serious one.

I now could see a waning moon through the fanlight above the front door as it emerged for a moment from behind night clouds. As I reached the foot of the stairs and started to cross the hall, I heard a sound and stopped in my tracks. Soon afterward I heard the tiny explosion of a spark from the remains of a charred log in the drawing-room fireplace. That seemed to explain the former, less identifiable, sound. The embers of the evening's fire, safely behind a spark guard, were gradually settling into themselves, adding a small warmth to the chimney that rose behind the drawing-room wall to Grandmother's bedroom above.

The candle flame protected by my hand, a necessity that reduced the available light, I pushed through the baize-covered door and went along the service passage into the kitchen. Oonagh was asleep in front of the range; she opened one eye and, seeing it was no one likely to feed her or put her out the back door into the night, closed it again. I paused, surprised by her presence, having thought that she slept on Grandmother's bed, making her exits and entrances onto the dark gray slates of the veranda through a window kept open even in the coldest, wettest weather.

My boots were no longer beside the kitchen door. I had come downstairs for nothing. Bridie had put them away with the other boots in the gun room, and, even if I had brought them upstairs, as I had intended, she would have taken them down to join those belonging to my mother, who no longer hunted, and to my grandmother, who had not worn hers during the past twenty-five years, perhaps for longer. It occurred to me that after I had grown out of my beautiful new boots, I would grow into my mother's and, in time, Grandmother's. There would, of course, be a couple of sizes between my boots and those of my mother's, and another between hers and Grandmother's: My grandmother was a tall woman.

So I should go back to bed. I retraced my steps. All went well until I had almost regained the landing. Then I trod on the hem of my night dress, stumbled, and dropped the candle, which immediately went out.

I sat in the dark on the top step, collecting myself and groping about for the candle. One of my bedroom slippers had come off as I lost my balance and was now out of range of my searching foot. Below I heard a door open and saw a very faint glimmer of light.

"Don't wait for me," I heard Grandmother say.

I thought she was going to the kitchen to look for Oonagh. I also thought my great-aunt would wait for her; the question was where she would do so. If she came to the foot of the stairs, her candle would, in all likelihood, provide enough light for her to see at least some movement as I crept away. I had three or four seconds to gather myself up, scurry around the corner, along the corridor, and back into my bedroom.

But first I had to find the candle and the candlestick. They had separated when I dropped them. I felt along each carpeted step and the polished wood at either side—very carefully along the edge next to the banisters, since I didn't want to knock either candle or candlestick through the railings and have it fall noisily on the stone flags below. I found the candlestick first; it had a square base and so had not rolled any distance. As my fingers searched further afield, they touched a patch of something smooth and soft. Candle grease. I wasted a moment scraping at it with my fingernails before I heard footsteps in the hall—Grandmother and Aunt Katie both walking in my direction. Desperately, I crawled down a step or two, found my slipper, groped around a little wider, and felt the candle. My hands full, I scrambled to the top of the stairs, got to my feet, and tiptoed around the corner. Once inside the door of my room, I waited for the old ladies to reach the top of the stairs; I wanted to hear if they had noticed me. As I waited, my heart thumping, I pushed the candle back into its stick; I still held one slipper in my hand. It took a little time for Grandmother and Aunt Katie to gain the landing. To my surprise, instead of turning right toward their rooms, I could hear their footsteps coming closer. I scampered back to my bed, kicked off my slippers, put the candle on my bedside table, flung my dressing gown at the foot of the bed—using a few seconds to take the box of matches out of my pocket and return it to its place—and scrambled into bed. I was lying still, eyes closed and trying to make my body appear relaxed when the old ladies paused in my doorway.

I could hardly breathe; if they had seen me they must have known I wasn't asleep, if they had not, what were they doing in the doorway? I was considering speaking and was trying to think of something more substantial than "Hello, Grandmother," when Aunt Katie said, "You see. She's fast asleep."

It seemed to me at that moment that Grandmother must have caught sight of me and that Aunt Katie had said that it was only her imagination. I lay quite still and waited for them to go.

"Why do you think she does it?" Aunt Katie's voice again, somewhat closer. She straightened my bedroom slippers and put my dressing gown neatly over the rail at the foot of my bed.

"It's probably seeing that woman today. She hasn't done it for months."

"She'll grow out of it, won't she? Doctor Jacobs——"

Dr. Jacobs? Dr. Jacobs was the family physician, frequently coming to the house to tend Grandmother and Aunt Katie. I had never had cause to meet him.

"Yes, but suppose it's part of the other thing——" Grandmother's voice trailed off. She sounded unsure of herself for the first time since I had come to live at Ballydavid. I sensed that her unsureness did not pertain to my physical health, whether or not Dr. Jacobs had been called to diagnose me in absentia; it seemed as though some moral dilemma had presented itself and that I was somehow the cause.

After they left, I lay awake for some time. I understood that I had avoided reproof for my misdemeanor because the old ladies had thought I was sleepwalking. And I had learned that I did sleepwalk; the discovery causing both pride that I was so interesting and an unsettling awareness that I was not quite in control of my own body.

It took me much longer to consider the possible significance of several mysterious moments during the day. I understood only that my grandmother and great-aunt had looked at me differently, with almost a touch of deference, and that this change had nothing to do with anything I had done. I had an uneasy feeling, similar to that I had felt when I discovered that my place in Grandmother's affections owed a good deal to some similarity in my features and coloring to those of her dead son. I suspected that she and Aunt Katie now mistakenly attributed some action—I could think of no origin for it other than the hunting field—or quality to me and that I was getting, and would get, special treatment as a result of their misapprehension.

It seemed important that this misunderstanding, whatever it was, should not miscarry. I was determined to be strictly accurate if asked how I had done in any future riding lessons. I also determined that allowing my aunts to be deceived or to deceive themselves—as in the sleepwalking incident—would never happen again. I already had the feeling of being swept, probably to my advantage, into something I didn't understand; when it became clear—as it would—that there had been a mistake, I did not want to seem to have knowingly taken advantage of it. At last I fell asleep.

When I woke up the sounds from downstairs suggested it was a little later than I was usually encouraged to sleep. I dressed quickly and hurried along the corridor toward the stairs. The wax I had spilled the night before had already been removed.

April 1916

Chapter 7

IRISH HISTORY IS FULL of heroic gestures and blind incompetence. Bad luck also plays its role. Communication, or lack thereof, is frequently part of these disasters. Leading up to the Easter Rising and the tragedy and debacle of Casement's last mission, the poor—in some cases, nonexistent—communication between the various arms of the revolutionary movement was in contrast to the efficient manner in which the British Admiralty, who had broken the German code, were intercepting wireless transmissions and deciphering their contents.

It was already the afternoon of Friday, 14 April, when a message from the Irish Revolutionary Brotherhood's headquarters in Dublin was received in New York at the offices of the *Gaelic American*. In code, it read: "Arms must not be landed before midnight of Sunday 23rd. This is vital." The twenty-third was Easter Sunday, nine days away.

By the time the message was decoded, it was too late to deliver it that day to the Germany Embassy. On the fifteenth, the Embassy sent a message by wireless to Berlin and, unknowingly, to London. Although the wretched Casement in Berlin had been kept in ignorance, the same was not true of British Intelligence. The U.S. Secret Service had come across plans for the rising in the course of a raid on a German agent in New York and the information had been passed to London.

By the fifteenth, the *Aud,* the trawler carrying the arms—obsolete, in poor condition, and far too few—was already well on her way to Ireland. Since she didn't have a wireless, there was no way to communicate the change of plan to the captain.

That it was too late to intercept the *Aud* was not, in turn, communicated back to New York (and thence to Ireland), and the committee in Dublin, believing the altered plan in place, prepared to meet the trawler and unload the arms on Easter Sunday.

Earlier in April, Casement and two companions—Robert Monteith and one of the Irish Brigade recruits—had boarded the submarine that was to take them to Tralee Bay off the west coast of Ireland where they were to meet the *Aud.* Casement now hoped only to reach Ireland in time to warn the revolutionary leaders that there was no meaningful aid to be expected from Germany and to urge them to cancel the revolution planned for the Easter weekend.

It had been for some time clear to the German military and diplomatic authorities that the increasingly neurotic and obsessive Casement was more trouble than he was worth; he was increasingly fragile psychologically and his lack of judgment had become apparent. The Irish Brigade had been, from its inception, an unmitigated disaster. Not even the most optimistic senior German official any longer considered sending the Brigade to Ireland; there had been doubts about sending Casement himself. Robert Monteith was the man the Germans preferred to deal with by then. Monteith worshipped Casement and had known him for a short enough time to be worried and sympathetic rather than disillusioned.

The three men boarded the U-20, the submarine that had almost a year before sunk the *Lusitania.* After a day and a half at sea, there was a mechanical failure, and they were forced to turn back. Casement, high-strung, suspicious, and obsessive, suspected the German authorities of faking the failure in order to prevent him from landing in Ireland in time. His suspicions were unfounded; when they arrived in Heligoland he saw for himself the broken shaft. It was decided that they would travel by another submarine and one was summoned from Emden.

On 15 April, they put to sea once more. The new submarine was under the command of Captain Raimund Weisbach, who had been the torpedo officer on the U-20 a year before. It was he who had fired the fatal torpedo that had sunk the *Lusitania*.

A little after midnight, during the early hours of Good Friday, the submarine, traveling largely on the surface and carrying the exhausted, seasick Casement; Monteith, who had injured his wrist; and the never-very-promising Irish Brigade recruit, arrived at the point where they were to meet the *Aud*. The conditions were perfect for the rendezvous: a calm sea and moonlight. But the captain of the submarine found no trawler, no signal light—nothing to suggest that they were expected and no indication of what they were to do next.

Captain Spindler, in the *Aud*, reached the part of Tralee Bay where he expected to find the submarine at midnight. He, too, found no one waiting for him, but he didn't realize he had made a navigational error and was several miles away from the meeting place. He waited for a few hours, and then, following orders, cruised up and down the Irish coast until, in the morning, he was intercepted by an English naval vessel. The *Aud* was scuttled, and the load of arms intended for the rising sank to the bottom of the sea.

The U-20 also waited for about three hours; then Casement, Monteith, and the recruit loaded themselves and some equipment and a few personal possessions into the dinghy and made for Banna Strand.

IT WAS TOWARD the end of Lent (I had, not entirely of my own volition, given up chocolates), the hunting season was over, and Grandmother was composing an invitation. Although Aunt Katie's presence was required and it was she who would write the letter, her suggestions were neither solicited nor welcomed.

I, too, was in the library, but there was no question of my role being greater than that of audience. Although the day was cold, the windows were open—a short-lived fresh air fad had further reduced the chilly temperature in which we lived—and I could smell the salt in a damp wind off the sea. I huddled in a corner of the sofa with a book on my knees and watched a small bird in the ivy outside the window, its body in constant motion as it cocked its head from side to side and pecked at something unseen— berries, insects—under the new green leaves.

The invitation was ostensibly to come from Aunt Katie. It was in the nature of a last resort. Although either or both the old ladies had attended each meet of the local hounds (I had turned out to be more useful than they could have imagined), we had never again chanced on the Countess.

"Dear Countess," Grandmother read aloud. There had been some discussion of the appellation. Words unknown to me such as *soi-disant* had been doubtfully murmured, and it was only when Aunt Katie had said, reassuringly, "just a Polish countess, after all," that the letter passed the stage of salutation and prelim- inary compliments to come to the point. It was an invitation to tea surrounded by coded hints, each requiring much thought—most of it aloud—by my grandmother. "Such a pleasure meeting you at Ballinamona Park." "If you have time on your hands while Mrs. Hitchcock is hunting——" (There was much discussion on this hint, since it was impossible Aunt Katie should not know the hunting season had been over for some time.) "O'Neill, of course, could fetch you and take you home." All were included in the final draft. The end result, Grandmother and Aunt Katie hoped, was an invitation based on adequate acquaintanceship and firmly excluding any suggestion that Mrs. Hitchcock should accompany her. Both the old ladies feared, nevertheless, that because of the Countess's inexact grasp—through no fault of her own, they hastened to add—of the English language and Mrs. Hitchcock's coarseness, ignorance, and probable lack of attention to the conventions of Anglo-Irish social life, that the hint that Mrs. Hitchcock should not accompany her protégée might not be understood. It seemed to me, silent on the sofa, that they had little to fear from that direction: The American divorcée's wish to spend an afternoon at Ballydavid, drinking nothing stronger than tea with two old ladies, would surely be even slighter than Grandmother's willingness to allow her to cross the doorstep.

At last composed, revised, rewritten, and sealed, the letter was not entrusted to the post, which would have guaranteed delivery at breakfast the following morning, but sent with O'Neill in the Sunbeam on the next occasion Mrs. Hitchcock could be counted on not to be at home.

An anxious couple of days followed, during which the Countess was not mentioned by either Grandmother or Aunt Katie, before a letter arranging a day for the visit came in the post. They had, I imagine, expected O'Neill to bring an answer back with him. I could see that the Countess's letter strained Grandmother's fastidious taste to its fullest extent. Aunt Katie muttered "Polish" and "things done differently there" several times as they read the untidy handwriting on pink writing paper.

"They write with little pictures in Manchuria," I said helpfully, not quite sure of my facts but having seen examples of beautiful Chinese brush-and-ink characters in my schoolbooks.

Both the old ladies looked at me with some gratitude for a possible excuse for the Countess's vulgar missive. I had not seen the letter in question and thought they were having difficulty reading it because it was not in English. Pleased with my success, I forgot a basic maxim of childhood—that a cheerful, uncomprehending silence is the best and safest demeanour.

"Mrs. Coughlan might be able to read it," I continued helpfully.

"I dare say," Grandmother said icily, making it clear that, while Mrs. Coughlan might indeed be more acquainted than they were with vulgar writing paper and ill-educated writing, she would not be the one to whom they would go for assistance.

I thought their reaction rather unfair. I had taken some trouble to find out exactly where Manchuria was and could see that it was convenient to both Russia and China. The Chinese purse that Mrs. Coughlan had given me (I believed that she had bought it herself in Singapore, and it is possible that she had), let alone her familiarity with Cairo, almost halfway to Manchuria, should surely have made her the person to consult.

There was a large globe in the schoolroom at Glenbeg. I had asked Miss Kingsley about Manchuria and she had told me to find it on the globe. Miss Kingsley taught us most of what we learned by referring us to standard reference sources; she rarely imparted information of her own. At the time it seemed to me a valid if rather irritating approach to education, but I now realize that most likely she herself had received no more than cursory schooling. I had been happy enough to study the globe, since I also wanted to see how close Manchuria was to Russia and the Balkans.

The day the Countess came to tea, Bridie put out on my bed the smocked wool dress I wore on special occasions. I was pleased with how smart it looked and how nice it was to have had new winter and summer frocks since I had come to Ballydavid, and I didn't think how similar my role was at this tea party to the one I played when, the previous year in London, Mara used to come to visit my mother. My presence providing an illusionary protection for my family against an unknown foreign quantity and, at the same time, making them guiltily aware that I was being exposed to unsuitable information and a possibly corrupting influence. Suspecting that this tea party was an occasion on which I might soon be excused, I also was interested in the iced walnut cake I had seen on the tea tray in the kitchen, and hoped I would last in the drawing room at least until it was served.

For a moment it seemed as though I might not even achieve the drawing room, let alone tea. I had been loitering in the hall, watching through a window for O'Neill to drive up the avenue. Running into the drawing room, I announced the Countess's imminent arrival to Grandmother and Aunt Katie, but neither of the old ladies rose until they heard the Sunbeam draw up at the front door. When they went into the hall to greet their guest rather than let Bridie announce her arrival, I followed and waited in the gloom by the stairs—officially present but, although curious, shy and unwilling to be involved in any of the possible misunderstandings or embarrassments of the first few moments of the Countess's visit. I was still more reluctant to be the cause of an awkwardness.

The first surprise—shock—was that, after O'Neill had opened the door of the Sunbeam for the Countess, he had gone around to the boot of the motorcar and, opening it, taken out two battered suitcases and several untidily wrapped packages. I watched the old ladies' eyes flicker toward the baggage he was unloading and saw them decide not to comment. Instead they greeted the Countess and led her back into the drawing room. Lagging behind, I caught O'Neill's eye, his lack of expression telling. I watched him set what might well have been the Countess's entire worldly possessions as neatly as he could just inside the hall door and go back to the Sunbeam. I wondered if he would put the motorcar into the garage, assuming it would not be further needed that afternoon, or whether he would wait and see; I was quite sure, though, that he would alert Bridie to the luggage in the hall and that there would be a discussion of what the proper procedure would be for the apparent arrival of an uninvited guest and no instructions from Grandmother. I, wide-eyed, followed Aunt Katie into the drawing room and reluctantly closed the door on the only slightly less interesting scene developing behind me.

Any hope Grandmother and Aunt Katie might have had that this tea party would proceed along conventional lines—at least to start with, their ultimate goal being not so conventional—was shattered before Grandmother had a chance to invite their guest to sit down. The Countess just managed to contain herself until the door was closed before drawing a deep breath and pouring out a garbled story of scandal and outrage. It was, at first, difficult to understand, although the luggage in the hall served as a pretty substantial clue.

Gaping at the Countess, I was nonetheless aware that Aunt Katie did not want me to witness any more of this scene. I studiously avoided her eye and remained by the door—I hadn't bothered to sit, knowing I would not be present for long—until the Countess paused for breath. I hadn't understood what she was talking about, although certain repeated words and phrases— "guns," "men with guns," "Mrs. Hitchcock," and "house on fire"— would allow me to piece together a possible scenario when I had time to think about it.

"Alice, dear, please tell Bridie to bring tea in——" Aunt Katie paused, trying to weigh the reviving qualities of tea against the likelihood of Bridie's witnessing such a scene and of the ensuing gossip, "——in fifteen minutes. And ask her to give you tea in the kitchen."

I left reluctantly, going out the door into the hall rather than the one to the passage and the kitchen. The Countess's trappings were still by the front door; Bridie and Maggie stood in the open service doorway regarding them with interest. I delivered my message and together we went into the kitchen.

"Aunt Katie said to be sure to give me a slice of cake with my tea," I said, reasonably sure that a slice out of the cake would not, in the current drawing room atmosphere, be remarked upon.

When I went to say good night to Grandmother and Aunt Katie, they told me that the Countess would be staying for a few days, since Mrs. Hitchcock had left for Dublin and the race meeting at Fairyhouse.

IT SEEMED FOR the next day and a half that no one would tell me the full story of what had happened at Mrs. Hitchcock's house. I gathered that armed revolutionaries had come looking for guns and had threatened to burn her house down. Most country houses at that time would have had a sporting gun or two on the premises, although, as far as I knew, Mrs. Hitchcock didn't shoot. I listened carefully in the drawing room and gathered only that censorship was more than usually in place. Even in the kitchen, where the Countess's character was freely discussed—not always entirely to her credit—I was sure I was not hearing everything.

While I was trying to puzzle out what had happened at Mrs. Hitchcock's house, a new set of rumors, these about Sir Roger Casement's arrival in Ireland and his subsequent arrest, began to circulate. Wild, often inaccurate, and telling of ignoble acts: Casement had been accompanied to the Irish coast by a German ship flying a neutral flag; under arrest, he had offered to inform on his companions in return for his life.

At about the same time that the Casement stories joined the colorful speculations about what had taken place at Mrs. Hitchcock's house, I heard Nicholas Rowe mentioned twice; on neither occasion could I fit him into the account of the Countess's quarrel with Mrs. Hitchcock or connect him to Casement's arrival and arrest. The second association seemed the more likely, since I had heard that Nicholas Rowe was the local head of the Irish Revolutionary Brotherhood. But an awkwardness that accompanied mention of his name led me to suspect there was a third drama or scandal of which I knew nothing.

It was Sonia, as I was by then calling the Countess, who, when we first found ourselves alone, filled in the details of her last night at Mrs. Hitchcock's house. I was at the time flattered that she should trust me to such an extent, although it now occurs to me that she may have been less than discriminate in her audiences. Even so, there were nuances and inferences I didn't catch until later, one of which was the state of play between Mrs. Hitchcock and the Countess the night before the former went up to Dublin and the latter sought sanctuary at Ballydavid.

It seems relations were already strained between my new heroine and her former hostess. The Countess had failed to divert Mrs. Hitchcock for more than a couple of weeks, and the older woman, discontented, now wanted more dramatic results or a new plaything. The Countess had thought herself rescued, no longer in the precarious position of a refugee increasingly worn down by living on her charm and ability to amuse. It is also possible that, although temporary male protectors may have made more explicit demands on her, they were easier to manipulate. As I was later to realize, men saw her more clearly than women did, but tended to be amused rather than distressed by her shortcomings.

It seems that Sonia had retired very soon after supper on the night in question, the atmosphere perhaps cool enough for her to have eaten her supper on a tray in her room. Mrs. Hitchcock was entertaining several men with whom she had been to a race meeting at Clonmel and the atmosphere was noisy, with a fair amount of drink consumed. The Countess liked a small brandy from time to time as a restorative, but I have the impression that she did not regard alcohol as a social aid.

Sonia had been asleep for some time when the sound of male voices from below awakened her. She didn't know how late it was, but outside it was pitch dark. She didn't get out of bed or light a candle, assuming the noise came from Mrs. Hitchcock's guests, some conceivably from Mrs. Hitchcock herself.

After a little while, the sounds becoming louder and more clearly not celebratory, Sonia wrapped herself in a shawl and crossed the dark room to the window. Some of the voices seemed to come from outside. Slipping between the curtain and the window, she looked through the glass and listened. Standing in front of the house were five young men. Two of them carried rifles, and the others had put down on the gravel objects she could not immediately identify. Sonia could not understand what they were saying, the heavy local accents unintelligible to her, but she could see they were shouting up to someone above them. Pressing her cheek against the cold pane and looking sideways, she managed to see—the front of the house a gentle bay—her hostess, in a dressing gown and with a shawl wrapped about her, leaning out her bedroom window.

The voices were becoming louder and the gestures more threatening; Sonia, who had probably seen her share of angry mobs, was afraid. Still not understanding and with a survivor's reluctance to get involved, she remained, quietly, invisibly, where she was.

"All right, for God's sake, wait. I'm coming down," she heard Mrs. Hitchcock shout.

The men below became quieter, muttering among themselves. Sonia took advantage of the few minutes during which she assumed her hostess was dressing to put on some warm clothes and boots herself and to gather a small bundle of her more valuable possessions. Then she heard the scrape of the hall door against stone. Although she again pressed her face against the glass, she could not see Mrs. Hitchcock, who stood under the porch, but she could see the men approach her, their voices less loud. After a moment they all went indoors.

Sonia, now fully dressed, tiptoed along the corridor to the top of the stairs, where she stood, listening. She could only make out Mrs. Hitchcock's part of the conversation; and her hostess was now speaking less loudly. She could, however, smell the petrol that one of the men had spilled when he set down the metal container he was carrying on the hall carpet.

While Sonia descended the stairs as far as the dark landing from where she could see the entire group, the men conferred briefly and shuffled toward the library door. Becoming more confident in her invisibility, Sonia crept halfway down the remaining flight of stairs and leaned over the banisters. Mrs. Hitchcock had not changed out of her dressing gown, and Sonia could see that her hostess's embroidered pink kimono, with its wide silk sash, embarrassed the men and made them awkward. She could also glimpse Mrs. Hitchcock's little slippers trimmed with swan's-down, and she saw that her hostess had taken a moment to brush her hair and to apply her usual dark red lipstick.

There was enough time for Sonia to admire the older woman's courage and how she acted as though she were in control of the situation. Despite herself Sonia was now almost at the foot of the stairs, close enough to be able to see the backs of the men as they followed Mrs. Hitchcock, whose hand now lay on the ornate glass knob of the library door. Close enough, when the door was opened, to be surprised that the room was lit by at least two lamps and that the embers of the fire still glowed in the grate. Sonia had time to think—illogically, since the smell of petrol had become stronger—that it was irresponsible of Mrs.

Hitchcock to have left the oil lamps alight and not to have raked out the fire before going up to bed, before she saw, sitting immobile in an armchair, a tumbler of whiskey and a soda siphon on the small table beside him, the man she later learned to be Nicholas Rowe.

No one, other than Sonia, ever told me the part about Nicholas Rowe. Not surprisingly, the implications were improper and troubling for a variety of reasons. Grandmother, for instance, would have felt betrayed, her friendship with the powerful Republican no longer so interesting or flattering if he were in the habit of visiting fast women under cover of darkness. The maids were reluctant to discuss Nicholas Rowe's late-night presence at Mrs. Hitchcock's house in part because he was for them a symbol—a land-owning Roman Catholic in a position to look any Protestant in the eye—and they would have been shocked by the thought of him consorting with a scarlet woman. A scarlet woman most likely Protestant—not that she had been seen going into a Protestant church, but anyone could tell she wasn't a Catholic. Even less than Nicholas Rowe's morals did they want to discuss the identity of the young revolutionaries, who had discomfited themselves, although, I suspect, not much embarrassing their superior officer, when they had raided a house in which he was being entertained. Incipient revolution in the air, the young men—or more likely boys—looking for guns became a sinister and unnerving story. And one far too close to home.

HER FIRST MORNING at Ballydavid, Easter Sunday, Sonia slept in. I could see, even as they tried to conceal their irritation, that Grandmother and Aunt Katie considered not getting up in time for breakfast to be decadent, self-indulgent, sloppy, and rackety. I was both admiring that the Countess, like Jarvis de Courcy, should take so lightly the conventions of Anglo-Irish society and impatient because I had not seen her since I had been sent out of the drawing room the afternoon before. Early in the day it was harder to dispense with my presence.

Eventually the Countess came downstairs. It was a little after twelve o'clock, and, despite her prolonged rest, she seemed sleepy and distracted.

"Would you like a cup of tea?" Aunt Katie asked. "You must be famished."

I knew the correct response to that offer. Anyone who had not appeared at breakfast was supposed to wait until lunch for refreshment, unless she were offered a biscuit and a glass of sherry at the moment deemed appropriate. To ask for a cup of tea while lunch was being prepared was thought to be "giving trouble." The transgression of giving trouble was unconnected to the high-handed way servants were treated by the very employer now taking offence on their behalf.

"Coffee, please," the Countess said.

Grandmother rose to ring the bell for Bridie. She seemed to hold herself even more straightly erect than she usually did, and, although she did not allow herself to purse her lips, her nostrils seemed drawn in a little.

I supposed that a certain arrogance was inevitable if you had spent your life as a Countess, and I thought my grandmother and great-aunt might be inwardly struggling to accept that explanation for Sonia's behavior.

There was a silence during which neither of the old ladies asked their guest if she had slept well. It was broken when Bridie came in, and it resumed after she left. Sonia, dull and puffy, did not seem to notice the lack of conversation. I could see she was not as young as I had thought her.

"Do you have a lot of yaks?" I asked, adding when I saw surprise on the adult faces, "In Manchuria?"

The Countess looked at me; for a moment she did not seem to have understood my question. I wondered if mentioning Manchuria to her was as tactless as bringing up Cairo seemed to be when Mrs. Coughlan was present.

"Yes, many," she said, glancing toward the door, desperate for Bridie's return.

Grandmother held off asking even the most subtle question until Sonia had drunk an entire pot of coffee—black with a lot of sugar—and had accepted, shortly afterward, a glass of sherry. She refused the biscuit.

"I see you are looking at the work of Sir Oliver Lodge," Grandmother then said, not quite accurately.

We were sitting in the library; newspapers and magazines lay on a low table in front of Sonia. They included literature from the Society for Psychical Research and books by its founder, Sir Oliver Lodge. Sonia's eyes flickered with no apparent interest over what Ballydavid offered her to read. I wasn't surprised she should think it dull. Neither Grandmother nor Aunt Katie read for pleasure. I wondered what Sonia read and decided after some thought that French novels would be to her taste. My own ability at that time to read French had not gone further than *Madame Souris,* and I had only recently started to read full-length novels in any language.

Sonia's answering smile was polite but bemused and did not suggest a pressing need to follow that line of conversation. After a moment, Grandmother approached the subject in a slightly different way.

"Katie and I are also devotees of Madame Blavatsky."

"Madame Blavatsky?" Sonia sounded bewildered and desperate.

"You are not interested in Theosophy?" Aunt Katie asked gamely, now that Grandmother had carried that conversational ball as far as she could take it.

"I have heard the name, also that of your Madame, but I am afraid that I don't—such things, names are not known in Manchuria."

It seemed that Sonia's English had taken a turn for the worse; her accent had thickened and she stumbled and searched for words.

The impasse was broken by Bridie coming to announce lunch.

Sonia was silent and gloomy throughout lunch, although she seemed to have a good appetite. The cooking at Ballydavid was good, the household not suffering through one of the fad diets that Grandmother and Aunt Katie from time to time embraced.

Sonia had eaten dinner with Grandmother and Aunt Katie the evening before, but the dining room had been lit only by the candelabra on the table and the candles on either side of the looking glass on the chimneypiece. Now sunlight streamed in, and my uncle Sainthill's portrait on the wall opposite the windows was clearly lit. Sonia finished her *oeufs en cocotte* before she looked up and saw it. Her face lost its habitual look of preoccupation, and she regarded the painting with an expression of affectionate pity and recognition. The old ladies, without moving, seemed to stiffen their spines.

"Your poor uncle," she said to me, "you remember him, of course."

I nodded. Not quite truthfully.

"His medals—the Military Cross? You have them?"

"In the glass case in the drawing room," Grandmother said faintly.

"With the cigarette case," Aunt Katie added firmly.

In the silence that followed, both the old ladies looked meaningfully at the Countess. But she added nothing more, merely nodding her head as though something she knew well had been confirmed.

"So young," she said a little later while Bridie offered her roast duck. "So beautiful, and all his life before him."

She had the attention of every person at the table, and I could see that Bridie was missing nothing.

"That poor girl. Now she will never marry."

Grandmother said nothing. Since her son's death, she had tended to minimize Uncle Sainthill's relationship with the young woman from County Clare whom, although they weren't engaged, it was believed he had intended to marry when the war was over. Since her son's death, Grandmother had become jealous of Margaret. Instead of shared sorrow making the two women closer, Grandmother went out of her way not to see Margaret and never, if she could help it, to mention her; on the rare occasions it proved necessary to speak her name, she would refer to her as Miss Hall.

"Oh, I expect she will," Aunt Katie said, her social instincts carrying her back toward safer waters and away from where she wanted to be. "Later on, of course."

"Never," Sonia said firmly.

There was another silence while the old ladies considered Sonia's pronouncement, unable to decide whether it was prophecy or merely cheek.

"Like Cordelia Hitchcock," Sonia added.

"She will never marry again?" Aunt Katie asked.

"She will, of course, marry again. That sort of woman always does." This seemed to be an observation rather than a prediction. "She thinks she will sleep tomorrow night at her hotel, the—ah———"

"The Shelbourne," Aunt Katie suggested helpfully.

"The Gresham," Grandmother said simultaneously.

"The Shelbourne," Sonia said.

The Shelbourne was where Anglo-Irish women stayed in Dublin. (Men not accompanied by their wives stayed at the Kildare

Street Club.) The Gresham, on Sackville Street, was also a handsome and well-run hotel but lacked the tradition of the Shelbourne. I remember, when I was older, my mother's words: "Oh, the Gresham—Americans and priests." The question now before the old ladies at Ballydavid was whether Mrs. Hitchcock should score a point for staying at the Shelbourne or lose one for aping the behavior of the Anglo-Irish. While they considered this, I thought of Sonia and the confident way she was predicting the future. Not that her first two pronouncements exposed her to much risk: Until Margaret married or Mrs. Hitchcock died unmarried, she could not be proved wrong. Now it seemed as though she were going to stick her neck out and predict something for the following day. I wondered if what she was about to tell us would be not easily verifiable.

"Cordelia thinks she will spend tomorrow night at the Shelbourne, but she will not."

"Why not?" Aunt Katie asked, her eyes sparkling. I could see that, although Grandmother was enthralled, she was also disapproving. Possibly the mention of hotel bedrooms in the context of a woman who had just lost her already shaky reputation upset her; she was probably about to suggest I should leave the table before pudding was served.

"She just won't," Sonia said and popped a forkful of duck into her mouth.

"But where will she sleep?" I piped up.

Grandmother and Aunt Katie looked at me disapprovingly; Sonia smiled and said nothing.

UNCLE WILLIAM CAME to tea that afternoon. The following day he was going up to Dublin for a committee meeting of the Kildare Street Club, where he was planning to stay for a week to take care of some minor business and to have one of his periodic breaks from rural life and the limitations of Waterford society.

Sonia, despite the hour she had come downstairs that morning, had gone back to her bedroom after lunch to rest. Grandmother and Aunt Katie were simultaneously pleased that Sonia's absence would allow them to discuss her with Uncle William and less pleased to be denied the opportunity of watching Uncle William handle Sonia, or vice versa. They were also less than happy about the way their guest was "treating the place like an hotel." Although I didn't care if Sonia treated Ballydavid like an hotel, I worried that she might have nocturnal habits that would prevent me witnessing her next pronouncements.

I set off obediently for my rest and walk; I did not intend to appear until Uncle William had arrived and was comfortably settled in front of the drawing-room fire, drinking tea from his special outsized cup. I was looking forward to his masculine, forthright way of speaking and thought he might have brought me an Easter present. I was also aware it was difficult for Grandmother and Aunt Katie to dispense with my presence on one of Uncle William's visits, although he had no difficulty in sending me out of the room if there was something he wanted to say to the old ladies in private.

Returning from my walk a little early, I entered the house through the kitchen, confirmed to my satisfaction that Maggie had gone all out to please Uncle William, and ran up the back stairs. In my room, I carefully brushed my hair, changed my dress, and composed myself to appear demure and innocent while avoiding the dangerously similar expression that suggested deep stupidity.

Ready for tea, I quietly closed the door of my room behind me. Although it was only midafternoon on an April day, the corridor was almost dark; a monkey puzzle, planted too close to the house, reduced the light that filtered through the opaque window and its stained-glass border. A gloomy halflight that came from the hall windows below guided me to the landing at the top of the stairs.

I didn't at first see Sonia looking over the banisters. She was still and her shawls blended into the sepia light. They covered more of her than they usually did and, were it not for a patch of flimsy lace and silk at her ankle and her bare feet on the thin landing carpet, I would not have guessed that she had come straight from her bed. I assumed she had got up when she heard the noisy masculine arrival of Uncle William. The hall was now silent, so I knew Uncle William must have gone into the drawing room. Sonia was looking straight ahead, her expression thought-ful; in front of her there was nothing but a large painting of a battle at sea. Since the picture had not been deemed good enough for the hall and was only just visible through the gloom, I sup-posed her thoughts to be elsewhere.

It had been instilled in me soon after my arrival at Ballydavid that, although I was expected to be quiet, I was not to approach an adult so silently that I might give her a fright—the maids had de-scribed in graphic detail what the consequences would certainly be—so I cleared my throat as I stepped off the carpet onto the wooden floor. I wasn't sure she had heard me, but I suspected it would take more than my unanticipated presence to give Sonia a heart attack. I stood beside her, looking down the shadowy and empty staircase.

"That is your uncle—Uncle William?" she said presently.

"I expect so. They went into the drawing room?"

"Your Aunt Katie was married to his father? And he lives alone?"

There was a brief confusion caused by my having considered Uncle William not to live alone since his house was heavily staffed.

But it didn't matter since Sonia had already seen Ballinamona Park and only wanted to confirm that there was no Mrs. Martyn in the wings. A few more questions followed along the lines of how much land was attached to Ballinamona. I think now she would have asked me how much money Uncle William had if she had imagined I could have known the answer. But there were also questions that baffled me: Where had he gone to school? What was the name of his dog? His favorite horse? I wondered if I should warn her to be careful of splinters from the uncarpeted floor.

Although I did not consider any time spent with Sonia wasted, I also did not want to miss too much of what was passing between the old ladies and Uncle William. When I came into the drawing room Uncle William was laughing.

"Adventuress?" He didn't hear me quietly opening the door behind him. "An adventuress and clairvoyant at Ballydavid? A fortune teller! What would Uncle Percival have said?"

My entrance, of course, put a close to that topic of conversation, but I thought the old ladies welcomed the interruption; they knew very well just what Uncle Percival would have said.

Uncle William had brought me presents, a small, ornately packed box of chocolates and a wooden puzzle. The chocolates would, I knew, be rationed—one after lunch each day—and I made no attempt to open them. But the puzzle, interesting enough in its own way, was of immediate use. I could take it a little away from the adults and play with it as soon as I had finished my tea.

Gradually, after a tea that relaxed and lowered guards, conversation drifted back to the subject of Sonia. I thought that Uncle William had probably heard the story of the cigarette case before and had not been quite as impressed as we all had been. Now the additional lunchtime predictions were recounted to add credibility; I was interested to see how firmly and loyally

Grandmother and Aunt Katie were lined up behind their resident clairvoyant.

But Uncle William refused to take any of it seriously. He tended to amuse himself by teasing the old ladies when he came to visit. I think that in a general way they enjoyed his gentle banter; it was a different form of attention and it made them feel young.

"Big earrings?" he asked. "Crystal ball? You cross her palm with silver?"

Both Grandmother and Aunt Katie laughed while protesting Sonia's authenticity. It seems possible now that Uncle William enjoyed these visits more than I imagined; it is unlikely he ever faced a less critical audience.

Soon Sonia joined us. I was more surprised than the others since I knew how quickly she must have dressed. We all looked at her with interest. Uncle William might have seen Sonia before but not in a place when he could observe her at his leisure or ask awkward questions. Grandmother's and Aunt Katie's feelings were mixed: a balance of the curiosity they felt in her presence and a fear that Uncle William would make her appear ridiculous or discredit her.

Sonia had again dressed suitably for afternoon tea at Ballydavid without sacrificing that touch of the exotic that complemented her image. The two large suitcases with which she had arrived at Ballydavid contained all that remained of her worldly possessions. I was once in her room and saw how meager her wardrobe was. Lady Ottoline Morell, famous for her elegance and her beautiful clothes, achieved her distinctive look partly by the way her shawls were draped and expertly pinned by her maid. Sonia, poor and worn around the edges, took, with a fair degree of success, a similar approach to her dress. Her shabby skirts and frayed blouses were covered with layers of shawls; the ones she now wore might well have been those I had fifteen minutes before seen covering her nightdress as she stood barefoot on the landing.

Conventional introductions followed.

"Countess," Uncle William murmured, taking her hand and bowing over it so low that he could have kissed it.

I could see, as could my visibly tense grandmother and greataunt, that Uncle William was going to tease Sonia, while behaving in a manner upon which he could not be called.

Sonia, who knew as well as the rest of us what he was doing, smiled modestly and sat down beside me on the sofa. She made no attempt to instigate conversation. I couldn't help thinking she had come out of the introductory exchange rather better than Uncle William had.

"Aunt Katie tells me you are from Manchuria?" Uncle William called his stepmother "Aunt Katie," perhaps further confusing for Sonia a family tree already accommodating remarriage and, in my case, the apparent loss of a generation on its lower branches.

"Yes," Sonia said, her eyes lowered, her hands folded on her knees, her posture emphasizing her tall, slight figure. "I am."

"Never been there myself," Uncle William said. He paused and looked thoughtful as Grandmother gave Sonia a cup of tea. All eyes remained respectfully on him as he nodded slowly; it was as though a respectable career in the Indian Army was to be considered the equivalent of having discovered the source of the Nile.

"I hadn't been aware that Count and Countess were titles in Manchuria, too?"

Even I understood that he intended to expose Sonia to the old ladies. I don't think he intended to do so from malice, but only in order to protect them. And to have a little fun. Sonia raised her eyes until she was looking at him.

"My title is not a Manchurian one," she said. "I was not a countess until I married."

"I see. Your husband...?" Uncle William left the question open enough for Sonia to volunteer information about her husband's aristocratic antecedents, nationality, profession, or character—and whereabouts. Although I was as curious as I knew my grandmother and great-aunt to be, I—as I suspected they, too—would have been satisfied for that afternoon with the revelation that Sonia had, or at some time had had, a husband. In a relationship as fascinating and delicate as ours with Sonia, we, unlike Uncle William, felt each additional scrap of information should be mulled over and digested before the next question was asked.

I knew that Sonia was not only the source of fascinating and pleasurable stories and of exotic information, but of a view of the world I was unlikely to encounter elsewhere. But I also knew—perhaps because I had seen Mara display her whole bag of tricks too quickly—that Sonia intended to reveal only as much as was completely necessary in order to keep a roof over her head. I appreciated the artistry of her small, well-timed revelations.

"My husband was Polish; he's dead," Sonia said quietly, and her eyes once again turned to her immobile hands. Despite the embarrassment of the moment, I found myself wondering whether the Count had been murdered. Possibly by Mara, I thought in a moment of wild confusion.

"I'm sorry to hear that," Uncle William said, possibly including the nationality Sonia had gained by marriage in his condolence.

Not surprisingly, for a little time the silence was broken only by a log dropping a few inches in the fireplace and some sparks falling on the metal tray beneath the grate. There was unanimous agreement, requiring not even a quick glance between the females in the room, that it was up to Uncle William to be the next to speak.

But before Uncle William was forced to retreat to a meaningless social banality, Bridie came in with a jug of hot water and the afternoon post. The passage of time makes necessary an explanation of the arrival of post on Sunday. In those days post, which was quick and reliable, arrived seven days a week.

Aunt Katie took the silver jug and added a little water to the teapot while Grandmother waved away the post. Bridie hesitated long enough to allow Grandmother to see that the top letter was from my mother.

Grandmother opened the letter as Aunt Katie refilled Uncle William's cup. My attention was entirely on the letter; the others, too, remained silent.

"Really, the most extraordinary thing," Grandmother said after a little time, during which she read the letter and then parts of it a second time. "Mary says she's had a letter and a call from a young woman who appears to claim to be engaged to Hubert."

We all stared at Grandmother, but no one said anything. Even Sonia seemed fascinated. Aunt Katie, the incurable romantic, was the only one who showed any sign of enthusiasm; Grandmother clearly thought that this roundabout way of learning her widower son was contemplating remarriage was at least disrespectful if not disreputable; Uncle William tended to disapprove of most decisions made without his advice.

"Who is she?" Aunt Katie asked at last.

"She seems to come from a respectable family. Gwynne. From Suffolk. Her name's Rosamund."

"I was at school with a Gwynne," Uncle William said. "I wonder if it's the same family."

"Mary says she doesn't much care for her. A rather bossy young woman."

Aunt Katie sighed while Grandmother reread the letter.

"And it doesn't seem quite clear that they *are* engaged. No ring, no announcement in the *Times*. She was, apparently, not willing to say definitively that there was an a engagement—of course, Mary could hardly question her——"

I imagined my ineffectual mother, embarrassed, worried, her own disastrous lapse rendering her deeply conventional and reasonably sure she would be closely questioned by her mother and held responsible for the answers. No wonder she "didn't much care for" this new complication to her life.

"But she says Miss Gwynne gave the impression that she and Hubert would either be married on his next leave—well, that's four years away—or that she would travel out to Canton next year and they would marry there."

"No word from Hugh himself?" Uncle William asked.

"You know how the post is. And yet this must have been going on for some time. They met when he was last on leave, but he didn't introduce her to any of the family or even mention her."

Grandmother read the letter again, for the third time, while we watched, waiting for her to find an overlooked detail that would offer some explanation. Beside me, Sonia seemed to have turned to stone.

Grandmother looked up and shook her head.

"For all we know she's a madwoman and making this up. Or perhaps Hubert——"

Even I knew what she meant. Perhaps Uncle Hubert had led this unfortunate woman on and then gone back to China without proposing marriage, assuming his five years' absence would make clear his lack of intentions. Leaving his family—in this case my mother—to deal with any mess he had left behind.

"Mary says he brought a woman with him to visit once or twice. But not this one."

"Definitely not?" Uncle William said, as though he thought my mother couldn't be trusted to tell the difference.

"Definitely not, quite a different situation. The woman was a refugee, not young, rather painted, Mary said. And she said Hubert had suggested she'd had rather a—an adventurous past."

I glanced at Sonia. Her lips were pressed together; she did not seem to be breathing.

"I liked her very much. She was pretty and very nice," I said, astonishing myself with my own daring. I could feel that something was happening that I should try to stop before any more damage was done.

Only Sonia seemed to hear me. Her hand crept out and touched mine.

"Better than that, anyway," Uncle William said.

"I suppose so." Grandmother sounded discouraged.

"What does she look like?" Aunt Katie asked. "Is she pretty?"

"Plump. But pretty. Mary said she asked a lot of questions."

"And the adventuress? What happened to her?"

Uncle William's bluff, man-of-the-world tone and his evident amusement in the whole situation was now in one way or another painful to everyone else in the room, and Grandmother merely shrugged.

"Well, this isn't so interesting for our guest," he said, with an extraordinary lack of perception, perhaps realizing further amusement at my uncle Hubert's expense was unlikely. For a moment, he did not propose a change of subject; his eyes sparkling with malice, he looked at us, each silent in her own distress.

"I am told," he said eventually to Sonia, "you consider Alice to have psychic powers?"

Everyone now looked at me, although Sonia was the one under attack. I was surprised to learn that the brief reference to "a gift" some time ago, with only Aunt Katie as a witness, had been taken seriously and had had so wide a circulation.

"It's not unusual in a sensitive child of her age." Sonia sounded exhausted, but her tone was matter-of-fact.

I wondered if Uncle William would say something about the

increasingly scandalous Mrs. Hitchcock, surely the next step in reminding the old ladies that they were harboring an unsuitable guest. But instead, after some small talk while Bridie cleared away the tea tray, he continued in the same vein.

"Well now," he said, rubbing his hands, "what shall we do? We're too many for a hand of bridge—so given the wealth of psychic powers at this tea party—what about a séance? Or should we see if Aunt Molly's table has a message for us?"

"William, what a—a—an unsuitable idea." Aunt Katie was not sure if she was being teased or not. "On a Sunday—with a child—and anyway you're an unbeliever so, of course, no good could come of it."

"I have a completely open mind. I'm a little choosey about what I believe in, but I'm open-minded. Open-minded, not incredulous."

Another small silence while the three women in the room unhappily resented the not very subtle insult to Sonia.

"In fact I've seen things in India that—that cannot be accounted for with a conventional Western explanation."

A frosty silence greeted this offering. Grandmother, Aunt Katie, and Sonia were still offended. I, however, sat on the edge of the sofa, gaping admiringly at Uncle William, thrilled to find myself with someone who might be persuaded to describe the charming of snakes, the Indian rope trick; here was someone who had seen scantily clad natives walking on coals, sitting on beds of nails.

"Oh, Uncle William, tell us, please," I piped up bravely when no one else spoke.

"One night in the Officers' Mess," he started unpromisingly—I had supposed the tale would be set in the desert or at least the marketplace. "Chap there took the heaviest man in the room—Tiny Harrington—and four subalterns. He had them, the subalterns, make a sort of tower with their hands above

Tiny's head. He was very careful that they shouldn't touch each other's hands because what they were doing was—ah—interrupting gravity. Then each of the four subalterns put a single finger under Tiny's arms and under both legs at the knee, and they lifted him high into the air. Tiny weighed all of eighteen stone, but he went up easily."

I was surprised and pleased by Uncle William's story, with its suggestion that life, even among the dull kind of people we knew, might turn out to be more interesting than I had so far had any reason to imagine. Sonia and the two old ladies looked at him without expression.

"Did it again later with the Colonel, only he sat on a chair. Got him up high enough that he signed his name on the ceiling with a silver pencil."

Despite my satisfaction with this story, it was followed by the final short silence—there would be longer ones—of the afternoon. Uncle William wanted to draw Sonia into the open; Grandmother and Aunt Katie were longing to communicate with a spirit from the other side; and I, although uneasy at being part of this adult recklessness, wanted to see what would happen next. Only Sonia's wishes remained unknown and, as she did not say anything, choosing instead to act as though none of this had anything to do with her, we quite soon found ourselves sitting around what Uncle William had referred to as Aunt Molly's table.

Aunt Molly was the elder sister of Grandmother and Aunt Katie; she had died many years before. Her table—various pieces of furniture around the house commemorated previous owners—normally stood with a Chinese shawl draped over it beside Aunt Katie's chair. Now that it was uncovered, I could see that it was pedestal-based and the papier-mâché top was black with an inlaid border of time-darkened flowers; there were small chips around the edge, and someone, a long time ago, had carelessly marked the surface with a wet glass.

Uncle William carried the table to an open area of carpet and arranged the chairs around it; no one had rung for Bridie, who would have been the usual person to perform such a task. The seating required no discussion. Uncle William sat down and gestured firmly to Sonia that she should sit on his left where, it was inferred, he could keep an eye on her. Grandmother sat on his right, then Aunt Katie. I sat between Aunt Katie and Sonia.

None of us, except for Uncle William, would have thought this attempt at table turning a good idea. We sat silently around the table, our fingers—following Uncle William's instructions— resting lightly on the papier-mâché surface. Nothing happened for a while, and I had plenty of time to consider the awkwardness of Grandmother's and Aunt Katie's position. They knew that even my mild mother would have been shocked that I should be so exploited. What my father would have had to say beggared imagination; his complete skepticism would have in no way mitigated his outrage that I should have been exposed to the perils of this kind of irresponsible charlatanism. Even more than what my parents would have thought or said, the old ladies had their own consciences to face. They had been angling, without success, to enlist Sonia to help them communicate with the other side. She had not only shown no enthusiasm for such an enterprise but had seemed not to understand their hints. They had become aware that it would take Uncle William or someone else capable of a similarly blunt approach to force Sonia's hand.

Not only did I feel that it was cruel of Uncle William to press Sonia and to place Grandmother and Aunt Katie in a morally indefensible position while crudely trampling on the small flowering hopes and possibly necessary self-deceptions of the two grief-stricken old ladies, but he had offended me by coarsening the mystery that Sonia offered. He appeared to equate Sonia's subtle arts with the crude antics of an officers' mess and I, for the first time, saw the thoughtless, clumsy, literal-minded way that men destroy the fragile, not always rational, structures that women build and depend upon. The damage inflicted by my father and O'Neill, I now understand, was a condition of their masculinity as well as of their individual natures.

What would have happened had we sat down in a spirit of faith and cooperation? I imagine that some random letters would sooner or later seem to have been tapped by the table; that Grandmother and Aunt Katie would have divined from them some small and hopeful symbol; that Uncle William would have been bluffly dismissive and matter-of-factly triumphant; that Sonia would have remained detached and not quite interested. Instead we sat tensely around the little table—even I, the one with least responsibility for our dubious undertaking, more aware of the tension around me than of any tentative spirit hovering in the ether. Some more sparks fell through the grate. I was beginning to wonder who would call a halt to the proceedings, or whether someone in a spirit almost of social obligation should give the table a little nudge. Nothing. And then the silence was broken by a small cry from a source unseen to all of us, apparently close to the fire. Aunt Katie quickly rose from the table—I had a feeling that she was, perhaps dangerously, breaching spiritualist etiquette—and crossed the room.

"It's Oonagh," she said, quickly scooping Grandmother's cat from the sofa. Banished for the afternoon, since Uncle William loathed cats, she must have slipped into the room when Bridie came for the tray. Aunt Katie took her to the door to the service passage and put her down outside. "She was asleep—dreaming," she added, as she firmly closed the door.

Then something happened. Or rather nothing did, but I was filled with an unreasoning terror quite unlike anything I have since experienced. There have been moments of extreme fear and not inconsiderable danger during my life, both as an adult and as a child, but my memories of these occasions are quite different. When, for instance, crossing the Irish Sea during the Second World War, I watched the periscope of a German submarine cut through the cold dark waters, I froze, time slowed, the moment observed, as from a distance, with a horrible clarity. Or during the Blitz in London, my fear suspended in a manner not wholly dissimilar to how it had been on my first day on the hunting field, the full extent of my emotions to be understood only later. To fears of a longer lasting but less immediate nature—those, for instance, of loss and loneliness—my terror was even less similar.

That afternoon in the darkened drawing room, I experienced fear in its purest abstract form. It had no image and no object, its provenance only our invitation to the spirits of the dead—even though that invitation had apparently been ignored. I didn't move or make a sound, and it should have been some time—the lack of light in the room, all eyes on Aunt Katie, the stillness of the other three at the table—before anyone noticed my distress.

Beside me Sonia sighed; then she drew in a breath and I felt, rather than saw, her body stiffen.

"I fear——" Her voice was not quite her own, so deep it might have been a man's, the accent, too, not completely hers. "I fear there will be no orange blossoms for Mademoiselle."

And that was all. Her words froze us in place. Then she sighed again and we all seemed to know that she was finished. Aunt Katie returned to the table.

It wasn't completely dark. The curtains had not been drawn—not only, I now think, because the light outside was fading but because of the undignified necessity of opening them again before ringing for Bridie to bring in the lamps and close the curtains. There was also a glow from the fire that faintly lit the area around it.

I sensed, though, that Aunt Katie knew something was wrong before she could see my face. She hesitated as she reached the table, but she may have been unsure whether the natural interruption—at that stage no one was giving any particular significance to Oonagh's cry and not much to Sonia's cryptic but apparently irrelevant utterance—might not serve as a way to extricate the group from their failed attempt without further fuelling Uncle William's ridicule or admitting the defeat of those whom he had bullied into testing, under unfavourable conditions, dearly held beliefs.

"Alice——" Aunt Katie said, her voice low but strained.

Grandmother and Uncle William were, I could feel—I did not dare turn my head or move in any way—also looking at me. Perhaps they could hear the change in my breathing. Neither moved; of Sonia's presence I was unaware, it was as though she were no longer in the room.

Slowly Grandmother and Uncle William stood up as Aunt Katie approached me.

"Alice——" she said again, and stretched out a hand toward my shoulder.

I shrank away from her. I still can't explain why I was afraid of her touch. I felt as though there were something amorphous that, without touching me, floated around me and that Aunt Katie's hand would disturb it, endangering and contaminating both of us. I could not see it, feel it, hear it, but I knew that nothing in our real, visible world could protect me or anyone else from it. I remained in the position I had withdrawn into when I flinched, and Aunt Katie took a step backward.

Uncle William stepped back noisily from the table.

"Where's the light, damn it?"

Then, remembering he was not in his own modernized house, he crossed the room and tugged at the bell rope beside Aunt Katie's chair.

"William——" Grandmother's voice was uncharacteristically tentative.

Even in my frozen state I knew Grandmother wanted to avoid Bridie witnessing this unfortunate scene. She need not have worried on that score. Uncle William might be crass in his dealings with the psychic world, but his understanding was perhaps greater than Grandmother's of the lives and minds of those he employed. He intercepted Bridie at the door.

"Would you bring some brandy?" he said, taking the two oil lamps she had been carrying.

Uncle William put one lamp in its usual place on the table behind the sofa in front of the fire and rested the other, the one that usually sat on Aunt Molly's table, on the sideboard. I hadn't until then been aware of how cold I was but, now that the room was lighted and the furniture was efficiently restored to its usual place by Uncle William, I felt suddenly warm and completely restored to safety. Aware that I was still the center of attention, I stood up. I didn't know what to say and I didn't have the words to describe what had just happened. I also had the sense that it would not be a good idea to attempt an explanation—that whatever it was I feared would not wish me to speak of it.

Bridie came back at that moment with a decanter of brandy, the soda siphon, and a bottle of white port. As she closed the curtains, Uncle William poured glasses of port for the two old ladies, a stiff brandy for himself and Sonia, and, as Bridie closed the door behind her, a small amount in a sherry glass for me.

ON EASTER MONDAY, we sat in the library after lunch. Throughout the colder months of the year Grandmother and Aunt Katie alternated where they spent the greater part of each day between the library and the drawing room. On the first of every month Bridie would set the fire in the room that had been left largely unused the month before. In this manner the damp was kept at bay, if not dispelled. The arrangement was flexible: A small morning fire would be set in the library if Grandmother wanted to write letters or review her accounts; if visitors were expected we would have tea in the drawing room; and sometimes in the middle of the month Grandmother, on a whim or for some never questioned reason of her own, would decree the change.

My temporary status—since my brush with the spirit world, I was being treated as though I were recovering from a not very serious illness—even with its potential for exploitation, was not a comfortable one. Aware that the situation could be turned to some advantage, I didn't know what I wanted, and that in turn frustrated me and made me more wretched, as though I had been told while I was feeling slightly sick that I could eat as many chocolates as I wished. I didn't want indulgence; I wanted the safety of unquestioned rules and a return to the belief that my grandmother's strictures, although often inconvenient, were infallible. It was a day I would have been happy to spend in the schoolroom at Glenbeg, but Clodagh and I were on holiday from lessons for another week.

Rain fell intermittently all that day; normally it would not have excused me from some form of outdoor exercise. But that afternoon neither Grandmother nor Aunt Katie sent me upstairs to rest or outdoors for a walk. I sat on the sofa opposite the fire and read *The Thirty-nine Steps*. Aunt Katie was reading *A Man of Property*, Grandmother the memoirs of the Duc de Saint-Simon. The clock ticked and from time to time embers fell through the grate; these sounds apart, the silence was broken only by Aunt Katie's asking me, when the light outside changed from gloom to dusk, if I had enough light. The ornate box of chocolates Uncle William had given me the day before remained unopened in the drawing room.

Chapter 8

THE FOLLOWING MORNING, Tuesday, I woke to a gale blowing in from the sea. Hard points of rain smashed against the windows of my bedroom. I lay in bed for a few minutes on the assumption that the normal unquestioned necessity for punctuality was in abeyance, and wondered how long the current atmosphere of laissez-faire would continue and whether the resumption of the often exhausting rules that composed and restricted my life at Ballydavid would be gradual or sudden. I considered the likelihood of another long day in front of the fire in the library, quietly reading my book and growing old beside Grandmother and Aunt Katie. What if on Wednesday morning I also awoke to an unchanged situation?

I need not have feared an imagined eternity of uneventful days. For one thing, I seemed to have forgotten Sonia. She had spent Easter Monday in bed, diplomatically ill, perhaps assuming that responsibility for the previous day's debacle would be laid at her feet and trying to think of a plan that would put someone else's roof over her head.

The atmosphere at breakfast announced business as usual. Grandmother's eye fell on me as soon as we had all exchanged greetings and I had taken my place. I could sense her looking for something to criticize, and I sat up straight, elbows by my side, and concentrated on my table manners. She gave me the minimal nod with which she bestowed temporary approval and asked me when I had last written to my mother. I saw Aunt Katie blink.

I realized that the old ladies needed to see what, if anything, I would tell my mother about our attempt at table tilting. I nodded obediently, if unenthusiastically; letters to my mother were another area in which I struggled and failed to come up to Grandmother's standards. The contents were not censored, the knowledge that she would read them censorship enough, but often the letter would be rewritten, sometimes more than once, on grounds of poor handwriting, poverty of description, or inelegant wording. On this occasion, since there had been no discussion of what had taken place two days earlier, I would have welcomed a hint as to the party line.

Since my grandmother's question constituted a suggestion, not an instruction, I had, by my reckoning, until teatime to present to her a draft of a neatly written, adequately expressed account of those events my mother might be interested in having described and of a reassurance of my health, well-being, and continuing affection. I also remembered that Miss Kingsley had given me the holiday task of tracing a map of Ireland. Again, there was no urgency; lessons wouldn't resume until the following Monday, but experience had taught me that when I had grandmother's full attention she would sometimes, if the mood took her, review every aspect of my life: Questions as to the regularity of my prayers and bowel movements might be followed by a quiz on French verbs and multiplication tables, an inspection of my fingernails, and an instruction to listen to the way she pronounced a series of words and then to say each word back to her five times—the latter exercise a precaution against my acquiring an Irish accent.

After breakfast I retired to my room. So far as I can remember, Sonia had not appeared in the dining room, and I left Grandmother reading the *Morning Post* to Aunt Katie. The alacrity with which I excused myself and set off toward my tasks was less a sign that I was conscientious than that I was developing political opinions at odds with those expressed in the *Post*'s editorial pages. It had taken me a little time to understand that the "grateless Irish," about whom Grandmother read in tones of scorn, included Bridie and Maggie and the two men who worked on the farm; even the *Morning Post,* I assumed, would not dare so to describe the formidable O'Neill.

Tracing the map seemed the more appealing of the two tasks before me, and I spent the next hour following, with a sharp pencil on a piece of tracing paper, the jagged indentations of the Atlantic on the west coast of Ireland and the smoother outlines of the rest of the island. I retraced the outline, pressing harder with my pencil, the tracing paper on top of a sheet of drawing paper, and then I followed the faint impression on the drawing paper with a pencil until I had reproduced the coastline for my map. After that came the most satisfying part of my task: shading the outline of the coast in blue to denote the sea; for this I chose the darkest blue in the box of colored pencils Uncle William had given me for Christmas.

I started shading the easier east coast, working my way down from Ulster—Belfast, Dublin, Wexford and round the corner to the south coast. I carefully shaded Hook Head which lay on the far side of the estuary from Ballydavid—the origin, I had been told, of the expression "by Hook or by crook." Someone—I now forget who—had told me these were Cromwell's words, spoken when he declared his intention of taking Waterford. Later I questioned the story when I learned Cromwell did not approach Waterford by sea. He came instead from New Ross, a town at the confluence of the Nore and Barrow, the rivers that later joined the Suir to flow past Ballydavid into the Atlantic. He failed to take Duncannon, on the Wexford side of the estuary, but captured the fort at Passage, the village a few miles up the Suir from Ballydavid where the ferry crosses between the Waterford and Wexford shores. Waterford held out against Cromwell, aided by the winter weather and sickness—a form of malaria, spotted fever, and dysentery—in the Commonwealth army. It fell to one of his generals the following year.

After Hook Head, I went back and carefully shaded around the tiny Saltee Islands which lay on the other side of the head, at the far end of Ballyteige Bay; it was my secret ambition to visit them one day.

Some time had passed, and I started to feel restless and a little lonely. I took my pencil down to the kitchen to be sharpened.

The request was legitimate; if I had been at Glenbeg I would have taken the pencil to Miss Kingsley, who would have sharpened it with her silver penknife, a possession I had the impression was of some sentimental value to her. Bridie took a knife from the drawer of the kitchen table and with two or three uneven strokes put a point on the pencil. She seemed impatient, and I, an expert, sensed tension—not extreme—in the kitchen. I wondered if Aunt Katie had decreed a late change to the menu for lunch; I knew better than to ask. Reluctant to go back upstairs, I wandered out the kitchen door.

It was still raining, but not heavily. I thought that I would go and see if Patience was in her stall. The hunting season over, Patience and Benedict spent most days in a paddock close to the stables, but it seemed unlikely that O'Neill would have turned them out in the gale that had been blowing that morning. A lack of exercise followed by a scoop of oats in Patience's evening feed could result in an unsatisfactory riding lesson the following day. My visit was as much placatory as sentimental.

I glanced back at Bridie and Maggie before slipping out the door; I hadn't changed my shoes and I wasn't wearing a coat. But Bridie and Maggie didn't care if I got my feet wet or came back cold; they were, in their way, as keen on cause and effect as were Grandmother and Aunt Katie, but different causes, different effects.

I glanced toward the gate to the back avenue; I hadn't seen the red-haired boy since the September afternoon that Grandmother and I had taken a walk through the Ballydavid woods. Although Jarvis de Courcy had replaced the young Clancy in my affections—the events of my birthday party having provided more material for fantasy—I remained curious about the boy with the mocking smile, his soldier brother, and the letters he read to Mrs. O'Neill. But I was alone.

Patience was in her stall. I wasn't tall enough to see her through the bars, so I slid back the door a little; she looked at me with a complete lack of interest. I wasn't sure what to do next. I could have stepped inside and closed the door behind me, crossed the stall, and patted her, but I was still frightened of her and knew her capable of biting or kicking me if I gave her the chance. After a moment or two, I thought that my mistake was to come empty-handed, so I closed the door and went in search of a treat. I knew she would like a lump of sugar, but the kitchen atmosphere was not conducive to a request for sugar for a pony. There was a store-room where apples from the previous summer, now wrinkled and softening, lay on slatted shelves, and carrots, equally soft and unpleasantly limp, were buried in a heap of sand on the concrete floor. Both commodities were in diminishing demand for human consumption, and I knew it would be all right to take one of either for Patience. An apple would have to be taken to the kitchen to be cut into quarters, but the sand on a carrot could be rinsed off under the yard tap; I weighed the disadvantages of each: kitchen and bad temper, or yard tap and wet shoes.

Mrs. O'Neill's door was open as I came back through the passageway and hesitated in its dry shelter, regretting now that I hadn't put on boots and a coat before coming out. She called out to me. I entered her kitchen shyly; despite her invitation I was ready to sidle out again if O'Neill were sitting at the kitchen table. But Mrs. O'Neill was alone.

"Come in and sit by the fire," she said. "You must be perished and you out with no coat on you."

The fire and chimney wide above it were set into the wall; on either side of the open hearth was a ledge wide enough for me to sit on, and I gratefully perched myself there, warming my legs. On the other side of the fire, a heavy, flat iron rested on its end, and there were some pots and implements involved in the meal Mrs. O'Neill was preparing. On the wall, to one side of the hearth, was a framed photograph of Tom O'Neill in uniform, his pose stiff, his expression proud and uncertain. I would have liked to say something to Mrs. O'Neill about her son, but I didn't know how.

Mrs. O'Neill looked cross. Usually an expression of anger or irritation on an adult face was enough for me to take myself into another room. But an invitation to come into her kitchen was by no means her automatic response to seeing me pass by. I wondered if she was bored or if she wanted someone to complain to. It crossed my mind that she might have recognized me as someone who would provide a sympathetic ear if she wished to unburden herself about her husband's shortcomings.

The meal cooking on the fire—I could tell from its smell— was boiled bacon and cabbage. A large black pot hung just above the embers, attached to a hook suspended from a cast-iron arm that swung across the fire. The lid of the pot was upside down and in it a cake of bread was cooking. I watched as Mrs. O'Neill leaned in to poke the fire, the glow from the turf illuminating her already heat-reddened face.

Mrs. O'Neill was famous for her hair and I took this opportunity to stare at it. It was, of course, pinned up—red, thick, shining—without either a gray hair or the fading of color that usually comes with middle age. How Mrs. O'Neill kept her lovely hair in this condition was a question I had heard discussed in both drawing room and kitchen. Years ago, a widow of a Bagnold cousin and thus, as Grandmother invariably remarked when her name came up, no blood relation, had asked Mrs. O'Neill to unpin her hair. Mrs. O'Neill had done so, not offended by the impertinent request, and had shaken it out, displaying it in its full glory. It had reached, uniformly thick, to a few inches below her waist. I had been told that the secret was that it had never, ever, been washed. The idea was slightly shocking to me; I sensed the grown-up reaction was more complicated. Logically, I suppose, either the explanation was not true, in which case there was nothing to be shocked about, or else it was true, and Mrs. O'Neill's beautiful hair vindicated the disregard for hygiene. But I now think the source of information was the root of the drawing-room discomfort; it seems more than probable that Cousin Dorcas, who had asked Mrs. O'Neill to display her hair, was also the one who had asked for the secret of its beauty.

From the distance of time it is hard to see that Cousin Dorcas had done any harm by showing curiosity about Mrs. O'Neill's beautiful hair, but the disapproval was so strong that I still remember it as an example of the kind of behavior that condemned Cousin Dorcas to a life of loneliness and genteel poverty. I don't know whether Mrs. O'Neill was flattered by the unfortunate woman's admiration or thought of her as not being quite a lady, but I am certain that O'Neill shared Grandmother's and Aunt Katie's disapproval. As, it would seem, even now do I.

Mrs. O'Neill felt no need to entertain me. She knew, I think, that I was happy to sit beside her fire and interested enough in what was going on around me without an attempt—hard even now to imagine what form it could have taken—at conversation. To the virtue of silence instilled in early childhood and reinforced almost daily since I had come to Ballydavid, I had added my own observation that the less I said the more I was told or, at least, allowed to observe. I sat by the fire, my feet now warm and my shoes drying, admiring the cheerful decoration of the wall surrounding the fireplace. The wall had been painted a strong blue, the paint not the kind employed on the interior of Ballydavid: It was of a thicker consistency and shinier. On it, in an equally strong red, a pattern had been superimposed—a not quite regular shape, more oval than round, divided into four quarters by thin strips that crossed in the middle. Mrs. O'Neill saw me touch one of the red shapes with the tip of my finger.

"I did it meself with a potato," she said. I could see she must have painted the wall blue and then cut a cross on a potato and dipped it into red paint and applied it to the wall. I envied her the freedom to express herself in such a satisfying way.

I looked around the kitchen, trying to understand the O'Neill living arrangements. The kitchen was where they ate, sat, and spent their indoor waking hours. At one end was a wooden door, but I thought it led only to a cupboard. I knew it was not a bathroom; the privy was separate and lay behind their quarters. On the other side of the passage lay two bedrooms. There was a large stone sink against the wall under the window that overlooked the kitchen courtyard. I wondered how they washed and whether Mrs. O'Neill had to carry all the water she used for cooking from the pump in the yard. I wondered if she used the laundry on the other side of the kitchen, where our clothes and household linens were washed. I wondered if she had a tin tub to set in front of the cheerful fire to bathe in and where such a tub would be kept. I imagined for a moment Mrs. O'Neill sitting in a hip bath, her pale shoulders lit by the fire, her lovely hair pinned on top of her head. I wondered what the kitchen would look like at night lit by the oil lamp that now stood on the well-scrubbed wooden table, and whether it would make the oleograph of the Sacred Heart on the wall over the table seem even more disturbing.

"The Major will be over for his dinner," Mrs. O'Neill said, glancing toward the window. There was no clock in the room, and I thought she was looking at the angle of the light in the courtyard to gauge how close it was to when O'Neill would be in for his dinner and Uncle William would arrive for the meal Grandmother would describe as luncheon. Then I remembered that my uncle had gone to Dublin.

"But——" I started.

"He was turned back. At Athy."

I remembered the increased tempo and bad temper in our kitchen and wondered if the altered lunch menu was the result of an instruction from the drawing room or information passed from the stable yard. I thanked Mrs. O'Neill for her hospitality and, avoiding the kitchen, went back into the main house through the side door. As luck would have it, no sooner had I opened the door and stepped inside than I met Aunt Katie carrying Oonagh and about to put her outside.

"There you are. Where's your coat—and your shoes——" She shook her head. "Run upstairs and wash your hands. Uncle William is coming to lunch."

I scurried past her, hurrying to avoid further discussion of my inadequate outdoor garb.

"And brush your hair," Aunt Katie called after me, but I could tell she was thinking about something else.

Sonia was at lunch. She looked her best, with her hair becomingly done and a little color in her cheeks. After Grandmother had glanced once or twice in her direction, I began to understand there might be a little too much color in her face; it seemed possible that rouge had made its debut at Ballydavid. In anticipation of some subtle communication of disapproval, I sank an inch or

two in my chair. In a different way, each of these adults held some
influence over my life: I answered to Grandmother; but it was
Aunt Katie who oversaw my well-being; Uncle William, a man
whose every whim was deferred to, could and sometimes did intervene in any way he chose; Sonia was the weakest link, unless
one was dealing with the supernatural, and since I was far from
sure we might not be, I did not discount her.

Uncle William had been describing the frustrations of his
aborted journey to Dublin. The train, as Mrs. O'Neill had told
me, had been stopped at Athy.

"I told the station master I would spend the night at the hotel
and travel on the next day. But he said it might be several days before the train was running again."

"But why didn't they tell you at Waterford?" Aunt Katie
asked. "Before you set off? Surely they must have known? Or
had there been an accident?"

There was a moment of silence. Something about Aunt
Katie's question did not ring true.

"When I got home I telephoned the Kildare Street Club, but
the telephone was out of order."

Grandmother's and Aunt Katie's expressions were expectant—a telephone that didn't work was not so unusual; Sonia
seemed to be thinking about something else.

"On the way over I saw two telegraph poles cut down. I didn't
get any post that wasn't local this morning. Did you?"

Grandmother paused a moment, thinking, then shook her
head.

"Newspapers?"

"Sometimes the mail boat's late—submarines, they say. But
that wouldn't affect anything from Dublin."

"I think something may have happened," Uncle William said.

Chapter 9

SOMETHING HAD HAPPENED. But it took days before we found out what it was and longer still until the hysteria and rumor abated. Gradually the facts became known; and depending on the class, political affiliation, race, or religion of the speaker, they were interpreted. As time went on, views and opinions changed, almost all to a position of greater sympathy with the revolutionaries. Now they are patriots and heroes. Rightly, I think, although only a few saw them as such in the days and weeks following the revolt that became known as the Post Office Rising.

At the time the rising was not generally popular. 150,000 Irishmen had enlisted in the British Army, and their families were strongly opposed to the revolutionaries. The more conservative patriots who believed Home Rule would be granted at the end of the war thought this revolt could only hurt their cause; the Home Rule bill had twice been passed in the Commons, although it had been struck down in the House of Lords. Even those who shared the beliefs of the revolutionaries could see that the rising, first planned for Easter Sunday, officially cancelled, then reignited by a splinter group to take place a day later without the promised German arms and lacking public support, was another doomed sacrificial gesture. That the war had made Ireland more prosperous than usual meant the level of discontent was lower than it had been.

The reception Casement was given on his arrival in Ireland could be seen as a metaphor for the gap between the idealistic desires of the revolutionary leaders and the wishes of the greater part of the citizenry. On Good Friday, Casement, Monteith, and the solitary member of the Irish Brigade landed at Banna Strand. It was early morning, not yet light. Their dinghy had capsized in the cold, rough water and they had had to scramble ashore. Casement hid himself in the ruins of an old fort, and the other two left and tried to make contact with the local Volunteers. Within hours of his landing Casement was under arrest. He had not met with any practical sympathy since he landed in the country he wanted to liberate. Every one of the Irish country people—the farmer walking along Banna Strand who saw the sunken dinghy and informed the police, the servant girl who saw the strangers and reported them, the small boys who saw Casement surreptitiously drop the shredded piece of paper on which the code was written and who retrieved it and took it to the police station—had treated him as an enemy. The jail in which Casement spent the night was a small, far-from-secure room attached to a country police station; it would not have been difficult to rescue him, yet no one did.

By the night of Good Friday, the government in Dublin believed an edgy moment had safely passed. Casement was in jail; two of the men who were to meet him had, mistaking their whereabouts, driven off the end of a pier and drowned; an advertisement by the IRB calling off the parade scheduled for Easter Sunday had appeared in the newspapers. Since the parade was where the authorities assumed the rising would have begun, military leave cancelled in anticipation of a revolt was now reinstated and British officers stationed in Dublin were looking forward to a day's racing at Fairyhouse.

But on Easter Monday, the revolutionaries took over the General Post Office on Sackville Street and made it the center of operations. They also occupied the Royal College of Surgeons, the Four Courts, Jacob's biscuit factory, and Boland's Mills; and there were isolated local risings in the countryside.

The besieged Post Office held out for five days before the survivors surrendered and walked out onto Sackville Street with their hands above their heads. The crowd that watched as they were led away was not sympathetic. Similar surrenders took place at other strongholds. A small local rising in Ashbourne, in north County Dublin, was successful enough to hold out until the order to surrender came, but those at Enniscourty, Athenry, and Ferns had already been quelled. We had little reliable information, and these facts came to us in dribs and drabs and in the form of rumor. A week after the Rising, many telephone exchanges were still not operating, the trains were not running, and there were restrictions on where motorcars could be driven. But by then we knew that a not-popularly-supported revolt had taken place, that there had been blood spilled and buildings burned, and that the surviving ringleaders had been arrested. And we already feared that the authorities were going to make a bad situation worse.

The government forces prevailed: The rising was put down, the leaders imprisoned, the populace largely unsympathetic. That should have been the end of it, but it wasn't.

Terrible damage to life and property had taken place. By the time of surrender 450 people had been killed and over 2,500 wounded. Sackville Street, a particularly good example of urban Irish architecture, had been looted and much of it burned. Liberty Hall was shelled by a gunboat; martial law was declared; and Sir John Maxwell, given absolute powers, arrived from England. Large-scale arrests, courts-martial, and imprisonments followed.

In my family there was no sympathy for the revolutionaries, either those executed or imprisoned, but there was also a feeling of disdain for the high-handedness of the government and the stupidity of its actions. Whatever the shortcomings of my family, naïveté was not one of them, and they knew well enough that although the power of the British Empire was great enough to absorb the consequences of most blunders and brutality, there would now be a changed relationship between the Anglo-Irish landowners and the government in Westminster. Over which lay the unresolved and shifting shadow of Home Rule.

And there was at least one death that sat very badly with the Anglo-Irish and that was not dismissed as an unfortunate occurrence of war. Francis Sheehy-Skeffington, a popular Dublin figure, had been shot. Sheehy-Skeffington would have been considered by my family and most of the Anglo-Irish we knew as, at best, an eccentric. He was a campaigner for all sorts of ideas whose time had not yet come, most of them unsympathetic to the stratum of society to which he belonged. He was a vegetarian and a teetotaler (eccentric), a socialist (unacceptable), an advocate for women's rights and a pacifist (beyond the pale). While he was alive he could be laughed at as an eccentric unwilling to exclude any bee from his ethical bonnet, but dead, he became an Anglo-Irish Protestant who had been shot by government forces. And not by a stray bullet. He had been randomly arrested on a Dublin street, used as a hostage, and had witnessed the shooting of an unarmed boy. He had then been, with two journalists, shot on the orders of Captain Bowen-Colthurst, an Anglo-Irish officer in the English army. Bowen-Colthurst eventually stood trial and was found guilty but insane. No one was placated.

The Countess Markievicz, from an old and distinguished Anglo-Irish family, had been one of the actual revolutionaries. She was another eccentric; but, when one included Casement, there were suddenly three of our own dramatically before us, in the news and their names on the tip of every tongue.

Every member of my family was distressed and uneasy, aware that the political situation was tenuous and inflammable. It did not occur to them that they were in any physical danger, and I think they were right in that assumption. Even later, when houses were burned, almost always the family was given a short period of time to remove itself and as many valuables as could be saved before the house was set alight. Grandmother and Uncle William were respected by the country people, and we all knew that if Ballydavid or Ballinamona went up in flames it was more likely to be caused by a chimney fire or one of the faulty paraffin lamps used to light the large, shadowy rooms.

EACH DAY THAT WEEK Uncle William came to lunch. Each day he told Grandmother and Aunt Katie what he had learned since the day before, separating—fairly accurately as it turned out—hard fact from unpleasant fiction. The stories, too quickly disseminated to be genuine misunderstanding, reflected badly on those who told them and those who believed them; it was now evident what each religion, class, and faction thought the other capable of. The ugliest stories, owing more to imaginative fear and anger than to fact, pertained to Sir Roger Casement.

Uncle William, it seemed to me, was more embarrassed by than angry with Casement. He was dismissive of the stories of Casement offering to betray his fellow revolutionaries in return for his life, and outraged that these rumors could all be traced to the same source: the car that had come from Dublin to take a schoolmaster from Gort back to face charges of gunrunning. Uncle William's outrage, embarrassment, and confusion after Casement had landed in Ireland and been arrested were a pale foreshadowing of things to come.

It is hard for me now to gauge how aware Uncle William, Grandmother, and Aunt Katie would have been of Casement prior to his arrest. I think that since Casement came from the north of Ireland and from a respectable Protestant family they would have known and been pleased that he had been given a knighthood for his humanitarian services in the Belgian Congo and the Putumayo. Their train of thought would almost immediately, I imagine, have taken them to condemnation of the Belgians, whose rapacious colonization was responsible for the atrocities in the Congo. The unspoken thought, by these children of the Empire, would have been that it was this kind of behavior that gave colonialism a bad name.

Grandmother and Aunt Katie thought Casement a traitor. Uncle William at this stage held the same opinion as Casement's friend, Sir Arthur Conan Doyle, the creator of Sherlock Holmes. Conan Doyle maintained and would maintain—long after the explanation was acceptable to the British public (it always enraged Casement himself)—that Casement, his health destroyed from exposure to the climate of the Congo and the Putumayo, had also suffered mentally and emotionally from the horrors he had witnessed and could no longer be held accountable for his actions. Even now, with Casement's sparse remains in their hero's grave at Glasnevin Cemetery, I am sure Conan Doyle was right.

Sunday had been the afternoon of our attempt to contact a spirit on the other side. Monday, Uncle William had been turned back at Mullingar; and although we still did not know it, revolutionaries had seized the General Post Office on Sackville Street. On Tuesday, Uncle William had invited himself to lunch and warned us that a revolution might have broken out.

During lunch on Wednesday, having sifted through the rumors we chose not to believe—as much, I now think, on aesthetic grounds as those of probability—for any aspect that might contain plausible fact, Grandmother and Uncle William discussed what the English government would do with Casement now that it presumably had him under lock and key in Dublin. Uncle William said that, whether or not Dublin was in the throes of a rising, the authorities would get him across the Irish Sea to face justice in England as quickly as possible.

"The last thing they need at Dublin Castle right at this moment is a man like Casement as a prisoner," Uncle William said. Although he had spoken with the authoritative tone he used when delivering an opinion on political or military matters, he now paused. His thought—that none of us knew whether Dublin Castle was still in government hands—was implicit, unspoken, but shared by every member of the family. And, probably, by the subdued and completely silent Sonia. During the lull in the conversation, a policeman bicycled up the avenue.

I was the first to see him. The local representative of day-to-day law and order was a handsome young man with curly hair. The son of a Fermoy farmer, he was, I had been told, a great favorite at the local dances. I expected him to go around the side of the house to the kitchen entrance. But when he reached the part of the avenue where the slope became steeper, he got off his bicycle and pushed it up the remaining few yards of the avenue onto the gravel and past the dining-room window to the front door.

Aunt Katie, I think, must have seen him go by, but Uncle William, having expressed himself fully on Casement and having little interest in dissenting views, was now lecturing Grandmother on the benefits of installing a wind charger at Ballydavid. I listened for the knock on the front door. Beside me, Aunt Katie stiffened her neck and turned her head. Several moments passed. I imagined the policeman dismounting his bicycle, adjusting the small metal stand that would allow him to leave it upright without leaning it against one of the pillars of the veranda, removing the bicycle clips from the cuffs of his trousers, fishing a notebook and pencil out of his pocket, and taking a moment to compose himself before knocking too loudly on the front door.

"Whoever can that be?" Grandmother asked, ready to be irritated by a tradesman's delivery boy who should have gone to the back door, or by a call from a neighbor naïve enough to eat her midday meal at some outlandishly early hour and ignorant enough to assume that the denizens of Ballydavid also did.

A long pause followed the knock; this time we all waited, listening. I imagined Bridie coming from the kitchen, tying her apron, crossing the hall, opening the front door. I thought Bridie, who could be stern, might be lecturing the policeman on his misguided approach and timing. If this was the case, she failed to carry her point.

"It's the police, Your Ladyship."

"The police, Bridie?"

Grandmother became a full inch taller. It was not clear to me whether she was expressing disapproval of the breach of etiquette in the time and place of this visit or if she were about to rephrase the question in the manner she would, in the future, expect Bridie to employ the next time she found a policeman on our doorstep.

"I'll deal with this, Verena," Uncle William said, wiping his mouth and moustache with his napkin as he stood. Although Grandmother and Uncle William were not closely related, they were part of the same family—not only because her sister was Uncle William's stepmother but because he was a distant cousin of her dead husband—and he occasionally addressed Grandmother by her Christian name. I'm not sure he was ever entirely comfortable doing so; at any rate, he didn't do it often.

"Really, William, I think I——"

But Uncle William was already almost at the dining-room door. Grandmother expressed her disapproval of his high-handed manner with a sniff and by saying "really" once more.

Again we waited. I thought, inconsequentially, that if we were to have the wind charger that Uncle William was advocating—repeating his arguments at each visit as though it were only Grandmother's inability fully to grasp its benefits that prevented its immediate implementation—there could be, instead of the door knocker, an electric bell by the front door that rang in the kitchen. The idea seemed appealing, but I would have found it difficult to say in what way it would be an improvement over our present arrangement.

I could hear male voices in the hall, but not clearly enough to have a sense of the tone of the conversation. Beside me Aunt Katie fidgeted nervously.

"It's not—it couldn't be about—anything to do with those—those pheasants?" she said at last.

"What *are* you talking about?" Grandmother said crossly.

I think she knew as well as I did that Aunt Katie had a bad conscience about the pheasants she from time to time bought at the kitchen door, usually from my red-haired hero. Aunt Katie used to make an uncomfortable joke about their having been poached from the Ballydavid coverts; she was now, I think, considering the possibility that it wasn't she who had been robbed but that she had instead been a receiver of stolen property.

Grandmother was as well aware as I was that it had been some time since a pheasant had been bought at the kitchen door and that no local boy would offer us game after the end of the shooting season. But her irritation at having been treated as a child or an incompetent by her younger sister's stepson rankled, and she felt no need to reassure that sister that she was unlikely to face arrest as an accessory after the fact to poaching.

I listened and waited. There was the disquieting association of an unexpected knock at the front door with death and violence: the telegram that told us my uncle Sainthill was dead, the men with guns and petrol cans arriving at Mrs. Hitchcock's house late at night. I did not think the policeman himself a threat, but I was afraid his arrival might mark another dramatic change in our lives in some not specified but unpleasant way. I knew his visit had nothing to do with pheasants.

I thought also about how Grandmother's seemingly boundless power had been checked—casually, in her own house, by one of her guests—because he was the eldest male member of the family. I had thought of Grandmother in the same way that I thought of Queen Victoria; it had not occurred to me there could be a limit to her power and moral authority. At Ballydavid she was Victoria, O'Neill her Melbourne.

"He—your son—liked to shoot pheasants?" It was the first we had heard from Sonia for several days, her tone as much an observation as a question.

As she spoke, she indicated Uncle Sainthill's portrait with a movement of her head, looking from Grandmother to the painting. Her eyes did not return to Grandmother but remained thoughtfully looking at the man whose loss even I now felt. Grandmother did not reply but made a small nod.

"He, ah, had a gun? He was a good shot." Neither was quite a question, it was more as though she were leading Grandmother's thought gently in some not specified direction.

"Of course," Grandmother said, and waited for Sonia to reveal her thoughts.

Uncle William returned to the dining room, closing the door behind him and bringing his hands together in a gesture that told us he had dealt with the policeman in a satisfactory manner.

"He came for the guns. I told O'Neill to take Saint's and Hugh's guns down to the police station—and his own shotgun; he'll have to give the crows a temporary cease-fire—keep them safe until this all blows over."

My uncle then sat down and readdressed himself to his bread-and-butter pudding, apparently unaware of the chilly silence that greeted his words. Sonia nodded slightly and thoughtfully; Aunt Katie looked at her plate; Grandmother drew herself up another half inch and stared at Uncle William. I watched carefully while sitting quiet and still; it was a moment when I would have welcomed being excused from the table.

"You told O'Neill to take the guns to the police station? Without consulting me?"

"It's dangerous to have guns in the house. You know that. It's just asking for trouble. Much safer if everyone knows you don't have any."

"And your Greeners? Are they at the police station?"

Uncle William colored slightly. But he recovered himself.

"They'll be taken over this afternoon."

"So," Sonia said thoughtfully, "all the guns will be in the same place."

Two nights later, four men in a stolen car, already well armed, raided the police station and met little resistance. They took away with them a good selection of sporting guns and ammunition. Grandmother, when she was told about it, did not comment, although one side of her mouth twitched in the beginning of an angry smile.

UNCLE WILLIAM WAS NOW constantly at Ballydavid. He came every day for lunch, arriving in the late morning and staying until after tea. I wonder now if in this protective mode he had offered to stay overnight at Ballydavid or if he had suggested we should all move temporarily to Ballinamona. I think it unlikely that he did for a variety of reasons, among them an unwillingness to admit the possibility of danger as well as the greater vulnerability of a house whose occupant was away from home. He may also have felt a reluctance to show lack of confidence in the authorities, the social order, or the position of either householder in his respective community.

In the meantime, it was necessary for everyday life to be carried on as though nothing were out of order. Some small changes in routine and a greater carefulness about how one talked and in front of whom were the only outward signs of watchfulness. The short Easter holidays were over, and on the Monday morning a week after the Rising, Clodagh and I were to resume lessons in the Glenbeg schoolroom.

Grandmother did not usually concern herself with arrangements, and it was rare for her to issue instructions herself rather than delegating them to Aunt Katie. I was surprised when she announced a change in my daily routine while we were sitting in the drawing room, engaged in the minor pastimes that made up our daily lives. Sonia's lack of handiwork during these stretches of time seemed to emphasize how temporary her status was within the household.

"Tomorrow morning you'll be riding over to Glenbeg. Patience will be ready for you at quarter to nine."

As with all changes at Ballydavid, particularly ones that entailed some aspect of privilege or promotion, a whole range of questions was raised, but I did not ask any of them.

"O'Neill will accompany you," Grandmother added.

That answered my first question, and my feeling was one of relief. The prospect of riding a couple of miles along the road without an adult to intervene on my behalf if Patience took it into her mind to go her own way seemed better addressed in the future. I was also, most of the time, afraid—in an unspecified way—of revolutionaries. These fears were at their most extreme at night, while I was lying in the dark, the only person upstairs, listening to the old house settling on its timbers and to unidentified noises caused by the wind or small animals outside. The sound of a mouse in the attic overhead would leave me rigid with fear, imagining a troop of rough men armed with my uncle's beautifully made guns, each carrying petrol and rags, waiting only for me to fall asleep before descending to kidnap me and burn down the house. It would have seemed almost willful to have given them the opportunity of scooping me up, and possibly Patience, too, as, conveniently alone, we trotted along the Woodstown road.

"Times are uncertain, but there is nothing for you to be afraid of. I'd like you to be careful of what you say to O'Neill or in front of the maids."

This was an unnecessary instruction but, remembering my tactlessness on the subject of Roman Catholicism on the way to the graveyard at the Abbey Church, I blushed.

"Yes, Grandmother."

I would have liked to have known how I was to be dressed when I came down to breakfast the following morning, but I thought I would ask Aunt Katie about that later. It was hard to imagine that I would spend the day at Glenbeg dressed much as I would for a day's hunting, but it was equally hard to imagine hopping up on Patience in a neat skirt with woolen stockings and my new shoes that buttoned across the instep.

"And it would be better to be seen and not heard if you eat lunch in the dining room at Glenbeg." Grandmother's tone was not the warning against bad or ignorant behavior that her words might have suggested. I understood her to be advising me about how to behave in the presence of people less worldly than she and, by implication, I were.

Uncle William came in and all discussion of domestic arrangements stopped. I had come to dread his arrival since he was the one most likely to have some new and unsettling news, announc-

ing it in a semi-humorous manner that only accentuated its horror and his anger. I had begun to think wistfully of the boredom
of our recent uneventful lives. But that afternoon his amusement
seemed, if not entirely good natured, genuine.

"Strangman, at the club, told me that it took Mrs. Hitchcock
three days to get back to Dublin from Fairyhouse."

"Three days? However did she——" Aunt Katie was shocked
and confused, and slightly disapproving. I thought she might be
imagining, as I was, Mrs. Hitchcock, fashionably dressed for the
race meeting, making her way back to the city. And wondering
how she had done it. I pictured her making her way along back
roads over the Wicklow Mountains wearing her little slippers
trimmed with swan's-down.

"It took most people four," Uncle William said with a grin.
"And of course when she got there—she'd been staying at the
Shelbourne——"

The Shelbourne Hotel was the tallest building on St. Stephen's
Green, and government troops had taken it over when the revolutionary unit, of which the Countess Markievicz was second-in-
command, had occupied the nearby Royal College of Surgeons.

"Revolutionary martyrs are a small enough group for a certain open-mindedness about the sanity of their recruits to be necessary," Uncle William began. I tried not to listen. Countess
Markievicz was in prison.

When we first learned the Shelbourne had been occupied by
the army, with shots fired and returned, we all thought of Mrs.
Hitchcock. Then we thought of Sonia's words and wondered, but
we had said nothing. Looking back, I can see that this prediction,
so quickly and dramatically fulfilled, bought Sonia a little more
time at Ballydavid. Although the political situation itself would
have made travel arrangements difficult—and where she would
have gone I still cannot imagine.

May 1916

Chapter 10

THE MONDAY FOLLOWING the Rising was one of the
most beautiful days of the year, a "pet day," Bridie said, as
she put into a soft bag the skirt and shoes that I would change
into at Glenbeg. I wore over my jodhpurs a navy blue jersey that
my mother had knitted. It was short at the wrist: I had grown
since I had come to live at Ballydavid. There were two badly retrieved dropped stitches on the front, and I hoped the jersey would
soon be replaced by one from Aunt Katie's more reliable needles.

Swallows had built nests in the barn and under the eaves,
and, while Patience stood uncharacteristically still beside the
mounting block, they darted about the stable yard, in and out of
the barn through the wide, open doors. The morning was cool
and sunny, and a low mist still lingered at the foot of the pasture
below the house. It seemed as though tender new leaves had come
out during the night. I felt a wave of gratitude and happiness to
be part of the most beautiful place on earth. Patience was on her
best behavior and I rode her with a new confidence. It was as
though I saw, for the first time, spring. I longed to walk through
the woods which now seemed full of, not hobgoblins and revolutionaries, but young animals and pleasant surprises.

Jock followed us down the avenue, along the road and to Glenbeg. He went home with O'Neill. Later, when I rode there by myself every school day, he would sometimes come with me and would spend the day in the stable yard or on the lawn outside the schoolroom window.

I didn't like Clodagh, but I liked and admired Miss Kingsley. I had tried to like Clodagh; she was the only candidate for a best friend or playmate, and I was sometimes, although not often, lonely.

Miss Kingsley was clever, funny, and subversive; these admirable qualities were *faute de mieux* restricted to the schoolroom. For a governess, self-effacement was a quality at least as important as being able to read, write, add, and teach basic French and the piano. Her story was not an unusual one. She was the youngest child of a rural dean and his consumptive wife, and there had never been any question but that she would stay at home to look after her parents in their old age. She was, I suppose, lucky that her father did not long survive her mother's death, although life as a governess to Clodagh Bryce would not have been most people's idea of freedom. Despite the prospects her life held— employment as a kind of upper servant until she was too old to work and a lonely, poor old age, dependent perhaps on handouts from the fund for Irish Distressed Ladies—Miss Kingsley behaved as though she were merely biding her time until her real future revealed itself.

The morning was spent in the usual pattern of lessons. We started with a reading from the New Testament, mild religious instruction being part of the basic curriculum; then arithmetic, requiring no great effort on my part since Clodagh still had not caught up with what I had learned in London; spelling; geography, coloring in each province on our maps, marking the rivers and principal cities and some of the smaller towns close to where we lived; French (we struggled through a page of *Madame Souris*); and history. We were learning about the Crusades: the history book we studied described brave Christians attempting to free the Holy Land, slaughtered by Infidels and dying of foreign diseases, good intentions gone sadly wrong; Richard Coeur de Lion the epitome of the good, the noble, the brave. Our governess took a different view.

Before lunch Miss Kingsley dictated a paragraph of *Children of the New Forest*. Clodagh and I then each read a page aloud, and Miss Kingsley read us the rest of the chapter. For me this was one of the most pleasurable times of my day. I loved the book; I enjoyed being read to; and Miss Kingsley was one of my heroines. For Clodagh, the chapter of Captain Marriot's tale was of no interest at all; I glanced over at her once and saw that her thoughts were far away.

"Mummy, Miss Kingsley says Richard Coeur de Lion was a thug," Clodagh said at lunch, her apparently innocent statement filling one of the dreary silences of which conversation at the Bryce's dining table largely consisted.

"A thug? Surely not, darling." And Mrs. Bryce glanced enquiringly at our governess.

"Thug. From *thuggee,* a Hindu word," Miss Kingsley said, her tone that of one who takes pleasure in imparting knowledge.

There was a moment of silence, more loaded than those, punctuated by rain against the window and the sound of knives and forks on plates, that had already taken us through most of lunch.

"I see. Well. Really."

And Mrs. Bryce decided to take it no further. I wished Captain Bryce were there, but it was some time since he had been home on leave. A good deal less exciting than Mrs. Coughlan, he, like she, bore the interesting label of an adult slur. I was still trying to work out the properties of what comprised "a temporary gent," but this was not Captain Bryce's only charm. I was very keen to listen to anything he might care to tell me about the beliefs of the British Israelites.

The British Israelites, although they still exist, may now need a word or two of explanation. To sum up their beliefs in a few sentences, their central tenet is that Anglo-Saxons are the true Israelites, the descendants of King David's daughter Zedekiah, and—making the theory irresistible to me—"the isles of the sea" to which she and her followers escaped was Ireland, whence they reached England and became, in a way I no longer remember, the English royal family. A mathematical proof of this belief and the source of several prophecies could be found in the measurements of the Great Pyramid. Once exposed to this truth, I was astounded that no one except me and Captain Bryce was prepared to be interested in it. Aunt Katie and Grandmother were amused and dismissive; Uncle William, entertained enough to make it a running joke at my expense, hurt my feelings; even the maids, who had shown an initial interest, shunned it once they realized it to be a Protestant heresy.

"What news from the pyramids?" Uncle William was sitting by the fire in the drawing room when I got home from lessons. As the days passed, he had started to look and sound discontented. The role of head of the family in a time of crisis was wearing thin. Especially since news had started to seep down from Dublin.

The Kildare Street Club, bastion of the Ascendancy, and where Uncle William, had the rising not taken place, would have been staying, was close to the center of events; those members in residence at the time unable to leave. I had at first wondered if my uncle was happy to have escaped the rising or if he rather wished he had been in the thick of it. When I heard that page boys had been sent out with tea and trays of bread and butter for the soldiers and that a member had narrowly escaped a bullet (a government soldier had seen him at a window of the club and thought him to be pointing out the location of government soldiers on the roof to revolutionary snipers), I no longer wondered. I knew Uncle William was deeply disappointed to have missed the excitement, the male camaraderie, the illusion of a return to military life, youth, and adventure. And he would have been happier away from Grandmother's disdainful eye. There was no statute of limitations on the subject of the stolen guns.

"Captain Bryce is in France." I sighed before I answered.

Uncle William looked at me for a moment; he recognized dumb insolence when he saw it but was not quite sure whether to reprove or ignore it. He glanced at Grandmother; I, too, watched her from the corner of my eye. But Grandmother appeared to have noticed nothing.

"And what did you learn at school today?"

"We learned 'Lord Ulin's Daughter.' Would you like me to recite it to you?"

"Alice, dear, run upstairs and change for tea," Aunt Katie said, looking up from her tapestry work.

When I came back a few minutes later, Bridie had brought in the tea tray and with it the second post that O'Neill and I had stopped for on the way home. Grandmother was reading a letter. It was the first mail we had received since the Rising that included letters with English stamps. Aunt Katie poured me a cup of weak tea and I went to sit beside Sonia.

Sonia was quiet. She didn't look well. She seemed smaller, paler, and older, as though she had subsided during the past week. She patted my hand and asked how Patience had behaved; her voice was quiet, almost weak, and I felt she was looking for a smile or a kind word.

"Did you ever meet the Countess Markievicz in Paris?" It was a question I had wanted to ask for some time.

Sonia looked at me vaguely, but before I could reframe my question—how many countesses could there have been in Paris?—Grandmother spoke.

"Rosamund Gwynne," Grandmother said, when she had finished reading her letter. She folded it and put it back in its envelope. "Rosamund Gwynne writes that she would like to visit."

Uncle William laughed; it came out as a kind of bark. "She seems rather an inconvenient young woman. An odd moment to ask oneself to stay, or perhaps she's merely unobservant and hasn't noticed they're mopping up after something damn like a revolution at the moment."

"It seems she's already in Ireland—she's stopping with some people—an army family—in the North. She had been going to go to Dublin, but now she's thinking of changing her plans."

"I suppose we'd better..." Aunt Katie's voice trailed off; she seemed to lack the energy necessary to set in motion the domestic arrangements of hospitality. "Does she say anything—anything that...?"

Again she left the sentence unfinished, but we all knew she was asking her sister whether the letter contained any clarification of the unofficial engagement.

"No. Just that she is *so* looking forward to meeting us. And that she's going to be staying with the Bryces. Apparently she is an old friend of Elaine Bryce—oh dear." Grandmother sighed, then drew in a deep breath and sat up even straighter. "I shall write to her and say we look forward to seeing her and then I shall write to Mrs. Bryce and ask them to come to lunch."

"But don't you think we're meant to—?" Aunt Katie sounded increasingly unhappy.

"I'm quite sure we are. But this Miss Gwynne will be in the neighborhood in ten days, and, if I have a letter from Hubert in the meantime, I shall write to her again and ask her to stay. Otherwise we'll wait and see. I know nothing, and it will be up to her to tell me if she is engaged to my son. She won't find me as easy to manipulate as Mary."

"I'm sure she won't," Uncle William said. "She sounds quite a determined young woman—maybe Hugh won't get away so easily this time."

He made it sound as though Uncle Hubert had a wake of broken engagements and breach-of-promise suits behind him. Grandmother was not amused. Her son had been a widower for little more than a year and he had also lost a child, although I don't remember that ever being spoken of, the death of small children born in foreign climes a sad but not infrequent occurrence. But Grandmother knew that if she protested she would be giving Uncle William a cue to be funny about the Russian Adventuress.

"And imagine having a daughter-in-law on cozy terms with the Bryces! I think I prefer the sound of the Russian tart he took to meet Mary."

"William, dear," Aunt Katie said faintly.

"So did you—did you ever meet the Countess Markievicz in Paris?" I asked Sonia.

She looked at me, every bit as puzzled as she might well be. It took her a moment to answer.

"No," she said. "She is a girl from a good Irish family and I was a poor refugee. We didn't move in the same circles."

And she started to cry. A handkerchief held to her face, she rose and left the room.

"And now she's in prison in Dublin," Uncle William said grimly. "A girl from a good Anglo-Irish family waiting to be shot."

It was my turn to burst into tears and run out of the room.

THE FIRST WEEK in May. It seems to me now the change in seasons used to be more beautiful: warmth and fullness, the small green buds now open and pale, the farmyards and fields full of young animals and birds, the first fragile shoots of the year's crops pushing through the earth. It is not imagination only that makes sweeter the memory of the fresh, light smell of the countryside, the flowers and blossom on the trees; this was a time before motorized vehicles were common, and the fields were still fertilized with manure from the stables and cow shed, and, if a potato field lay close to the sea, long-tendriled seaweed would be spread over the ridges.

But the first week of May 1916 was also one during which we all waited for the next horrible thing to happen. We went through the motions of our day to day lives behaving as though the world as we had known it would continue if enough of us pretended nothing irreparable had taken place. We flinched when we learned of each new horror and, although we were still angry at the revolutionaries who had willfully caused so many to be killed and who had destroyed so much of Dublin, now we were appalled at the authorities who were compounding their initial mishandling of the Rising. And then we went on with our lives: lessons for me; the running of the household for Aunt Katie; for Grandmother, letters to my unfortunate mother— who, I like to imagine, was more concerned with her daughter's well-being in the wake of a revolt than in trying to remember some additional nuance of Rosamund Gwynne's visit that would allow the family to decide whether to clasp her to its collective bosom or turn to her a cold shoulder. Only Sonia behaved in a natural—to us unacceptable and foreign—way. She spent most of the day in her room, appearing only for meals and the immediate time in the drawing room before and after them. Listless and pale, she would occasionally venture the opinion that we would all be murdered in our beds.

Casement, imprisoned in London, would not stand trial until the end of June, but the Dublin authorities believed, as did most of England and some of Ireland, that quick, decisive, and stern measures would be the best way to deal with the first real Irish rising against British rule in more than a century.

The first rebels were shot on Tuesday, the day after I went back to lessons at Glenbeg. Ninety of those who had taken part in the Rising were condemned to death, and fifteen of them were executed the week afterward.

The most bloody war in English history was taking place in France, the newspapers scanned for war news and the casualty figures read aloud. Death in the abstract I understood. Uncle Sainthill was never far from anyone's thoughts. I had the usual morbid imagination of a child whose family life was less than conventionally secure, and I would lie awake wondering what would happen when Grandmother died and occasionally torturing myself with fears about unforeseen disasters that would deprive me of either or both of my parents. But the executions in the aftermath of the Rising were different. It was as though the headmistress of the school I used to attend in London had announced at prayers one morning that several of the less satisfactory pupils would be shot that afternoon and—this was where it most felt like a nightmare—although everyone agreed how terrible this was, no one did anything to prevent it.

The executions were spread out over the week. We waited for each day's announcement. In the end, of the ninety sentenced, only fifteen were executed. But at the time it seemed as though the executions would continue day after day until ninety prisoners—eighty-nine men and one woman—had been shot. These harsh realities made no rumor improbable; grim truth accompanied the wild stories about how the secret trials had been conducted. I waited each day for the announcement that Countess Markievicz had been executed.

Constance Markievicz was forty-eight years old at the time of the Rising, closer in age to Grandmother and Aunt Katie—who I considered to be enjoying venerable old age—than to my

mother. But in my imagination the Countess was the age she had
been at the time her portrait was painted. The portrait—painted
well before I was born—was by her husband, Casimir. It shows a
tall woman in an evening dress. Her pale skirt and one slim white
arm dominate two thirds of the painting. She is in profile against
a dark interior with some faintly but effectively painted furniture, and one can see a fine jawline and the kind of distinctive
nose that Grandmother admired. Her hair is, of course, up; a
loose knot on top of her head. I wonder where I'd seen the portrait: most likely as a reproduction in an illustrated magazine.
The daily newspapers had printed photographs of the countess in
military uniform but, though I studied them carefully, I always
thought of her as a tall, slender beauty in an evening dress with a
long skirt and a bodice of a darker material, her shoulders draped
with a light shawl. If such a person should now be waiting in a
cold dark cell for soldiers to take her out at dawn, stand her in
front of a firing squad, and kill her, anything was possible. I was
far, far more frightened of the forces of justice and order who
could do such a thing than I ever was of the revolutionaries whom
Sonia feared.

Public sentiment throughout the country began to change
when it became known that the dying Joseph Plunkett had been
shot and that James Connolly, too badly wounded to stand, had
been tied to a chair for his execution. Anger and horror soon took
the place of apathy and disapproval. Even Grandmother and
Uncle William were shocked and appalled, although mainly
at the stupidity of the authorities. The executions continued all
through the week: Patrick Pearse, schoolmaster and poet; his
brother Willie; Tom Clarke; John McBride, who—an inspiration
to Casement—had raised a brigade in the Boer War to fight the
British. Michael Collins was imprisoned; de Valera was spared
the death penalty—the American Consul claimed him, not quite

accurately, as an American citizen. After the first fifteen, the executions stopped, and by the end of the year the greater part of the prisoners had been released. But the dead were dead. The harm had been done.

It was a time of great uncertainty. We didn't know then that England and her allies would win the war in France, that a second and bloodier revolution in Ireland would not break out any moment, that we would not, as Sonia feared, all be murdered in our beds. I was afraid but not sure what I should fear most. There was no one to ask. I instinctively spent little time in the kitchen those days and was aware of tension when I did visit. It felt as though I'd been pushed out of the kitchen-and-children camp and into that of the drawing room.

The atmosphere was equally dark at Glenbeg, but there my curiosity was once again in play. At Ballydavid, I now dreaded hearing the latest developments in Dublin, but at Glenbeg the new light cast by the views and beliefs of schoolroom and dining room was novel enough for curiosity to balance fear. And it was here that I—and, through me, Grandmother and Aunt Katie— was most likely to learn something to add to the little we knew about Rosamund Gwynne.

Not only was I afraid the Countess Markievicz and Sir Roger Casement and the other condemned revolutionaries would be executed, but I was afraid that Miss Kingsley would lose her job. I knew that she had no home other than Glenbeg and no family of her own. I worried that Mrs. Bryce would send her away without a reference, and then what would become of her? Either Miss Kingsley did not share my fears or she no longer found her disdain for Clodagh and Mrs. Bryce, held in check during less tumultuous times, possible to conceal.

It is likely that Miss Kingsley would not have lasted the weeks following the Rising were it not for Mrs. Bryce's anticipation of

Rosamund Gwynne's visit and my own presence at the lunch table. Mrs. Bryce and Clodagh were proponents of a hard line— a minimal waste of time on the processes of justice and a speedy execution—for the revolutionaries and for Sir Roger Casement. Miss Kingsley was a passionate admirer of Casement—his handsome appearance, I now think, as much a part of her reluctance to think him a traitor as his heroic stand on the Congo and the Putumayo.

No one at Ballydavid, of course, suggested I listen for a few more details about the uncomfortable woman who might be about to marry into our family, but my arrival home from lessons now occasioned a greater level of attention than that to which I had previously been accustomed. Inquiries about my day and what I had learned were no longer absentminded, and any mention on my part of lunchtime conversation made me the center of attention.

"Miss Gwynne and Mrs. Bryce were at school together," I remarked on Wednesday, coming home from my third day of lessons. The Delphic Oracle could not have had a more gratifying reaction.

"Really, dear. And where was that?" Aunt Katie asked, and all eyes looked at me expectantly. I didn't know.

"They both played hockey. Miss Gwynne was captain of the first eleven."

"Was she indeed?" Aunt Katie said, with apparent polite interest. Grandmother closed her eyes briefly and Uncle William laughed. Sonia was resting upstairs: I imagine her immediate future was another subject much discussed while she slept and before I came home in the afternoon.

At Glenbeg, Mrs. Bryce had only me as a source for any clue as to how Miss Gwynne was regarded at Ballydavid. I can't estimate how close the friendship was between Mrs. Bryce and

Rosamund Gwynne, nor can I decide whether Mrs. Bryce was merely curious or if she were trying to discover the lie of the land on behalf of her friend. Since I was a child, I was obliged only to answer direct questions and, since I was partisan, any hint or leading observation of hers could be met with the look of blank, attentive incomprehension I had by now mastered.

Rosamund Gwynne arrived at Glenbeg earlier than we at Ballydavid had expected. Some of her arrangements had fallen through, not surprisingly in light of the troubled state of the country. But it also seemed to us that the unrest and the difficulties of travel caused most people—Sonia, a good example—to stay put longer than they had planned or were expected to stay. Grandmother was of the opinion that at least one hostess had used the Rising to cancel an invitation to Miss Gwynne and another had failed to press her to stay on.

Even I, desperate for excitement not allied with fear or death, was unenthusiastic about the woman who might be about to become my aunt. My mother's disapproval and the unsatisfactory lack of clarity as to an actual betrothal were not the grounds for my reservations; if anything, they offered a possibility of some moments of always welcome drama. I thought it unlikely I would become fond of anyone who was a close friend of Mrs. Bryce—a consideration I knew also counted for something with Grandmother and Aunt Katie—but even more I felt that the interloper, as I thought her, had ousted Mara, of whom I still thought fondly, and that she had, in some way I didn't quite understand but was not prepared to forgive, caused pain to Sonia.

I was the first member of our family apart from Uncle Hubert (although I had entertained myself for an hour the previous evening with the idea that Uncle Hubert was quite unaware of her existence and that the woman claiming to be his fiancée was a German spy) to meet Rosamund Gwynne. I don't know how she and Mrs. Bryce had spent their morning, but Clodagh, Miss Kingsley, and I arrived exhausted at the lunch table. History had, as usual, been where the trouble began. That morning we had read about the Princes in the Tower: the boys, incarcerated in the Tower of London by their uncle, Richard III, and then murdered by him. There was an affecting illustration, not devoid of sentimentality, which upset me more than I was prepared to show. Clodagh, whose imagination it was almost impossible to engage, was merely bored. It may have been frustration with her pupil as well as her own emotional state that caused Miss Kingsley to make an inflammatory remark.

"The Tower of London is where Sir Roger Casement is even now imprisoned," she said, her tone carefully suggesting nothing more than the introduction of a topical reference to make more immediate an historical moment.

"Serves him right," Clodagh said. "He's a traitor and a coward."

There was a moment of silence, during which I once again thought how much I disliked Clodagh and during which Miss Kingsley drew in a slow breath.

"That brings up an interesting ethical question," Miss Kingsley said, "and we might pause for a moment to discuss it. The logical implications of whether a man who is prepared to die for his country can be a traitor. Or a coward."

Clodagh looked at our governess with an expression of dull, offensive boredom. She preferred pronouncement to discussion and shared her mother's disdain for logic. I, too, failed to concentrate on the point Miss Kingsley was making, partly because I was in my imagination placing Casement in the surroundings illustrated in our history book. I could see that the Tower of London was a cold, dark place, and I pitied anyone unfortunate enough to be imprisoned there. I thought of the little princes, of Queen Elizabeth, Sir Walter Raleigh, Lady Jane Grey. I was sympathetic to all of them—although only to Elizabeth during the earlier part of her life, since it was she who later imprisoned and then beheaded her cousin, Mary, Queen of Scots—and I had formed a very poor impression of those who did the imprisoning. Photographs of Casement, a tall, unusually handsome man with a closely trimmed beard, had appeared in the *Morning Post*. I had studied them for a long time. He did not look like a traitor; he wore a tweed suit and his posture was straight and proud. He looked like a gentleman, and his expression, calm, gentle, patient, was that of a saint.

Half listening to Miss Kingsley, I was also struggling with an idea of my own. My family had been soldiers and builders of empire for several generations, and it did not occur to me to question the moral implications of colonialism. The sun never set on the British Empire; most of the map of the world was pink. Christianity and the benefits of British law and government were justification enough—were any needed—for conquering distant, primitive, hot lands and subjugating their inhabitants. I still did not question the right and might of the Empire, any more than I did the standards Grandmother set for herself and imposed upon the rest of us. But it now felt to me that there might be other standards and beliefs that were almost as right, valid, and worthy of self-sacrifice. My sympathy for Casement, Constance Markievicz, and the revolutionaries executed in Dublin that week was also, I was beginning to see, in some way connected to my protective feelings for Mara and Sonia; all of them, I was beginning to think, sacrificed, discarded, or excluded to preserve an order that benefited me and my family. It was with these subversive, if not completely formulated thoughts, that I arrived at the lunch table.

Rosamund Gwynne was about thirty, far too old, it seemed to me, to be engaged to anyone. Had I considered it, I would have realized that she would be the same age as Mrs. Bryce and also

that Uncle Hubert, a widower, was not of an age to marry a debu-
tante. Miss Gwynne, the woman I was apparently to start thinking
of as an aunt, was quite pretty—later I would hear her described
unfairly as "chocolate-boxy"—but she was devoid of any of the
feminine qualities I found attractive or admirable. I studied her
during lunch—not an easy task, since, when I allowed my eyes to
creep in her direction, I often found her looking at me, only, it
seemed, to find me lacking. I studied her in order to be able to describe her to my family and to understand what it was that I found
unlikable. The first and most obvious reason was that I could sense
Rosamund Gwynne did not like me. Why, I wondered. Had Mrs.
Bryce perhaps said something? Or was the antipathy predestined,
mutual, and instinctive? And what was it exactly that I didn't care
for? She wasn't soft or tender like my mother, and her voice wasn't
gentle; she wasn't vulnerable or exotic, emotional or affectionate,
like Sonia; she wasn't straight and noble and admirable like Grandmother or maternal like Aunt Katie. I thought of Bridie, of Mara,
even of Mrs. Coughlan, and knew I would have welcomed one or
all of them into my family rather than this interloper who was
talking not quite comfortably to Mrs. Bryce.

Miss Kingsley, Clodagh, and I remained silent while the conversation between Mrs. Bryce and Miss Gwynne passed from a
dull exchange of memories of girls with whom they had been at
school to, inevitably, the war. By the time we had finished our
shepherd's pie, Miss Gwynne had mentioned the dangerous and
painful word "conscription." I saw Mrs. Bryce look at the maid
who was setting the rice pudding and stewed plums on the serving table, and I was pleased to see that Miss Gwynne's views, with
which I knew her to agree, were causing her discomfort.

"Unmarried men in England have to go. I don't see why
Irishmen shouldn't, too. We're all in it together."

Irishmen were not being conscripted, but, while Miss Gwynne
was outraged that they were exempt, there was widespread and

dangerous anger at the prospect that they might be, and the possibility had led to a new spirit of cooperation between the various nationalist factions. My family believed, as did many others, that conscription was not only likely if the war continued, but that the introduction could lead to a popular revolution.

The maid's face was expressionless; it was impossible to know what she thought or where her family stood politically. The war had made Ireland more prosperous, and farmers who supplied food and wool to England were better off than they had ever before been. Her family might be nationalist and among those the government feared might revolt if conscription were introduced, or they might be prosperous loyalists, perhaps with a son serving in France. I wondered how O'Neill felt, and I remembered the tense moment between him and Nicholas Rowe outside the pub the day of the meet at Herald's Cross. I thought also of the maids telling me that Irish soldiers were more likely to be sent to certain death at the most dangerous parts of the front than were their English counterparts. I thought of Uncle William's anger at what he considered Kitchener's stupidity in refusing to form specifically Southern Irish regiments.

"*Pas devant...*" Mrs. Bryce said faintly, nervously fingering her pearls.

Miss Gwynne looked at her, surprised and, it seemed, not quite sure that she wanted to be interrupted.

"*Pas devant les enfants ou les domestiques,*" Miss Kingsley said pleasantly.

There was a moment of silence while the maid closed the door behind her and while I looked at my place mat. No one had risen from the table to help herself to pudding.

Miss Kingsley continued in the same pleasant conversational tone, still in French: just a couple of sentences—she knew and they knew she knew it—that no one else at the table understood. The only word I recognized was "mademoiselle," but, since my vocabulary was limited to simple descriptions of the domestic life of middle-class mice, it would have been unreasonable to have expected more. For good measure she finished with a smiling, "*N'est-ce pas?*" Another silence ensued before Mrs. Bryce spoke.

"Rosamund," she said. "Rice pudding? And plums. From the old tree at the bottom of the garden. I bottled them myself."

"SHE ASKED ME to call her Aunt Rosamund."

"'She,' Alice?" Grandmother asked.

"Miss Gwynne asked me to call her Aunt Rosamund." I thought it unfair that Grandmother should treat me as a child while benefiting from my almost adult reporting skills. At the same time I was grateful she hadn't asked, as my schoolmistress in London used to, "Who's 'she'? The cat's mother?"

"I don't think that's a very good idea," Grandmother said.

I hadn't thought she would. I didn't think it a very good idea myself.

"So what should I call her?" I allowed a note of weariness, not entirely simulated, to creep into my voice.

"Perhaps you should continue to call her Miss Gwynne, at least until we know her better."

Grandmother's words condemned me to the inconvenience of never addressing Miss Gwynne by name and confirmed my assumption that Uncle Hubert had not been heard from and that my mother had neither remembered any further telling details nor had she added anything that had gained importance in translation at Ballydavid.

"We should ask her to lunch on Sunday," Aunt Katie said. I could see that she was retreating into the reassuring world of food and domestic arrangements. "And the Bryces, of course."

Grandmother allowed her eyes to close for a moment, and I saw Aunt Katie flick a glance at Sonia. Sonia sat, as she now did all the time, in a corner of the sofa. She seemed to have become each day a little smaller and more bedraggled, like a bird losing its plumage. She had said nothing since I had come home, but she followed the conversation with interest. Now she began to cough and held a handkerchief to her face. After a moment, still coughing, she left the room. Uncle William, who had not contributed much to the conversation, although he had seemed somewhat interested and amused by it, watched her speculatively.

"Mrs. Bryce, Miss Gwynne, Clodagh," Aunt Katie said, counting on her fingers, "you, William———," and she continued silently.

"And Miss Kingsley?" I asked timidly. It was less a suggestion than a way of introducing my governess's name into the conversation. I was worried about Miss Kingsley's fate and was seeking reassurance, and, should that not be forthcoming, then information about what might become of her. At the back of my mind, I mingled kitchen stories of eviction, famine, and death with the less dramatic but also horrifying cases for whom Aunt Katie collected subscriptions for the Irish Distressed Ladies Fund.

"An excellent suggestion," Uncle William said, to my surprise. "Miss Kingsley. That could dilute the vulgarity level by quite a lot."

"William," Grandmother said faintly, as though she had not already clearly intimated that the Bryces fell short of her social standards.

"Mrs. Bryce said *pas devant* at lunch today, and Miss Kingsley said quite a lot in French. I don't think they understood her."

Grandmother managed to purse her lips and smile at the same time. Uncle William laughed.

"Roast beef and Yorkshire pudding, of course, and since there will be Alice and Clodagh, perhaps charlotte russe," Aunt Katie said. "I'll write to Mrs. Bryce."

———

"ALICE, DEAR, YOU HAD a bad dream last night. Do you remember what it was about?"

It should not be inferred from my great-aunt's question that any influence emanating from Vienna had wafted west as far as Ballydavid. Nor had Aunt Katie's curiosity about my dream—as would have been the case had it been Bridie asking—been in anticipation of prophetic content. She was, tentatively and euphemistically, attempting a discussion of my resumed sleepwalking, in which she hoped to learn something without telling me anything I didn't already know.

I hadn't known about the sleepwalking until that morning—it was Bridie who told me I had resumed my somnambulistic habits—but for a little time I had been having nightmares; two or three times a week I would awaken during the night so frightened that I did not dare to sit up and light my candle and I would lie immobile until the first light came through my bedroom window.

Aunt Katie had the night before, Bridie told me, come into the kitchen to reassure herself that the house had been properly locked up for the night and had found me at the back door, turning and tugging at the doorknob in an apparent attempt to leave the house. This had occurred early enough for Bridie to be still awake and for her to creep down the back stairs into the kitchen. I had not been able, Bridie said, to open the back door since it was secured with heavy bolts at both top and bottom. I wondered if this was something she should have kept to herself, or perhaps the information she imparted to my sentient waking being would be inaccessible to my sleepwalking persona if I were to make another attempt, while asleep, to leave the house.

Aunt Katie must have known that, if Bridie had seen me, my sleepwalking could no longer be kept secret, but she chose to approach the subject obliquely.

"I had a nightmare," I said, playing the same game.

"What was it about?" she asked.

I shrugged helplessly. Had I been capable of talking about my nighttime fears I would probably have been able to stay put in my bed.

"Monsters?" she asked. I could tell that she was uneasy about even this suggestion, torn between the possibility that she might be offering a new subject for fear and the hope that whatever disturbed me was one of the usual childhood terrors of the imagination. She could have been more convincingly dismissive of, say, witches than she could have of armed revolutionaries.

"I don't know," I said, untruthfully.

Aunt Katie seemed almost reassured. She patted my arm.

"Something chasing you? Running away and not being able to—cry out?"

I nodded; acquiescence seemed the easiest course. My nightmares weren't abstract. They were clear and always the same, although each took its theme a little further and each was a little more specific in its details.

In my dreams I had been condemned to death. The circumstances of my life had not otherwise changed. I was not imprisoned, but I had only four days before I was to be executed. It seemed that no one could help me, and, although everyone was sympathetic to my circumstance, I never had anyone's full attention. Implicit in every one of these nightmares was the never-quite-present Countess Markievicz, who, in her beautiful pale dress, waited in a condemned cell. Roger Casement, with his ascendancy tweed suit and his saintly smile, farther away, made a less substantial member of our condemned trio.

UNCLE WILLIAM HAD NOT been consulted about the placement; for a moment I thought he was going to protest under the guise of modestly pointing out that Grandmother, rather than he, should sit at the head of the table, but, after a moment's hesitation noticed by everyone except possibly Clodagh, he said nothing and pulled back chairs for Mrs. Bryce and Miss Gwynne. Mrs. Bryce sat on his right, Rosamund Gwynne on his left. Sonia and Miss Kingsley were separated from him by Aunt Katie and the dual buffer of Clodagh and me. Grandmother, far from sanguine about her lunch party, was not taking any unnecessary chances.

Uncle William carved. He did it very well; it was a skill he had learned as a senior boy at Repton. When I had first been told this—my father's brief education in New Zealand had not included such refinements—I'd imagined a classroom with a joint of beef on a large platter on every desk, behind which each boy stood with a carving knife and fork while a master at the front of the room demonstrated the proper way of carving a sirloin. It had been explained, to my disappointment, that "learning to carve" merely meant that at lunch the senior boy at each table sliced and dispensed the meat as best he could, learning by trial and error. Uncle William's performance kept him happy. I watched his preliminaries: testing the knife on the edge of his thumb, sharpening the blade noisily, and then stepping up to the sideboard and assessing the joint as though there were several schools of thought as how to approach it. Bridie stood patiently to the side, waiting to carry around the plates.

There was plenty going on and no awkward silences while Uncle William questioned our guests about whether they would prefer rare or better-done beef and gave unneeded instructions to Bridie. It meant, however, that Mrs. Bryce and Rosamund Gwynne were conversationally isolated until he sat down, with only Aunt Katie, herself preoccupied with the serving of food, to encourage small talk. Grandmother was already regretting her decision to place Miss Kingsley and Sonia to either side of her. Sonia remained silent and sipped her wine. A small glass had been poured for each adult guest, and I saw her flick her eyes toward the sideboard to see if a second bottle stood open beside the decanters of port and brandy: None did; wine at lunch was only a token offering, the amount served about the same size as the glass of sherry each had been given in the drawing room before lunch.

Aunt Katie, who should have taken responsibility for entertaining Rosamund Gwynne at least until her stepson sat down, had instead engaged Miss Kingsley in conversation. Miss Kingsley, provided one kept off the current political and military crisis—and assuming one did not choose to steer the conversation into the dangerous waters of Sonia's expertise—was probably the easiest person to talk to at the table. But Aunt Katie, more unnerved by Rosamund Gwynne than I could have otherwise discerned, had managed nothing better than a governess anecdote. I missed her opening gambit, since I was unhappily aware that Sonia, between me and Grandmother, seemed shabbier and less substantial than ever.

"My cousin Florence," Aunt Katie was saying, "when her father was Ambassador to St. Petersburg, was asked to tea by one of the archduchesses, and the Archduchess took her to the nursery to see her children and asked Florence to let her know how they were getting on with their English. Florence told us the little archdukes and duchesses spoke excellent English, but with a strong Waterford accent!"

Miss Kingsley smiled; otherwise no one seemed to find the story amusing. Fortunately at that moment Uncle William returned to the table.

"The Archduchess's children," he said, sitting down heavily, with a hearty laugh, "a strong Waterford accent!"

"What did your cousin tell the Archduchess?" I asked Aunt Katie. I had the feeling that this particular meal was one during which any innocuous conversational gambit, even from a child, would be welcome.

"Oh, I expect she said their English was perfect. What else could she say?"

I now wonder if Aunt Katie had, consciously or not, introduced the subject of accents because she knew I was worried about Miss Kingsley's future at Glenbeg. Was she hinting to Mrs. Bryce that, if she wanted her daughter to grow up to take a place in Waterford society, a good governess could steer the girl past some of the vulgarities and ignorance of social conventions that held back her parents? I don't know, but it seems possible that Uncle William, at least, was making that point.

Before lunch we had had a full account of Rosamund Gwynne's travels around Ireland, and Grandmother, without betraying a glimmer of the curiosity that so appalled her in Mrs. Bryce, now knew the full extent of her putative daughter-in-law's friends and acquaintances in Ireland. She had been staying in the politically more stable—in the sense that those loyal to England were more firmly in charge—north, and I could tell that she found the atmosphere there more sympathetic.

"When did you last hear from Hubert?" Uncle William asked Miss Gwynne, as soon as he was comfortably settled in his chair and had eaten enough of his beef to be certain it met his rigorous standards. (The butcher was a character of some importance in our lives, and our convention was to make sure that the relationship was adversarial enough to keep him on his toes. The butcher with whom Aunt Katie had maintained such an arrangement for years had recently been "left" by her—the word uttered with the same gravity and outrage as though it had been a husband rather than an unsatisfactory tradesman with whom she had severed relations—and both the old ladies and Uncle William watchfully anticipated the moment when the honeymoon period with the new butcher would be over.) "We haven't had a word for over a month—the post is terrible, of course."

"Terrible," Rosamund Gwynne agreed. "And, of course, I

have been traveling and I have had to change my plans, so I'll probably get a whole stack of letters all at once."

Grandmother didn't say anything and her expression remained one of polite interest, but I could see the idea that her only surviving son, from whom she received one letter a month, was inundating this ordinary young woman with "stacks" of what we were supposed to infer were love letters was not one that sat well with her.

I wonder now to what extent Mrs. Bryce and Rosamund Gwynne had planned the course of conversation. I have to assume that Miss Gwynne had confided something close to the true state of affairs to her friend and that Mrs. Bryce had described to her—while glossing over Grandmother's attitude of distant condescension toward herself and her family—the generally haughty and cold atmosphere of Ballydavid and the imperious character of the woman Miss Gwynne planned to have as a mother-in-law. I was very aware that no member of my family had so far mentioned the words "engagement" or "marriage" and that Uncle William was the first to volunteer a reference to Uncle Hubert. I saw Mrs. Bryce gather herself, much in the uncomfortable way that Patience did approaching a jump, for this opportunity to take the conversation to the next stage. It occurred to me that Grandmother would not have given either of her guests the cue they needed to make some reference to the unofficial engagement that, if unchallenged, would establish Rosamund Gwynne's position in our family. Grandmother would score an enormous victory if she could get through the visit without ever acknowledging that my mother had written to her about the engagement. What she wished was to be able to say goodbye to Rosamund Gwynne on the doorstep, with the polite sentiment that she hoped they would meet again sometime. If she could succeed in that, she was capable of allowing Miss Gwynne to stay at Glenbeg for a month without any further contact. Uncle William's approach was different. He believed in getting to the bottom of things, and since, once started, he was prepared to worry his quarry with the single-mindedness and lack of inhibition of a terrier, he often did, even if the process left bystanders bemused and embarrassed. Mrs. Bryce, of course, didn't know this and consequently felt compelled to do something to advance her friend's cause.

"Rosamund has never been to the East," she said.

"When are you planning your visit, Miss Gwynne?" Uncle William asked.

"Oh, please, do call me Rosamund," Rosamund Gwynne said, as she had an hour before in the drawing room. "I don't expect I'll go until Hubert and I are married. But it's such a long time until his next leave that maybe I won't be able to wait——"

Aunt Katie managed a polite and sympathetic smile; Grandmother stiffened as though Rosamund Gwynne's hint that she might not be able to wait was faintly indecent; Uncle William was, or seemed, confused—but again no one picked up the cue.

"But you will be married in London, won't you?" Mrs. Bryce asked, a note of desperation in her voice. "I'm counting on it. St. George's, Hanover Square and clouds of orange blossom."

The silence that followed this was broken only by Aunt Katie's indrawn breath as she glanced involuntarily at Sonia.

"Orange blossom," she said eventually, then tried to collect herself. "June, then—that's the season, isn't it?"

"I'm sure it's grown in greenhouses now for London florists," Uncle William said absentmindedly.

Although each one of us who had been present on Easter Sunday remembered Sonia's words, words that had come seemingly from nowhere, only I had heard Rosamund Gwynne since referred to—by Miss Kingsley at the Bryce's dining-room table—as Mademoiselle.

"Alice will be a dear little bridesmaid." Mrs. Bryce seemed to have lost her head completely.

"I don't think Alice's uncle much likes the scent of orange blossom." It was the first time Sonia had spoken since we sat down to lunch. She said it quietly but clearly, the words hard and graceless.

For a moment no one said anything, but it felt as if everyone in the dining room had been sucked away from the table to either end of the room to form two opposing teams: Rosamund Gwynne, Mrs. Bryce, and Clodagh at one end; my family, with Sonia as a visiting center forward, on the other; Miss Kingsley alone unallied, but no one in much doubt as for whom she would cheer (for her sake, I hoped, silently).

"How do you know?" Clodagh asked in the same unpleasant and superior tone that had made me dislike her when we had first met at my birthday party.

"How would you know?" Rosamund Gwynne asked simultaneously, and in much the same tone. I hated her.

Sonia smiled faintly and looked at her plate. The Ballydavid team knew that Sonia's pronouncements were never expanded upon or clarified. It now occurred to me that Sonia might be speaking metaphorically, and, although I enjoyed a challenge to the claims of Miss Gwynne, I feared for Sonia in the same way that I feared for Miss Kingsley when I saw her overplay her hand.

"Really!" Mrs. Bryce said, her disapproval apparently aimed at Grandmother who she seemed to imply was not able to ensure the behavior of her dependents.

It was Grandmother's turn for a faint smile.

"I'd forgotten," she said. "How odd. Of course. Hugh doesn't like orange blossom; it gives him hay fever—it makes him sneeze and his eyes water."

I wondered, and I wondered if everyone else wondered if what Grandmother said was true. Had she invented Uncle Hubert's allergy to the flower on the spot? She was unlikely to be challenged: Uncle Hubert was on the other side of the world, and, even if

Miss Gwynne wrote to enquire—and unless the engagement was somewhat more definite than it appeared to be, such a question might be hard to word—a denial of his distaste for *Citrus sinensis* could be some months away.

In fits and starts, short silences and shorter banalities, we finished lunch. I ate the charlotte russe without quite tasting it. Soon we were crossing the hall to the drawing room where I imagined our guests would linger for a token moment or two before making their excuses, and then their pony and trap would be brought round to the front door. But it didn't happen like that. The post had arrived while we were eating lunch, and a letter with my mother's handwriting lay on top of two or three others. I saw Grandmother's eye light upon it.

"Katie," she said to her sister. "Why don't you show Mrs. Bryce and Miss Gwynne where they can wash their hands?"

Aunt Katie and Mrs. Bryce turned obediently toward the stairs. The only downstairs water closet in a house inhabited solely by women, the owner not in her first youth, was designated the gentlemen's cloakroom and, thus, women who needed to relieve themselves had to climb the stairs and avail themselves of one of the two drafty bathrooms on the upper floor.

"I don't——" Rosamund Gwynne started to say, before Grandmother interrupted her.

"My room is at the top of the stairs on the right. You'll find—" she said, making a vague gesture that suggested that her guest might wish to readjust her hairpins in front of the winged looking glass on her dressing table.

After a moment, Miss Gwynne followed the others up the stairs. Grandmother picked up Mother's letter and took it into the drawing room. When Mrs. Bryce and Rosamund Gwynne came downstairs, Grandmother was waiting for them in the hall.

"Would you like to see the garden?" she asked, with a quick

glance at Miss Gwynne's feet to make sure she hadn't come to lunch in satin slippers. "It's a little early for there to be much to see, but a stroll after lunch might be nice."

"I think I'll just go and have a word with O'Neill about the wind charger," Uncle William said. The excuse was more genuine than it seemed; Uncle William's answer to political unrest was to improve his house and land: the Rising seemed to have lifted him to a level of determination that would allow him to overrule Grandmother and to install electricity at Ballydavid.

Uncle William disappeared to the stable yard. Sunday afternoon was a time that O'Neill might well have thought his own, but he was always pleased to see Uncle William, and each found in the other an enthusiastic collaborator for his plans, schemes, and projects, both large and small.

Clodagh and I also went round to the stables, pausing only long enough for Miss Kingsley, not included in the original expedition, to run upstairs before we went to visit Patience, an animal that now spent a large part of the day at Glenbeg and was thus hardly a novelty. Somewhere between the dining room and the front door Sonia seemed to have evaporated.

"I don't see why we have to go and see Alice's pony," Clodagh said crossly.

"What would you rather do?" Miss Kingsley asked.

"I want to go home."

"Your mother and Miss Gwynne are in the garden with Lady Bagnold. If you like, you and I could walk home. I don't know how suitable your shoes are, though, for such a long walk."

I was well aware of the inadequacy of the entertainment I was offering, and, after I had given Patience a quartered apple and stroked her lovely, soft nose, we turned back toward the house. A cloud-laden wind was blowing from the west and I could feel a light drizzle on my face.

"Why do you have that woman living with you?" Clodagh asked. "My mother says she's some kind of fortune teller."

"Clodagh," Miss Kingsley said warningly.

"Your grandmother doesn't go to church, does she?"

I muttered something about Sonia being a guest rather than a permanent feature of our household, but Clodagh's last question cast an entirely new light on how Sonia was seen by some of our neighbors. I was worldly enough to have gathered on my own that Sonia was rackety, down on her luck, inconvenient; now I understood that the Bryces and presumably other of our narrow-minded and generally disapproving Protestant neighbors considered Sonia's powers and our exploitation of them wrong and possibly sacrilegious. A grossly exaggerated version of her capabilities had probably circulated through the parish, and doubtless her earlier connection with the scandalous Mrs. Hitchcock had not been forgotten.

The drizzle also brought the grown-ups back to the house, and shortly afterward Grandmother was offering Mrs. Bryce and Rosamund Gwynne tea. The invitation was not intended to be accepted. (I could see on the hall clock that it was not quite three o'clock.) Soon Bridie was dispatched to have the pony and trap brought to the front door.

"Well, this has been delightful," Grandmother said. "We must see each other again soon. Is there any possibility that you might come and stop with us after your visit with Mrs. Bryce?"

Uncle William came into the hall from the door behind the stairs in time to hear this invitation. I flickered a glance at him, but his face was as politely and pleasantly expectant as I hoped mine was.

Rosamund Gwynne was going a few days later to Tipperary and after that to stay with another friend in Queen's County and then back again to Waterford—she seemed to have a large range of hospitable acquaintances—but she would be delighted to visit us in August.

We stood, protected from the light rain by the veranda, as the Glenbeg party got into their trap. Good-byes and thank-yous were mingled with the polite pleasant anticipation of the longer summer visit as Mrs. Bryce took the reins. We waved until they had left the graveled sweep and the pony was trotting down the avenue. For several moments after they had left earshot and after even an unusually long-sighted lip reader could have interpreted our conversation, no one said a word.

"I take it there was something germane in Mary's letter?" Uncle William said eventually, his tone expressionless, as if demonstrating exemplary calm in the face of disaster.

"Not entirely," Grandmother said. "She had a letter from Hubert saying a young woman called Rosamund Gwynne might get in touch with her and that, if she did, Mary was to be nice to her."

"'Might get in touch'?"

"Yes."

"Well, one thing's sure—that woman will have to go."

"Yes," Grandmother said, "but—I don't see quite how. Or where."

"Oh, leave it to me."

And so, casually, Sonia's fate was sealed. Even I saw it could not have been otherwise.

June 1916–August 1916

Chapter 11

"DEATH BY WATER." Maggie, reader of tea leaves and an artist in both the interpretation and pronouncement of what she saw, nodded and sighed.

She held out the cup—mine—to show the sparse pattern of dark asymmetric leaves loosely stuck to the inside and repeated, "Death by water." One or two leaves rested on some particles of dissolving sugar, and it seemed to me they might shift if given time. Could that small adjustment alter my fate? Changing death by water to perhaps a dark stranger from over the water? I knew better than to ask.

The Hanged Man. Fear death by water. Years later when I read *The Wasteland,* the scene in the kitchen came back to me as vividly as though I could see and smell it: Maggie sitting at the head of the kitchen table, the threads in the wood scrubbed into bleached grooves; the dark brown kitchen teapot in front of her; a kettle hissing gently on the range; the room dimly lit by the window over the sink; and the smell of paraffin from the pale lamp on the dresser.

Death by water. The Hanged Man. Casement, transferred from the Tower of London, was awaiting trial in Brixton Prison. (Countess Markievicz, the unseen presence in my continuing nightmares, had by now had her death sentence commuted to penal servitude for life—she would be free of this, her first prison term, by the end of the following year—and my dreams and my conscious fears were now both focused on Casement.) I had that morning found in a drawer in the library a pack of tarot cards. The cards fascinated me, even though I understood only vaguely what they were. It required no special knowledge to guess that the picture on each card had a symbolic significance, and, since I saw Aunt Katie's conventional pack of playing cards used, if not to predict the future, as a conduit of omens and portents, I had a pretty good idea of how they might be employed in the right hands. That they lay neatly at the back of a drawer beside some pads for scoring bridge and half a stick of sealing wax suggested that the right hands were neither Grandmother's nor Aunt Katie's. I wondered if Sonia had been asked to read them, and if she had, with her practiced, vague incomprehension, avoided doing so. It had been the Hanged Man and the association with the fate of Casement that had driven me for company and comfort to the kitchen. I had for the moment forgotten that it was in the kitchen that I had first learned of the means by which Casement, when he had—as he undoubtedly would—been found guilty, would die. Until then, I had assumed he would be executed in the way that the revolutionaries in Dublin had and would face a firing squad—a grim enough prospect in itself but, in my imagination, far short of the hangman's rope.

And my fortune: death by drowning. I didn't immediately understand that it was my own fate that had been foretold. The reaction around the kitchen table to the reading was dramatic rather than serious. No time for my demise had been set. The prospect of death by water when I was an old woman, I was young enough to bear with comparative equanimity. But, even more, I believed that, although Maggie had the gift of reading tea leaves and what she saw in my cup would take place, it would affect me rather than happen to me. There would be in my life death by water, but it would not be my death. And until the situation became clearer or I had a reading that gave me six children or some other guarantee of longevity, I could with a little forethought remain on dry land. I wondered if Uncle William had a plan to send me, too, back to England the following night with Sonia. It seemed unlikely, not because I hadn't been told about it but because I knew my uncle capable of the expulsion of an unwanted guest without going to the trouble and expense of sending me as a companion across St. George's Channel.

It was Sonia, then, who would drown—and with her the passengers and crew of the mail boat. It was with a sense of great responsibility that, later in the afternoon, I entered the drawing room. And it was with a sense of shame that I allowed tea to end without my having broached the subject. It seemed as impossible that I should add to the awkwardness of Sonia's not entirely voluntary departure with the suggestion that Grandmother and Aunt Katie were sending her to her death as it would be to ask about the tarot cards in the desk drawer. Uncle William, with masculine cowardice, or perhaps feeling he had done his bit, was not at Ballydavid that afternoon.

I have in recent years thought just how dangerous those wartime crossings of the Irish Sea were, and wondered how dangerous they had, at the time, been perceived as being. Just before the end of the war the *Leinster* was torpedoed a few miles from where I now live with the loss of hundreds of lives, and on one night in December, 1917, two steamers—the *Conningbeg* and the *Formby*—both out of Waterford, were sunk without survivors. Contemporaries of mine, recalling childhood crossings, remember spending the entire night on deck wearing cork life jackets.

I, perhaps alone in the Allied countries, felt relief rather than grief when, next morning, the day of Sonia's departure, the *Morning Post* arrived, its entire front page and large black headlines devoted to the disaster that had befallen England: Kitchener was dead. Drowned.

Two nights before, the *Hampshire,* carrying the hero of Omdurman to Russia, had struck a mine a little west of the Orkneys. His body was never found. Grief, loss, and fear (many believed he was a military genius who would lead the country to victory) followed Kitchener's sudden and dramatic death. The nation, stunned, mourned the loss of the man whom, although he died as Secretary of War, they knew better as the face on the recruiting poster. It seemed a personal as well as a public loss.

I sat quietly at the breakfast table. From time to time Grandmother read aloud from the newspaper. I looked at the large black headlines and listened.

"Broad daylight," Grandmother said. "Eight o'clock in the evening. The seas were very high and the lifeboats couldn't be launched."

Aunt Katie glanced at the window. In the distance we could see white crests on the estuary. She turned to Bridie who had brought in some fresh toast.

"Please take up some tea and toast to Madame Debussy. And see if she needs any help with her packing."

Grandmother and Aunt Katie had arrived at a graceful solution to the embarrassment of Sonia's dubious title. "Madame" was to Bridie (who knew as well as Grandmother did that Sonia was still asleep) not only an appropriate way of describing a foreign, ostensibly widowed woman, but at least as distinguished a title as "Countess," since "Madam" was how the wife of the holder of one of the older Irish titles would be described.

IT WAS YEARS before I understood the mail boat was not called the Great Western but was merely one of several passenger ferries operated by the company that provided train service throughout the south and west of England. The Anglo-Irish families whose children traveled to and from school on it called it the "Pig Boat," the basis of its nickname apparent as Uncle William and I stood on the Quay, seeing Sonia off at the end of a lovely summer day. Pigs, squealing in furious protest at the drovers' switches, were being loaded into the holds. More pathetic and upsetting to a child or any imaginative adult were the cattle, panicked by the shouts and yells and cutting swipes from the drovers' ash plants, slipping and falling, as they were herded into the bowels of the ship. A dark, airless, and terrifying night lay between them and an English slaughterhouse. I tried not to think about this example of everyday casual cruelty to animals. I glanced at Sonia, but she seemed to be thinking of something else.

Uncle William had, at the very least, paid Sonia's travel expenses. Common sense, overheard sentences, and a later conversation with Aunt Katie allowed me in time a fairly clear picture of how Uncle William had dealt with the problem of Sonia. Once again a blunt masculine approach that ignored nuances, details, and areas of sensitivity had solved a problem far more efficiently than would have either of the more intelligent and thoughtful old ladies. Money, of course, was the key. Neither Grandmother nor Aunt Katie would have known even how to approach the subject; Uncle William understood that Sonia was staying at Ballydavid only because she lacked the means to get herself somewhere else. Life as a poor relation in a fairly comfortable country house was not her goal; preferable by far was a marginal existence in a rackety boarding house. There her charm, wiles, and flare for the dramatic would keep her head above water until she could charm the occasional gentleman caller, who would enliven her life with moments of luxury and the occasional present that could, if necessary, later be pawned.

Uncle William had, I must assume, in addition to Sonia's fare, also pressed on her a small sum, in my mind ten guineas, to cover out-of-pocket expenses incurred by her sudden change of plan. I can only imagine the conversations that would have taken place if Grandmother and Aunt Katie had had to word the proposal, let alone decide how much it was appropriate to pop into the discreet envelope that clinched the deal. What did Uncle William demand in return? He would not have balked at the ten guineas, if that was indeed the amount, and it is hard to imagine casting Sonia adrift with less. But, even allowing for Uncle William's being a little better off than his elderly female relatives, it was not an inconsiderable sum. With it he bought Sonia's immediate departure and, although I cannot be sure of this, a conversation in which she told Grandmother and Aunt Katie that, although she had had small, comforting intimations of Uncle Sainthill's existence in the afterlife and she was sure they would all be reunited after death, there was no way she or anyone else could help them communicate with him from this world.

Uncle William summoned a porter. I watched Sonia and realized that at some time in her life she had been in the habit of giving instructions. It is difficult now to separate what I really thought from the myth that I enjoyed. Manchuria and the title of a dead husband I don't think I even then took to be literal truth; if I had, I wouldn't have been so taken by her new air of authority. She was as sure and confident as Uncle William himself, as she had the porter rearrange her baggage so that her portmanteau was on top, tipped him, and gave him the cabin number, in the time it would have taken Aunt Katie, in similar circumstances, to open her purse and gaze uncertainly at its contents.

Sonia and I embraced; she shook hands with Uncle William. It had been agreed that he and I would watch the boat go past from a field behind old Mrs. de Bromhead's house, at the point where the Suir divided to flow on either side of a wooded island. Uncle William had brought an extra pocket handkerchief for me to wave.

"She must once have been a different person," Uncle William said thoughtfully as he turned the motorcar into the Mall. I had noticed earlier that he was capable of driving and conducting a conversation at the same time.

"Yes," I said. "Uncle Hubert———"

"How much did you tell her about Uncle Hubert?"

I hesitated, aware that we had been at cross purposes. "Nothing," I said.

"Did she ask you about him, or about Uncle Sainthill?"

"No." I realized he had taken my hesitation for a prevarication, and, since providing Sonia with information about those uncles was not on my conscience, I answered with the firmness of relief. It seemed a moment when frankness might pay off with some reciprocal information, and I added, "She asked me about you, though."

"Did she, by Jove." Uncle William sounded interested and rather pleased. "What did she ask?"

"She asked me the name of your dog and if you were married." I thought, without quite understanding why, that I would not mention her curiosity about how much land he owned.

Soon we drew up beside the wrought iron gates of Mrs. de Bromhead's villa. A dower house, it was small with pretty proportions and a view of the river as far as Waterford. The mail boat was not yet in sight, and I picked a bunch of cowslips while Uncle William strolled over to look at some rust-colored bullocks.

"Tom O'Neill is come home," I said, when we had chosen the highest part of the field clear of the trees and stood, handkerchiefs in hand, watching the boat steam slowly down the river toward us.

"I'll come over and see him next week. See if we can find him a job. There'll be some kind of pension, of course." Uncle William tied a knot in one corner of his silk handkerchief to remind himself.

"He lost his leg," I said.

"I know. Terrible business. Gangrene."

There was more I wanted to say, but I didn't know how. I sensed that my uncle, too, was awkward. Now the boat was abreast of us, and we waved our handkerchiefs and tried to spot Sonia among the people at the rail. Unfortunately, we had not agreed upon a specific place for her to stand. We waved affectionately to a figure in a dark coat near the bows until the boat disappeared gradually behind the trees on the north end of the island.

We were again in the motorcar before I plucked up courage to ask my uncle a question about something that had been troubling me since that morning.

"They said in the kitchen"—Uncle William raised an eyebrow; he knew I was not supposed to hang around the kitchen—"that Tom O'Neill said a boy who worked on Mr. Rowe's farm was shot in France."

"Yes?" Uncle William said. "I'm sorry to hear it."

"Tom O'Neill said an English officer shot him."

"He was shot by an English officer?" Uncle William asked, his voice grave.

"Yes, Tom O'Neill said."

"I see. I'm afraid he may have been a deserter."

I looked at him and he, reluctantly, went on.

"If a soldier runs away under fire, he is shot. It's horrible, but necessary. So that other soldiers don't run away when they're afraid."

"He was shot for being afraid?"

"Everyone's afraid in a war. It's a horrible thing. But this war is necessary."

"But his mother—his brother——" I was afraid I would cry, but I needed an answer and I pressed on. "His brother is the boy who comes to the door with pheasants."

"The boy with red hair?"

"Yes. He had red hair, too. Tom said."

"One of the Clancys, then." Uncle William's voice was cold and sad. I knew that he was horrified, too, but I thought he understood the terrible thing that had happened. I didn't.

"It's horrible for the man who does the shooting, too," he said after a moment.

I hadn't thought of that. I wondered, from the flatness of his tone, whether he had ever been the one who had done the shooting. I didn't ask. I was already too ashamed to go into the kitchen.

As we drove through the gates of Ballydavid, Uncle William broke the silence.

"I hope Sonia's a good sailor. She's out on the estuary now. It could be quite rough tonight."

"Is she going to be all right?" I forced myself to ask. It was rare for me to be alone with Uncle William, and there were so many questions I couldn't ask my grandmother and Aunt Katie.

"Oh, yes," he said, and laughed. "Don't worry about Sonia, she'll always land on her feet."

I MISSED MY MOTHER and I longed for her visit to Ballydavid that summer. It was now more than a year since I had last seen her, and since my Uncle Sainthill's death. I scarcely missed Edward and had no particularly warm feelings toward my so far unmet younger sister; I missed my father not at all. London was to me inferior in every way to the small part of County Waterford that I now thought of as home. Unusually for a child my age (and it probably does not reflect well on my nature), place seemed as

important as people. Ballydavid, the old and slightly shabby
house and farm, fields and woods that I was, that glorious summer, old enough and independent enough to explore and enjoy by
myself, took first place in my affections. I did not want to be in
London now that the eggs in the blackbird's nest had hatched,
while the hedgerows were in bloom, during the time that Miss
Kingsley and I, trailed by a sullen Clodagh, looked for wild orchids in the undrained boggy fields behind Woodstown Strand.
And there was Patience. And Jock.

I missed my mother not only because I was a little girl and it
was a year since I had seen her, but also because I was guilty and
confused. I was guilty and confused for a whole range of reasons,
some of them not logically connected to me. I would lie awake at
night and worry. I would think about the brother of the red-
haired boy, who had been shot because he was afraid. I would
think sadly of his family. Then I would wonder if Bridie and
Maggie blamed me as part of the society responsible for the boy's
death. How could they? And yet, since I was a beneficiary of that
society, how could they not? I felt guilty about Sonia and worried
about her future. Uncle William had said she would be all right,
but he was given to broad definitive statements. And should I
have told Grandmother and Aunt Katie that Sonia and Mara
were the same person? They were too alike in too many ways not
to be, but at the same time they were different. I had never—
apart from a Christmas pantomime in which most of the characters had been animals—been to the theatre, and so I had no
experience of seeing a great actress, whose face was familiar to me
and thousands others, play one dissimilar but completely convinc-
ing role after another. Had I failed Sonia—now adrift in a world
I increasingly understood to have little respect or compassion for
the underdog? Or had I failed my family by keeping silent about
her identity? What would have happened if my mother had arrived before Sonia left and if she had looked at her and said,

"Why, Mara, whatever are you doing here?" But maybe Sonia would be a complete stranger to her with only a similarity— common perhaps to every female between the ages of thirty and fifty born east of the Balkans—to someone she had once known briefly. I would have been less uneasy if I had not heard Uncle Hubert tell my mother that Mara had murdered her husband. If Sonia were Mara, then I had been party to Grandmother having harbored, if not literally a fugitive from justice, then someone who was clever and devious enough to avoid that unenviable state. But then again, as my mind went round and round, perhaps England was awash with slightly desperate, aging adventuresses with Slavic cheekbones, any one of whom might easily drift off course and find herself in the rural south of Ireland.

I worried, too, whether my mother would come to see me that summer. My paternal grandmother was in London, visiting her son. (Raising the question, unanswerable at this distance of time, of how and when she had made this wartime voyage from New Zealand. Or had she already been in England when war broke out? Perhaps visiting another long-forgotten relative?) I even worried, although in this instance confusion played a larger part, about my sleepwalking and its supposed connection to a "gift" that I knew I did not have. But I had not known I walked in my sleep, itself something that suggested I was unusual; might I not also have psychic powers of which I knew nothing? And what about Tom O'Neill, who would live out his days with a wooden leg? I now guiltily avoided the stable yard as well as the kitchen.

The guilt and confusion I felt closer to home did nothing to alleviate my morbid fear and increasing preoccupation with the fate of Sir Roger Casement. It seemed to me that Kitchener's death and Casement's trial filled the summer. I heartily disliked Kitchener; I connected the wave of patriotic emotion following his death with a greater emotional determination to see Casement also dead. Nothing I have learned about Kitchener since has moved my opinion; the man who gave us concentration camps during the Boer War turned out to be more adept at recruiting soldiers than at keeping them alive once he had them in uniform.

At the time I felt uneasy about my lack of patriotic grief for Kitchener, but it was nothing compared to the guilt I felt for my unpatriotic sympathy for the man being tried and for my horror at his trial—Casement pale, handsome, sad, dignified, and sick; his persecutors smug and brutish bullies. I hated them, and I feared them.

Casement's trial began on 26 June. The proceedings were short, sharp, and to the point. There was an assumption of guilt that made the trial little more than a formality. Soon after Casement had been brought to England and incarcerated in the Tower of London, a member of the House of Commons had asked Asquith if it was true Casement was in custody and whether the Prime Minister could assure him that Casement would immediately be shot for treason. The question had been greeted with cheers. The newspapers, as soon as Casement's arrest was made public, had referred to him as a traitor, and the combination of evidence and the emotions of a country at war left little doubt as to his eventual fate. It seemed inevitable that he should be executed.

But Casement still had a few friends, and there were also those who remembered his work in the Congo and with the Putumayo Indians; Sir Arthur Conan Doyle, who had known Casement socially during happier times, contributed £700 to his legal expenses. Bernard Shaw, staying in character, did not give any money but drafted a line of defense that argued that Casement, as an Irishman, had no allegiance to the Crown and could therefore not be a traitor. It was a line of argument, one of several, that for a moment appealed to Casement.

Many of Casement's notes and suggestions to his counsel were concerned with the peripheral, much in the way that he had frittered his time and the patience of the German authorities on the Findlay-proposed kidnapping scheme. His pride was hurt by the suggestions that he had been too grateful for his knighthood, that he had taken money from Germany, or that he had been drawing his English pension. Understanding that he would certainly be found guilty, he concentrated on defending himself from painful sneers and slights on his honor.

On the fourth day of his trial, Casement was found guilty and condemned to death. Horridge, one of the three judges, had a nervous tic that made him appear to grin as the black cap was placed on his head. The newspapers made much of this macabre touch. The execution was set for 3 August.

There was still the appeal to come, but before that Mother came to visit. On the morning of her arrival I was allowed to postpone my breakfast and accompany O'Neill to the mail boat. There followed the tradition of O'Neill's welcome, the drive through Waterford and the countryside, with the smell of hay and the summer sounds of birds and insects, meadowsweet in the hedges and larks above us, through the gates of Ballydavid and up to the front door. Edward and Emily were, I assume, with her, but I remember nothing of them, not even my first impression of the baby whom I no longer felt so keenly to be an interloper.

Even I, uncritical and with the eyes of childhood adoration, could see that my mother looked older and very thin; new lines had appeared on her forehead and to the sides of her mouth. But that morning she was happy to see me, happy to see her mother and aunt, happy to be at Ballydavid.

Grandmother and Aunt Katie were happy to have my pretty, amusing mother home; their talk and laughter in contrast to their dark clothing. Mother, since she had a husband to please and a year had passed since Uncle Sainthill's death, was no longer in mourning; Grandmother and Aunt Katie were in the black each would wear for the rest of her life.

Mother was happy to be home and, perhaps because Grandmother had lost one child, was now forgiven for her unsuitable marriage. And I, clinging to her side, was rarely sent away when they talked. Sometimes Uncle William was there; sometimes he wasn't. Sometimes they would recall my presence, and a subject would be changed or an opinion withheld. But usually the conversation would circle around, and, with a glance in my direction, Mother—for it was usually she who offered the indiscretion— would pause in midsentence to substitute a word or phrase and then, with a laugh, continue. Away from her literal-minded husband and her visiting unsympathetic mother-in-law, she bloomed. And it was most often of her mother-in-law that she spoke indiscreetly.

"I took her," Mother said, laughing, "to see the Changing of the Guard at Buckingham Palace, the Tower of London, and Kew Gardens. Bobby took her to lunch at Roehampton Golf Club and to a music hall. Then I took her to see the Albert Memorial, Nelson's Column, the National Gallery, and a concert at the Albert Hall. Then I found out that what she really wanted to do was to see Casement tried."

"Madame Defarge," Grandmother said.

"Madame Defarge," Mother said, and laughed again, happy to be with people for whom simple literary allusions did not require explanation. Then, after a moment, she realized that this one, in my case, did. "Madame Defarge is a character in *A Tale of Two Cities*. It's a novel about the French Revolution by Charles Dickens."

"I have a copy upstairs," Grandmother said to me. "I'll give it to you later."

"I think perhaps, dear——" Aunt Katie said, "I wonder if it is quite suitable."

"Absolutely not," Mother said, still laughing at the image of her mother-in-law as a latter-day Madame Defarge, "We don't want Alice roaming the upper floors of Ballydavid all night like a miniature Lady Macbeth."

There was a moment's hesitation, and then both the old ladies laughed. It was a moment I could not afford to miss.

"Is it true that if you wake a person who is sleepwalking that you kill her?" I asked in a voice that sounded unnatural to me. As soon as the words were out of my mouth, I regretted the use of the feminine pronoun.

"Of course not. Why would you think so?" Grandmother said.

"Need you ask?" My mother said, and laughed again.

Bridie had, of course, been the source of this fear. She had not intended any harm and doubtless believed what she was telling me. My mother reassured me, first by telling me that what I had been told was not true, then by saying that no one would wake me if they met me out on a late night ramble. She added that it was well known that somnambulists, even those who slept in less hospitable surroundings than I did, never hurt themselves.

The subject drifted—any association of ideas not conscious—to Kitchener's death and a bizarre phenomenon in its wake. Some—those who thronged the séances and consulted mediums and became the willing prey of charlatans—could not accept the tragedy, and rumors, ridiculous but understandable in the circumstances, began to circulate: Kitchener was not really dead but a prisoner of the Germans or lying in an enchanted sleep in a cave on the Shetland Islands, a sleep from which he would, like a mythic hero, at some moment of his country's even greater need, awake to save England.

I had the impression that Mother was on the edge of being tempted by this idea, but Grandmother and Aunt Katie were disapproving. It is possible they appreciated how narrowly, as a direct result of an unsuccessful attempt to communicate with the other side, they had escaped Sonia as a permanent member of the household, but I think it more likely they were afraid of Uncle William's anger and ridicule if he caught them again flirting with the occult.

"Almost every culture has some superstition———" Grandmother started, but Aunt Katie, laughing but outraged, was now describing the deep mourning into which, following Kitchener's death, Mrs. Coughlan had temporarily plunged. Her choice perhaps intended to mitigate an earlier sartorial *bêtise*. Of all her eccentricities, the one that had most alienated Waterford society had been the scarlet dress she had worn only days after the death of Edward VII. Red was, she had explained, the Chinese color of mourning. Although that year the beautiful and fashionable clothes and hats at Ascot had all been black, nowhere was mourning for the king more rigidly adhered to than among the Anglo-Irish, the political sentiment behind the black as marked as the grief.

"A huge black hat with a veil like a beekeeper—you could hardly see her face. Indecent. It was as though she thought she was his widow or—I don't know what———"

"Or his mistress. You don't suppose...?" Mother said, playfully.

"And then," Aunt Katie continued, "after three days she got tired of it all and went back to her usual outrageous fashions."

I was sorry that I had missed this sight and wondered if Mrs. Coughlan had carried a black parasol.

That evening Mother came up to my room a moment or two after I had climbed into bed.

"Would you like me to read to you?" she asked, and sat down beside me.

A copy of *Ivanhoe* lay on the table beside my bed; I found it slow going and was aware Grandmother had chosen a book for me without fully considering my age. I would be grateful for a chapter read aloud and some help with the longer words. But Mother had brought her own book.

She looked at me for a moment before she asked, gently, "Do you have bad dreams?"

As well as having nightmares, I used sometimes to dream that my mother was dead, but I didn't know how to tell her about either, so I shook my head.

"Are you happy enough?" she asked, and took my hand.

I had often thought, lying awake and missing my mother, about the moment when she would come to take me home again. What she was supposed to do now was to tell me how much she missed me and that her other two children in no way made up for my absence. At the time I had felt that these fantasies were shameful and self-indulgent; now they seem perfectly reasonable. I suppose I also wondered whether she intended to take me with her when she returned to London at the end of the summer. It was not a possibility anyone had thought necessary to discuss with me. Now I was aware that in the highly improbable event that my wishes were consulted, I wouldn't know what to do. I knew what I wanted: to live at Ballydavid and have my mother live there, too.

Choosing to take my silence and smile for assent, my mother asked no further question and instead opened her book.

"This is a grown-up story," she said, "but I think you'll rather enjoy it. Lots of adventures but nothing frightening. It's quite funny, too, but I'm not sure if you'll see all the jokes until you're older."

And she began to read. I still remember the book and am now, even more than I was then, pleased by her selection. Both Mother and my grandmother were admirers of the work of Arnold Bennett, a novelist not much read today, who wrote books that usually described life—and often a preoccupation with money—in the

Potteries. *The Grand Babylon Hotel* owed nothing to the new French realism that influenced his more serious, regional novels.

Mother read it, her tone not so exaggerated as to mock the story, which had originally been written as a serial for a newspaper, but with sufficient expression to reflect the suspense and surprise with which each chapter was amply laced. I lay wide-eyed, lips parted, excited by the description of high life, intrigue, and extravagance in an hotel "like a palace incognito." It was while following a plot that never paused for breath or balked at improbability that I first became aware that a book, if sufficiently powerful, could provide an alternate world into which I could, now and in the future, escape. The fear, guilt, confusion, and helplessness that I felt, even as I enjoyed the long summer days spent out of doors, became as distant and unreal as though they, too, existed in a novel.

At the end of the second chapter, my mother handed me the book.

"Why don't you read to yourself for a little while? I'll come up again after dinner."

I read until I heard a footstep that might have been Grandmother's in the corridor, and then I fell asleep, happily considering the adventures of Nella Racksole as she foiled villains and pursued adventuresses in the luxury of her father's hotel and in Dover, a "port of ill repute, possessing some of the worst-managed hotels in Europe."

WITH CASEMENT'S APPEAL came the petitions. There was a small but strong campaign for mercy. I pinned my hopes on it. I was constantly aware that a man with a gentle face and a dignified bearing, a gentleman, was in prison waiting—once the pro forma appeal had been heard—to be hanged. It seemed impossible that it should be so and even more impossible that my mother should accept this as a merely unfortunate, and Grandmother a not undesirable, inevitability.

America—still neutral and with a large Irish vote—strongly advocated the commutation of Casement's death penalty. From Washington, Sir Cecil Spring Rice, the British Ambassador—and father of Mary Spring Rice, who had been part of the Childers' gunrunning adventure—advised strongly and repeatedly against making a martyr of Casement. The weight of American public opinion was probably that which most concerned the English authorities, but the stance of senior members of the Church of England clergy worried them also. The Bishop of Winchester had been one of the forty distinguished names that had signed Conan Doyle's petition. Bernard Shaw drafted his own petition, also counseling the government against making Casement a martyr and suggesting that executing him would only make worse the Irish situation. Although the British man in the street had less sympathy for Casement than for the revolutionaries who had been executed in Dublin following the Easter Rising, there were still those who thought Casement should not be hanged. It was at this time that photographs of pages of what were later called the Black Diaries began to circulate.

Soon after Casement had been brought back to London in custody, he was interviewed by the Assistant Commissioner of Police, Basil Thomson. During the interview a policeman asked for the keys to some locked trunks in Casement's former lodgings that they wished to search. Casement told them they might break the locks and there was nothing inside except for some old clothes. The police found some diaries and account books: Casement was in the habit of recording transactions of even small sums of money. The diaries, which have only recently been unsealed to historians and scholars, contain a full and explicit account of Casement's homosexual private life.

There may have been those who thought that Casement's sexual life—although illegal—was a separate issue from the question of whether he was or was not guilty of treason, but, if there were, they held their peace. It is almost impossible, in the permissive moral climate of the second half of the twentieth century, to describe the attitude toward homosexuality of the generation before my own, but one comparison may illustrate the difference. At approximately the same time that Oscar Wilde was sentenced to two years in jail for homosexual offences, Sir Charles Dilke (who as a Member of Parliament had supported Casement's report on Belgian colonial atrocities) was able to return to politics. Dilke had spent ten years out of public life following a scandalous divorce case in which he had been cited. A prurient and fascinated public had heard Mrs. Crawford, the defendant, claim that a housemaid had been added to the already adulterous bed. For Wilde, such a return to society would not have been imaginable.

We can, I think, assume that Scotland Yard had the diaries in their possession from the afternoon of Easter Sunday; F. E. Smith, the Attorney General, had copies of some pages before the beginning of the trial. The first reference to the existence of the diaries seems to have been in the newspapers reporting the conclusion of Casement's trial and his death sentence. Photographs of excerpts from the diaries began to be circulated during the weeks between the end of the trial and the beginning of the appeal. The king—according to Dean Inge in a letter to Alfred Noyes, the poet and Casement apologist—showed "the Diary" (by which I think he meant a photograph of a page or pages of the diary) to Canon Henson, who in the past had preached in Westminster Abbey on Casement's Putumayo report. Copies were shown to the press (especially American correspondents), politicians, clergy, and to other influential people who might have spoken up for Casement—and nowhere with more effect than in Ireland.

Since the point that Casement's perceived moral turpitude was irrelevant was not one that carried much weight, the only other line of defense was to claim the diaries were a forgery. It was a popular partisan theory for a while although too many Casement sympathizers who knew his distinctive hand, Michael Collins among them, saw parts of the diaries and acknowledged the authenticity of the handwriting.

The appeal was heard on 17 July before five judges. One of them, Mr. Justice Darling, invited the painter John Lavery to paint the scene and gave him the use of the jury box. Lavery had painted a portrait of Darling some years before in legal robes and the black cap that was placed over his wig when he pronounced the death sentence. F. E. Smith, a man whom I have never thought oversensitive, had found the portrait offensive; he was still less pleased when Lavery was invited to paint the Court of Criminal Appeal.

It is a large painting, with many people, some quite detailed, although there is no distinctive foreground figure. Casement, too small for us to see the expression on his face, is in the exact center of the painting. A clock light enough and large enough to draw the eye is above him, high and a little to the left. The room is paneled; the occupants, with the exception of Casement, are dressed in dark clothing—wigs, collars, and papers making white or pale contrast with the dark wood and foreground shadow. We can see part of three windows above the hall and a smaller one above the section of gallery at the top of the painting, but the room seems to be lit by twelve gas globes suspended from an ornate circular fixture. The judges sit on a platform behind a raised desk on the left of the painting, below them four men at another desk; there are books in front of the judges and papers in front of the four men. To the right, facing them, is a table at which sit three men and three women, the women somewhat concealed. The right of the painting is filled with the crowd, some standing behind the seated and wigged lawyers, one of whom—Serjeant Sullivan, Casement's counsel and, like him, dark-bearded—is on his feet, addressing the court. The man in front of him is half-turned, not looking up at him but in a position from which it seems he can hear more easily. Two warders, one seated, one standing, to each side of Casement, peer through the double row of bars that enclose the dock and obstruct their view; Casement, tall and straight, looks out between the upper bars, his beard and black tie contrasting with his light-colored suit.

The appeal took two days. Lavery, in his memoirs, recalls the drowsy monotony of the proceedings on which depended a man's life and the casual way in which Darling pronounced the words: "The Appeal is dismissed." He writes that Casement waved to someone in the gallery before he turned and was taken away.

Chapter 12

AUGUST BEGAN WITH a heavy threat of thunder, the dark skies and thick, oppressive air portentous. We waited for the storm to break. There was nothing to limit the named and unnamed fear we all felt. It semed now that anything might be possible.

Each sultry day, I was conscious that Casement was soon to be hanged. For others the war was about to enter its third ghastly year, and, although it had as long again to go, it could already be seen to be one of the great tragedies of the world's history. Ahead of us, unsuspected in the specifics, lay the Russian Revolution and the influenza epidemic of 1918 that would kill more than the war and the revolution put together—with anything that would happen in Ireland thrown in for good measure.

Even though I was too young to read the newspapers and my family felt no need to dwell on the horrors of the moment in history in which we were living, I began to understand that, although the rules that governed my life still applied, they were no guarantee of consequence.

———

CROWDS GATHERED outside Pentonville on the morning of the third of August. There was no last minute reprieve, and, at about the time we sat down to breakfast at Ballydavid, Roger Casement was hanged. Severing another tie with his background, Casement died a Roman Catholic, received into the church during the weeks before his death. The English newspapers would carry the story of his execution the following day; the day after, the second anniversary of the outbreak of war, we would read it at Ballydavid. The Irish Sea put a buffer between the immediacy of the news and our sheltered drawing room; the Irish newspaper read in the kitchen would, of course, offer a somewhat different account a day sooner. Despite the lack of written confirmation, and, although we did not speak of it, the horror of what had happened in London that morning hung over the household. The kitchen no longer a haven for me, I spent much of the day alone, some of it praying that Casement would be granted a last minute stay of execution. That afternoon Rosamund Gwynne came to tea at Ballydavid.

If Mother had, as I suspect, pleaded Grandmother's ill health as an excuse to escape her mother-in-law and for her sudden visit to Ireland, her letters home must have been full of half-truths, evasion, and omission. Not only was Grandmother as healthy, cheerful, and energetic as she was ever to be after Uncle Saint-hill's death, but she was engaged in a whirl of social activity. Rosamund Gwynne's promised visit to Ballydavid was imminent; she had brought her trunks and hatboxes south and was now staying on the other side of Waterford with a friend whose father commanded the garrison.

"She seems to be rather a favorite with the young officers," Aunt Katie had said at lunch, her tone benevolent.

Grandmother said nothing. I could imagine the weight of disapproval she would have conveyed with the same words. It seemed that Aunt Katie's essential good nature and her reluctance to think ill of anyone with whom she was connected now included her prospective niece, Miss Gwynne. Grandmother, with one son dead and her daughter unsuitably married, did not share her charitable outlook; that the young woman who would in all probability become her daughter-in-law was apparently a flirt did not sit well with her.

Nevertheless, the Ballydavid tennis party was an annual event, and this year it was to be slightly expanded and to some extent in honor of Rosamund Gwynne. Although most invitations had already been sent out, Grandmother had not yet completely finished with the guest list.

When I came downstairs to tea, the sun was shining, and Mother, my grandmother, and my great-aunt were sitting outdoors with Miss Gwynne. I followed Bridie who was carrying the tea tray out to the veranda. My mother gestured for me to sit on a footstool beside her.

"So Alice, still on holiday—you must be missing Clodagh."

With her first sentence, Miss Gwynne managed to offend me. While she had been in the north of Ireland and after it had seemed inevitable that she would become one of the family, I had considered the likelihood of being a bridesmaid when she married Uncle Hubert, and had gone so far as to prepare myself with a couple of suggestions as to how I might to the greatest advantage be dressed. Now I felt the wave of instant dislike that, looking back after all these years, I think Rosamund Gwynne managed to induce in most members of my family—with the presumable exception of my uncle. There were few people I wanted less to see than Clodagh and, surely, it would have been more graceful—although equally improbable—to suggest that Clodagh was missing me.

I smiled politely, but said nothing.

"And that unusual woman—who was staying when we came to lunch—how is she?"

I resented not only her description of Sonia but also the amused superiority of her tone.

"Sonia?" Mother said. "I'm afraid we've rather lost touch."

"I'm sorry to hear that," Miss Gwynne said. "I was hoping to hear what she was up to now."

"Yes," Mother said. "I'm afraid I can't help you. I saw her one afternoon at the Dorchester and wanted to thank her for her kindness to Alice, but she was having tea with Lady Dartmouth and I didn't want to seem pushing."

"Lady Dartmouth!" This was not good news for my adversary, but she recovered herself quickly. "The Dartmouths are relatives—distant—on my mother's side."

"Oh, good. Well, I'm sure you'll see her there and you'll be able to catch up."

It is to my mother's credit that she had made her fabrication on Sonia's behalf (whom she had never met, or if she had, I realized a moment later, entering my usual labyrinth of anxiety and confusion, it had been unbeknownst to her while Sonia was traveling under another name) seem less unlikely than what was probably only a slight exaggeration on Miss Gwynne's part.

"I hope Miss Critchley will be able to come on the twenty-third," Grandmother said, the tennis party still in the front of her mind, as it would be until the guest list was completed. In front of us the tennis court, mowed, rolled, and the lines freshly painted by O'Neill, lay ready. The summer had been dry, and the court was baked hard and the yellowing grass in need of rain.

"Oh, yes, indeed, she is looking forward to it," Rosamund Gwynne said, her friend's enthusiasm intended to flatter Grandmother. She did not understand that Grandmother was less seeking reassurance that Miss Critchley would be able to attend than airing her displeasure that no written response had yet arrived.

When Miss Gwynne had climbed into her dogcart and trotted briskly down the avenue, Grandmother returned to the table in the drawing room at which she wrote her letters. We sat in silence, Aunt Katie at one of her ritual games of patience, Mother watching as I played with Oonagh. After a little while, Grandmother stood up, two sheets of writing paper in her hands.

"The Bryces, of course, will have to be asked, but leave their invitation for a day or two. I've added Inez de Courcy, and she can bring that badly behaved little brother of hers to keep Alice company. And you should also write to Major and Mrs. Coughlan. You have already asked Rosamund's list from the garrison, all those young men?"

"Inez de Courcy?" Aunt Katie said, not questioning Grandmother but musing on the wit and originality of her choice. I assumed that since Jarvis was, to my delight, to be invited, Aunt Katie had given Grandmother a modified version of his behavior on the afternoon of my birthday party; certainly his discourtesy toward Oonagh must have been omitted. None of us remarked on the reinstatement of Major and Mrs. Coughlan on Grandmother's invitation list; we were relieved that the Bryces, whose invitation had been in doubt, were, after all, to be invited.

"She's a very pretty girl and the best tennis player in the neighborhood," Grandmother said quietly, and we understood that she did not intend Rosamund Gwynne to have it all her own way.

GRANDMOTHER RETURNED to her books and letters; Aunt Katie sent out the remaining invitations, then rolled up her sleeves and set to work on the preparations.

Aunt Katie had planned, ordered, and helped make tea for the Ballydavid tennis party every summer—except for the year before when it had been postponed following the sinking of the *Lusitania* and cancelled after the news of Uncle Sainthill's death. Each year her guests had been offered bridge rolls filled with egg and cress, cucumber sandwiches, and the Ballydavid sponge cake. They had been refreshed with lemonade, barley water, tea, or a light punch, the mixing of which Uncle William supervised. This year the tennis party would run along the same lines, but there would be ten or more additional guests: Rosamund Gwynne, Miss Critchley— the friend with whom Miss Gwynne was staying—the Bryces, Inez de Courcy and Jarvis, and half a dozen officers from the Waterford garrison. The Dean and his wife, on the other hand, had been pointedly excluded from Grandmother's list.

It was the inclusion of the young officers that prevented Aunt Katie taking the arrangements comfortably in her stride. A seemingly endless supply of perfectly presentable, young, unmarried men of good family arrived in Ireland, performed a modicum of military duty, and made themselves socially available. These young officers were a boon for the average hostess, especially for those with unmarried daughters. When one young officer married or transferred to other duties, a new one would immediately take his place. In time each officer, each man, each regiment would go to France; Ireland was for them a rural, unsophisticated, largely out-of-doors equivalent to the Duchess of Richmond's ball on the eve of the Battle of Waterloo.

While there were certainly nationalists who regarded these soldiers as an occupying military force, and others with husbands and sons fighting in France who thought the officers were having a comparatively easy war—many of those who put down the Easter Rising had been enjoying a day's racing at Fairyhouse when the General Post Office was seized—these were not views I ever heard spoken aloud. Officers were socially useful, and they had not previously been entertained at Ballydavid only because Grandmother had no young unmarried woman to launch into society and because she chose to limit her social circle to the county families she had known all her life.

Aunt Katie wasn't used to entertaining strange young men; if she had known these officers from their childhood, she would have been in her element. She would have produced their favorite boyhood food—a preference for gooseberry fool or treacle tart, even in a small boy, was never forgotten. But these young men were unknown to her, and she worried that they might expect the fare to be more sophisticated or in a greater quantity than she had planned to provide. Uncle William was consulted, but, apart from allowing that the Colonel (he hadn't been invited) should, if he stayed for any length of time after tea, be offered a whiskey and soda, he took the view that plying young men with rich food and strong drink was unnecessary and, if it were done simultaneously with encouraging them to play tennis in hot weather, an actively bad idea. Aunt Katie, who was unsure if he was hinting at the dangers of drunken and licentious soldiery, did not argue, which isn't to say that she was reassured.

The preparations began several weeks in advance. O'Neill tended the tennis court and painted the wrought iron chairs and tables that were arranged on either side of it. Aunt Katie told him how much butter and cream she would need and gave similar instructions to Pat, the gardener, about tomatoes and cucumbers. Bridie scrubbed the canvas deck chairs and left them to air in the sun. O'Neill's underlings clipped hedges and waged war on dandelions.

Even I was set to work at small pleasant tasks. Churning butter on a summer day fifty years ago is a clear memory. The sound of that day: the wind—the end of a gale blowing itself out—in the elms, the lazy clucking of hens, the bees around the lavender hedge, and butter churning in the dairy. And the smell: the scent of flowers beside the gate to the kitchen yard, bread and cakes baking in the kitchen, the slightly unpleasant damp smell of the dairy. I remember that afternoon as an interlude of pure innocence, my fear, guilt, and horror suspended. The Clancy boy, like Casement, was dead; his brother, my red-haired hero, had not, Bridie told me, visited either Mrs. O'Neill or the Ballydavid kitchen door since his brother had been shot; Tom O'Neill was maimed; the war in France was going badly; but that afternoon everyone, except possibly Grandmother, was caught up in the excitement of preparation for the tennis party and the ritual of the churn.

Noreen, related in some way I no longer remember to Bridie, was the butter maker. The wooden churn stood on iron supports, away from the cool marble slabs over which hung the skimming pans and ladles. Turning the handle for the necessary length of time became hard work, but it was not only to relieve Noreen that I was pressed into service; it was believed that sometimes a change of hand would bring about the heavier sound inside the churn that told us the butter was about to come.

When at last we heard and felt the butter become solid, I was sent to tell Mrs. O'Neill and the men in the farmyard there was fresh buttermilk. The men came in and were given large mugs of the cool liquid, and Mrs. O'Neill filled an earthenware jug to make soda bread. I took a taste from my own small cup; I didn't like it, but it was worth a sip or two to be part of the ritual.

THE TENNIS PARTY was to be held on the twenty-third of August. Even without whatever local excitement may have been generated by the festivities at Ballydavid, the twenty-third was an historic day for Ireland. It was the day the clocks changed—not changed in the sense of the daylight saving plan, which had that year, as a wartime measure, been enacted. On the twenty-third of

August 1916, the Irish people were robbed—as some of them felt—of twenty-five minutes as their clocks, for the first time, were set to Greenwich Mean Time. There had been some discussion at Ballydavid about whether the invitations should be issued for new time or old time and if it should be specified. In the end Uncle William said that, since it was a tennis party not a horse race, twenty-five minutes wouldn't signify one way or the other and that those who arrived first would play first and that tea would be served whenever it was ready and Aunt Katie chose to serve it.

Still, the day was felt to be special, and on the stroke of noon—the moment of enactment chosen by Grandmother rather than by the government in London—the hands of every clock at Ballydavid were moved to show twenty-five past twelve.

THE GREATER PART of Grandmother's and Aunt Katie's guests were of necessity spectators rather than players. There was one tennis court, and the convention was that mixed doubles, each match one set, would be played while the remaining guests watched. Some of them had little interest in tennis; a few were probably even vague about the rules or how the game was scored, but, of the forty or so invited to Ballydavid, a couple of dozen turned up with tennis racquets and the expectation of a game.

It would not have been unreasonable to have expected some rudimentary plan as to who should be partnered with whom and that, at least after the first match (in which players would be determined by their time of arrival), some thought should have been given to the level of skill of those playing before they were allocated partners and sent onto the sunbaked court—not only for their own sake but for that of the spectators. But this aspect of the tennis party did not seem to have been anticipated either by Aunt Katie, who thought the afternoon was about food and drink, or by Grandmother, who had thought no further than who should, and who should not, be included in the party.

After the clock-adjusting ceremony and the realization directly afterward that there was not quite as much time as had been previously imagined for a quick and unambitious cold lunch, I had been sent upstairs to rest. No one seriously expected me to sleep and I was happy to lie on my bed with a book. I was reading *Anna of the Five Towns.* The day before, after my initial disappointment that, although by the author of *The Grand Babylon Hotel,* the novel was not a tale of glamour and intrigue, I had become sympathetically engrossed in Anna's dreary life. But that afternoon I was too excited to concentrate.

The evening before, Bridie had washed my hair. She and I had gone with a large jug to the barrel in a corner of the stable yard into which rain water drained from the gutter. I had peered dubiously into the butt: Because of the drought, the water was low and didn't look as clean as I might have wished. But I didn't complain. My hair was long, and the washing and combing out of tangles afterward was a lengthy and a painful ordeal, and the rainwater was softer than the water pumped from the Ballydavid well.

The dress that I had been given for my birthday the summer before, the hem let down, was hanging, freshly laundered and starched, in my room. After my rest, as I put on my dress, I wondered where I should be for my birthday; it was not so far away. Then I thought that Jarvis de Courcy and his sister might be among the earlier guests, and I hurried downstairs.

The earliest guests were mostly old ladies. But soon the first game of the afternoon was underway: the curate, who had still to discover that his dean and the dean's wife had not been invited; two middle-aged sisters who lived near Corballymore who came to Ballydavid once a year for this very gathering; and a young Waterford airman home on leave. Their game was the backdrop for the arrival of the greater part of the guests.

The old ladies sat, their large, shady hats protecting their faces, on the newly painted, wrought-iron garden seats. Some wore silk dresses in pale, lighthearted colors; for others, half-mourning was their concession to a festive occasion. Among them were women who were seen in society only once or twice a year. They were either too poor or too old to go about much and, not able themselves to entertain, were usually forgotten. The tennis party at Ballydavid might well have been the social highlight of their year. Grandmother had arranged for some of her guests to bring one or two of these old ladies, and O'Neill had been dispatched to drive two elderly, impoverished sisters, who lived in a cottage with a lovely garden in a neighborhood not along the route of anyone with a spare seat.

Overhearing discussions on this aspect of the guest list had given me much solitary thought, reinforced by *Anna of the Five Towns,* much of it on the subject of money and the fate of women who did not marry. I had the sense that a great change was coming, although I did not then know that each generation sees itself as both the end of one way of life and the beginning of another. Not only was the Great War going to change the world forever, but it would in all probability be followed by some form of Home Rule for Ireland. I was dimly aware that, when Grandmother died and Uncle Hubert married Rosamund Gwynne (although he still had not given an entirely satisfactory answer to any of my mother's increasingly pointed letters), I would no longer live at Ballydavid. I was too young to have much of a sense of the future and, apart from moments of fear and self-pity when I woke during the night, the inevitability of my expulsion from paradise did not much occupy my thoughts. Still less did I dwell on an alternate, less probable scenario, although I had been, since I'd overheard Mrs. Bryce's "heiress" allusion, dimly aware of its possibilities. In it Uncle Hubert did not marry Miss Gwynne, and after his death—in the distant future, although I knew that in the

East sudden death from a variety of deadly diseases was in no way unusual—I became chatelaine of Ballydavid. I would have liked to live the rest of my life at Ballydavid, but I could not quite imagine myself, a few years older and a couple of inches taller, dressed in long black garments similar to those Grandmother wore, giving orders to O'Neill and Maggie.

Since I was about to be, as it were, disinherited, a different view of my future had to be generated. One that included marriage—the only alternative to a life spent looking after my parents in their old age, followed by genteel poverty and the hope that someone would be as thoughtful to me as Grandmother was to the less fortunate of the old ladies sitting on either side of the tennis court. Much in the way that the youths who had come to Mrs. Hitchcock's house carrying a petrol container had anticipated the burning of the big houses (the first of these houses would not go up in flames until 1919), I knew that after the war growing Irish nationalism would change the way the Anglo-Irish lived and, in time, remove much of their privilege. I already knew I would never marry an English soldier, and Jonathan, the boy who had spent the greater part of my birthday tea party under the dining-room table, was the only Protestant male of my age I had met during my year at Ballydavid.

Jarvis and his pretty, athletic sister arrived as the first of the matches limped toward a close, the curate and one of the sisters hopelessly outclassed by the other sister and the young airman on leave who, in happier days, had been awarded his blue at Cambridge.

"Alice, dear, why don't you take Jarvis away and play with him. And Inez, maybe you'll play in the next set——" Grandmother paused, glancing down the avenue. "Or the one after."

Her glance seemed to suggest that she expected to see a player worthy of Inez de Courcy arrive, and we all followed her eye. I most eagerly since I was playing for time, wondering where I was supposed to take this terrifying boy to play and what exactly it was we were intended to play at. I had the sense that anything short of robbing a bank would seem a tame afternoon's sport to Jarvis. Fortunately, at that moment a painful grinding of gears announced a sporty open motorcar driving up the avenue. All eyes, few of them approving, watched an unknown young officer drive past the front door of the house, spraying gravel on the grass, and come to a stop in the shade of the large beech. Rosamund Gwynne, laughing, dusty, and clutching a straw hat almost secured by a long, wide motoring veil, stepped out of the car. Under her motoring coat she wore tennis clothes, and she carried a racquet.

How to entertain Jarvis was no longer an immediate problem; hands in his pockets, he strolled over to take a look at the car. I followed him. Miss Gwynne, crossing our path, failed to notice me.

"That's a Lancia," Jarvis said to me, looking at it judiciously. "It should be able to do more than fifty miles an hour. Although probably not with yer man driving it."

I said nothing but stood beside him, looking at the motorcar. It was green, a more interesting color for a car than the stately black of the Sunbeam, a vehicle I had never seen driven at more than fifteen miles an hour. With its canvas top laid back flat, and lacking even a windshield, the Lancia was open to the elements. There was a good deal of brass trimming around the radiator and headlamps. I could imagine that it was capable of tremendous speed.

Despite the novelty of the Lancia, Jarvis remained the center of my attention. It seemed unlikely, though possible, that he would spend the afternoon inspecting the motorcar. I feared that he would jump into the driver's seat and simulate driving it; fortunately these were the days before the self-starter, so there was no question of Jarvis making a sudden Mr. Toad–like move and the Lancia disappearing into the Ballydavid woods, leaving me to explain. I began to remember that, however heroic Jarvis seemed to me, being responsible for him was exhausting.

After a minute or so, Jarvis having done nothing more provocative than stroll around the Lancia and kick its tires, I again became aware of the progress of the party behind me. The first set was finished, and Grandmother was organizing Inez and Rosamund to play in the second match. Rosamund Gwynne was—if she were indeed to marry into our family—rather too much the center of attention. The noisy arrival of the car, her companion, her loud and unattractive laughter now followed by the demand that Captain Blaine should be her doubles partner, were earning her disapproving looks from the old ladies. Inez, well able to take care of herself and better acquainted with the conventions of provincial Irish life, summoned the Resident Magistrate—a middle-aged bachelor whom I recognized from the meet at Herald's Cross, the owner of the horse with the red ribbon on its tail—from the shade in which he was standing with some other men, smoking to keep away the midges. He arrived at Inez's side as Grandmother glanced around randomly for a partner for her, and a moment or two later all four were on the court.

Grandmother was now free to greet Mrs. Coughlan, to whom she had not spoken a word since the day I had run away from Ballydavid and found myself a favored guest in her house. Mrs. Coughlan was dramatically dressed, but as I remember it, not in a contemporary fashion. There was always a suggestion of a costume party in her choice of clothing; it seems to me now that at some point in her life—most likely before Major Coughlan married her and brought her home to Ireland—she had admired a picture of an eighteenth-century portrait in an illustrated paper and decided that, if she ever found herself in a position to dress in such a manner, she would. Which is not to say that, when the opportunity presented itself, she abandoned such other dramatic possibilities as her crimson mourning dress or the widow's weeds she had worn for Kitchener.

I wondered if I should say how-do-you-do to Mrs. Coughlan, but guests were arriving all at once, among them the Bryces. Aunt Katie indicated my presence to Clodagh, and she and Miss Kingsley came to join Jarvis and me beside the Lancia.

Clodagh and I greeted each other with tepid enthusiasm—moral cowardice on my part and, I think, an already ingrained conventional streak on hers. Jarvis glanced at her and said nothing, although he answered some question Miss Kingsley asked him about the car politely enough.

"Mrs. Martyn said we should go and play rounders on the other lawn," Clodagh said. Her voice seemed unenthusiastic, and I remembered how deliberately she could refuse to be entertained.

"Did she say we had to?" Jarvis asked.

"No." Clodagh was startled. "She thought we might like to."

"Well," Jarvis said, "then I'll just stay here and watch my sister win the Brits."

"'Beat', I think you mean, Jarvis," Miss Kingsley said. "One wins a race, one beats one's opponent."

I glanced at Miss Kingsley and saw she was going to correct only Jarvis's choice of words. She sat down beside Jarvis on the grass at the top of the incline that enclosed the tennis court and the area in which the spectators were sitting. We had the equivalent of balcony seats and the advantage of a cool breeze.

For the first time in the annals of the Ballydavid tennis party, the attention of the guests was completely focused on the game. The symbolic aspects of the match were apparent to everyone, although what it symbolized may have varied slightly, depending on the spectator. From where we were sitting, it seemed clear enough. The brash, unquestioningly self-confident interlopers were being challenged by a member of a no longer powerful old Irish Catholic family whose children showed a tendency to revert to a former primitive natural state, and by a representative of the Crown who, although charged with upholding the law and supervising the dispensation of justice, understood his place in the subtle hierarchy of Irish society. Major Spenser, the RM, lived a quiet life, largely devoted to sport, in a plain, gray, famously cold house on the Dungarvan road. He was a good fifteen years older than Captain Blaine, but he had kept fit and knew how to pace himself.

Rosamund Gwynne played well; I was surprised how well. I had expected her to be less physical. I had, I suppose, thought her strength to be that of the will. We watched the game silently. Clodagh, I assume, was on the side of Rosamund—her mother's friend, a woman who made no bones of preferring her to me—and her partner, upholders of the standards in which she believed and which, if they lasted, would benefit her. Jarvis, of course, supported his sister, but with an intensity I would not have expected. Miss Kingsley and Mother, who drifted over during the second game, remained on the surface neutral, applauding volleys and the better shots of both sides, but I knew they wanted Inez and the RM to win and, even more, for Rosamund Gwynne to lose.

In Mother's wake came Noreen, sent by Aunt Katie with a rug for us to sit on, although it had been a good week since the grass had last approached dampness, and, soon after refreshments had been served to the more formally seated spectators below us, Bridie brought us a tray loaded with tomato sandwiches, cake, and lemonade. I remember the next hour and a half, sitting on the rug in the sun with Mother and Jarvis, watching the match, as one of my life's moments of pure uncomplicated happiness. I was comfortable beside my gentle mother and happy in Jarvis's unspoken approbation—happy with the picnic and the warm summer afternoon and the excitement of being part of a festive grown-up party. I was proud of Ballydavid at a moment when the house and household was shown at its old-fashioned hospitable finest.

This memory marks for me the beginning of loss: an hour or two on a sunny afternoon of pure happiness of a kind we would never again find. I am not yet sixty years old, but of that afternoon Clodagh is the only one that I know still to be alive; we, perhaps because of that, still exchange unenthusiastic Christmas cards. The happiness of the moment is not even an entirely accurate memory; much had already been lost. Although I remember Grandmother and Mother both taking pleasure in the party, they had already lost my uncle Sainthill and pure happiness could never again exist for them. The Great War had taken him; when it ended—a little more than two years after that August afternoon—the way we lived would change forever with the Anglo-Irish War, a time popularly and euphemistically referred to as the Troubles, a time of assassination and the burning of houses. Then would come the Civil War. There was already a foreshadowing of these unhappy times in the isolated incidents of violence—or the threats of violence—that occurred in the wake of the Rising. Even if all that had not lain before us, even without a second great world war to slaughter the finest of another generation of young men, the best it seems to me we can, even in the happiest of times, hope for is gradual loss.

Inez and the RM prevailed. It was a popular victory, although, apart from Jarvis, the spectators were too polite to appear partisan. I don't think that Rosamund and her partner were beaten only by their opponents' greater experience of the uneven local court. The two couples were more evenly matched than was usually the case at Grandmother's tennis parties. Rosamund may also have become gradually aware, as the excitement of the drive from Waterford in the open Lancia wore off, that her appearance on the court with the dashing young officer was not admired by the intolerant and judgmental old cats who were watching. Her tennis dress, the height of fashion in England and even perhaps in closer Dublin, was shorter and more revealing of the outlines of her attractive young figure than County Waterford was used to; it seemed immodest beside that of Inez, by local standards a modern young woman, who wore a skirt long enough to reveal only her slim ankles and buckskin shoes. The old ladies thought Rosamund fast. I now think she was, instead, arrogant and had seen no reason to sacrifice the fun of flirtation and attention to make a good impression on a bunch of shabby old ladies. Rosamund was from a good family, but a good English family. It cut less ice in County Waterford than she supposed.

She didn't, I think, imagine that the old ladies' opinion would make any difference to her life, and, as it turned out, she was right. But it makes me wonder how much she really cared for my Uncle Hubert. Was her less than discreet behavior that afternoon merely the manifestation of high spirits? Or was she, without Uncle Hubert completely hooked, prepared to entertain the possibility of another choice? Or was she merely flirting?

Inez and her partner thanked each other and separated after they left the court. Captain Blaine fetched a glass of lemonade for Rosamund; I saw a silent moment between them before they became part of a larger group that almost immediately dispersed as the new game, of a staid and known middle-aged quantity, began. There was a general movement, further refreshments were offered, and some of the guests wandered toward the garden.

Major Spenser, still tightening the screws on the press of his racquet, came over to greet my mother who congratulated him on his game. Clodagh, discontented, went to look for her mother; Miss Kingsley did not rise to accompany her. Instead, she and I lazily picked daisies from the less recently mown grass behind us, and she made them into a chain she draped around my neck. She was, I could see, aware of Major Spenser's presence.

"Cubbing begins next week," Major Spenser said to my mother. "I hope you're planning to come out with us."

I glanced up at Mother. The question was of some interest to me and I wanted to read her expression as well as hear her reply. Cubbing began the following week; my birthday was the week after. So was the beginning of the new school term. I didn't know whether I—we—would still be in Ireland for my birthday. If we were, I hoped that in recognition of my greater maturity and as part of my birthday celebrations, I would be allowed to go cubbing.

Mother laughed.

"I don't know," she said. "O'Neill has clipped my hunter and the pony, but they're both a long way from being fit."

I was trying to pluck up courage to add my voice to that of Major Spenser's when I became aware of Mrs. Coughlan's approach. She was carrying a lovely pink parasol. I stood up to greet her.

"My little girl," she said. "It's been a long time since I last saw you. Wherever have you been?"

"Hello, Mrs. Coughlan," I said breathlessly. I had not seen Mrs. Coughlan since my birthday party, and I was not sure of the current state of relations between her and my grandmother. Jarvis slid silently past me; he seemed to be going in the direction of the front door.

"Let us go for a little walk," she said, twirling her lowered parasol so that I could admire it. The pink silk was covered with white embroidered rosettes; I wondered where she had come by it. "You can tell me all about what is going on in London. Have you seen any good plays?"

I experienced my usual mixture of flattered delight and confused alarm at Mrs. Coughlan's assumption that she and I would converse on equal terms; after a moment I remembered that my part of the conversation, not a significant one, was largely ignored by her. Instead of being forced to admit that we hadn't seen each other for almost a year not because I had been leading a busy social life in London but because Grandmother had not considered herself to be on speaking terms with Mrs. Coughlan, I was, a moment later, listening to an account of a concert at which she herself had sung and after which attention had been paid to her by a duke. I longed to ask where—in a drawing room or at Wigmore Hall? Waterford or St. Petersburg? They all seemed equally probable. And when? A week ago or when she was a girl? And if the latter, how long ago was that? Then we were interrupted by Captain Blaine.

"Seraphina," he said, kissing the back of her lace-gloved hand. "How enchanting and cool you look. Who is your little friend?"

"My name is Alice," I said quickly, in case she hadn't remembered.

"The last time we met," Mrs. Coughlan said, "you promised to take me for a ride in your motorcar."

"So I did," said Captain Blaine. "Why don't we go for a spin now? We'll take—Alice as a chaperone."

Mrs. Coughlan's cries of girlish laughter—I wonder now how old she was; maybe she was still young enough to have been attractive to Blaine—were interrupted by the arrival of Rosamund. She was red in the face and her hair was damp and frizzy. Her expression told me she was still suffering from defeat, and she looked more determined than usual.

"Good afternoon, Miss Gwynne," I piped up politely, but, when she seemed not to hear me, I added, not quite so innocently, "I am sorry you were beaten."

She glanced at me briefly, her expression more one of distraction than dislike.

"And Rosamund, of course," Blaine said.

Introductions took place; it seemed the Bryces and the Coughlans did not know each other socially. I took note of that fact and of Mrs. Coughlan's first name and that Captain Blaine had addressed her by it and stored it at the back of my mind for consideration later. Then we all strolled toward the Lancia.

There was a pause, slightly awkward, while Blaine decided how to accommodate two large egos and a superfluous little girl in his motorcar.

"You," Captain Blaine said to Mrs. Coughlan, "will sit here"—he indicated the back seat—"like the Vicereine. Alice will sit beside you. Rosamund, you sit next to me."

He opened the doors and a moment later we were all seated. Despite the heat, Rosamund allowed him to drape his khaki greatcoat over her shoulders so that she should not catch a chill after her exertions. While Captain Blaine went round to the front of the car to start it, Rosamund turned the collar of the coat up and put on his uniform cap, adjusting it to a saucy angle. She looked very fetching in a boyish way, but I knew her action would earn her a couple more black marks from the critical eyes of the old ladies. It was not until Blaine had swung the starting handle vigorously a couple of times that anyone seemed to notice what we were doing. He leapt into the car as the engine caught, found the gear, and the car lurched forward; all eyes turned to us as he drove across the gravel. I saw O'Neill and Jarvis just outside the hall door, O'Neill's expression stern as he addressed Jarvis. A moment later, Jarvis launched himself across the gravel and, like a monkey, gripped the canvas of the folded down roof of the Lancia, and, with a foot on the fender, attached himself to the back of the vehicle before it gathered speed. As we swung onto the slope of the avenue, I saw Miss Kingsley still sitting on the rug with Major Spenser beside her.

Patience and Mother's hunter, grazing in the field by the avenue, raised their heads for a startled moment before turning and dashing to the far end of the pasture; I imagined O'Neill would have something to say on that subject when we came home. I wondered how far we were going and for a nervous moment whether Captain Blaine was planning to return. Perhaps he would leave me with Mrs. Coughlan at her house, while he and Rosamund Gwynne, sulky from their defeat, returned to the garrison in Waterford. Maybe Grandmother and my mother would again have to come and take me home.

We passed out of sunshine into the shade of the avenue as we turned the bend and drove out of sight of the house. The speed was exhilarating, but the noise of the motorcar and the lack of any barrier between me and outside made me afraid; that Jarvis was insecurely attached to the back also terrified me. I sensed, when we came out onto the road, that Captain Blaine would drive faster and that his other two companions, competing with each other, would encourage him to show off. I began to wish I had stayed at home.

Rosamund Gwynne laughed and with one hand held her military cap in place. Mrs. Coughlan, upright, towered above me; she had taken Blaine's reference to the Vicereine to heart. I turned to look at Jarvis, unsure whether it would be more dangerous for him to try to clamber over the back into the seat with me and Mrs. Coughlan or to continue hanging onto the back while Blaine gathered speed. That the folded canvas projected more than a foot from the back of the Lancia made his position more vulnerable and less easy to negotiate.

My head was turned toward him when the first shot was fired. It didn't have an immediate significance for me; it seemed one more loud noise emanating from the engine of the Lancia. I felt the car swerve and saw that we were not going to clear the gateposts that marked the end of the avenue, behind which lay the Waterford-Woodstown road. I huddled down instinctively for protection and found my face in the lace of Mrs. Cochlan's dress as I heard the second, third, and fourth shots.

WHEN I BECAME conscious again, I was lying on the grass verge that Pat had so carefully mown the day before. Since I could see the greater part of the tennis party streaming down the avenue— only three or four men, two of them in uniform, and Inez de Courcy were already with us—I knew that very little time had passed. I was most aware that sound had begun to come back into the summer afternoon. After the car had bounced off the open wrought iron gate, it skidded across the stony packed earth of the avenue before hitting the opposite gatepost and turning on its side. And after the crash there was silence; only a hiss of what might have been steam escaping from the damaged engine filled the silent afternoon, taking the place of the usual, hardly noticed sounds of birds and the countryside. I felt an intense awareness of every detail of my surroundings; of every passing moment, which seemed to take place at half the speed of normal time, before I floated away into the feeling of a slow, calm dream.

I was lying on the grass, a man's jacket over my legs. I could hear Jarvis's voice close by. Although the words he was speaking did not at first arrange themselves to have much significance, I knew—long before I understood what he was saying—that Mrs. Coughlan, Captain Blaine, and Rosamund Gwynne were dead.

A moment later I opened my eyes again and saw my mother crouched, wild-eyed and pale, above me.

"Are you all right, darling?" She gasped breathlessly, one hand on my shoulder, the other supporting herself on the grass.

I nodded and smiled a little to reassure her. I felt as though I were somewhere else, floating over the scene, and that the physical effort of speaking was for the moment beyond me.

"There were three men. They were wearing masks," I heard Jarvis say. I allowed my head to fall a little to one side so that I could see him. He was sitting on the grass. The side of his face was grazed and bleeding. Someone had given him a large white handkerchief. The skin had been scraped off both his knees and the side of one leg. He was shivering as though he were very cold, and the way he held one arm I would later, on the hunting field, come to recognize as a broken collar bone, but his voice was clear and confident.

That Jarvis had chosen to lie about what had happened did not in my dreamlike state seem surprising. Nor was I surprised that he knew I would not betray him. I closed my eyes again, as much to avoid having to speak, even to continue reassuring my mother I wasn't hurt, as to have to answer questions about what had happened. I wasn't even playing for time; I knew what I would say: I would, a habit already invisibly in place, follow Jarvis's lead but, as always, I would be one step behind. I would not contradict his lie; he already knew that. Instead I would say I had seen nothing. It would prevent a good deal of questioning; or, if it did not, it would at least simplify my answers. I closed my eyes because I wanted to prolong a little the time before it would all become noisy and urgent and confusing. And if I said and did nothing, I knew that, after the noise, urgency, and confusion, I would be put quietly into my bed where I could lie still and think about what had happened.

There had been two boys, not three men—it had all taken place in a moment, and then they were gone. Through the bushes, onto the Fox's Walk and into the woods. And, although they had worn masks, it now seems to me—I have had a long time to consider every aspect of those moments—the masks had been worn more to dramatize the event, to give them courage, than as an effective disguise. They had surely not expected to leave a witness—or witnesses—alive. One of them was the red-haired Clancy boy. I wondered if he had seen Jarvis and me. I had seen him, but maybe he hadn't seen us. But if he had, he must in that moment—having already shot at two khaki uniforms—have decided not to kill us. And who was his companion? And if he had seen us, why had he, too, spared us?

And during the time I have spent thinking about what happened, there is another question I have had to consider. If Jarvis had not lied, if he had not been there, what would I have done? I am fairly sure I would have said I had seen nothing. Three people, one of whom I had been oddly fond, were dead. I, through half-closed eyes, had seen their blood-stained bodies being covered with jackets, a shawl, a rug from the motorcar. But I was a child and, although I understood what had happened, there were limits to my understanding. And my instincts and reactions were those of a child. And my loyalties and values were not as clear as they once had been. While I wouldn't side with the assassins, I no longer trusted the forces that would hunt them down if I spoke up. And if he had seen me—surely he had—the red-haired boy had spared my life; did I not now owe him his? And Jarvis, why did he lie? Not often, but from time to time, until his death early in the second war, we would talk about that afternoon. But I never heard him say anything more concrete than that he wasn't an informer.

I kept my eyes closed and breathed in the smell of mud and crushed grass. I listened to Jarvis tell his story once again. It felt as though everything was still and at a great distance, even my breathing had become so slow that it seemed a conscious effort. I thought I would lie still and feel the short grass on my cheek and my mother's hand stroking my hair. I knew that as long as I did not open my eyes I would have a little time.